Fast & Hard

Kat Ransom

Fast & Hard
Copyright © 2019 Kat Ransom.

One

Mallory

"In the interest of full disclosure, Ms. Mitchell, I do want to reiterate the responsibilities and expectations of the position, one final time."

Smile, Mallory, smile. Do not yawn at the Marketing and Communications Director, no matter how tired you are from the red-eye to London or the fact that it's gray and gloomy and a soft rain drizzles down the office windows. It's London, of course it's raining, should have expected that.

Smile, damn it.

"Thank you, Mrs. Alix," I start.

"Ms. It's Ms. Alix, no Mrs.," she interrupts, peering at me over the frames of her oval tortoiseshell eyeglasses.

Of course, it's Ms. and not Mrs. I should have known that, too. Not that Sandra Alix is an unattractive woman, she's just... cold. Like this room. Or the frosty cocktail I am going to imbibe in as soon as I finally get this job.

I will get this job.

"My apologies, Ms. Alix. I appreciate you being so thorough and I assure you I am confident in my ability to deliver the results you require." I look Sandra square on, straighten my spine, and make a mental note to stop tapping my foot lest she know how much I want this job. She could tell me that standing on my head and spitting nickels out of my mouth was a key performance indicator and I would convince her that I'll spit dimes.

"Yes, well," Sandra leans back in her squeaking office chair and I feel like I'm a piece of fruit being sized up at the market, "it's imperative to Celeritas that we succeed this time in bringing the right person aboard."

"I understand," I nod. I understand fully that my predecessors were either shit-canned within days or ran screaming from this job. I do my homework. I'm not stupid. I just want this job that badly. And after flying here a second time for my final interview, they're going to give it to me.

"Do you? Do you understand Ms. Mitchell?" Sandra sneers.

I see what's happening here. This is the portion of the interview where they try to scare the naive little American girl and force her to retreat to the safety of New York.

Not happening.

"Yes, Ms. Alix. I am good at what I do. I have done my due diligence. I have familiarized myself with the challenges of the client. I have read all the news stories, seen the social media incidents, and I have developed a multi-point strategy to reform the brand to meet Celeritas Racing's expectations."

Take that, you shrew. Like I'm intimated to work with a difficult, if not obscenely good looking athlete. Well, I'm not. Seen one musclebound dick in the locker room, you've seen them all. This one just comes with a Scottish accent and drives a car versus throws a ball, color me unimpressed.

"Yes," she starts, "I have no doubt you have talent or we would not be here. You have been successful in managing the images of troubled athletes in the past, we know that. You've also had a misstep, however, and I'd like assurance that will not happen again."

I knew Sandra Stick Up Her Ass would bring that up. Even though we're in Europe and I was hoping my sins of America would not follow me here to haunt me. But I'm still prepared. Because I'm always prepared.

"You have my word, Ms. Alix. I learned a valuable lesson with the client you're referring to and Lennox Gibbes will not be let out from my sights. The situation will be under control at all times."

"You're going to control Lennox Gibbes?" She leans forward and chuckles. "And how do you propose to do that?"

"I will put him on a leash if necessary," I mash my teeth and announce boldly.

Time for games is over, lady, give me the job. I'm tired, I've been here twice and through rounds of Skype interviews, I'm well aware that Lennox Gibbes — the 'Paddock Playboy' — is another skeezeball athlete running around sticking his dick in anything that moves and embarrassing the company.

And I. Don't. Care.

"Oh," Sandra starts, actually proving that she does, in fact, have the facial muscles required to break a smile, "I like you."

"I will not let you down." *Seal the deal, seal the deal.*

"Formula 1 is quite a bit different from what you're used to, Ms. Mitchell, I suspect you'll have quite a learning curve ahead of you."

"I look forward to meeting that goal, as well."

It's in the bag, right? She said I *will* have a learning curve, not I *could* have a learning curve. Damn it, spit it out, you wanker! I've been practicing British slang and have always wanted to call someone a wanker.

"Right, then. Let's get down to brass tacks. There will be extensive NDA's, you understand." Sandra starts shuffling papers on her desk and this is it, it's happening. The job is mine. I don't care if the tacks she's offering are brass, gold, or made of tinfoil. This is my chance.

"Yes, of course." Working with athletes, NDA's live in my back pocket at all times. They're all the same.

Every single one of them who can hit a ball or kick something into the end zone is the same type of manwhore who thinks he's god's gift to women. On some mission to knock up half of the Eastern seaboard and disgrace their team and their sponsors then they act surprised when their contract is cut and their newfound riches evaporate.

Oversized man-children, all of them. Not interested.

"On the matter of compensation," Sandra pulls a sheet of paper from her stack and slides it across her meticulous, empty glass desk toward me.

Holy shit. This is double the salary range initially offered. This is… this can't be right.

"I'm sorry, is this figure correct?" Please let it be correct.

"This job is more than just Publicity Management, Ms. Mitchell. If you review this sheet," she slides more sheets of neatly typed paperwork at me, "you'll see there are additional duties of new sponsor recruitment and partner engagement."

I study the sheet, so many zeros behind so many dollar signs. "I see."

Oh boy, do I see. Requirements to achieve new corporate sponsors for the driver with minimum financial investments and benchmarks, expectations of investor events, product launch parties, this is a lot.

"You're not going in cold, don't worry." Sandra tries to breeze into this like it's a simple task to acquire all the zeros staring at me on these pages. "Celeritas has all the connections. All you need to do is ensure that Mr. Gibbes is a property worthy of the investors' endorsements and backing. Create the public image our business partners want to see from a world champion. Guarantee that Mr. Gibbes represents them, and Celeritas Racing, well. Get him to the required events on time and keep him from making a jackass of himself." Sandra purses her lips and bites out the final sentence and I know this has been a thorn in her side for some time. She's frustrated.

"This is quite extensive, Ms. Alix," I stumble, still skimming over the printed details. I hate stumbling, hate that she caught me off guard. I'm a social media whiz and I reform the public opinion of ill-behaved celebrity athletes. I'm used to sponsor requirements and endorsement deals. But even for top tier athletes, this is a lot.

"Yes, well, as I said, you have a great deal to learn about F1. This is the playground of the elite, not a football field." Sandra makes air quotes for the word football and I don't know if she's making fun of American sports or, because here, football is actually soccer. I decide to ignore that thought, either way, as she continues, "I believe the salary more than compensates for the additional duties, does it not?

"The salary is quite generous," I agree. Ha, generous. That's a good one. The salary is enough to cement my dreams. I was in this to get the experience and contacts that only a behemoth of an industry like F1 can bring, to rebuild my reputation after that piece of garbage NBA player tanked me almost a year ago.

But this, this changes everything.

"In addition to the salary terms, you have your expense account agreement," Sandra starts whipping more paperwork at me from her bottomless folder, "corporate housing agreement, NDA as discussed, benefits package dossier, all of your work visa documents. Here, just take it all. Look it over tonight and tomorrow morning we will meet with Mr. Sanders, the HR attorney, to finalize everything."

"Ms. Alix, I want to be very clear. Are you offering me the position?" I'm fairly sure this is a redundant question and she's made it obvious, but I need to hear it. I need to hear the words so I can internally scream and then start plotting how I am going to stuff my success down everyone's throats. Maybe after I celebrate tonight with that frosty cocktail. Or during. Definitely during.

"Yes, we are officially offering you the position. After the paperwork is finalized tomorrow I will show you to your flat on premises and make introductions to Mr. Lennox and other personnel."

I stand from my chair and reach to shake Sandra's hand. "Thank you, Ms. Alix, thank you."

"Get your affairs in order quickly, we leave for Australia in ten days. And good luck to you, you're going to need it."

Ah, but Sandra, you cantankerous shrew you, I don't need luck. I make my own success and Paddock Playboy or corporate sponsors be damned, I will rock this job and everything I want will fall into place.

Two

Lennox

"I," grunt, "hate," grunt, "you." I sputter as I pull my head and up and over the chin-up bar over and over again in the gym at headquarters. Sweat is running down my back because the heat is turned up to mimic race weather conditions. Or terrorize me, one or the other.

"Uh-huh, cry me a river, Lennox, another 20," Matty mumbles from his stationary position on a weight bench beside me, crunching down an apple with extra gusto because he knows I hate the sound of food slurping. "Less than two weeks left, you need to pick it up."

"Don't see you up here," I groan in between pulls.

"I'm already in peak physical condition," Matty replies while chewing and in his customary tone where most people can't tell if he's being sarcastic or serious. I've known him long enough to know that he's not making a joke right now.

The stereo is loud in the background and I've been running and rowing and heaving myself over assorted bars for hours. Just need to make it through this set and then my sadistic physio will let me eat something again. Perhaps another delicious helping of quinoa and kale or whatever the last bowl of slop was.

"I love when you two squabble, you know it gets me hard." Jack is sitting on the floor in front of me with his back against the wall, face glued to his iPhone and fingers tap-tap-tapping on the surface.

"Jesus, why are you even here?" Matty calls to him over the stereo and rolling his eyes.

"Making the Melbourne travel arrangements, getting his promo materials in order, picked up his new helmets from the designer. You know, being good at my job." Jack sashays his head back and forth though he still hasn't lifted it from the iPhone.

I give Matty shit for putting me through these grueling workouts and making me stick to the world's most boring diet plan, but he and Jack are like an old married couple, constantly at it. Gives me something to get my mind off of, anyway. Makes things interesting.

"Also, I want to meet the new nanny," Jack adds like this is a secret afterthought he's letting slip out.

I drop from the pull bar and beads of sweat break off me and hit the floor. "What new nanny?"

"Yes. Do tell, Jack," Matty pitches his apple core into a trashcan several feet away and leans forward on his seat to hear the latest gossip that neither of us knew about.

"Well," Jack lifts his head and comes alive because there's gossip. He's obnoxious like that. "From what I hear, this one is American and she…"

Jack is cut off when the stereo stops and all three of our heads turn to the door. Sandra, the main dragon lady from Marketing, has cut the stereo and beside her stands, I'm assuming, the latest pawn in her bullshit scheme of 'restoring my image.'

Jack pops off the ground and Matty stands from the weight bench while my eyes flicker and my brow creases. This better not be another new babysitter.

"Well, don't just stand there," the dragon lady squawks as she begins her approach with the wide-eyed doe next to her, "Come meet Mallory."

Jack and Matty circle in, the new chick's heels clacking on the tile gym floor. Dressed in a tight little fawn-colored pencil skirt that ends mid-calf and a white blouse, she's wearing the official uniform of new employees everywhere. I scowl.

"Mallory," Sandra starts pointing like the rude bird she is, "this is Matthias Vitanen who is Mr. Gibbes' physio." Matty shakes her hand and smiles a little more than is normal for him.

"This is Jack Addair, the personal assistant," Dragon Lady points to Jack.

Jack wraps both his hands around the nanny's outstretched palm and gushes, "So nice to meet you, Mallory! Welcome!" He's being a sarcastic ass but the new chick doesn't know it yet and gushes back at him with a naive and hopeful smile that I'm going to enjoy watching fade.

"And this," Dragon Lady's tone drops and her lips purse, "is Lennox Gibbes."

I stand with my hands on my hips and my gym shorts riding low and make no effort to pull them up or put a shirt on.

"Lennox, nice to meet you. I'm Mallory and I'll…"

"The fuck is this?" I refuse to look in new chick's general direction and continue to stare at Sandra the Dragon Lady.

"This, Mr. Gibbes, is your new Publicity Manager, Mallory Mitchell. Please be a gentleman and get acquainted, she'll be joining you in Australia and with you this season." Sandra's arms cross over her chest like she's preparing for a showdown.

If it's a showdown she wants, it's a showdown she'll get.

"Did you not learn from the previous dozen nannies, Sandra?" I glare at her.

"Did you not learn from reading the fine print in your contract, Mr. Gibbes?" She snarks back. "While we may not be able to release you from it, yet," she paused and emphasizes, "Celeritas is well within its rights to protect its brand and will continue to take aggressive action until you get with the program or get out."

I smirk at Sandra and take a step closer. She takes one step back. "Sandra, Sandra, Sandra," I shake my head. "You don't get it. You can send one hundred nannies. You can send one thousand nannies. She'll be out of here the first week, like all the others and you'll still be stuck upstairs in your barren office with your barren life quibbling about Facebook engagement rates. At some point, Sandra, would it not be easier to simply remove the stick from your ass?"

New Nanny — Mallory, I guess — gasps and covers her mouth with her hand.

Jack is trying hard to stifle a giggle.

Matty stands next to me like a lifeless statue, as always.

Dragon Lady's eyes bead and her face gets red and her lip is trembling ever so quietly. That's right, Sandra, piss off back to your office with all the other greedy little suits who chew people up and spit them out to get what you want out of them. Scurry along to have more meetings about what to do about me, call me a property or an asset like humans are disposable cogs in your machine to bring in more and more sponsors of trashy products none of us on the track would ever use in real life.

Sandra takes a step back and makes an attempt to disguise how uncomfortable I make her. The poor lass probably hasn't been laid in a decade. A dick would freeze right off it came anywhere near her.

"We'll see, Mr. Lennox, we'll see. I have confidence that this nan... uh, Publicity Manager will work out. She says she's going to put you on a leash!" Sandra aims her pointy little finger at me then turns and makes her retreat to the door like the coward she is.

I turn to the new nanny who is standing calm and collected with her shoulders back. We'll see how long that lasts. "What's this about putting me on a leash now?" I ask her.

"Oh shit," Jack giggles, watching with rapt attention.

"Do you prefer I call you Lennox or Mr. Gibbes?" She asks in a stern voice, trying to sidestep my question and act authoritative while reaching a palm to me in an attempt to shake my hand. It's adorable.

I ignore her hand. "I'd prefer you run back to whatever small Americana apple pie baking country town you flew here from and save us all a few days. Go see London Bridge and Big Ben on your way out so it's not a total loss for you."

"Oh good, you do still have some firing neurons left in your head and know I'm American. Excellent. You should be aware, however, that I'm from New York so you'll have to try harder to insult me."

"OH EM GEE, I love New York," Jack claps.

I turn to Jack and look at him like the numpty he is. "Did you know about this?" I bark at him and point to New Nanny.

He shakes his head at me and tries to reign in a smile by biting his cheek. I can't believe I sign his checks. Why, again, do I sign his checks? Oh yeah, because I can't be bothered to book flights and fetch coffee or keep track of where I'm supposed to be on any given day. Or that's what I said when I hired him, anyway.

Matty comes forward trying to be the peacemaker of the group, or trying to get into New Nanny's pants, which is more likely the case. "So yeah, I'm the physio. You can call me Matty."

New Nanny sees an olive branch extended and she brightens, but she's in way out of her depth and doesn't know that branch is a dry-rotted twig capable of snapping at any time. "Physio, that's great. My roommate in the States is a personal trainer."

"That's not a real thing," Matty replies flatly. And here we go. I couldn't have asked for anything better than New Nanny launching into Matty's biggest pet peeve.

"I'm sorry?" New Nanny asks.

"That's cute and all but that's not a real job. What I do is science and medicine, not aerial yoga and smoothies for bored housewives."

Jack is beside himself with glee over the drama that's unexpectedly entered our workout session today.

"Don't mind him, New Nanny," I deliberately run a hand over my naked pecs for her, "he's Finnish. That's just how they are."

She doesn't take the bait and ogle my chest, that's interesting. But she does tilt her head and retort, "What's your excuse then?"

"Oh this is amazing," Jack beams. "New Nanny is sassy! You and I are going to be friends!"

"You will not befriend the new nanny!" I roar.

"I am not your nanny," the nanny steps toward me as I raise my eyebrows in amusement. "I am a Publicity Manager and a damned good one at that. And, by all accounts, you've made a mockery of Formula 1 and need all the help you can get!"

Jack is right, this one does have sass. The others don't even try to talk back or give me a challenge. This might be fun, for the day or two it lasts. "I need your help, really? Do tell, Nanny, what do you know about F1, hmm?"

I'll bet anything she's done some two-bit work in NASCAR or fancies herself a car enthusiast, like the last one. Though, by the look of her, she's never gotten dirty or near an engine a single day in her life. She looks like she just stepped out of a Harrod's ad meant for budding new professionals trying to make a good impression.

See, I do know something about marketing.

"I don't need to know anything about Formula 1 to know you're a joke." She puts one hand on her hip and cocks it to the side.

"Oh, that's cold," Matty interjects.

"A joke?" I cackle. Joke? I'm a bloody world champion! There may have been a string of bad seasons lately, but a joke? Hardly! This little American princess needs to run back home to daddy before she breaks a fingernail and starts crying. "I'm a world champion, love, I have records to my name that would make a grandmum cream her panties."

"Yes, I've seen your records all right," New Nanny doesn't back down, flips her long chestnut hair over one shoulder, and continues this ridiculous debate she knows nothing about. "Like your arrest record for drag racing down the Strip in Las Vegas."

"God, that was fun," Matty nods knowingly.

I'm about to educate her that there was no arrest, technically. Money goes a long way into making problems go away. But New Nanny launches into the next thing on the mental list she's obviously created to try and prove her point.

"Or the newspaper records of your implication in the extramarital affair resulting in the divorce of the Duke and Duchess of Osland."

"Those were amazing days," Jack gushes, "Not true, but amazing! Swedish royalty, can you imagine?"

New Nanny is all fired up now and her chest, from her neck down to where her blouse buttons finally start closing just above her tits, is getting flushed from yelling. I'm trying not to look directly at it. Not because it's not worth looking at — it appears to be very worthwhile — but I'm not going to give her the satisfaction.

"Records of all your fines and citations from the FIA. Is it true they created a new system of fines for excessive swearing over team radio because of you, Mr. Gibbes?"

Matty snorts next to me and I clench my jaw to keep from laughing with him because I'll give the point to New Nanny, that one was kind of funny. Like I give a shit about fines. Oh no, a one hundred pound fine. I'm under contract for fifty million a year.

Plus the extra sponsorship money, though admittedly that's largely dried up. But I don't need it, and I don't need this.

I decide to change tactics.

I take a step toward the nanny so we're face to face and I can smell whatever is wafting off her hair, jasmine maybe? To her credit, Nanny's feet stay planted and she doesn't back off, despite the fact that I've been sweating for hours and probably smell like something a lot worse than flowers.

"Tell me more about this putting a leash on me thing," I look down and smolder at her. "That's not usually my thing, but I do like an aggressive woman from time to time."

She looks up at me and squints before she growls back, "You're a pig, Mr. Gibbes."

"Call me Lennox, love" I whisper back to her and move half a step closer.

Her head barely reaches my chin and she has to strain her head all the way up to look me in the eyes from this angle. If I were a real pig I'd run a finger down the side of her cheek, trace it along her neck, and into her cleavage which I can see perfectly from my vantage point.

But I'm not, and Mum would smack me upside the head for that kind of shit.

"Ok, Lennox" she starts, cute little hazel eyes all on fire with anger from trying to keep up, "You need to know this isn't going to work, either."

"It's ok. I'll do all the work, you can just lie there."

"What is wrong with you?" She hisses before she takes a step back.

I grin and cross my arms over my chest, gloating. That's right princess, this point goes to me, you took the step back.

She must realize she lost that round because her shoulders go back and she lifts her chin and takes a brave step right back, almost up against me. "You listen up, this is not my first rodeo and…"

"Now see, me playing a cowboy and you riding a rodeo bull, I can get behind that. Keep going with your John Wayne fantasy, baby."

I know I'm being an asshole but she's making it so much fun. Also, I am an asshole. That's just a fact if you ask anyone. Except Mum.

"You are far from the first athlete who's come onto me and," she pauses her rant and catches herself, beating me to my punchline, "do not make a joke about coming on me now!"

"Dirty," I hiss. For which I get a stab in the chest with one of her stereotypical light pink manicured nails.

That brings a dark smile to my face. I'm happy to be manhandled by the New Nanny during her short stay here in the UK. More than happy. That's gotten rid of at least a handful of previous nannies. The condom isn't even off and they've grown feelings and within 24 hours they're all packed up and crying their ways back home. It isn't like I didn't warn them.

Bottom line is, no new nanny is welcome here.

"You're not special and it's not going to work. I'm not quitting. So give it up."

She's taken her finger back from my chest, pity, and both hands are back on her hips as she glares at me like I'm a piece of gum on the bottom of her shoe. I've been called worse.

"I don't ever give up, love," I smirk back at her.

"Yeah?" She recoils with surprise and proudly states to the room, "That's not what I hear."

Both Matty and Jack let out a collective "ooooooooo" from behind us. Those two eejits are still apparently here, I hadn't noticed.

"I'm in for 50 pounds, Bahrain," Matty says to Jack.

"Mmm, she's got fire. I'll say 50 pounds by Baku." Jack answers him back.

New Nanny swings out from in front of me to my side to confront the two clowns behind us. "What are you two doing? Are you taking bets on when I will quit?" She seems surprised by our juvenile ritual.

"Aye," I confirm for her. Better she finds out now that there are no friends here, no one to trust in the world's most expensive traveling circus known as F1. I nod to the only two people who come close to being trustworthy and that's probably a step too far since both are here because I'm paying them, "I'll split ya both and say 50 pounds by China."

"You're all children," she shakes her head at them. "And you're disgusting and dripping sweat on me!" She shakes off her blouse where apparently some drops of my toxicity have touched her delicate, unspoiled skin.

"Love, when I get you all hot and sweaty, you won't be protesting," I smirk and give her a little wink.

New Nanny eases a step backward to take all three of us crass assholes in and shakes her head, "Well suckers, you're all going to lose. I'm here to stay. What's the last race of the year?"

"Abu Dhabi," Jack helpfully educates her.

"Great. I'm in. 50 bucks on Abu Dhabi." She crosses her arms over her chest and I pretend not to notice that it pushes her cleavage up even more when she does it.

Not one to let a statement go by without fact-checking it, Matty taunts her more, "You realize with the conversion rate that's more like 62 US dollars."

"Perfect," she snaps back and I chuckle because this is going to be fun.

New Nanny stands back tall and claps her hands, "Well gentleman, this has been delightful. I will see you in Australia."

And with that, she turns and makes her way to exit the gym, shoulders back and doing her best to stride with confidence.

"I enjoy the view of you leaving, New Nanny!" I call to her because I need to get the last word in. Also because that ass is on fire. She raises an arm without looking back and flips me the bird.

"Bye, Nanny," Jack calls after her.

"Bye, Nanny," Matty joins in.

Three

Mallory

How many sweaters do I need? London can be chilly but I can't fit all the sweaters into my moving boxes. Plus, we'll be traveling all over the world and it'll be warm in a lot of those locations. I pull one sweater back out and put it into the 'donate' pile.

Lots of flying, I need more leggings and comfy pants for flying.

"Aria," I bellow toward the hallway from my tiny bedroom back in New York, "do you have my favorite black leggings?" I swear she's going to be naked and starve to death when I leave and there's no one to grocery shop or do the laundry.

"What do you need, babe?" Aria comes sauntering into my bedroom, staring into the screen of her rose gold laptop and paying me no mind.

I sigh. Aria is a bit... flighty, but she's my bestie and I'd walk through fire for her. We went to college together and she's been my roommate for ages. Leaving her is the hardest part of taking this job.

"Focus, Aria," I scold her, "my black leggings. Do you have them?"

"How can I focus on leggings when I'm looking at this?" She huffs and flips the laptop screen toward me. The full resolution is a paparazzo picture of Lennox Gibbes walking on a beach, god knows where in the world, looking like he's auditioning for Baywatch. Except Lennox has blue trunks on and I think they were red on Baywatch.

"Seriously? We're doing this again? I barely have time to pack and get everything sorted before I leave and all you've done is Google that jerk and show me every photo you want to drool over."

"But I'm so jealous," she whines and flops onto my bed, on top of the heaped pile of donate clothes, and continues scrolling around on the laptop. "He's so hot."

"Nothing to be jealous of, he's a huge asshole." And that is a mouthful. All athletes have egos and act like every woman in existence sits around waiting for them to grace her with his penis, but Lennox Gibbes is next level asshole.

"Huge dick, too, if the rumors are to be believed. Look at this perfect little treasure trail." I turn to look at her, not the laptop, and she's petting the screen. If I roll my eyes any harder they're going to circle back around and start spinning like I'm in need of an exorcism.

"The fact that he has dick pics online should tell you everything you need to know about him, Grade A douchebag," I move onto my closet and start rifling through hangers and more sweaters I can't possibly bring with.

"I haven't found the dick pics yet but I'm not done searching. I need more visuals, Mallory, give them to me. Spare no detail." Aria turns on the bed and puts an elbow under her head.

I haven't found the dick pics either, but I'm not getting into that with Aria. It's my job, I was looking for work reasons, mostly.

"I already told you, sweaty, gross, total pig." Tall, sturdy but lean, half-naked in the gym, electric green eyes and abs for days. But still, total pig.

"Tell me the story again about how he said he was going to get you all hot and sweaty," she begs like the horny twenty-something she is. Aria tends to have a different guy every week but she has high standards and apparently, none of the guys she brings home have measured up yet. I've certainly never met one who deserves her.

"Which scarf?" I ask, ignoring her request and holding up two possible wool options. In reality, I probably need neither but I like to over-prepare.

I'm leaving NYC to go straight to Melbourne but my moving boxes should be waiting in my flat when we return to London. It's a small but lovely little unit in an old brick building Sandra said is corporate residence housing. The drivers, some staff, and some executives have units there for staying at headquarters which is in a sleepy British town about an hour outside of London. It's the kind of place where one reads a book and drinks tea while rain drips down the leaded glass windows.

I need to learn about tea. I smile that I can now call my apartment a flat, too. Tea, flats, and wankers.

Speaking of wanker, Aria continues her lewd googling and turns her head sideways to try and make out whatever photo she's found of him now. God knows there's enough material. Lennox at the beach with a supermodel. Lennox at a club with several supermodels. Lennox autographing women's breasts. Or my personal favorite, Lennox drunk at a New Year's Eve party doing a Facebook Live video with some fan who is trying to, as far as I can ascertain, clean out his inner ear with her tongue.

And I get to clean all this up.

He's got the horny women fans on his side, I'll give him that. But that's all he has going on for his reputation and that is not what Celeritas is looking for to bring in sponsors. Unless they want me to pursue condom brands or Axe body spray - actually, scratch that, we should look into a sponsorship by whatever magic cologne he uses that so successfully masked his sweaty pig scent last week.

"The gray one," Aria brings me back to reality and makes my scarf decision for me. "Promise me you'll send me nudes, of him obviously, as soon as you can." She's dead serious.

"Stop it," I giggle because she's so outlandish I can't help it. "There will be no nudes sent from me and hopefully not on Google anymore, either."

"You won't be able to resist, I'd climb this man like a tree."

"I'm sorry to disappoint you but I've never slept with a client and I'm not going to cheat on David so you'll have to get your celebrity porn from someone else." That much I can guarantee with absolute certainty. I'm a lot of things but I am not a cheater like these entitled athletes I'm paid to rebrand.

"Is David coming tonight?" Aria asks.

"I don't know, he said he might have to work late." I don't want to get into this, too, with Aria. We don't have much time left before I leave and I don't want to spend it arguing with her about David, who she has never liked.

"But it's your going away dinner," she sits up on the bed and looks at me disapprovingly.

I'm aware that it's my going away dinner at my parent's house and it would seem reasonable to expect my boyfriend to be there and not cite work as an excuse, especially since he works for my father, but it's... complicated.

"I'm glad you're going to be there, though" I smile at my obnoxious bestie. I really will miss her.

"Duh, I'm not leaving you alone with those sharks."

We arrive at my parent's Upper East Side townhouse as late as I could manage without getting reprimanded. I don't want to be here longer than absolutely necessary.

My sister's pristine white BMW and my brother's sleek black Mercedes are parked on the street so they're here already. Aria and I, we circled the block for half an hour then finally found a place to park her ten-year-old Toyota Corolla which is still a step up from my car. Which is no car at all. Because normal people do not need cars in New York City. Aria only has it because it was left to her when her grandmother died and she trades the building super personal training sessions for free parking.

"Let's get it over with," Aria slaps my thigh and we make our way past the manicured potted hedges and enter the double-wide white doors.

I hate this Georgian nightmare home.

"Darling," Mom calls as she greets us in the foyer and gives me a kiss on the cheek. Lydia Mitchell is dressed to the nines even though this is just a family dinner. Nothing is more important than appearances to Mom.

She has a new little white dog in her arms that is yipping and wiggling about at the commotion and I think it may have peed a little on her white Chanel, which pleases me.

"Aria," Mom's voice drops an octave and she plasters a fake smile on to greet my oldest friend, "don't you both look lovely. Come in, your brother and sister are in the sitting room."

The foyer is mint green this month and there's a new abstract modern art piece on the wall which sums up Lydia's sense of style and decorating sense. If it's expensive, it must be good. It doesn't matter that it defies logic and looks ridiculous amongst the gold plated mirrors and chairs that are for looking at, not for sitting in.

"Hey hey, there's our little English muffin!" My brother, Cody, leaps to greet me when we enter the gaudy sitting room. Who needs a room just for sitting?

He's got a tumbler full of cognac in one hand because he's also a prepared person like I am — I pregamed this little shindig, even — and he wraps his free hand around me and pulls me into his side. "So proud of you," he whispers into my hair as he kisses my head.

I knew I could count on him to say it, anyway.

He gives Aria a big bear hug and musses up the long hair she had

18

piled neatly on the top of her head. I always hoped Cody and Aria would get together but it's never happened and both feigned repulsion whenever I brought it up in the past. I think they doth protest too much, but alas.

"Girls, nice to see you," Dad greets us from a tall leather chair next to a plush settee, which also looks wildly out of place in the room. "Join us for a cognac?" He asks.

"Yes," Aria and I both answer in unison.

"I got it, Dad," Cody tells him so he doesn't need to get up, and sets to filling tumblers for us from the glass bar cart. My father, the distinguished Robert Mitchell, is used to people waiting on him.

My sister, Emma, is sitting in the settee next to Dad but doesn't bother to glance up from her phone. Her wine glass sits empty on the coffee table in front of her. Looks like everyone is on top of their coping mechanisms this evening.

"Dinner will be in ten," Mom sing songs back into the room and sits on the armrest of dad's chair, new little dog still in tow.

"Oh Mallory," Dad says, "David won't able to join us this evening. He sends his regrets but deadlines wait for no man."

Aria sighs and I swallow down my first gulp of cognac, which is disgusting but gets the job done.

It's not enough for David to miss my send off but he calls my father to let me know. Mom and Dad think we'll be getting married soon and I'd like to tell them that the last time David even fucked me was three months ago. So I don't see wedding bells or grandbabies in their near future.

Or ever.

"Make sure you make time to see him before you leave, Mallory. Leaving a man like David behind is a risk and you'll want to give him something to remember you by, if you know what I mean." Mom winks and Dad chuckles and puts a hand on her knee seductively.

Gross. Gross. Gross.

The thought of Lydia and Robert banging is perplexing. If she didn't have three children, I'd swear Lydia Mitchell was far too prim and proper to ever be caught naked or in an unsavory position. And when would Dad have time?

"Jesus, Mom," Emma shudders and makes a vomiting face even though she never stops swiping through her phone.

By the time we're halfway through our gluten-free dinner meal even though no-one has celiac disease, the whole table is several coping mechanisms into the cognac and wine and the nitpicking has started. I can feel the argument coming like a train rolling down the tracks.

Emma's hair is looking rooty and needs a touch-up. Cody needs to choose a wife already because he'll do better at work if he appears to be a family man. And me? I'm throwing my whole life away chasing my naive dreams, running around to Europe like a "high school student on her gap year."

"All your father means, Mallory," mom says swirling the wine around in her glass so vigorously that some has already spilled onto the tablecloth but she doesn't notice, "is that this social media thing was fun while you were young, but David isn't going to wait around for you forever."

"What does David have to do with my career?" I take the bait, fueled by liquid courage.

Aria starts to make some comment about David not deserving me at all if he can't support me or be faithful while I'm gone, but Dad interrupts her as if she's a ghost at the table and he can't hear her. Aria has always been far beneath Robert and Lydia Mitchell.

"I wouldn't call social media a career, dear," Dad chortles.

And here we go again. Because the whole family, Cody and Emma included, work in the traditional print media corporation that Dad built, my stepping foot outside it into a new marketplace is a grave offense. A total waste of my journalism degree. An offense worthy of shunning their youngest child.

"Oh yeah? Tell me, Dad, what would you call it then?"

"Well, at this point, I'd call the whole stunt a disgrace," he extolls without an ounce of hesitation.

"Dad, come on," Cody tries to reason with him like he always does. But there is no reasoning with my parents. God knows I've tried over the past 26 years.

Still doesn't stop me from arguing with them because I don't need this crap. I've never needed any of their crap. I graduated from college and then refused to take one more penny of their support because it comes with strings attached, like all shitty gifts from shitty people.

"This is not a stunt," I growl and slam my glass tumbler to the table, "this is my life!"

"Mallory, please, after the last public embarrassment working with that hoodlum basketball player don't you think it's time to stop this?" Mom's eyes are glazed over but she's dead serious. For months I had to hear about how her snooty friends at the club kept bringing up her poor misguided daughter and she never once defended me even though I had nothing to do with the debacle.

"Just wait Mom, I'm going to bring all the shame upon our name now. So much shame you'll need a pitchfork to shovel it all. I have a much bigger platform now and by the time I wrap up this job I'll be able to open my own firm and then shame will rain down from the heavens!" I realize I'm slurring my words and should probably quit with the cognac but fuck them.

"Your own firm!" Emma snorts and heckles me, "You're drunk!"

"And you're a bitch," I seethe back at her. She's said a dozen words to me all night and now she only throws gas on the dumpster fire.

"Enough!" Dad roars. "Mallory, enough is enough. You need to grow up. Your mother and I agree, this ends now. Or," he pauses.

"Or what?" I challenge him. What else could they possibly do to me?

"Or we'll have no choice but to disavow you, update the will and remove your inheritance," he finishes.

Inheritance, is he serious? "That the best you have, Dad, huh? I was never going to see a penny of that anyway and I don't want it!"

"I'll take her share," Emma smirks over her wine glass.

Cody has his head in his hands over the table, rubbing his temples.

"Alrighty then," Aria stands and shoves her chair back, sending it toppling over sideways onto the floor. Lydia clutches her actual pearls. "This has been a lovely evening but I think we'll bid you a fond adieu now," she says in a faux French accent and tries to take a dramatic bow but only ends up drunk stumbling onto Cody.

I stand to join her and Cody walks us both to the front door so he can call us a cab since neither of us are in any condition to be driving anywhere right now.

"Why do you put up with them, Cody, why?" I ask him as we stand outside trying not to fall over as we wait for a cab. Cody works for Dad too but he's not like them, he never has been. He was my only salvation growing up in this gauche mint-colored house of horrors.

"Shit, I don't know," he scratches his head, "I just don't have the energy to fight with them all the time. Always respected that you do, though."

He wraps his arms around me and rests his chin on my head. "You don't have to leave you know, don't run away for them," he says.

"I'm leaving for me, Cody. For me." I mumble into his side.

"Then you do you, little sister. Go find what you're looking for. See the world. Run far enough that you find yourself."

I squeeze him harder and nod. I refuse to cry over my parents, though. They don't get my tears anymore. "I'll come home and visit you when I can."

"Pfft, I love you but I kind of hope I never see you back here again," he chuckles.

"Ugh, me too!" Aria announces and launches herself into us to join the group hug and the three of us nearly fall onto the sidewalk giggling.

Thank god for her comic relief and a big brother who never lets you down.

Four

Photo: Lennox Gibbes and Celeritas Arrive in Melbourne

staceyq1998: how can anyone be so hot after a 20 hour plane ride? sigh…

llamalover4life: he's washed up and needs to retire. and maybe shave.

fortytwodogs: Nooooooo! No shaving! He's so delicious when scruffy!

purplelipstick99: girl, did you see the pics of him with Kate Allendale?! I'm so jealous. :(

fortytwodogs: Yes! I'd cut a bitch to be that close to him. I wonder what he smells like.

michael650004: smells like failure

mustbetoast: hasn't driven well in two years, fire the loser!

atsronautfeet11: I don't care how he drives as long as he does it naked

kiltsandkites: Scotland stands with you, Lennox! Bring us home a victory!

ieatlemons: speak for yourself, mate. dude's an asshole.

Lennox

There's a loose thread on the hem of my black Cerelitas polo and I've been picking at it endlessly. I want to pull it off but it's cinching the seam up instead and won't budge.

"Lennox? Lennox?" I glance up and one of the crackpot F1 journalists in the pre-race driver press conference is standing with a microphone looking at me like he's waiting for me to deliver an epiphany.

"Sorry mate, can you repeat the question?" The crowd giggles because it's no secret I don't pay attention during these, not that any other driver does either. They're all bullshit with the same tired questions and we deliver the same tired answers.

Or, I used to deliver the same tired answers. Now I don't give a shit. That's what happens when your loyalty is abused and you're stabbed in the back enough.

Case in point, the first burning question from this reporter comes, "What is your strategy for the first race here in Melbourne?"

"Well, I just came up with this late last night and I've been thinking a lot about it so I'm glad you asked." The twenty-five or so journalists in the room all quiet themselves and dial into the profound words I'm about to speak. You'd think they'd learn. "I thought, and this is pretty radical, I thought I might try to win the race."

The journalist huffs audibly into the mic and sits back down with a smarmy purse of his lips. The two drivers sitting behind the media table with me chuckle.

Every single interview is the same and has been for all the years I have been driving. They ask the world's most inane, boring questions or they purposefully exploit the smallest mistake or weakness to sell their bloody rag sheets in the grocery aisles. All of them out for themselves with no regard for anyone else.

Creating drama where there is none.

Pick pick picking at the scab.

"This question is for Lennox," another one of them stands and is handed a microphone by the F1 Press Coordinator. "Lennox, is this your comeback year? Is this the year you're going to make a run for the championship and return to your previous form? And the second part of my question is…"

"What kind of question is that?" I interrupt him. "Do you think I, or any of the drivers sitting up here," I wave my arms toward them, "set out to not win a race? Do you think that's why we got into racing, to not win?"

"I just, I mean," he stutters, "I just thought we'd like to hear your thoughts on being relegated to the Number Two driver at Celeritas and if that team structure still exists this year."

This fucker.

The correct answer, the one Celeritas wants me to give, is that this is a team sport and I have the team's full backing and I will do whatever is in the best interest of the team. That's the canned response. I know this because they give me actual printed materials of acceptable answers.

And those go right into the bin.

Because the real answer, the one I should give to this asshole, and all his asshole colleagues, is that my team hasn't had my back in two years and I no longer give a shit about them beyond ensuring they deliver large sums of money into my bank account on a regular basis. I should tell them that the team would happily tie me up and light me on fire in a blazing effigy if someone paid them enough money to do so.

I should tell them that I still race to win because I fucking love this sport, the one I have dedicated my entire life to, but that my own team doesn't really want that. They don't want me to win. I'm welcome to come in second place, of course, but winning is frowned upon.

But instead of that, I answer in the only way I can possibly muster and still have some sense of dignity - with sarcasm. "Is this my year?" I start, "Probably not. Might want to try back next year."

The journalist sits back down, or maybe he's still standing, I don't know. I've gone back to picking at my loose thread.

My phone starts buzzing in my pants pocket so I pull it out while half-listening to the journalists terrorize the other drivers and I'm grateful for whoever this is that's sending me a text or an email, anything that is more interesting than this press conference.

Text Alert - New Nanny: STOP IT!

I pick my head up from looking at the phone hidden in my lap under the table and there's my eager little babysitter scowling and shaking her head at me from the back wall of the press conference room. She's standing with Jack who is oblivious to these ongoings by now and is as bored as I am.

But Mallory's pissed.

I was split fifty-fifty on whether she'd even show up in Melbourne. I was rather hoping not. A grown-ass man doesn't need a full-time babysitter, regardless of what Celeritas makes her official job title. I guess I need to try harder to get rid of her and send her back home to New York or New Jersey or wherever the hell.

I grin at her mischievously and fire back a text, the journalists still droning on about some new regulations and how we feel about them. As if anyone cares how we feel about them. We just drive the cars and dance like monkeys when ordered.

> **Lennox:** You look hot in that little team uniform.
> **New Nanny:** Act like an adult and answer the questions appropriately!
> **Lennox:** Undo a button on your shirt and I will.
> **New Nanny:** Are you insane? What is wrong with you???
> **Lennox:** is that a no?
> **New Nanny:** Of course it is a NO, you pig! Do your job! This isn't funny!
> **Lennox:** Ok then.

I continue staring at Mallory and refuse to take my eyes off her even when the next mundane question from the next bloodsucking wanna-be journalist comes my way.

"Lennox, it's obvious there's been tension in the team since DuPont came aboard, is there anything you want to address with us today on that matter?"

A corner of my mouth quirks up and my eyes are still locked in on Mallory's as I answer, so much that some of the people in the room are looking over their shoulders to see what I'm staring at. Mallory fists are clenched at her side and daggers and ice explode from her eyes.

"I'd say I'm more focused on *undressing* things right now, mate," I say into my mic while still locked onto Mallory like a heat-seeking missile.

Alessi, one of the drivers from Anora Sport who's sitting next to me at the press table, snorts and hangs his head as he laughs trying to hide it from the press.

The room is giggling as several of them turn to look at Mallory who is absolutely livid. Jack is giggling next to her and as the room quiets and everyone turns back to face the front she whips an arm across her and smacks Jack in the side.

I expect her to race out of the room and finally go home to whatever vanilla office job she belongs in but she stays, in quiet rage, for the rest of this dull press session. As soon as it's over she tears out of the room though.

Good, she's on her way home. She's a sexy babysitter in her little black team shorts and a tight polo shirt, but it's time for her to go, just like all the others.

Celeritas doesn't get to win this fight.

Alessi and I are shooting the shit on our walk out of the press conference down a long hallway headed back toward the garages when he taps me and points. The goddamn nanny is waiting for me at the end of the hallway and it doesn't look like she wants an autograph or a selfie.

"Don't leave, mate. We'll need a witness when she murders me and throws my body into the bay," I grumble to him.

"Dude, you're on your own with that shit," he replies before abandoning me in the hallway.

She's so mad it's actually cute. Her long hair is tied onto the top of her head and even the tips of her ears are red with anger. I'm six foot something and she's five foot nothing, yet she's looking at me like she's going to take me outside and beat the shit out of me.

"Nanny!" I smile and exclaim as if I'm overjoyed to see her. "Do you need a lift to the airport? I could have one of the guys pull a car around."

Mallory takes in a long, deep breath and squares off with me. "We aren't going to the airport, Lennox. We have a photo session with Choman Palé so let's go." She grabs me by the elbow and is trying to drag me along, which is so comically adorable I let her.

"Choman what? The watch company?" I ask her as she pulls me along, not releasing my elbow because she must think I'll run off and she must believe herself capable of stopping me.

"Yes, the watch company, Lennox. You know, one of your sponsors?"

"I wouldn't wear one of those gaudy watches if you paid me," I grumble.

And I wouldn't. I don't. I'm not above buying expensive things if they make me happy. I have supercars and for a while, I had a yacht. I can be a rich bastard when it suits me. I just see no value in a £50,000 hunk of ostentatious gold on my wrist that does nothing more than advertise to the world 'I'm a douche.'

"They do pay you, Lennox. That's the point. They pay you several hundred thousand dollars," she rolls her eyes.

"No, they don't. They pay Celeritas. Not me."

"What is the difference? Same thing!" She turns and yells at me.

"No," I bark and crowd into her space. She takes a step backward and bumps into the wall behind. "You listen up, my naive little American nanny. It is not the same thing. This isn't some kumbaya feel-good festival. Every single person you see here is out for one thing and one thing only — himself."

Her hands are flat on the wall, her chest heaving, and she's searching my eyes back and forth. "Including you," she snarls.

I inch closer to her and she sucks in a breath. "Especially me."

We hold this position for several beats until her shoulders drop and she softens ever so slightly, which is the last thing I expect someone in her position to do when I'm in her face and yelling. She looks small and vulnerable and for just a split second, I feel guilty for raising my voice. But she needs to know.

She's nothing but another pawn, no different than I am.

"Why are you like this?" She whispers.

"What am I like, love?" I revert to my smoldering facade that never fails to drop panties and this time I do reach up to touch her cheek with the back of my fingers. Not in a sexual way, I just want to feel the heat causing the red fire alighting her face, remind myself of what it felt like to be that passionate about anything.

She turns her face into my fingers just a millimeter, a fraction of a second, but I think I felt it. It's over before I can be sure and instead, she says, "You're such an asshole!"

I can't help but step back and chuckle, "Aye, I am. Don't forget that."

She pushes off the wall and starts back down the hallway and because I need to go take pictures with ugly watches now, I follow. Or that's what I tell myself.

"And go home," I say to her back as she continues marching ahead.

"Not going home, Lennox, deal with it!"

Five

Mallory

The sweet burn of top-shelf rye whiskey in my throat has never felt so good. After the day I had today, this is medicinal whiskey I'm enjoying in the hotel bar. I've earned it.

After Lennox treated the press conference like it was open mic night at a standup comedy club, I dragged him to the photo session for a high-end watch manufacturer. He threatened to tell them their watches were 'as ugly as a shaved ape on a catwalk' unless I introduced myself to the photographer as his lovestruck fangirl stalker.

I debated whether caving was the right thing to do, or not, but it was better than him asking me to unbutton my shirt again and the press conference proved that Lennox Gibbes does not bluff. Getting fired on my first trip for the new job was not an option so I proudly marched up to the photography crew and introduced myself as one of his insane groupies.

To prove a point and take back some control of the situation, I even hammed it up and twirled my hair, spoke like a valley girl, and told them I've been following Lennox around the globe for years now. I'm sure they thought I was a complete idiot, especially with Lennox embellishing with more fictional details of my prowess as a stalker, as I gave them my tale.

And then he actually did as asked, kept his part of the bargain.

I got some great photos of him to post on social and I think I can spin them as a take on a luxury product for a rugged kind of man. Lennox certainly doesn't fit the normal demographic of older rich snob, with his tattoos and bad boy persona, so I'm hoping to gain some traction on my actual job duties since I got an hour of partial cooperation out of him.

Of course, as soon as the photo session ended and I wanted to discuss his social media accounts, so I can do my job and manage his publicity, he was back in his standard form of egomaniacal asshole.

I do feel slightly accomplished that I got the photoshoot done and I have all the info I need now to tackle all of the online platforms. Come hell or high water, I am not being run out of this job by a tyrannical playboy. I have enough spite and hostility toward my family that I will put up with damn near anything to prove them wrong.

It would be nice if Lennox Gibbes didn't make it his life's mission to push those boundaries, but that doesn't appear to be an option for him.

Stupid, sexy asshole.

I sip my drink and try texting David again. I sent him a photo of downtown Melbourne when I arrived and he replied, hours later, "That's cute. Hope you're having fun."

Fun. Like I am on vacation.

He's never said congratulations on my job, never even expressed that he would miss me when I left. When I tried to discuss how we'd manage a long-distance relationship given my travel schedule, he simply said he wasn't worried about it. In my heart, I know the writing is on the wall.

I think the only reason I've been ignoring it is because breaking up will cause another fight with Mom and Dad and it was an easy enough relationship to tolerate. It wasn't bad, he hasn't cheated or treated me poorly. But it wasn't good, either. It's just kind of there, existing but not adding much to life, like plain white bread… technically full of calories but it doesn't leave you satisfied.

I deserve good. I deserve earth-shattering, someone that gives me spark. And honestly, someone that supports who I am, doesn't try to tame me or make me complacent like David who will always side with Dad over me.

"I see you're hitting the hard stuff." I glance up from my medicinal cocktail and Jack has pulled up a stool next to me at the bar and is flagging over the bartender.

As far as I'm concerned, Jack, Mattias, and Lennox are one and the same, the three of them some sort of band of assholes. Lennox is certainly the ring leader, but they are grown men who should know better. They're all stupid attractive too, it's ridiculous.

"Mmmmm," I mumble at him. "Have you also come to ask me to portray a stalker or take my shirt off?"

I just want to drink my drink in peace without more annoyance, insults, or irritation but Jack is making himself plenty cozy on the stool next to me and orders a local draft beer.

"Nanny, if you haven't noticed, I'm gay, so no, I don't want you to take your shirt off. I mean, unless you want my opinion on your goods, in which case I'm happy to offer constructive feedback. I've seen a lot of breasts, for a gay man," he tells me, waving at my chest with his fingers.

Jack is a good looking man, tall, fit, blue eyes and brown hair with a bit of curl to it. He has dimples which would be attractive if only I didn't see them when he was cackling like a schoolboy every time Lennox antagonized me. He's decidedly less attractive then. He has the same gorgeous Scottish accent that Lennox does and I decide then that all men should have accents.

I ignore his comment about my chest and snark back at him, "isn't it a little cliche to have a gay assistant these days?"

"Yes, definitely," he nods. "But Lennox didn't hire me because I'm gay so I don't think it counts. Well," he pauses, "no, technically he did hire me because I'm gay."

"I've been drinking, Jack. You'll need to make up your mind and be more clear if you insist on harassing me while I'm drinking."

"Harassing? No, I'm here for gossip. Tell me all about New York, I love it there." Jack's beer has arrived and he downs nearly half of it in one chug. I see I'm not the only power drinker in the bar this evening.

"I'm sorry," I crane my neck and face him, "are we friends now? What is happening here?"

A few guys from a competing team walk in and take a hightop table in the corner and Jack watches them suspiciously and lowers his volume. I've only just arrived but there is an awful lot to keep up within this environment and I need to figure out all the dynamics. I'm used to one player and his team goes up against one other team. Here, there are 10 different teams, each with two drivers, and they don't seem to fraternize with each other much. It's odd.

So I take Jack's cue and turn my back to the other team members and keep my voice down.

"There's no reason we can't be friends, Nanny."

"I seem to recall Lennox telling you exactly that you were not allowed to be my friend." He yelled it, in fact, when he was half-naked in the gym, but I leave that part out.

"Please," he spurts, "you can't take everything so literal. If you survive long enough you'll see he's not that bad."

With the courage of two tumblers of Masterson's whiskey in my belly, I bark out a laugh. "He's awful! He is a chauvinistic man-child and I don't think he is hiding a single redeeming quality!"

"I'm sorry," Jack puts his hand on mine atop the bar and glares at me sympathetically "have you not seen his abs?"

I can't help but giggle a little. Jack seems like a likable enough character but he works for the devil and I'm not foolish enough to let my guard down. Though, if he wants to engage in gossip, it might benefit me to let him keep talking.

"Abs are not a redeeming quality," I tell him.

"The hell they aren't." His beer is gone and he's waved a finger toward the bartender to get us another round, which is not a great idea but I'll nurse mine to keep Jack talking.

"Name me one redeeming quality. A real one. I dare you."

"Oh hell, the man has a house full of cats, for fuck sake. That counts for something, right?" Jack smirks like he knows he's being naughty revealing inner details about my enemy.

"Cats?" I exclaim a little too loudly. I don't know why I cannot picture tough guy Lennox Gibbes with cats. An aggressive, snarling large breed guard dog, maybe. But cats? I mean, I adore cats, all animals really. Except for the little dogs Mom is always carrying around and it's not even that I don't like them, it's that I don't get attached to them because she never keeps them past the stage when she finds them new and cute.

They're for showing off, just like her children.

I suppose this means Lennox is comfortable with his masculinity but that's not a big surprise, manwhore that he is.

"Mmhmm, the man is always bringing home strays. There's a good quality, Nanny.

"Stop calling me Nanny," I blurt out. I've had about enough of it from all three of these bozos.

"Maybe," he considers. "Tell me why you haven't quit yet. You're in the upper 50th percentile for nanny longevity, by the way."

"It's been two days…" I stare at him.

"Exactly, and you're still here. That's a long time, comparatively."

Nothing about that statistic is funny but I do giggle and am happy to have someone to talk to. I know absolutely no one on the team and the only people I converse with are hell-bent on sending me home on the next flight.

"Get on it with it," he continues, "tell me why you're still here."

"I need the job, Jack. Same reason anyone takes a job. Why are you here? What did you mean that Lennox hired you because you're gay?"

"That's technically two questions, Nanny — sorry, Mallory — but I'll allow it because you're new. As I said, always bringing home strays. I was one of them."

I'm happy he so easily caved on calling me by my name instead of continuing to address me as a babysitter when that is not at all what I see myself as. Perhaps Jack will end up being the reasonable one of the group.

"You were a stray gay assistant, how does that work, exactly?" I ask him. "Were you just wandering the streets of Scotland?"

"Oh hell, that's a story for another night with a lot more liquor, but let's just say that being gay in a family of Scottish Catholic zealots was not a good time." He takes a long pull of his beer and stares at the empty glass.

"Oh shit, I'm sorry, Jack." I have zero tolerance for bigotry and this makes my stomach roll. I know how it feels to have parents who shame you instead of support you. I want to put my hand on his to comfort him but I hesitate because it's not like we're besties and I don't want to get ahead of myself.

"Aye well, anyway, the fam' thought they'd send me away to be cured of my sinful ways. Lennox gave me a way out, more or less." He orders another beer and I realize we may be here a while. I'm ok with that.

"So you grew up together?"

"He's a few years older, but aye."

"And Matthias, was he also a stray?" I ask him.

"That's Matty's story to tell."

Interesting. I make a mental note about this theme of taking in strays, might be one good factoid to help counter the thousand negative pieces on him that exist on the internet.

"So, what's the real reason, Mallory?" He asks. "This is not an easy business to be in. Has to be more than the paycheck."

I take a deep breath and think for a moment of how to respond. I'm not naive, or drunk, enough to open up to the childhood friend of my arch-nemesis, but I suppose it doesn't hurt to keep the goodwill going. It's not like I am failing or quitting at this job no matter what Lennox or Celeritas think.

"Dysfunctional families make us all do strange things, I guess."

Jack nods at me knowingly and thankfully, does not push the issue.

He lifts his beer mug and clinks it against my glass tumbler, "Cheers to dysfunction."

We have one more round together and then I excuse myself before I say more things that I shouldn't. I'm the slightest bit buzzed and don't want to give anyone room to suggest I'm not professional. Plus, I need to dive into all these Facebook and Twitter and Insta accounts tonight. I have a feeling there's a lot of damage control awaiting me.

A long hot shower later, I'm camped out on my bed in my hotel room, which I do not have to share with anyone else, thank god. My laptop is out and Sandra sent me passwords to all the accounts today so it's time to get to work. Sandra's team at headquarters manages the company's pages but anyone Googling Lennox Gibbes comes across his personal accounts, too, so those are my first priority.

I log in to his Instagram account which he seems to have had enough sense to lock down to private. Still, there are over 6,000 requests to friend him and the direct message icon simply reads "99+". Oh, joy.

The last photo he posted was actually almost two years ago, but he's been tagged in hundreds and hundreds of photos. Photos of him driving on track, those are innocent enough. Then there are photos of him with cheerleaders, random women pressing themselves into the side of him for selfies and squealing about getting to meet him. A supermodel he was linked to a while back, hanging all over him and kissing him.

Yep, manwhore.

I spend nearly an hour untagging him from all of the posts I can and try not to read too much into the comments because they're either girls gushing about how much they want to bang him, or they're comments from armchair critics who leave messages ranging from constructive criticism to suggestions that he drowns himself in Loch Ness.

Social media can be ugly like that, I know all too well. As much as Lennox is a pig and a bully, as much as my other clients have also screwed up, no one deserves total strangers publicly decrying their value as human beings.

I open up Facebook next, his Public Person fan page. He says he doesn't have a personal account and Sandra says that's accurate as far as she can tell, so this should be easier and then I can go to sleep.

There are posts I can tell previous nannies, or Publicity Managers, have left more recently. The number of horny women throwing themselves at him compared to angry F1 fans seems to be three to one. I hide a gaggle of comments that the world is better off without, edit some of the previous nanny posts that I think were done poorly, and I make a new post from today's watch promo shoot.

"What happens when you annoy a clock? It gets ticked off. #LennoxGibbes. The time has come."

The attached photo features Lennox in a wide power stance, arms crossed over his chest so the watch on his wrist is prominent, and he is staring into the camera like it's going to get its ass beat. His eyes are emerald green and he looks intimidating as fuck with his forearms and biceps bulging.

Should appeal to the ladies, assuming they have a pulse. I want to avoid this man like the plague and it makes *my* lady parts tingly. And I think it might register with the race fans who are demanding a comeback. We'll see how it does overnight.

I cringe as I open up Messenger, knowing there will be more of the same and I am not disappointed. Pleas of bearing his children. Phone numbers galore, from every phone extension on every continent. I'm scrolling and deleting as I go when I almost delete one from Kate Allendale, the supermodel. It looks like it's from her real personal account and they're all unread.

Baby, please answer me.
Please answer your phone, we need to talk.
This is stupid, Lennox. I love you.
Did you block my number? WTF.

There are a dozen or so, all unread and unanswered from Kate the Waif, my new name for her, trying to get Lennox to respond. I knew they were linked a year or so ago because there are photos of them everywhere, but this must have been a relationship gone sour. Or else she's off her rocker and stalking him, which is also a possibility based on the messages I've read tonight.

In any case, it feels gross reading what are obviously private comments, no matter that a tiny part of me enjoys gossip as much as the next person. Aria would be squealing if she could see this, that girl is up to date on every celebrity gossip blog in existence.

I have to assume he cheated on her because, let's be serious, you can't throw a rock without hitting evidence of his philandering ways. Who cheats on a supermodel? Lennox Gibbes, apparently.

Six

Lennox

Ten years ago, my teenage self would have killed to be sitting where I am right now, behind the wheel of a Formula 1 car about to head onto the track. Now? Now I'm bored senseless.

The two choices I have are to be in a blind rage twenty-four seven or drown it all out and exist in a semi-conscious state of apathy, with the random snide remark to keep my heart pumping.

The only thing keeping me awake today in between runs during Free Practice is my NILF flitting around the garage like a kid in a candy store, in utter fascination with the big boy toys. She didn't find my new acronym for her, the Nanny I'd Like to Fuck, very funny but it hasn't stopped her from chasing me around like a harpy all day asking a million questions.

It might be cute if she weren't also taking pictures all day long for her cockamamie marketing ploys, and that gets on my nerves. The whole influencer generation grates on me. None of it is real, the bullshit people post to their profiles. Vacation photos of the happy couple who sleep in separate bedrooms and pray for the other to die so they can collect on the life insurance policy. But damned if they aren't going to post beach photos from the Bahamas and gush about how in love they are so they can try and one-up the neighbors. Are they really fooling anyone?

Everyone wants what someone else has.

"What about this button, what does it do?"

Nanny has asked about every button on my steering wheel so far and she's doing it because I am fully strapped into the car, helmet on, ready to go and can't get out. I'm being held hostage and begging the crew to release the car so I can get the fuck out of here. She's perched over me in the cockpit and deliberately flipping her long hair over me and leaning her chest in so I can see down her shirt. I know this game.

Unfortunately, she's winning it because being smashed into the car is not a comfortable time to have a semi.

"How about this button, and what does this dial do?" Her fingers are sneaking in trying to push every goddamn button the steering wheel.

"Fucking stop, you evil harpy!" I swat her hands away, but she keeps it up relentlessly.

"And this one, and this one, ooo what is that switch?"

"Matty, for fuck sake, pick her up and lock her in the motorhome!" I yell to Matty who is standing beside me with a cold air hose blowing on me, watching her with rapt fascination.

"You don't pay me enough for the sexual harassment lawsuit, sorry," he answers and cocks his head to the side in wonder at her obnoxious and unprecedented behavior.

Nanny manages to hit a clutch pedal behind the steering wheel and the car rocks forward a split second before I catch it. "Stop before you kill someone, wench!"

"I'll stop it when you stop calling me Nanny," she stands and puts her hands on her hip.

"You're mad," I shake my helmeted head at her, as much as one can shake their head with a HANS device on.

"Ok then," and she's back to double fisting every fidgety bit she can reach within the cockpit.

"You realize this car is worth about seventeen million pounds, aye? I guarantee that destroying it will get you sent back to New Hampshire faster than I ever could." I know she's from New York.

"Sounds like your problem." Push push push, fidget fidget fidget.

"FINE," I declare defeat and swat her away. She may have won the battle but I'll spend the rest of the afternoon making war preparations.

"Ha! That means no 'Nanny', no "NILF', no 'AU that's a great PAIR of tits ya' got there, none of it, Lennox!"

"Yeah, yeah," I wave her off and look straight ahead but it's impossible to miss her giant smile as she stands to my side, thoroughly impressed with herself.

The crew lowers the car from the dolly and sends me out moments later and I can finally adjust myself as soon as I pull out. Fucking hot nanny always arguing with me with that smart mouth. I can think of much prettier ways for her to use it.

I do a couple of dozen laps and run the programs the engineers call for, not that it matters, they'll see to it that I don't win the race anyway, and then I pull back into my garage bay. I've got twenty minutes before the next session so I hop out of the car and make my way into the back to find the bathroom because Matty pumps gallons of water into me every day.

Rounding the corner I hear Mallory giggling and I'm planning to announce that she neglected to ban the word 'babysitter' and I've come up with a few puns for that while driving around the track. But as soon as I see her, my jaw locks and my hands instinctively ball into fists.

My piece of shit teammate, Digby DuPont, is leaning against the wall with one arm above Mallory running a long strand of her hair between his fingers and she's laughing and smiling. Falling for his bullshit.

"Dickby!" I roar and march toward them.

Mallory jumps from the boom of my voice but Digby only turns to smirk at me like the manipulative little bitch he is and puts his arm around her shoulders.

"Ahh, Lennox, I see you're in caveman mode yet again. How charming. I was just introducing myself to the lovely Ms. Mitchell," and he glances down to smile at her with his smug artificially-whitened toothy grin.

"Get your fucking hands off the nanny," I seethe.

Mallory looks mortified and tries to slink out from under his arm but the prick tightens his grip on her shoulder and locks her against his side. She has no idea what kind of rat bastard is preying on her right now and I can feel my pulse ratchet up.

"Really Lennox, must you be so uncivilized all the time? It's tiring. Mallory and I were just having a chat about who makes the best cheesecake in New York City. Weren't we, Mallory?"

"Remove your hands from her or I will remove them from your torso."

"Oh good lord," his arms drop and he turns back to face Mallory, grinning with his full phony charm bullshit act. "Mallory, my apologies for having to witness this behavior. I do hope we can chat again soon in more pleasant company."

She looks between Digby and me and nods, unsure about what is happening here. We're supposed to be teammates. Fuckface makes his exit from the room going in the opposite direction of me, which is a really good call on his part.

"What the hell was that?" Mallory snaps at me as soon as he's out of earshot. "He was just introducing himself, not that it's any of your business!"

"Stay away from him."

"Why should I? You can't tell me who to talk to!" She's flustered and confused and I'm sure as hell not getting into it with her right now, or ever.

"I can and I will. Stay. Away. From him." I growl at her.

She shakes her head at me like I'm the world's biggest disappointment, which may be true, but I don't need this shit right now and she doesn't know what she's doing with Digby. "Piss off, Lennox," she says as she pushes past me and storms off.

Now I have two minutes to take a leak and get back in the car and I'm still fuming as the crew straps me back in, the guys cinching down my shoulder straps giving me a wide berth and knowing better than to make chit chat.

Dickweed DuPont is the reason my career is a joke, he embodies everything that is wrong with this sport now. He's a pay driver - Daddy in Monaco gives Celeritas enough money to let him drive a rocket around the track like the no-talent hack he is, endangering everyone else's life and throwing it in the faces of everyone who busted their ass to get here.

Oh yeah, and he fucked my girlfriend.

My car gets released from the garage and I tear out, needing to burn off this adrenaline before Digby gets his ass beat, again.

Two years ago I had one bad season, it happens. Small mistakes that add up. I was just coming off my world championship and I was a shoo-in to clinch it two years in a row, but shit happens. I own it.

But you make the smallest of errors here and the pundits and journalists and the suits blow it up like it's an act of war. As if I don't feel bad enough when I screw up, knowing hundreds of people back at the factory work their asses off every single day to get me into this car for a couple of hours on Sunday afternoons.

One bad season was all it took for Kate to move onto the next big sensation, the golden boy of the paddock, Digby DuPont. Walked into them fucking. On my bed, in my suite, in my on-track motorhome. He wasn't even on the Celeritas team then but he came into my house and fucked my girlfriend.

Didn't matter that Kate and I had been together for over a year and she was pushing me to get married. She was as full of shit as DuPunk. Just another user ruining people's lives for sport, stepping on them like rungs on her social-climbing ladder. It had been going on for months, all the while she posted those sickening happy photos of us all over the internet while I was an oblivious asshole.

Fuck her and fuck Digby DuPont.

The bruises on his pretty-boy face weren't even healed when Celeritas brought him aboard as a driver, courtesy of Daddy DuPont's deep pockets, which are deep enough for the team to dictate his position as the Number One driver, getting all the priority and strategy from day one.

My loyalty to the team, all the car development, the world championship I brought them, meant nothing once enough money flowed through their coffers. My commitment to Kate, the life we had together, meant nothing once a shinier new toy was dangled in front of her.

Matty calls Kate vampyyri, the vampire. It's perfect.

And Digby, the whole paddock calls him a piece of shit.

Celeritas has firmly cemented that he is the priority, he is to win. I'm to let him pass, give him tows down the straights, smile for the cameras like he's Mr. Personality and we're all a happy family. They can suck my dick.

I'll do my time and ride out my contract but I have zero fucks left to give. That's why I don't participate in their bullshit sponsorship events and fake ass media campaigns. That's when I became such an asshole.

At first, the playboy act was just to get back at Kate. Then it took focus over my shit season and the even shittier things happening at Celeritas and it just became easier to let people focus on my dick rather than my driving.

After the twentieth lap around the track, the engineers call me over the radio to come back into the garage. I 'accidentally' lock up the brakes to flat spot and ruin this set of tires. I'm a petty asshole, apparently.

I'm done for the day but I can't even go have a drink or six because I'm driving again within 24 hours and I won't be losing my super license over these clowns. Dickweed's car is in his bay in the garage though and I do want to ensure his hands are nowhere near my nanny.

I have no idea why I care besides the fact that Mallory is my plaything and he isn't going to steal that from me next. That's all the reason I need.

"Where is she?" I bark to Jack who is in the motorhome sorting cases of 5x8 stock photos for this weekend's autograph session.

"Who?" His head pops up from behind the tower of cardboard boxes.

"The bloody nanny, Mallory, where is she?"

"Ah, she took off for the day. She said, and I think these were her exact words, 'Lennox Gibbes is a primate who belongs in a zoo' and she stomped off. I didn't stop her to argue."

"Where's Dipshit?"

"With his physio, why?"

Good, as long as they're not together that suits me fine. I unzip my race suit down to my waist and think about how to handle this. Now that he knows there's a new way to get under my skin, he'll be relentless. Like a case of herpes.

"I want her hotel room moved, right across from mine," I tell Jack.

"Oh really," his eyebrows perk up, "Is that how it is now?"

"Don't give me shit, just do it."

"Like, tonight?"

"Aye Jack, tonight and every night thereafter. Right across from mine."

"The hell do you want me to say the reason why is?" Jack is trying to make sense of this and there's no rational explanation for him, it just needs to happen.

"Tell her the old room has bed bugs for all I care."

"Oh, that's good. Wait, does the hotel have bed bugs? They're insidious, you know."

Seven

Mallory

Since neither my parents, nor Lennox Gibbes, are driving me away from this job, I'm determined to find other sane and tolerable human beings in this environment to surround myself with. Preferably human beings without deep gravelly voices and Scottish accents that get thicker when angry, which is fairly often.

Yesterday was odd with Lennox and his teammate Digby, weird even for Lennox's standards. He has no business dictating who I can speak with and I don't see what he cares. He lets me know, often and in no uncertain terms, that my presence is a constant irritation to him. I thought we had made a tiny shard of progress — he seemed a little more playful versus malicious and agreed to stop calling me his nanny. But since the Digby incident, he's back to being a stone wall and all around crabass.

He's not going to kill my mood today, though. Sandra called this morning to give me sponsor engagement event dates but also to tell me she's pleased with my work so far on presenting a more... acceptable version of their bad boy driver. The watch post did better than I could have even hoped, the engagement was through the roof and it seemed to get a lot of people hyped up for the new season. Sandra said it did so well she shared it to their main marketing sites.

I got tons of usable material from free practice yesterday, too, including some candid video of him goofing about in the cockpit of his car with his crew and fans online loved seeing a different, more personal side to him.

So I'm patting myself on the back while sipping my coffee and I'm pleased, despite Grumpy Gibbes being back on the prowl today. Not only am I not fired yet, nor run out of here by Lennox's deliberate attempts at sabotage, nor failing as my parents and sister are waiting for me to do — I'm doing well.

Ha, take that, suckers.

So while the cars are running on track this morning, I'm making myself friendly and available for new friends in the team motorhome dining area. I'm coordinating Lennox's calendar with the sponsor engagements Sandra sent to me this morning and I have to say, I'm looking forward to some of these. There's a black tie affair or two in there. Part of me shivers in response to the thought of Lennox in a tuxedo and part of me shudders at the thoughts of all the ways he can, and probably will try to sabotage a formal event.

Two of the kitchen staff are chatting together and filling up coffee mugs from the self-serve beverage station in the dining area and as they scan the room for a place to sit I sit up tall and smile brightly at them like a new girl at school, desperate for someone to join her at lunch.

My lonely puppy eyes work and I'm thrilled when two younger girls make their way to my table with cheeks round from authentic smiles. Women are an obvious minority in the paddock — no equal opportunity hiring happening here — and I'm overly eager to just hang with girls and be normal for a few minutes. I miss Aria.

"Hi ladies, please join me!" I greet them when they make their way near my table. "I'm new and don't know many people here yet."

"Yes, you're the new media girl for Lennox, right? I'm Francisca!" Both girls take a seat and shake my hand. Francisca is maybe in her early twenties and has youth and perfect sun-kissed olive skin and a beautiful Latin accent. I have yet to meet another American, now that I think of it.

"Yes, his new Publicity Manager," I nod.

"I'm Tatiana," the second girl shakes my hand, "welcome to the team!" She also has a Latin accent, stunning eyelashes, and sleek black hair.

More importantly, both girls are smiling and chatty and behave like normal, kind humans when meeting a new coworker! Hell's bells!

"So what do you ladies do here?" I sip my locally roasted Australian bean coffee and ask them. The coffee here in Oz is no joke, I would sit here all day sucking it down if I didn't have a plan up my sleeve for this evening.

"We're both in catering," Francisca says.

"That has to be a lot of work to put out so much food every day for everyone at Celeritas," I say, wanting very much to make the kind of simple small talk and chit chat I usually hate.

"It's a lot of work," Tatiana says, "but there's a pretty big team back in the kitchen and it can be a lot of fun, too."

"Well, if the coffee is any indicator, you guys are doing an amazing job. This stuff is legit." I nod to them holding my warm mug up.

"I'm glad you like it. The catering team tries to incorporate as much local cuisine into the meals as possible so the food is always fresh and not the same thing over and over all season long." Francisca tells me.

"I didn't realize that. That's really cool." These two girls are immediately likable and super chatty. I feel like I'm back home for a minute, meeting with friends in an NYC cafe. It's a welcome respite until Francisca dips her head and pokes Tatiana in the side, nodding toward the main door.

In walks Lennox, strutting over to the beverage station to refill his oversized team water bottle. His back is turned to us and Tatiana is biting her lip and blatantly staring at his ass, which I will admit, looks delicious in his racing suit. Francisca is no better, twirling her long black hair in one hand now.

"Oh my god, you two are terrible," I whisper to tease them. They're not even attempting to hide their gawking and the pair of them doing it, sashaying their heads and making mmm-hmmm sounds as Lennox bends and stretches, fills my gut with laughter.

"Please, girl. That man is fine." Francisca says, her head turned away from me and refusing to unlock from its masculine target.

"The things I would do to him," Tatiana whispers under her breath. "Things that are illegal in my home country."

"I'll do the jail time for one hour with him," Francisca whispers back, her short unpainted fingernails mindlessly caressing over her neck as the peep show continues.

Lennox turns around with his water bottle and their two heads spin back away from him, though there's no way Lennox could have missed them checking him out. He's probably used to it, walking around all through the world with women staring and throwing themselves at him. It must be a hard life.

He spots us and Francisca gives him a little wave and squeaks out, "Hi, Lennox" and bats her eyelashes at him like an innocent southern belle, not the woman who just moments ago threatened to do illegal things to his body.

In three strides of his long legs, he's at our table standing behind his two gushing fans. "Francisca," he says and bends down to plant a kiss on her cheek.

"Tatiana," and he does the same for her.

Both girls are beet red and looking up at him like he's just hung the moon.

"You're both looking gorgeous as ever this afternoon. Thank you for the breakfast this morning, it was delicious, as always," he says to them.

"Lennox," Tatiana starts, vying for his attention next, "I asked Chef to make the New Zealand lamb tonight. I remember you liked it last year."

"You're too kind. Thank you for being so thoughtful but you know I like everything you prepare," he grins down on his adoring fangirls. "How is your mother, by the way? Is she feeling better?"

"Oh yes," Tatiana gushes, "you're so sweet to remember her. She's much better now."

I don't know who this thoughtful and charming man is that is standing in front of these lovestruck ladies, but I can no longer control a tiny snort at how taken Francisca and Tatiana are with him.

"Mallory," he states coldly in acknowledgment that I am also at the table with his fangirls. Half a second later he squeezes the girls' shoulders, says goodbye to them, not to me, and struts out of the room as both girls crane their necks to watch him go.

As soon as he's out of earshot I heckle them both, "You two are absolutely hilarious. Is he being so nice so that you don't poison his food?"

"What?" Francisca's face falls and I realize I must have upset her. "Why would we poison his food?"

"I'm so sorry, I didn't mean to insult you or insinuate you would ever poison anyone! I just meant because he's so nice to you guys." I hope I didn't make them both mad and run off the only two friendly coworkers I've found yet.

"What are you talking about? Lennox is nice to everyone," Tatiana nods, defending her man crush with fiery confidence.

"Nice to everyone?" I sputter. "Lennox? Lennox Gibbes? He's been nothing but awful to me! His teammate, Digby, is nicer to me than Lennox is!"

"No no no no no no no," Francisca waves her hand back and forth and shakes her head. Her words crash together in that beautiful rhythm I have never been able to recreate, no matter how many Spanish classes I took in high school. "No, all wrong girl, all wrong."

Tatiana crosses her arms and nods in agreement with Francisca, adding in a sassy "mmm hmm" while pursing her lips at me. "You want Lennox, not Digby," she adds.

"I don't want either of them," I chuckle. "I have a boyfriend."

"Good, more chances for me," Francisca laughs and slaps my hand. I'm so glad I haven't really upset them, they're just passionate Gibbes defenders, much like the fangirls online. "Anyway, break time is over, we have to get back."

"It was so nice chatting with you both!" I tell them hoping we'll be able to do this again.

"Come back anytime, girl, we're always in here!"

Today is getting better and better. My boss is happy, I found two new coworkers to chat with, and Lennox did not bite my head off or make any crass sexual comments about me.

Yet.

"Whispered something in your ear. It was a perverted thing to say. But I said it anyway. Made you smile and look away." - Cigarettes After Sex - Nothing's Gonna Hurt You Baby

"Who are you and what have you done with the real Lennox Gibbes?" I whisper into his ear at the autograph session I'm trying to pry him away from right now.

He's sitting behind a covered table with a box of Sharpies and I have just watched him spend an hour with an ongoing line of fans at the track who are queued up waiting their turn to have photos and hats and tee shirts signed by their favorite driver. The other drivers all did their scheduled twenty-minute sessions but Lennox has been here for an hour. He's had a smile on his face and made time for every single one of them.

"Stop speaking in riddles, Mallory." He answers, continuing to sign and take selfies with each person waiting for him. He's also stuck to his word and is calling me by my real name.

A very buxom blond is next in line and is bouncing with excitement, her low crop top straining to contain her implants. They must be implants, otherwise, at their size, her breasts would be down to her knees, not aiming toward the sky. Security lets her step up and she rounds the table and starts lowering her frilly blouse even further. Lennox doesn't bat an eye and stands so he can sign her chest as she claps and squeals. Cell phone cameras from the crowd start turning his way to capture Lennox and the bare boob incident that is about to unfold.

"Nope, tops stay on please!" I interrupt and put a hand between the woman's chest and Lennox's Sharpie.

The woman huffs and protests but security is on top of it. I only get a death glare from Lennox as he signs her phone case instead.

"You're a real buzzkill, you know that?" He says.

"Get your fill of silicone on your own time, preferably behind closed doors." I dismiss him.

"I'm not a silicone kind of guy, thank you very much."

"Oh, you prefer saline?" I clap back.

"Since you asked, I like natural tits, Mallory." His gaze drops to my chest and his deep voice lowers and he speaks slowly right next to me, "a handful of soft, natural tits. Fucking perfect."

"There are children," I scold him, as his stare slowly raises back up from my chest.

48

"Better hide those hard nipples, then," he says and turns back to the waiting crowd.

Oh my hell, my traitorous nipples are peaked and visible through my polo. Damn you, boobs, damn you to hell! I turn my back for a second and smooth my hands down the front of my shirt trying not to be obvious and give him even more satisfaction of knowing how he made my body betray me. It's the deep, gravelly voice and that damn accent. My nipples were powerless.

When I turn back around a second later, he's occupied with the next fans in line, a parent and a little boy in Celeritas team colors who is so excited he cannot speak and is so nervous he looks on the verge of tears. He can't be more than four years old. It's adorable.

Lennox crouches down on his knees and urges the tiny fan to come closer. Clutching his dad's hands, the tiny fan carefully starts toward Lennox and extends a Celeritas children's hat to be signed. Lennox signs it and talks sweetly to the little boy and gets him smiling within moments. Before I know it, the boy is being swung upward in Lennox's big arms onto his shoulders and the proud papa is snapping photos of this once in a lifetime moment for his son.

They scurry off after getting their shot and my mouth is agape. Why is he so nice to other people? Where is the pig that I've been working with?

Before he sits back down at the table, he towers over me and whispers, "Don't be jealous, you can ride on my shoulders later." My mouth clamps shut but I'm still bewildered about what's happening here and I'm keenly aware that his vulgar comments don't seem to offend me much anymore. More troubling, my attempts to deny what they do to my body when he whispers filthy things in my ear are getting harder to keep at bay. I'm only human.

I need to get my head on straight.

"Last person, Lennox, we have to go."

"Five more minutes," he responds. He's asked for five more minutes a dozen times now.

Five minutes later I put my foot down, pick up my backpack of gear, and pull him away from the line, begrudgingly.

"Where are you dragging me to now, anyway? I'm done for the day." He grumbles as I lead him through the maze of the circuit.

"We have a recent addition to your schedule, it won't take long," I tell him as we make our way toward the exit and the private parking zone behind the garages for the teams.

When we reach the parking lot I dig into my bag and pull out the key fob and hand it to him.

"What is this?"

"It's a key fob, Lennox."

"Yes, smart ass, I can see that. Where are we going?" He pushes the button on the fob and a sleek dark grey Ferrari convertible near us lights up and beeps.

"It's a surprise," I say. I hope this works. The fans must have rubbed off on him, he's not as combative as I expect him to be, so far.

"What kind of surprise?" One of his eyebrows raises playfully and his lips curl up.

"If you don't fight me on this, there may be pussy in it for you." I smile. I can play his game too if I get what I need out of it.

"Consider me intrigued, Ms. Mitchell," he smolders back.

We both sink into the car and he hits a button to roar the engine to life, a deep rumbling of the motor that I can feel through the soft leather seat and into my core. This Ferrari coupe would make anyone's panties wet, it's just a fact.

"Where to?" He asks as I pull out my phone and start giving him directions from my map app.

This car is obscenely sexy and it seems an intimate moment despite the passing freeway. We're rarely alone together for this long and he's never been this cooperative.

We're cruising in the convertible, my hair whipping around my face in the warm sun and I am having very impure thoughts about Lennox's hands working the paddle shifters on the steering wheel. Every sinew and tenon in his forearms flex as he guides the steering wheel and it's hot watching him drive this powerful car. If he would just shut his mouth, he'd be the perfect specimen of a man.

In a show of good faith, I decide to push my luck and try talking to him, like an adult, without any barbs or snide comments. "Want to know something?"

"You're a virgin? It's ok, I'll be gentle," he says and pats my knee.

"You're such an asshole," I grumble and turn away to look out the open window. I should have known.

He laughs, "Ok, come on, tell me."

"Are you going to be a dick?" I turn back to him and cross my arms over my chest.

"Probably, but I want you to tell me anyway." His brown hair is blowing and he's looking straight ahead under his aviator sunglasses.

If he wasn't a client and if I didn't have a boyfriend, I have to admit, I would also very likely do things to him that are illegal in most countries like Francisca suggested. Just for one night, of course, because Lennox Gibbes is not a man for keeping long term.

"I'm the worst driver in the world. Literally the worst. I wrecked four cars by the time I was 18 and my roommate won't let me near her ten-year-old junker. I'm that bad."

He open mouth laughs. I think it's the first time he's had a genuine positive reaction to something I've said and it makes me smile, in return. "Wasn't expecting that," he chuckles.

"Take exit 26B," I tell him. Should I push my luck even further since he's in such an unusual mood? What the hell. "Can I ask you something?"

"I may not answer, but you can ask."

"Why are you so nice to everyone else but so mean to me?"

He pauses for a long time and isn't speaking. I can't take the silence anymore so I continue even though I should know better by now, "The fans, the catering crew, you're so much different with them."

Finally, he answers. "Aye, I love the fans and most of the support crew. They're real people."

"So I'm not a real person?"

"Nope."

"Now who is speaking in riddles, Lennox?" This man is infuriating. He can't manage to get two sentences out of his mouth without insulting me.

He sighs. "Listen, it's not personal. I know you're just doing your job. But your job is as phony as mine. You're just collateral in the grand scheme, same as me."

"Care to expand on what that means?" I ask him. There's obvious tension between him and Celeritas, between him and Digby. He has a dream job, as far as I can tell, but I've also been around long enough to know that pro sports have a lot of politics and money thrown around that sometimes supersede ethics.

"Nope." He replies but then smiles. I'll have to settle for the crumbs he's thrown me and consider it a win that he's being civil and even moderately polite, for Lennox Gibbes.

"I liked your watch post." He mumbles so low I almost can't hear him.

I clutch my heart in surprise, "Did you just compliment me?"

"I've complimented you plenty. I said you've got a great ass, told you about your banging rack, there was something about your long legs wrapped around me," he starts counting off his accolades in commenting on my body parts until I interrupt him by reaching across the seat and slapping his chest.

Oh, that's a hard chest.

This is the first time both of us are laughing. It's kind of nice.

"The new media is doing really well, I think. People seem to really engage with a more personal side of you, some of the good instead of only the bad."

"If you think there's a good side of me," he jokes, "I need to step up my game and get tougher on you."

"God, please don't. I'm not quitting and I really can't get fired right now."

"I will never understand why the world cares about my personal life anyway. It's not that exciting."

"Looks pretty exciting if all the photos and articles are to be believed!" Club photos, beach photos, models and supercars, it's Lifestyles of the Rich and Famous with an extra helping of Insanely Sexy thrown in.

"If you believe everything you see online, you're not as good as you think you are. Left or right up here?"

"Oh sorry," I say and check my map app. I've been distracted trying to crack this six-foot enigma driving the hot car. "Left, right at the 2nd street, and then we should be there."

Lennox takes the next few corners and I point to a parking lot behind an old brick building just outside of Melbourne.

"What is this?" He asks. "You really a stalker and you're going to tie me up inside?"

"You'd like that, wouldn't you?" I tease and start climbing out of the low car once he's parked it.

"Aye," he grins, meeting me near the hood of the Ferrari.

I start leading him around to the front of the building. It's kind of a run-down neighborhood and the building is old, but quaint and charming, not unlike the little town outside of London where my new flat should be waiting for me to officially move into. Rounding the sidewalk, the street is only a block or two long with small shops and it's charming in a small town way.

"Ok, really, where are you taking me? I don't see any Mercedes dealerships or Rolex shops," he says, taking it all in.

"Nope, this isn't for Celeritas, no ugly watches today," I tell him and keep walking. Another few paces and I see the sign hand-painted on a large picture window — 'Heart of a Lion Cat Rescue'. "Here we go," I say and point to the door.

"I don't get it," he plants his feet and puts his hands into his front jeans pockets.

"Well," I tuck a loose strand of hair behind my ear and swing for the fences hoping this doesn't backfire on me, "I heard you have an affinity for cats and I came across an article about this rescue last night. They do good work and they're struggling, might lose their lease." I look up at him with my best puppy dog eyes and bite my bottom lip.

"This is the pussy I was promised?"

I nod at him and bat my eyelashes.

He presses his lips together and shakes his head at me. "So, you want me to write a check or something?"

"No, I wouldn't be that presumptuous. I do want to borrow your assets, though." He's crossed his arms over his chest and is cocking an eyebrow at me. Such a skeptic. "Come on," I grab his arm and drag him into the door.

Inside there are three small rooms and dozens of cats, some walking around freely, some in wire kennels, some missing an eye or a leg, all waiting for a new home. Each kennel has a card listing the name of the cat and how they came to be here at this rescue, their life story condensed to a few lines of handwritten text.

"Oh my goodness, you're here!" A short middle-aged woman rushes into the main entry room and clasps her hands together in excitement. "Thank you so much, Mr. Gibbes, Mallory, you have no idea how much this means to us! I got your phone call and oh, I just," she starts fanning her eyes as tears well up, "I just cried! You're angels!"

"That's Lennox," I smile and elbow him in the gut, "a real angel!"

He clears his throat and throws me his best side-eye while introducing himself. Mrs. Callister, the rescue founder I concocted this idea with late last night, gushes over his kindness and generosity.

"We're all set up in the back, come right this way," Mrs. Callister says as she rushes into one of the attached rooms.

I start to follow her and Lennox grabs my arm. "What have you done?" He leans and whispers into my ear.

Thirty minutes and a dozen more sarcastic comments whispered into my ear about how he'll get me back for this, Lennox Gibbes is shirtless and posing while cuddling different rescue cats and kittens. Mrs. Callister has a white sheet hung up on the wall behind him and has brought in assorted props she was able to source on the fly. Her daughter is taking photos on an entry-level camera borrowed from the high school photo lab. It is assuredly the most low budget photoshoot Lennox has ever participated in.

Mrs. Callister is carrying a construction worker hat for the next shot and passes Lennox "Brad Kitt," an orange kitten with a little blue cast on a hind leg and she tells us the story of how he was found after being hit by a car. Lennox takes Brad in his arms so carefully and gently brings him against his chest to cradle him. He's been trying to be macho but I hear him cooing every cat she gives to him, and there's been many.

I snort when she places the construction worker hat on Lennox's head but my ovaries are on fire. As he was with Francisca and Tatiana and all of his fans, Lennox is patient and kind with Mrs. Callister, even when she drapes an Australian flag around his shoulders and has him pose with an ancient, haggard-looking black cat that would rather maul him than be a part of this hilarious low brow photo shoot.

We wrap up after Mrs. Callister's daughter says they have enough photos for the charity calendar they'll be able to fundraise with and, with his shirt back on, Lennox spends some time walking around the shelter and meeting more cats, learning about the rescue that Mrs. Callister founded because there was no place in this small town for animals to go when they needed help. I don't rush him out the door this time, I just watch him, so very different outside of the racing paddock.

I wonder if I have him wrong but then again, photos don't lie and he has encyclopedia levels of incriminating evidence against him.

Eight

Headline: Lennox Gibbes Rescues Local Cat Rescue
Headline: Cocky and Cuddly F1 Star Makes Surprise
Fundraising Appearance
Photo: Big Dick AND Big Heart? A Sneak Peek at
Lennox Gibbes' Smoking Hot Charity Calendar Shoot

Lennox

"They're going to think this was a publicity act," I tell Mallory who is shoving her iPad at me to show me the results of her overnight work on 'reforming my image.' I don't know, or particularly care, what all the engagement rates and metrics are she's so excited about mean, but she's all plump smiling lips and touchy-feely this morning. I won't complain about that.

It was a sneaky trick; I give her props for that. I didn't hate the time spent with her, not that I'll let her know it. It was nice to get away from the track, that's all. Still, I may have paid a hotel worker handsomely to put a snake in Jack's hotel room toilet as retribution for telling Mallory about the bloody cats.

As soon as I got back to my hotel room yesterday and watched through the peephole of my door to make sure Mallory got into her room across the hall safely and Digby-Free, I told Jack to wire the cat rescue money. Not that I told Mallory about it. I donate generously to several charities but I do it anonymously because I don't want the attention. As opposed to the jackass in the garage bay next to mine who is a cheap prick and only performs the smallest act of charity when he gets credit and media for it. Not my style, not that Digby has any style beyond the latest fashions at Douchebag Unlimited.

"Do you need to personally verify these 'big dick' credentials this blog is talking about? I know you value integrity in your work." I rib Mallory while she keeps swiping through articles and photos.

"God, Aria would love proof of that," she says, not looking up from the iPad that has her so entranced.

"Who?"

Mallory stops her incessant scrolling and looks up at me, snaps a curvy hip out to one side and eyes me beneath her long eyelashes, "Promise not to make fun?"

"There's nothing funny about my dick, Mallory. I cannot emphasize this enough." I'm trying to put my race suit on in my suite in our motorhome before the race and I can already tell it's going to be another long, uncomfortable drive in the car thanks to my sassy nanny talking about my cock all the time. Or maybe it's me who keeps bringing it up when she's around.

"My roommate Aria is kind of obsessed with you," she rolls her eyes. "She texts me every day asking when I'm going to send her nudes."

I have one leg in my race suit and one leg out but I drop the suit to the ground entirely and take Mallory by the shoulders. "Wait, wait, wait. This is serious. Tell me now, is a nanny three-way a possibility?"

"You're such a pig," she laughs and shoves me in the chest making me nearly topple over my in the small room.

More touchy feely. More laughing.

I finish climbing into my suit and zip it up. Grabbing my helmet, I let her know I need to get to the garage and we'll table the three-way conversation until after the race. She follows me the entire way, chatting endlessly about what she's going to post next and reading me online comments from fans.

I suppose it's nice to hear some internet comments other than how much I suck, but my mind is drifting elsewhere as it does before every race now. Team strategy for this race is as usual: DuPont gets the priority strategy and pitstop preference, I'm to assist, block our rivals, and not overtake. New season, same bullshit.

I need out of this contract before I kill DuPont or kill my career altogether. More than that, I loathe what this has done to my fans, supporters, people who used to get joy from watching a good race on

Sunday. As the only driver from Scotland on the grid right now, every race disappoints my entire country. *I* disappoint my entire country. The Scottish flags being flown by diehard fans are fewer in number at every race.

Seeing them in the crowd, holding signs and screaming my name, was addictive. For a few minutes after a race win when I was on the podium spraying champagne and hearing the Scottish anthem played, I felt like a god. I was hooked. So when it all came crashing down on me, it crashed hard. Now I'll never reach those impossible standards I've set for myself again - not with Celeritas.

"Are you back to ignoring me, now?" I feel Mallory's hand on my arm and realize I've not heard anything she's said as we approach the garage bays.

"You talk so much sometimes I need to tune you out, for my sanity." I keep walking as her short legs hustle to keep up.

"Yes, well, not only am I a damn fine Publicity Manager, I'm a pretty good harpy, too."

"Aye, A+ on being a harpy. Your parents must be proud."

Her face falls and her smile fades and I wonder what that's about but I'm much more concerned about something else when I walk into the garage. "Dicklicker! Back onto your side of the garage," I point the correct direction to my pompous dimwit of a team member who is on my side, talking to my engineer, Seth.

"Ms. Mitchell," he croons at Mallory beside me. "Still stuck working with this ill-bred brute, how unfortunate!"

He takes a step toward Mallory but I head him off by putting my body between his and hers. Seth is quick to professionally shuffle him and his dumb coiffed bleach-blond hair back to his own bay and then the crew needs me on track so I grab my helmet and make toward my car that's parked and waiting for me.

"Hey!" I hear Mallory shout and I turn back at the last second. "Good luck!" She yells.

I'd like to shout back that luck has nothing to do with what's going to happen today but she's not my friend and this is not the time nor place. So I simply dip my head to nod to her then turn back around to keep marching toward the next shitty result I'm about to disappoint everyone with.

On purpose.

Mallory

Matty hands me an oversized set of black headphones from a wall charging rack and I join him and Jack in the far back of the Celeritas garage as the first race of the season is minutes from kicking off. I'm bouncing with excitement watching the cars lined up on the grid on the dozen live television monitors hanging in the viewing area. This is the first F1 race I've ever watched and I have so many questions.

All twenty cars roar to life as the clock ticks toward go-time and they start their formation lap. The whole building rumbles from the chorus of horsepower of these impressive cars making their way past. Matty, who seems to take satisfaction from correcting everyone's statements on nearly any topic with his encyclopedic knowledge of statistics and figures, is only too happy to point out what I'm watching and why the drivers are doing what they're doing.

"When they swerve back and forth like that across the track," he points as I watch all twenty cars weaving and bobbling across the tarmac, "they're warming up their tires."

"Because cold tires have no grip, right?" I've done as much reading as I can on the subject, but cars and I have never seen eye-to-eye, so my technical knowledge is limited. Plus, seeing it in person, hearing it, feeling the engines reverberating in my bones, is a much different experience.

The energy in the air is palpable as the cars line up on the grid and the overhead start lights come on above the drivers.

5,4,3,2,1 and lights out.

The cars take off like a shot, the whole pack bunching up as cars try to dart around each other, maneuvering into prime position for the first corner. It is beautiful, controlled chaos. Before the pack reaches Turn 1, two cars at the rear of the group have rubbed tires together and a plume of smoke arises between them, sending one car halfway off the track but the driver recovers after a partial spin and takes off after the pack again.

I gasp and cover my mouth with my hand but then the camera pans to the front of the group of cars and Matty lets out a roar, "Yes!", his clenched fists pumping into the air as he watches the television monitor.

"Run right into that foppish fuckboy," Jack joins in screaming.

Lennox has passed two cars and is now right behind Digby, inches off his rear wing. The two cars dance around the track, blasting down straights and swooping through chicanes as the pack separates and spreads out, the front-running cars pulling away from the slower cars at the rear. Lap after lap they chase each other.

One yellow car near the back has a tire blow out and the driver creeps it back into the pit lane, chunks of rubber flying off the damaged wheel. My fingers are clenched in front of me and my stomach is rolling in excitement and nerves. I had no idea this was so exciting and... fun! I jump and clap as both Digby and Lennox pass another car in quick succession. Twenty laps pass before I know it. Matty's doing his best to answer my questions and point out what's happening.

Digby's car darts into the pit lane and moments later he stops in front of the garage where ninjas in black Celeritas jumpsuits change his tires out in the literal blink of an eye, then his car takes off again. On the next lap, its Lennox's car in for fresh tires and as he stops the car for 2.3 seconds in front of us, I can't help but scream for him, even though he surely cannot hear me, "Go, Lennox!"

He re-enters the race right behind Digby on track again and Matty explains that was the goal, to put him back out right there in that position. They're back on it, Lennox so close to the rear of Digby's car I don't see how they don't touch and crash. Finally, on a long straight, Lennox darts out from behind Digby and pulls alongside him, both cars blasting along the street circuit at unimaginable speeds, neck and neck. "Yes! Go, go, go!" I bounce and grab Jack's arm in excitement. But Lennox just holds steady, squarely even with Digby's car, then falls back behind him as they take a sharp corner.

"Why didn't he pass Digby?" I shout to Matty over the noise of the circuit.

"He's not allowed. He was just showing DuPunk that he could," Matty closes his lips tightly and folds his arms over his chest.

"What, why?" I ask. That doesn't make any sense. I thought the whole point of racing was that the fastest driver wins. Matty just shakes his head knowingly and continues watching the television monitors. Jack slips one of his long, toned arms around my shoulders and gives me a little squeeze of comfort. We're commiserating, but I don't understand why. I have so much to learn.

Round and round they go, Lennox chasing Digby and the cars behind them occasionally changing positions and coming into the pit lanes, some cars break down and they retire from the race. Rounding a hairpin corner with just ten laps to go, suddenly the cameras pan to both Celeritas cars again and Digby has gone too fast into a corner. Blue smoke pours from his front tires which are locked up stiff. His car smacks the side of another one, and Digby goes off track, into a gravel pit, careening the nose straight into a barrier wall, bits of carbon fiber and plastic shards shattering off the car.

Matty and Jack both erupt into a ruckus of laughter but I'm wide-eyed and shocked. Is he hurt? Apparently not, as seconds later, Digby removes his steering wheel, climbs out of the cockpit, then spikes the steering wheel down into the gravel in a rant. The track marshals are there to escort him off the race track and Digby kicks one of the car's tires on his way past.

"Now's your time," Matty says to no one in particular, his head forward and locked onto the television monitors. We all watch silently as the laps tick down and Lennox comes to life, inching ever closer to the lead cars on every straight and into every corner. He passes one blue car and is in third place. Matty, Jack, and I squeal and jump and pump our fists. There's one lap to go and the television shows the crowd on their feet, erupting with cheers as Lennox overtakes one more red car on the final lap right before the checkered flag. Second!

My heart is beating so loud I can hear it pumping through my earphones. Jack and Matty give each other a one-armed manly hug and Jack pulls my head to his chest to muss up my hair. "Second, that's amazing!" I cry.

"It's not first," Matty quips, ever the pessimist and fact-checker, "but it's a win for Lennox."

As the cars cross the finish line and start making their way back into the pits, Jack and Matty take off to meet Lennox and to assist with the post-race ritual. I follow the group of pit crew and engineers to swarm beneath the elevated podium platform and by the time we arrive, the top three drivers are making their way onto the platform as their names and final positions are called. Hundreds of people clamor against the metal crowd barricades to get as close as possible and, for once, my small size helps me squeeze in upfront amongst other Celeritas crew.

Lennox is standing tall and proud on his second-place step, his hair soaked from sweat, drops of perspiration dripping from his dark brown locks down his face and into the neck of his race suit. His face is red from physical exertion but there is no hiding the emotion and glee in his eyes as he points to fans with a huge Scottish flag below the podium, taps a fist to his heart than points directly at them.

The drivers are handed their trophies by diplomats in swanky pinstriped suits and another man in with a British accent asks each driver a few interview questions but I barely hear them. I am captivated watching Lennox stand with his shoulders back and his head tall, hands behind his back as he scans the crowd and nods to pockets of fans screaming his name.

I feel my eyes start to fill with moisture and quickly dab them and clear my throat to get ahold of myself. I don't know why I'm so emotional. It's just seeing him up there, chest flexed, the wide stance of his hips, and the noble square of his jaw - I'm proud of him.

Music kicks off and each driver grabs an oversized bottle of Monet champagne and spray each other down, spray the British interviewer, and take long, deep chugs of the cool bubbly. Lennox comes to the edge of the elevated platform and sprays everyone below, several droplets of the sticky, cold sweetness hitting me as the Celeritas pit crew scream and celebrate.

As the drivers make their way off the podium, I fight my way through the mob and start jogging my way back to the motorhome so I can capture any celebratory moments with Lennox and be present during the post-race press coverage.

I'm winded by the time I arrive to the front of our the Celeritas motorhome where Lennox has also just swaggered up and is about to head inside, leaving a herd of cameramen and media just outside our door. "Lennox!" I call and he pauses his hand on the door.

He swivels just in time for me to pirouette on my tiptoes and throw my arms around his neck. "Congratulations," I exclaim into his neck as he bends to wrap one strong arm under my ass and lift me up to his full height, pulling me tight against him. It's only a second before he drops me back down but he's slick with sweat and filled with testosterone and adrenaline. Despite racing for two hours in the Australian sun, his scent of wood and moss and leather surrounds me.

I gaze up at his hollowed cheeks and chiseled jaw and I want to kiss this stupidly handsome, proud man.

Nine

MUST SEE: Gibbes Storms to Second Place Finish in
Cracking Australian Grand Prix
Headline: Lennox Gibbes Cinches Driver of the Day
Award by Sport Guild Readers
Blog: Give us More Gibbes!

"Gettin' robbed, gettin' stoned, gettin' beat up, broken boned. Gettin' had, gettin' took, I tell you, folks. It's harder than it looks." - AC/DC - It's a Long Way to the Top (If You Wanna Rock and Roll)

Mallory

"Can you see out the window," I ask Aria as I maneuver my laptop screen around my charming second-story brick flat at headquarters to give her the grand tour via Skype. "Sometimes there are sheep out in that field, sheep! How British is that?"

"I'm so jealous! I'm here looking out our window with a view of the sanitation station," Aria jokes.

We landed in London less than 48 hours ago and when I made my way back to my cozy new home in Aylesbury, I must have slept for the first 24 hours. I didn't even bother to unpack my boxes which have mostly arrived from the States. I need to ask Matty for tips and tricks for coping with jetlag because I am all kinds of out of sorts.

There are at least two housing buildings on campus, as far as I can tell. Both are old-world brown brick construction, original windows

62

with white shutters, and old slate roof tiles with occasional patches of green moss growing between them. They're tucked away from the other Celeritas buildings and overlook a meadow that is green with lush spring grass. It's quintessential small-town Britain. The kitchen and bath are both small but updated and manage to keep the old-timey feel.

According to Sandra, Lennox's flat is direct across the hall from mine and Matty and Jack share a flat on the first floor. The third floor above us has two flats for executives. I haven't seen anyone else in the building but me, but I've also been sleeping like the dead and wouldn't have noticed a rampaging moose roaming about. The campus is sprawling with a massive glass front factory building a quarter of a mile down a narrow red brick road, a modern office complex, and beyond that is a test track for the cars. I haven't had time to tour anything besides the office complex and meet some of the security guards who patrol the gated grounds.

"Did you get to do anything cool in Australia?" Aria asks, sipping her morning coffee while I'm thinking of another afternoon nap on my side of the world.

"There was no time, really. I was busy trying to make a good first impression and keep Lennox in line, clean up all of his social media accounts, beg him to behave at all the press conferences." I tell her.

"Did you have to get down on your knees while begging?" Aria winks.

"Hardy har," I curl my lip at her. "He spent the first several days trying to get me to quit but it's been better lately. I hope he's given it up. When he's not insistent on being a complete jerk, he's actually pretty tolerable."

"I bet he is."

"It's not like that at all and you know it. I'm not going to screw this job up. I can't," I shake my head and set my laptop down on the kitchen counter so I can still see Aria while I make my first official cup of tea.

"Have you heard from your parents or David?" Aria asks, yawning and rubbing her eyes.

"My mom texted me a news article a woman from the club sent her about a Melbourne climate change protest that was scheduled so I could avoid the 'riff-raff.' I didn't respond, obviously. I talked to David for a few minutes," I sigh.

"And how is he handling this?" She asks, picking up on the change in my tone as I drop an English Grey tea bag into the white porcelain teacup my flat came equipped with.

"I think I need to end it, Aria." I plop down on a barstool at my tiny kitchen counter and prop my head upon my elbow. "I thought about it the whole flight home, which is a very long time, let me tell you."

"And?"

"I just... he never called once. When I finally reached him, all he wanted to talk about was Cooper Media and how he and Dad are fighting with them, their stupid publisher rivalry, the same tired conversation. I started to tell him that Ms. Alix in Marketing here was really happy with my work and that I was proud of myself and he blew me off, told me 'that's nice' and went right back into the latest Cooper Media nonsense."

"He's a self-absorbed twat." Aria nods. She's told me this a thousand times, of course.

"This is a new start for me, you know? I need to focus on work and build something for myself, do something that makes me happy. And he just doesn't make me happy." I feel more alive arguing with Lennox, for god sake. My kettle on the stove starts to whistle and I stand up to turn it off, steam clouding the Skype session as I pour the boiling water and christen my first cup of Earl Grey.

"Your parents are going to go through the roof," Aria says.

"I know but if I do this now, at least I won't be home for them to make me miserable." I gave this a lot of thought and this really has been a long time coming.

"So what are you going to do, call him?"

"No, I should come home and tell him in person. I owe him that much. He isn't a monster, this just isn't working. I think I can swing a quick trip home after the next race." There won't be anything quick about the flying time from London to Bahrain in the Gulf, to New York, then to China in time for the next race, though. I don't know how everyone does it. It probably helps that Lennox, Matty, and Jack fly first class and I'm in the cattle pen section of economy. I make a mental note to sign up for frequent flyer programs so I can at least rack up points.

Aria and I chat for an hour and two cups of Earl Grey before she needs to head out to an appointment with a new personal training client she's signed up. Disconnecting, I was thinking about taking a stroll around the Celeritas grounds, but I hear a rumble in the hallway outside of my front door. Maybe I'm not the only one knocking around in this old building?

Prancing to the front door I peer out the peephole and see Lennox fiddling with his key at his door then kicking it open with his foot and shoving his large suitcase in before the door closes behind him. He has no media or events scheduled during this break between races and I only have a few meetings scheduled with the Marketing Team so it should be a little downtime for us. If Lennox cooperates and doesn't go on a bender making headlines we don't need, that is.

I can't deny the butterflies flapping in my gut at the thought that he's living right across the hall from me again. It was weird enough in the Melbourne hotel after I had to move so my room could be fumigated for bugs and the hotel stuck me right across from Lennox. Then again, it is comforting not to be alone in this old creaky building by myself in case Jack the Ripper is on the loose. This is certainly not New York where I'm surrounded by millions of people at all times.

Thirty minutes later, I hear his door open again. The building is old and has thin walls, apparently, which is not a good thing for sleep but it is a good thing for keeping tabs on him to make sure he doesn't do anything to get us both into trouble. That's *definitely* what I'm on the watch for as I race silently to my front door again and catch him exiting just in time, in gym shorts and a grey tank top that exposes his rugged shoulders and sculpted biceps.

Definitely not club apparel, we should be safe. Still, it is my job to prevent paparazzi slip-ups or media snafus so I should probably see what he's up to. In the interest of my job.

I throw on my favorite black leggings and a casual but cute off the shoulder tee and grab a hoodie I've unpacked because it's still cool in the evenings and the sun is almost down now. There's nothing to be done about my bedhead but a high ponytail and a coating of ruddy peach lipgloss cleans me up a little bit.

Outside, landscaping lights line the cobblestone sidewalks and they flicker to life as it grows darker. Security buzzes past me in a golf cart and gives me a friendly wave as I make my way toward the factory and office buildings off in the distance. Magenta and deep purple azaleas are thoughtfully landscaped along the paths weaving throughout campus and with administration personnel gone for the day, it's quiet and peaceful and downright romantic. I stuff my hands into my hoodie pockets and stroll on, grinning inside. It's everything I dared to dream of when I left New York and with Sandra pleased and Lennox relatively harmonious, in his own way, everything is right on track.

The administration building is up ahead and as I grow closer I can hear music and bass thumping inside, interrupting the solitude and silence of the grounds. They keycard in my pocket buzzes me in the door of the building that's closed for the night and dark save safety exit lighting. I recognize this building from my first day with Sandra and the music is growing louder as I reach the gym door.

Peeking in, the music blasts me as the door cracks. AC/DC is thumping out It's a Long Way to the Top (If You Wanna 'Rock n' Roll) at ear-piercing decibels. They were from Australia if memory serves, and Lennox's music choice makes me grin as I sneak in. He's alone in the gym with his back to me pulling cables through a strength training machine that's lifting and dropping heavy iron weights with every tug and release of the handles.

His grey tank has a band of sweat down the middle and I'm mesmerized watching his shoulders clench together over and over as I prowl into the room and take a seat on a weight bench behind him, watching like a total creeper. Thick black lines of a back tattoo peek out from under his shirt sleeves as he flexes. This is the best free entertainment the UK has to offer, I'm sure of it.

"See anything you like?" He calls with his back still to me. My eyes had moved down to his tight ass in those gym shorts but his voice booming over the music startles me and I look up and catch him looking at me in a mirror in front of his machine. Damn gym mirrors, why do they even exist? No one looks good at the gym, sweating, and puffing.

No one except people built like Lennox Gibbes.

He snatches a white towel hanging from his machine and wipes off his face and forehead before reaching for a remote nearby and turning the volume of the stereo down. I'm sure my face is flushed as I sit here with my legs crossed, obviously ogling the man before me. But he's hot and he knows it, so pretending I have only pure thoughts in my head right now is only going to make me look more ridiculous.

"I was just strolling around campus and heard the music," I bald-faced lie. He studies me silently, not even winded from that torture machine he's been abusing and, out of sheer nervousness, under the scrutiny of his stare, I keep talking. "I didn't get to talk to you after the race very much but I wanted to tell you I really liked the race and I was," I pause, rethinking saying something vulnerable and honest to him, "I was proud of you." My head lowers and I'm waiting for the sarcastic comment or barb from him.

"Why would you be proud of me? You barely know me and it was only second place," he answers as he looks down at his hands, wiping them off in the gym towel for longer than it should take. Is he nervous? Impossible.

"I've never seen a race before. Matty had to explain to me what was happening the whole time, but it was amazing. And then watching you pass all those cars... I know I don't understand how everything works, but I was proud of you for doing so well." I shrug my shoulders and realize I probably sound like an idiot fangirl.

Good job, Mallory. Now he's going to demand you go home, again.

"Well, I've got forty-five minutes left or your friend Matty will have my ass." He turns his back to me and returns to pulling the machine's cables, both at once this time with his arms going wide to the side and his forearms rippling with each elevation of the stacked weights.

"Most people say 'thank you' when they're complemented, Lennox," I chide him as I get off my bench and make my way to his side. Bad idea, now I'm up close and can feel the heat coming off him.

"I'll thank you properly in 45 minutes if you'd like," he muses in that delectable accent, arms still working the machine and the metal clink of the weights tapping down every few seconds.

Nope, he can be a human and thank me. Or respond with any variety of socially acceptable acknowledgment. I raise an eyebrow, fold my fingers together in front of me and stare at him. We're going to have an old fashioned Mexican standoff until he grows some manners.

After several moments in which it's growing harder to keep quiet and not gawk at him too shamelessly, he finally drops the weights and they slam to the base with an echo in the room. "Either join me or go back to your flat. You're creeping me out, you stalker."

"Join you? In what? I can't do that...," I point to the machine with what's surely sixty tons of free weights attached. I'm a treadmill and elliptical kind of girl, never could get those sculpted Michelle Obama arms.

Before I can protest more, he's grabbed me around the waist and has planted me in front of the machine. "Take this off," he takes the hoodie from my shoulders and pulls it down and tosses it aside. He's standing right behind me and I can see him in the mirror in front of us.

He puts the pulley handles in my hands and says to pull straight back. "Yes, haha, you're a big strong man, I get it," I groan as the weights don't budge an inch from their resting place even when I struggle with all of my body weight.

He chuckles and adjusts the weights on each side of the machine before returning to his stance of towering over me from behind. "Square your hips up," he says and steps closer, his two hands firmly gripping my hips, his long fingers wrapping around my pelvis and controlling my core. I shiver at his touch, the warmth of his hands penetrating my thin leggings.

"Pull," he commands and I do, watching him watch me in the mirror. This time the weights move up and then slam back down as I release them. "Don't let them slam down, controlled descent." His eyes are on mine in the mirror every time I dare to look. I can feel his breath on my neck and I'm going to soak through my panties if we don't stop this.

Stop this, Mallory.

Several revolutions more and my muscles are on fire from the weights, my body on fire from Lennox. "Keep your back straight," he says and takes a step closer to me then pressing his chest against my back to force my form. His feet are planted on either side of mine, his body swallowing mine up. I suck in a deep breath at the feel of his hard chest and stomach pushed against me, his body temperature and sheen of sweat making our tees cling between us.

My arms and shoulders go through the motions on autopilot but I'm speechless and dazed. Surely I look just like one of his awestruck groupies waiting for him to sign my breasts.

He stays pressed up against me and I start to feel what can only be his growing length getting hard and pressing into my lower back. I want badly to push back against it but this is insane, I cannot do this. "Lennox, unless that's a barbell between your legs, we have to stop this."

"Don't know what you mean," he whispers and drops his head to the side of mine, his nose lightly brushing my hair just above my ear. Oh god, he's going to make me say it.

"You're hard," I whisper, still watching him in the mirror.

His head lowers even farther until his lips are nanometers away from my skin, the warmth of his breathing just below my ear. "And you've got goosebumps," he whispers and runs his nose along the valley of my neck.

"Ok," I exclaim, dropping the pulleys and letting the weights slam down, "we're not doing this!"

God, I want to do this.

I step away from him and put my hands on my hips. The loss of his body heat is immediate and I'm sure my nipples are betraying me at this very moment and pointing at him like daggers.

"If you say so," he smirks and fidgets with the machine to put the weights back to his herculean levels, then he's right back in the swing of his workout while I stand like a statue trying to regain any sense of composure. So cool and controlled at all times.

Stupid sexy asshole.

I glare at him for a moment while he utterly ignores me, before I run my hands over my pulled back hair and pace a few steps trying to rid my body of these traitorous hormones coursing through my veins. I take several deep breaths and then step onto a treadmill. I'm already sweaty, I need to do something with this pent up energy inside me now, and goddamn it, I don't want to leave.

I push the buttons on the machine and ramp up into a decent clip, running and running the desire away, while Lennox continues his assault on the strength machine. In my peripheral vision, I can see he's still watching me in the mirror in front of him but I keep my eyes straight ahead and stare at a very interesting flaw in the drywall in front of me.

Thirty minutes later he finally lets his weights drop and I slow my machine down until I can step off. He wipes himself off with his gym towel and I do the same with a clean one from a wall rack. Both of us wipe our machines down. Neither of us speaks as he turns off the stereo and flips the light switch on our way out.

It's a slow, silent walk back to the housing unit with Lennox beside me in the dark, his arm occasionally brushing mine as we wind down the narrow pathways. He holds the front door open for me at our building and we march up the flight of old wooden stairs together, the hallways dimly lit by wall lanterns.

"You still never said 'thank you'" I mumble when we've reached our respective flat doors opposite each other.

"You wanna invite me in then, love?" He nods to my flat door.

"I can't," I shake my head. My knees are weak and my body feels like goo but I don't think it was the treadmill sprinting.

"Ok, then. G'night," he says and turns to open his door while I still stare at him like a stupid lovestruck schoolgirl until I realize I need to also get my key out and open my door. "See you in Bahrain, unless you're ready to quit now," he adds as I fumble with my key in the lock.

"Wait, what?" I don't even register his comment about me quitting.

We have over a week until Bahrain, what does he mean I won't see him again?

"I'm going home, I'll see you in Bahrain," he clarifies as his door opens.

"Home to your flat?" I point at his apartment.

"Home to Scotland." He must think I'm a total idiot. I *am* a total idiot.

"Oh, yeah, of course. Umm, no media, you'll behave?"

"Very unlikely," he grins and then his door closes shut behind him and I'm alone in the hallway.

Shit shit shit, I curse myself under my breath as my door finally opens and I rush inside, closing it behind me and slinking down to the floor.

Oh Mallory, you stupid, stupid girl. What were you thinking?

Ten

Photo: Gibbes Returns Home to Scotland, Fans Mob Ashaig Airstrip
angela.mickel99: is that his mom and dad with him?
nocarbsinlettuce: Aye, and his brother Bram.
maxpropulsion: Kick ass race in Australia, Lennox!
derbyhats4sale: swoon…
Headline: Driver Power Rankings: Gibbes Leads DuPont Ahead of Bahrain
Headline: F1 Arrives in Bahrain, Schedule of Events

Lennox

"Ha! That's fifty pounds, pay up!" Jack holds his open palm out in front of Matty as Mallory comes barreling into my garage bay at the Bahrain track, dragging her rolling suitcase with her and swearing up a storm. It's late and she looks a delightful wreck.

"Damn," Matty shakes his head and reaches into his pocket for his wallet to make good on the Nanny Longevity Bet he's just lost.

She's officially made it to race two now, looks like Mallory may be in this nanny gig for the long haul. After she showed up in the gym and sent me home with a raging case of blue balls, I wondered how this would play out. If she's not going to go home, she and I have unfinished business.

I didn't even get into trouble, that I know of, back home this past week. Not that there is too much trouble on the Isle of Skye, but sometimes trouble finds me regardless of where I am or whether I'm looking for it or not. Truth be told, I'm finding myself with more respect for this nanny because she fights back instead of shrinking like a violet, like her predecessors. Not that I'm going to admit it to her.

"Did you just get in, it's nearly midnight?" I check my watch and question why her suitcase is with. Her hair is pulled up again revealing her sweet little neck I almost had the opportunity to bite, and leggings, or yoga pants, or whatever they're called trace every curve of her hips. God bless whoever invented those things.

"Yep, my plane was delayed so I missed my connecting flight. Some pervert on the first flight kept running his hand up my thigh and then got drunk and drooled on me. Then no one from the team was at the airport to pick me up because my flight was so delayed and I had to wait for an Uber since cabs stopped running for the night. I couldn't even go to the hotel because Jack here, "she points and scowls at him, "apparently has my reservation and key. Total. Shitshow."

"Why didn't you call m… Jack? Jack would have picked you up," I wave at Jack who is giggling at Mallory trying to drag the suitcase around which is half her size. I don't think I care for someone manhandling her on Lecherous Pervert Airlines, either. If anyone's going to manhandle her and touch her thighs, it'll be me. She is *my* nanny, after all.

"I did call Jack! He won't answer his phone!" She roars at him.

Jack pulls his phone out of his back pocket as I glare at him, "Whoops, sorry about that," he says.

I need to talk to Jack about that later. Regardless of the sexual escapades I have planned for Mallory and those leggings in our very near future, we don't leave women alone at midnight in airports in other countries. We may be assholes, but we aren't monsters.

"Why did you fly commercial?" Matty asks her, stone-faced as usual.

"How else would you like me to get here, carrier pigeon?" She's on a tear tonight and clearly in no mood for Matty's trademark Finnish bluntness. "Will one of you muscle-bound apes please help me with my suitcase! Jesus, were you all born in a barn?"

Matty is closest to her so he picks up the heavy suitcase and puts it next to our bags to go back to the hotel. "I was born at home. It wasn't much different from a barn," he adds. "But, why didn't you come on the jet with us?"

"What jet?"

"We fly private unless it's too far, like Australia," Matty answers because he doesn't have the sense God gave a goose when it comes to women. Jack and I are already shaking our heads at one another knowing she's about to rip his head off. And Jack's gay so it would be understandable if his female prowess was subpar.

Mallory all fired up is sexy as hell, though. Her pulse racing, her face and neck flushed, the way she squares her shoulders like she's marching onto a battlefield. I like a little fight. And she has plenty of it in her.

Sure enough, Mallory walks up to Matty and pokes her little finger at his chest, "You three are monsters!"

"Don't take it out on me, Jack is the assistant. I'm the physio, remember? Also, Sandra should have told you to come with us. It would have been more economical for the company."

"Sandra is a troll and Jack will book your travel from now on," I announce amid the squabbling.

"What? Now I'm the nanny's PA, too?" Jack protests.

I shoot him a glare that says not to argue with me and he knows enough to drop it.

"Fine. The paid help is going to the hotel now," he says to Matty as the two of them start throwing luggage into one of the transport cars, "are you two coming?"

"We'll be there shortly," I reply, staring at Mallory as her face slowly registers that yes, I mean she and I will be staying, together, at the garage for the moment. It's late and almost all the support staff has left for the night.

Jack and Matty give each other knowing glances, Jack gives Mallory her hotel room keycards, and then they depart. I take a seat on a side pod of my car and sit in silence as Mallory takes a few deep breaths and then starts pacing the garage. She's frustrated.

"Listen, about the other night," she starts.

"Let's not," I cut her off. She's in no mood for anything fun right now and the last thing I'm interested in is a discussion in which she tells me that we will never, ever sleep together. We will. She just doesn't know it yet.

That's ok. I like a challenge.

"I think it's important we clear the air and acknowledge that while we may be attracted to one another..."

"Who says I'm attracted to you?" I interrupt, half teasing, half starting an argument just for the sake of it.

"I'm sorry, do you frequently rub yourself up against women you find *unattractive*?" She spits back.

"I wouldn't say 'frequently' but it's happened before, sure."

"You're disgusting," she growls.

I stand up from the car and stride toward her. She backs up a few steps then stops when she recognizes my modus operandi, plants her feet, and rolls her eyes at me. Once more, I'm inches away and towering over her, her head meeting the top of my shoulders, at best. I take a lock of her hair from her ponytail and run my fingers down it. "You don't really think I'm disgusting. Do you?"

"I have a pulse and a vagina, Lennox. I realize how attractive you are, but that doesn't mean…"

"I'm glad you have a vagina. That'll make things easier," I smile.

Ignoring me, she continues, "That does not mean we can do this. I am not quitting and I am not losing my job over you. I don't have that luxury. So please stop."

I pause a moment before stepping away and Mallory smoothes her shirt down nervously. I don't believe she wants me to stop doing this — whatever this thing is we're doing — but until I'm 100% sure, some lines don't get crossed. I'm not going to force her. I'm going to make her beg for it.

Onto Plan B.

"You need to learn a few things about the cars and the races," I change the subject with no finesse whatsoever and pace back to my car so I can explain. "You made a post the other day about DRS that wasn't correct."

"You read my posts?" A quiet voice whispers from behind me.

Uh-huh, not interested, my ass. She isn't going to lose her job over sleeping with me, either, but we'll cross that bridge when we come to it. She may lose her job, or more likely quit, for a thousand other reasons, but not because she gives in to what she wants from me.

"Aye, and I read the comments from the assholes making fun of you for saying the wrong thing." Because keyboard warriors and pussies around the world never hesitate to act tough when they can hide behind a screen and anonymity.

"See this flap here?" I put my hand on the rear of the car and open and close the carbon fiber wing a couple of times. "DRS—Drag Reduction System. At certain points in the race, I can open up this wing and reduce aerodynamic drag on the car. Gives me another twelve kilometers per hour, more or less."

"Oh," she comes over and fiddles with the wing herself, "so you want this open as much as possible."

"No. When it's closed there is more downforce on the car which is better for cornering. Plus, we can only use DRS in certain zones when we're within one second of the car ahead, and never on certain laps like right after a safety car or the first couple laps of a race."

"Wikipedia did not mention all of that," she looks up at me, her face softening and the tension melting from her stiff shoulders. The same porcelain shoulders that were bare for me last week.

"Aye, you confused DRS with KERS, Kinetic Energy Recovery System. See this reservoir here?" I kneel next to a wheel and she joins me to poke around under the car. I'm oddly turned on talking shop with her. She seems genuinely interested, like she's not just doing this to humor me or for some ulterior motive. And the damn jasmine smell is wafting off her again.

"This big metal thing?" She asks and touches the smooth titanium component.

"Aye. The KERS harvests energy produced by braking. It stores it and then, when I choose, I press a button and can use that stored energy for more horsepower."

"All the buttons on the steering wheel are making more sense now." She's biting her bottom lip as she contemplates and asks more questions. I want to know what those lips taste like, be the one biting her lip.

She asks a dozen more questions and even finds paper to start taking notes, halfway through. Pausing her writing, she lifts an eyebrow as if there's been a sudden rush of skepticism, "Why are you helping me?"

Because you smell like heaven and I want to see you naked in my sheets flushed with satisfaction that I give you. Because I want to run my tongue over every inch of you and I want to hear you scream my name. Because the way we argue is such a turn on I think the way we fuck will be cataclysmic.

Because I'm lonely and like spending time with you even though I have no business dragging you into my mess.

"You're supposed to be here to help me. If I help you, that only helps me. No?"

Lies. I can tell them, too.

Mallory nods, either believing my bullshit or pretending to. I can't tell.

"Most people here have dreamt of working in F1 since birth. You don't know the first thing about it. Why are you here?" I ask her, flat out. I have no right to ask, I know this. But Mallory feels oddly tangible to me, something real amidst the facade. There's no Botox, no duck lips stuffed with filler. No kissing my ass or trying to get me into bed so she can post it on Instagram. She could have done that on Day One.

The reality is, I don't particularly want her to leave anymore. Celeritas will just replace her with someone far less tolerable or fuckable. If she won't leave on her own, we're going to do this. And if we're going to do this, more than once, I need to know what I'm getting into. Besides her leggings.

Mallory hesitates for a moment then sinks to the floor and sits with her legs crossed, facing me and leaning up against a toolbox that separates the garage bays. "I'm new to racing but it's always been sports,' she fidgets with the hem of her shirt and avoids eye contact.

I pretend to inspect something on the car that does not need any inspecting. "Let me guess, you were a tomboy and this was Daddy's dream." Pretty sure that was the case with Nanny numbers two and six, though they didn't last long and it was just speculation. I certainly never cared enough to ask.

"Nope, my father does not believe driving is a sport and is disgusted that I'm here." She shakes her head. I guess she wants me to pull it out of her.

"So this is revenge. You're getting back at him?"

"He probably thinks so. I doubt he even realizes that I went into Sports PR because he got me hooked on it when I was a kid." Mallory slouches forward and rests her head on her palm, her hazel eyes sagging from her flight ordeal.

"Go on."

"We used to go to games with him when we were little - the Mets, the Knicks. The Jets once or twice. He had box seats and would entertain clients there."

"That sounds wholesome enough," I add. Daddy may be ignorant about driving not being a sport, but no skin off my nose.

"He quit taking us when we were 'too old to be cute' for the cameras photographing him there as a 'family man' and Mom decided it was 'unbecoming.'" Mallory makes air quotes around several phrases and her face twists up in bitterness. "We were just there to be seen. There was nothing wholesome about it."

"But now you do the same thing, participate in the media circus."

What an enigma, this one.

"I was fascinated by the athletes and wanted to know everything about them, how they got to be the best in the world at their craft. And I wanted to control the narrative of what got told. I guess that's why I can relate to your fans wanting to know about your personal life, little things about you. Media was in my blood, the family business, I just went a different direction."

"Let me guess," I smile, "they do not approve."

"They do not. You're a bunch of barbarians driving around in circles all day and my work in social media is an embarrassment. Working with disgraced barbarians on social media is a triple threat." Mallory is staring at the concrete ground beneath her, her face blank and zoned out, no fire. The paddock has grown quiet and it's getting chilly here in the desert now that the sun has long since gone to bed for the night.

"Here," I say, handing Mallory one of my team jackets that's hanging on a wall nearby. Again, asshole, not monster. "So this is a revenge plot, I can dig that."

"No, I just want what I want and this is how I'm going to get it." A little bit of sass has returned to her voice and some color to her face.

I reach for her hand to help her off the ground and she takes it. Her fingers are cold as I pull her up. I have several ideas on how to warm her up. Even if now is not the time, I want her sassy mouth back and I want her to argue with me. God help me, I don't know why I like her arguing with me. Last I checked, I was not a masochist and I have no mommy issues. "And what is it you want?" I ask and pull her closer to me than is just a friendly assist off the ground.

"I want you to behave this weekend and not insult the press," she puts both hands on my chest and bats her eyelashes at me, feigning innocence. The same trick she used to pull off her ridiculous cat shelter scheme. Unfortunately for her, my balls are still firmly attached to my body and not in her possession.

"I can't make you any promises," I say, putting my large hands over hers and holding them in place on my pecs.

"Right," she pulls her hands back and steps away, "You're not a promises kind of guy, are you?"

"What's that supposed to mean?"

"Nothing," she turns away, my jacket floating around her, far too big and long. But I like how it looks on her. "Can you take me back to the hotel, it's getting late and we have a lot to do this weekend."

Ah, classic deflection. "Aye," I nod and grab the keys to the loaner

Ferrari I'm driving this weekend from the local dealership. She's right, though. I don't do promises anymore. No one keeps their end of the bargain, so what's the point? She wants what she needs out of me to get back at Daddy, and I want what I need out of her — mainly her legs wrapped around me while I'm buried inside of her. Seems there's a contract negotiation to be made here.

Another day.

The ride to our hotel is starting to look like a silent one as Mallory's eyes get heavy and she struggles to keep them open in the warm, comfortable seats with the engine lulling a soothing lullaby. "How did you get here?" Comes a whisper as she curls up facing me.

"Private jet," I answer immediately.

"Don't be a dick," she replies in the same whisper as if it's a request to me, not a demand. As if she doesn't have the energy to fight. Shame.

"Worked my ass off." That's the honest truth, unlike DuPont who sailed in from Monaco on his money and family name and keeps his place on the grid only because he pays for it. It's a bloody insult to all the parents like mine who sacrificed everything for their kid to make it here.

"I can Google the facts, Lennox. How did you get here?"

I sigh, debate taking the long route back to the hotel so we can stay in the car together and I have a chance to swing the conversation back to my comfortable topics, but she needs sleep. "Pop built me my first kart when I was 3 years old. It was all downhill from there."

"Three? How can a three-year-old drive anything?"

"You were born being a danger to society behind the wheel, guess I was the counterbalance."

"I bet you were a cute kid," she yawns.

"You'd have to ask my Mum."

"Does your family ever come to races? The internet would love embarrassing photos of you as a kid."

"No, almost never. I'm not interested in sharing my family with a few million people who follow a phony version of me online, either." I also can't bear to see their disappointed faces when the truth of Celeritas is thrown into their faces, everything they sacrificed for me pissed away over greed and fame. I won't do it to them.

"I'm trying to make it less phony, you know," Mallory whispers so quietly I can barely hear her. Her eyes have blinked close and her head rests back into the leather seat.

I want to carry her up to her hotel room and tuck her into bed. Let her wrap her hands around my neck and feel her head tuck into my chest. Feel like a mighty hunter carrying home the spoils of victory. Her eyes are closed, long lashes folded over one another. Tiny, soft breaths pass over her soft lips.

But if I pick her up and carry her into this hotel, she'll be on every predatory celeb blog and gossip rag by tomorrow morning along with jealous women slut-shaming her or horny dudes leaving comments that reveal why, in fact, they'll never have a woman like Mallory in their lives.

"Hey," I whisper and nudge her. She stirs an inch and makes a tiny noise but she's still out of it. Trying a little louder this time, I tease her more. "Mallory, get your hand out of my pants, someone is going to see you!"

Eleven

Mallory

Ms. Mitchell,

Reports from today's sponsor event are promising. UG Petroleum was pleased with Mr. Gibbes' appearance. It seems you are doing a fine job keeping a leash on the dog.

Sandra Alix
Director of Marketing and Communication
Celeritas Racing

The email from Sandra is rare praise and even though my mouth is stuffed with the most delicious falafel, I'm grinning ear to ear.

This afternoon's sponsor event was painfully boring and consisted of Lennox driving executives around in a sports car that looked like a spaceship but they seemed to enjoy themselves. Round and round they went in a closed parking lot for hours. While Lennox was making people scream in terror as he did donuts in the car with them, I used the time to schmooze with the executives. Meeting the CEO of an international oil company never hurts when you want to launch a brand new PR firm.

Lennox did not have to do media today which is probably why he's been in a good mood all day. Digby was called to the press conference instead, where they grilled him about his error in the last race, which Lennox took childlike satisfaction from. I may have rolled my eyes, but

I'll take the win however I can get it.

"I will cut you!" I stab Lennox's hand with my fork as he tries, for the 100th time, to steal one of my falafel in the motorhome's dining hall. Tonight's feast is a buffet of fragrant rice and chicken, local grouper, falafel, and baklava drizzled with golden honey. The falafel is too good to share and I'm treating myself to all the carbs after my successful day ending in accolades from my ice queen boss.

"Eat your machboos," Matty pushes the pre-measured plate of chicken and yellow rice back toward Lennox. Matty has shoveled down a pound of shawarma and I've been inhaling everything before me while Lennox pushes his chicken around his plate like a toddler refusing to eat his vegetables.

"Oh my god," I moan around a mouthful of baklava, pistachios, and honey bursting out of the buttery phyllo dough. Lennox stabs a piece of chicken and chews it slowly, glaring at me as I embellish the sweet flavor to antagonize him.

"Luqaymay, Mallory?" Matty passes me a plate of little round dough balls on sticks, a Bahrain cake pop of sorts, the saffron sugar glaze covering them sticky and glistening.

"Don't mind if I do!" I pip. Matty and I have been having too much fun teasing Lennox. I didn't know Matty even had a sense of humor, but it seems to come out when he can badger Lennox.

"Both of you can piss off," Lennox blurts. "And you," he points at me with his fork, "quit moaning like that." Obviously, I moan even more when I pull the luqaymay off the stick with my teeth.

"Matty, Jack told me you and Lennox go way back. How did you meet?" Jack had told me Mattias was another 'stray' Lennox brought in and I've been wanting to hear the story.

"At Sisu Performance. I was in training while he was staying there," Matty gestures a barren cake pop stick toward Lennox.

"Sisu, what is that?"

"It's a company in Finland that works with elite athletes, some of the other drivers. A lot of fitness but also nutrition and sleep tracking and psychological training." Lennox says as he makes his peace with a forkful of rice.

"Is this where you learned your jet lag voodoo?" I ask Matty.

"That's where he learned all the ways to terrorize me," Lennox adds with no small amount of sarcasm.

"And then Lennox hired you?"

"Eh, something like that," Matty shrugs.

"Matty…" Lennox cuts him off and ticks his head.

"What? I don't care, it's not a secret," Matty replies, back to his monotone voice and stoic facial features.

"What's not a secret?" I pry. Lennox huffs and leans back in his chair, arms crossing his chest.

"I had some trouble with a girl. Went off the rails, got hooked on heroin." He says flatly as if this was a minor hiccup in his life.

"Oh, wow." I'm not sure what to say. I would never have guessed the tall Finn, straight-laced and toned like a blond adonis, and militant about Lennox's health would have said that.

"Went to stay with Mum and Pop — well, his Mum and Pop," Matty points to Lennox, "Figured my shit out. Then he hired me."

"Good for you, Matty. I'm so glad you're healthy now. I guess Jack was right, he really does bring home all the strays," I joke, trying to lighten the mood.

"Oh for fucks sake, not the cats again," Lennox rolls his eyes. "There are only two cats. Two."

"Two *inside*," Matty corrects him.

"The ones outside are not mine," Lennox argues.

"Mmhmm, that's why you feed them and make them houses and shit."

"Ok," I laugh, "I definitely need to know more about that, too, but Matty would you ever do an interview about how you came to be on the team and what you do for Lennox now?"

Before he can answer, Lennox barks at me, "No."

"I didn't mean anything private, I just think it's fascinating and the fans would love even a generic backstory…"

"I said no. My friends and family are not pawns, they aren't here for entertainment value," he snaps. His voice is low, his eyes are dark, and there's nothing playful about the tone of his voice this time.

"I'm sorry, I didn't mean…"

"Ignore him," Matty waves his hand to brush Lennox's tirade off, "he gets a little protective. Finish your chicken," he eyes the uneaten food and chides Lennox.

Two steps forward and one step back, Lennox stabs his remaining food and starts grudge-eating it.

"Matty, I'm sorry. I would never imply you should tell your private story. I just meant you're all old friends and I thought the fans would love that kind of personal insight."

Lennox is silent and leering at me.

"No offense taken. Mr. Privacy here wouldn't allow it anyway, though," he nods his head toward Lennox and pops another cake ball into his mouth.

"Nope," Lennox confirms.

"Duly noted," I eyeball him back. What a shame, Lennox hiring two close friends and all the tasks they do for him every day are fascinating to an outsider like me. It would make him seem so much more human, reveal some of the good I see in him, when he lets me see it.

I spot Tatiana refilling the buffet station and taking an empty tray back into the kitchen. Rather than sit here under Lennox's glare, I excuse myself to go say hello. Hopefully, Francesca is around too.

The kitchen is small but bustling with several cooks working and calling out refills needed in the dining room. Bussers are coming in with trays of dirty dishes as fast as more can leave with fresh food. It's loud and steam rises above the cooktops as the crew works to feed the entire Celeritas team.

"There were no onions!" I hear Francesca's Latin voice from the opposite side of a cook station. I step around a trash can and the backside of the cook station and Francesca has her hands on her hips, her face is scrunched up and she looks ready to murder Digby DuPont who is hovering above her.

"I saw them, Francesca. I saw the onions with my own eyes. Right there in my rice. Do you think I'm stupid?" Digby chastises her. A busser passes by them and sticks her tongue out at Digby behind his back.

I don't have many friends here, ok, any friends. And I don't think I care for the way Digby has Francesca cornered and is raising his voice to her. It's exactly the way Robert and Lydia Mitchell scold the help and treat them like subpar humans.

"Francesca!" I step between the dueling pair and give Francesca a quick hug. "I just wanted to thank everyone for dinner. It was delicious!"

Francesca harrumphs and gives Digby the universal face for 'neener neener neener.' "Thank you, Mallory. I'm happy *someone* appreciates our hard work."

"Oh gosh, Lennox and Mattias and I stuffed ourselves!"

"Ms. Mitchell," Digby interrupts and takes my hand to turn me toward him. He's wearing a polo shirt tucked into his tailored pants and has an aqua sweater hanging over his shoulders. He looks like he just left a golf match, not a Formula 1 race. "My apologies, good help is so hard to find," he mewls as Francesca scurries away.

I pull my hand away and tuck them both into my back pockets so he isn't inclined to grab them again. Digby DuPont is as wholesome and squeaky clean as they come, according to what I've learned about him, but I have no patience for people who berate service workers. "I don't know, the food is always amazing," I retort.

"Of course. Long day, that's all."

One of the men who's always with Digby, I assume his personal assistant, enters the kitchen and steps beside us, his iPad clutched against his torso. "Sir, the yacht is ready."

Sir? What a difference between these two teammates. The only time Jack would call Lennox 'sir' would be to make a joke.

"Ms. Mitchell," Digby puts his hand on my shoulder, "have you ever been to Bahrain before?"

"No, first time. It's beautiful, though."

"You must see it from the gulf, the city is stunning at night," Digby gushes and starts reaching into his back pocket. "I have a yacht in the marina here. Would you like to be my guest this evening?"

"Oh, umm, thank you but I have a lot of work left." I don't really have anything major planned but something about Digby is beginning to give me the creeps and also, I'm just not interested. If I was interested in someone, and I'm not - it'd be the tall tattooed sometimes-asshole in the dining hall. But that's neither here nor there.

"Yes well, perhaps afterward?" Digby pulls a card from his Armani wallet and hands it to me.

"Right, thanks," I say and smile.

Digby and his prim and proper assistant, who looks entirely dead behind the eyes, excuse themselves and I look at the card he's handed me. It's glossy black card stock with 'Digby DuPont' and an international phone number in elaborate embossed gold writing on the front. I snort at the pretentiousness that oozes off it and make my way back into the dining hall.

Matty and Lennox are still at our table. Matty is turned sideways talking to one of the other Celertias guys and Lennox is scrolling through his phone. I cruise past the buffet table and grab one falafel on a cocktail napkin. Skirting past so Matty doesn't notice, I slip Lennox the falafel with a wink. My peace offering.

He pops the whole thing into his mouth, cheeks stuffed like a chipmunk, and smiles at me as he chews. Good to know I can placate him with food, as well as sarcasm, jokes, and inappropriate sexual tension.

I sit back down in front of my open laptop and toss Digby's silly business card on the table next to me. Lennox swallows and picks it up, "What's this?"

"Nothing. Ran into your favorite teammate in the kitchen." I start browsing through my email again.

"Why do you have this?" Lennox is holding the card up and leaning over the table toward me with wide eyes. His jaw is stiff and I can see a vein pulsing in his neck.

"It's no big deal, he asked me to join him on his yacht tonight. I told him no."

Lennox launches to his feet and his chair screeches back against the floor. Before I know what's happening, he's halfway to the kitchen, cutting through the dining room crowd on a mission.

"What happened?" Matty turns to ask.

"I don't know. He saw a business card Digby gave me and freaked out." I reply shaking my head.

"Fuck," Matty curses and starts toward the kitchen after Lennox.

I snap my laptop closed and grab my backpack, trying to hustle my way through the dining room without causing a scene. This nonsense with Digby is getting tiresome. By all accounts, he seems a little douchey, but harmless enough.

"Where is he?" I hear Lennox roaring as I finally make it to the kitchen.

One of the chefs says Digby's already gone and points toward the rear exit of the kitchen. Lennox tears out the door with Matty in tow behind and I jog after them trying to keep up. We are not having a public altercation over a freaking business card.

Outside, behind the motorhome, Lennox and Matty are several paces apart looking up and down the road. "He's gone," Matty says.

"What the hell are you doing?" I bark.

Lennox stops his hunt and storms to me. He's absolutely livid and the sight makes me take a step backward. The angry Lennox Gibbes seems to grow in size and anger pulses off him in waves. "What exactly did he say to you?"

"Nothing! Calm down!" I yell back at him.

"If it's nothing why do you have this?" He waves the business card at me.

"I told you. He asked me on his yacht. I said no. Try to keep up!"

"Don't fuck with me, Mallory."

"Don't you talk to me like that!" I scream back at him and point my finger in his face.

"Ehh, keep it down guys," Matty makes his way to us and is looking around. It's dark and thankfully there is no one behind the motorhome along this service path, just piles of produce boxes and sounds from the kitchen bustling inside.

"Fuck off!" Lennox snaps at Matty next, who shrugs and walks away, cool and unfazed, as always.

Me, on the other hand, I've had enough. "Don't talk to him like that, either!"

"I'll talk to him however I want!"

"What is wrong with you? Nothing happened! You're acting like a crazy person, storming around like The Hulk! Why don't you just get it over with and piss a circle around me to mark your territory!"

"I am not a crazy person!" He roars back. His chest is heaving, his nostrils are flaring, and he looks like he wants to eat me, swallow me whole.

"Stop yelling at me!"

"You stop yelling at *me!*"

Before I have time to consider what I mean, I scream back at him, "I don't want to!"

"Good! I don't want you to, either!"

There's a brief moment where all I hear are crickets, a heartbeat of time in which we're both silent. My fists are clenching around my laptop bag, my breathing out of control, my pulse could keep pace with any one of the cars on track.

I am so fucking turned on.

In two long strides, he's on me.

My backpack and laptop hit the ground.

My hands lock behind his neck and as much as I'm dragging him down to me, Lennox is pulling me up to him. His strong hands are in my hair, holding the base of my skull with one and my jaw with the other. His lips smash into mine with all the aggression and power behind his frame.

My hands dig into his hair and god help me, I am kissing him back as hard as I can, climbing up him trying to get closer and closer. The heat of his body pressed up against mine in the cool desert air is electrifying as I smash myself into him. A strong thigh parts my legs and I grind my core into him, desperate for more as his tongue sweeps my lips.

I open my mouth and my tongue chases his. He tastes like sin, the original forbidden fruit, and I moan as he rolls his hips into mine. We're battling for dominance, his fist is wrapped around my long hair and I suck his bottom lip into my mouth, dragging my teeth along it as he pulls me closer still.

He growls into my mouth as I rake my nails across his neck and he grabs my ass with his free hand, dragging me up onto his bent thigh over and over while I writhe and grind against him. His mouth expertly explores mine, biting and licking, taking everything I give him and everything I didn't know I had it in myself to give.

This is not a sweet kiss, this is pure adrenaline and passion. My body is on fire, so wet I slide against him effortlessly. One of my hands snakes around his back to clutch his shirt, his powerful shoulder blades flexing and manipulating my body. He holds my head exactly where he wants it and slides his lips down my jaw, his tongue leaving a wet trail to my neck. He bites the soft skin above my collarbone and I let out a gasp, pulling his head into me harder, "Lennox!"

His tongue flattens over the bite and he sucks the tender skin into his mouth before he returns those skilled lips to my own. Pulling my hips in, I can feel his hard length against my stomach, I can feel the heat permeating my clothes, infiltrating my core, all my excuses and reason dissipating into the desert air.

Taking my head between his two hands, he brings his forehead to mine. "I want you," he growls.

"We can't, " I whisper.

"We are," he wraps both hands around my ass and keeps me close against him.

I put my hands on his chest and ease myself off his thigh. I can feel his pulse hammering through my palms. "You make me crazy."

"Back at you," he bends to nuzzle my neck.

In a moment of extreme self-control that my throbbing lady parts do not agree with, I push him back and separate ourselves an inch. "I can't do this, Lennox. I need this job."

"This won't risk your job, I won't let it." His green eyes are electric and glimmering under the light of the moon and the glow of the buildings next to us. In this moment, I could so easily believe him, be swept up in that kiss, those strong arms. If only I didn't have responsibilities and an agenda, and technically, a boyfriend back at home who no longer returns my calls or texts.

"Take me back to my room?" I ask him.

"With pleasure," he grins.

"Alone!" I laugh and slap his chest.

Lennox grabs my hand and pulls me into his chest and wraps his long arms around me. I tuck my head into him and he rests his head on the top of mine and sighs. I close my eyes, so warm and secure. "It's inevitable, Mallory."

Twelve

"Lightning in your eyes, you can't speak. You've fallen from the sky, down to me. I see it in your face, I'm relief. I'm your summer girl." - HAIM - Summer Girl

Lennox

"Seriously, Lennox?" Mallory's lips are pursed but she's biting her cheek trying to hide a smirk when I open my hotel room door. I may have forgotten to put on pants when I got out of the shower and am standing at the door now dripping wet with only a towel clutched around my waist.

Whoops.

"Let me help with those boxes," I nod to the packages she's carrying in her arms, the made-up task I've concocted needing her help with tonight to get her here.

"No! Do not let go of that towel!" She squeezes past me into my hotel room and I close the door behind her. "Go put some pants on!"

"Are you sure, love?"

Mallory piles the boxes down on the coffee table in front of the loveseat in the hotel's small sitting area next to my bed. "Yes! I'm here to help you get all this stuff mailed, not help you with other... stuff," she waves her hand in a circular motion toward the towel barely containing my dick, which is already getting twitchy with her here.

"If you say so," I reply and head into the bathroom to throw some sweatpants on.

After the race today, I agreed to 'behave' for the media if Mallory

89

helped me get several boxes of fan mail, postcards, and signed photos shipped out. I'm behind on it and I don't like to keep my fans waiting, but I could have had Jack do this like he normally does. That would be decidedly less fun, though. Now that I've had a taste of my smart-mouthed nanny, I need more.

Between the race and the obligatory team meetings, including the debrief afterward in which I claimed it was an accident running my front wing into Digby's rear tire to puncture it on track, I've not had a moment alone with Mallory. When I'd catch glances of her, she looked deep in thought but I caught a hint of blush creeping up her back when she'd meet my eyes.

My nanny wants me as much as I want her. There was no hiding it after she tried to climb me like a tree last night before sending me home, again, to jerk off in the shower like a teenager. Knowing what she tastes like now, the texture of her tongue, how her hands feel raking through my hair, I came in record time picturing those soft lips wrapped around my cock. Normally being fast is a good thing in my life, but this was a new track record.

"And a shirt," she says as I stroll out of the bathroom and take a seat next to her on the small loveseat.

"You said nothing about putting a shirt on, too. Negotiate better."

Mallory rubs her hands over her eyes and shakes her head and then starts opening the cardboard boxes, classic distraction. "Ok, so what's the procedure here?" She says, pulling out postmarked envelopes and small packages from the first box.

"One of these boxes should be blank envelopes and stock photos." I start opening up a second box looking for them. "I need to sign photos and then you can address the envelopes so they can get mailed out tomorrow."

"What about these packages?" She holds up a small padded envelope, half the front covered in postage stamps and written with Asian alphabet characters.

"Sometimes people send things they want me to sign and return. Start opening, here are the blank return envelopes."

Mallory starts ripping into packages and envelops like a kid on Christmas morning while I begin signing a stack of glossy photos. Normally after a race, I'd be out celebrating or drowning my sorrows but this is nice, her being here, not being alone in my room. I doubt few people know how much time we spend alone in hotel rooms across the world.

"Wow," Mallory sighs and leans back into the loveseat, reading a handwritten note, "this is so much fun."

"Read them to me?"

Mallory starts reading the letter a woman in Singapore has sent. Her husband is my 'biggest fan' and she's asking for a special message sent back as a gift for their wedding anniversary. I fulfill the request and jot a few lines on the photo for her and hand it back to Mallory to mail.

"Do you read all of these?"

"Aye. Someone took the time to write to me, I can take the time to read it." Mallory studies me, her face half-hidden behind the letter. "What?"

"The Paddock Playboy, bad boy Lennox Gibbes, reads and responds to all of his fan mail. If you aren't careful, the world may find out you aren't such an asshole, after all."

"I don't much care what they think." I shrug, toss my dried up Sharpie into a bin next to the television and uncap a new one.

"I don't believe you," she starts, "if you didn't care, you wouldn't do all this. You wouldn't make time for all the fans at every autograph session. You wouldn't wave at the people waving Scottish flags at each race."

She's right, of course, but it's far easier to pretend that I don't care. That way, when I disappoint them at every race, it kills me a little less. When I make a fraud of this historic sport every Sunday, it's far easier to act like I don't give two shits. When the media makes up ridiculous nicknames like the Paddock Playboy, it's easier to ignore them than to educate them that I'm alone in my hotel room at night more often than not. I'm far from innocent but it's easier not to argue.

Except for arguing with Mallory, which raises my blood pressure and gets my heart going, reminds me I'm alive, and for whatever reason, makes my dick harder than a rock. I keep silently signing photos, though. I still have balls and would rather they be buried up against Mallory right now than discussing my feelings.

"Running into Digby today wasn't an accident, was it?" She asks, changing directions after studying my silence.

"Nope," I admit to her, but no one else.

"You could have ruined your own race; you had to change your wing."

"My race was ruined anyway."

"I don't understand you," she sighs and reaches for a bubble mailer to open.

"I don't understand why you're still dressed," I counter, running my gaze up her body, bare legs peeking out from the black Celeritas knee-length skirt she wore today just to tempt me.

Ignoring me, she opens up the bubble mailer and pulls out a white thong and an attached note. Across the front of the thong are the ironed-on letters, 'Mrs. Gibbes.' "What is this?" Mallory shrieks and throws the thong at me like it's covered in ebola. Sometimes they do arrive covered in... something, which even I'll admit is disgusting.

I chuckle while Mallory reads aloud the index card note that came with the thong, thankfully free of any dry crusty patches. "I need you in my panties. Please sign and return."

I sign them across the small fabric front, add a smiley face, and toss them back to Mallory to return.

"You aren't seriously going to mail these back?" She objects.

"Of course. Unless you want to try them on," I wiggle my eyebrows at her. "Do you want to try them on, Mallory?"

"Absolutely not, that's disgusting!" She laughs and shoves them into a new plain envelope. "I'll stick to wearing only my own thongs, thank you very much," she adds.

Well, fuck, now that image is in my head. I toss my marker down. "What color are they?" She shakes her head and seals up the envelope, looking straight ahead and dismissing me. "You're the one who put the picture in my head so tell me, what color are they?"

She crosses her legs and fidgets with the mail for a few beats of silence, I can practically see the wheels turning in her mind. "Black," she finally gives in.

I lean back onto the loveseat and throw my arms over the back and side. "Show me," I deadpan.

"I will not!" She giggles until she turns to face me and sees that I'm dead serious. "Lennox..."

"Show me." The blush is back, creeping up her neck and her foot is wiggling nervously. When she bites her bottom lip, though, I know she's considering my request. "You have my word, your job is safe no matter what happens between us."

Her eyes dart to mine. "I have never, ever behaved this way with a client," she murmurs. Good, I don't want to think about anyone else touching her.

"Show. Me." My voice lowers and Mallory's eyes drop to the impressive tent in my sweatpants. She stares at the obvious bulge for a moment then meets my eyes and stands, watching me as she circles the coffee table and stands a few feet in from of me on my side of the loveseat.

I stay leaned back on the couch as she grabs the hem of her skirt and starts inching it up her hips, ever so slowly. The way she's looking at me, determination and pride over what she's doing to me - she's goddamn intoxicating. I keep my eyes fixed on hers but the creamy white of her thighs is exposed, her breath picking up. The hotel room is silent but the sexual intensity between us beats like a snare drum.

A few more inches and the skirt is up around her curved waist revealing a tiny patch of black fabric covering her perfect little mound. I suck in a breath and lean forward with my elbows on my knees as I envision burying my tongue inside those folds I can scantly see the outlines of. I lift a hand and rotate my fingers instructing her to turn.

She pirouettes and looks back at me over her shoulder, her juicy peach-shaped ass facing me. Two flawless, milky cheeks are totally exposed, just the thin string of her thong run between. My cock is throbbing with the need to sink my teeth into her ass, to bend her over this couch and bury myself deep inside her.

"Fucking perfect," I growl at her as she turns to face me again. Her nipples are hard beneath her shirt and as I lean back on the loveseat and wave my finger for her to come hither, she runs her hands up her torso and cups her tits in her hands. The way she holds my gaze, not even a little intimidated by me like most women, ignites the competitor in me and I reach out to pull her onto me.

Grabbing her bare ass with both hands, I drag her over my lap to straddle me and her hands wrap around my head as I bite and suck at her pebbled nipples through her shirt. She gasps and pulls me in harder, thrusting her chest at me. I slip my hands under her shirt and over her smooth skin and start to pull her shirt off.

"Lennox, wait." She gasps and puts her hands on my bare chest and leans back to look at me.

"I swear to christ, Mallory, if you give me the job excuse again..." I don't know what I'll do if she gives me the job excuse. Probably go beat off again, in reality, but that's a piss poor substitute for the smoking hot woman with her barely covered pussy an inch away from my dick.

"No, that's not it. I mean, that's also bad, very bad, but..." she mumbles and takes my face in her hand, thumbs running over two days worth of stubble I haven't had the inclination to deal with.

"But what? We have twenty-two races, Mallory. Seven more months together. You want to keep fighting this for seven months?" My poor dick will be chafed and raw in another week, much less seven months.

"No. Just not yet, ok?"

I'm conflicted because she's not arguing and this is technically a win for me, but what the hell are we waiting for? Mallory does not strike me as the kind of girl who's waiting. Unless she's looking for a commitment from me, which we would need to get to the bottom of now. I want Mallory but I don't want to hurt her if she thinks this is a long term thing. "Why?"

Her hands drop to my shoulders and her eyes lower, "I have a boyfriend. Technically."

"What?" I drop my hands from her sides and her head lifts at the elevation of my voice, the surprise in my tone. What boyfriend? We've been dancing around each other for weeks playing this game, and she's never once mentioned a boyfriend. The memories of Kate fucking around behind my back left scars I'd rather forget and hell if I'm going to be her back-up dick while she's away from home. "What does 'technically' mean?"

"It's over. And not because of you—it was over a long time ago. I just need to tell him." My eyes squint and I cross my arms over my chest in front of me, which makes her lean back further. "I should have ended it before I left, it's been done for months."

"Then why didn't you?" I question her skeptically.

"I'm going to catch so much shit from my parents," she sighs, "and I don't know, I guess it was just easier to go through the motions and pretend than it was to deal with the real problem."

Fuck, can I relate to that. I exhale a deep breath and my shoulders relax; I didn't realize they were flexed and tensed up from her revelation.

Mallory puts her hands back on my chest and I let my hands fall back to her hips. "Call him and do it, then."

"He won't answer my calls or texts," she says, warm little hands running over my pecs.

"What sort of pussy is he?" I don't know what kind of man doesn't answer calls from a woman like Mallory who is overseas and away from him, much less working with a bunch of F1 drivers. It's a full-blown sausage fest and, at a minimum, you'd think he'd want to check in that she's safe. We're in a different country every other week, for fuck sake. No clue who this prick is, but he's a pussy.

Mallory giggles but doesn't disagree. Her skirt is still hiked up around her waist, exposing the black triangle of her thong to me. I'm pissed but I'm dying to know if she's bare underneath it or if she has a patch chestnut curls. "I'm going home tomorrow to deal with it."

"Tomorrow?" Again, I knew nothing about this. I don't know why it pisses me off. Jack is supposed to be making her travel arrangements now, he should have told me.

She nods, trails one finger up and down my chest, and bats her long eyelashes at me. Little minx. "You gonna send me home like this?" She teases.

"Get rid of him," I order.

"I will," she whispers and lowers her head to my neck, one soft kiss under my ear. One soft kiss on my collarbone. One soft kiss on top of my shoulder.

"Mallory..." I warn her.

"It's ok," she runs her tongue from my shoulder all the way back to my earlobe. Boyfriend or not, my cock is ready to tear a hole in my sweatpants to get at her. "I'm sure another gentleman on the long plane ride home can help me out."

"Fuck that," I roar, grabbing her ass cheeks and dragging her up against me, creating friction of her hot core against my throbbing dick. She laughs at first, thinking she's won the game of making me jealous until I rotate my hips into her and her eyes slam shut and she gasps. "When are you going to be back?" I ask her, watching her neck arch and her chest heave as she starts grinding against me.

"Ch-China," she moans.

Two more goddamn weeks. I don't share women and I'm not doing this until it's officially over with her pussy boyfriend. I'm not Dickless DuPont running around with other men's girlfriends. It may be over in Mallory's head, but I need confirmation for myself.

From the moans and the way Mallory is digging her nails into my shoulders, she's as hot as I am. I know she's full of shit about finding some rando on an airplane but still, it would be ungentlemanly to leave her in this condition. I'm an asshole, not a monster.

I pull her in all the way up against me and I tilt my hips. She's pushing down on my dick and I can feel her moisture through my sweats. Wrapping my hands around her hips, I drag her up and down my shaft. Dry humping was never this hot the last time I did it, which was probably high school.

I latch my mouth onto the swell of a breast that's heaving out of her shirt, the first few buttons undone. If she's going home to see some other guy, she's going home marked. I bite and suck until I'm sure she's got one hell of a reminder of me while she's gone.

"Lennox, oh god," she pants. Her legs are trembling around me and her motions are getting sporadic, twitchy.

"Come for me," I growl.

"Ah, fuck, I can't come like this. I need you," her eyes are clamped shut, her fingers are pulling my hair so hard she's going to have a fistful soon.

"You can and you will." I push into her harder with my cock. She needs to come for me before I blow my load in my pants like a novice. My length separates her folds and I can feel her clit rubbing up and down over me.

I squeeze her ass tighter and bite her neck and Mallory tenses up and drags her nails into my flesh. She throws her head back and screams for me, screams my name, screams gibberish, I don't know. I'm too busy watching her come apart on my cock, her face flushed, her breathing hard, before she collapses onto me and wraps her arms around my shoulders.

I hold her tight as she comes down and rides out the final waves of her orgasm in tiny shudders and soft sighs. Her breathing returns to normal in a few seconds and she starts giggling against me.

"What, exactly, is so funny?" My hard dick finds nothing amusing about its condition right now.

"I can't remember the last time I did that," she laughs.

Wrapping my hands under her ass, I stand up, taking her with me, and then dump her off onto the loveseat. Looking down, my grey sweats are soaked and the purple head of my dick is staring at me over the waistband. Lying on the loveseat with her skirt still around her waist, Mallory starts laughing hysterically.

"I'm glad you find this so entertaining," I wave to my very unsatisfied dick.

She sits up and stares at her handy work, "Let me take care of that."

"Get rid of him Mallory, I'm warning you." I point at her and turn to find a clean pair of gym shorts in my suitcase. From the bathroom, as I change, I can still hear her giggling. I think about quickly taking care of the ache in my balls, but I still have some sense of pride.

"I think I kind of like this, Lennox," she calls from the loveseat.

"I bet you do," I call back, splashing cold water over my face.

"You can be my sexual servant, my dick-on-demand!"

Staring at myself in the mirror, I don't know how I've lost the upper hand here, but I sure as hell have. China cannot come soon enough, "I'll give you dick on demand," I mumble to myself.

Coming out of the bathroom I make my way to the phone by the bed and call room service. If my dick is going to be miserable tonight, at least my stomach can be happy. I order a burger and fries for Mallory, always a safe bet, and whatever kind of grilled chicken and vegetable dish the kitchen can concoct for me.

"Rather presumptuous of you to assume what I want to eat," Mallory smirks as I return to the loveseat.

"Really? You're going to complain?" I wave at her, her face still flush and her body slumped with contentment.

"Nope, no complaints. Just like to argue with you," she smirks and pokes me in the side with her toe.

"Do not argue with me, Mallory. My balls cannot take anymore." I find the television remote on the table between our cardboard boxes and click the TV on. "Get back to mailing," I toss an envelope at her in jest.

"Yes, boss," she teases and tries to run her foot up my side before I slap it away.

I will remember this. She doesn't realize it yet, but she'll pay for this. Never in my life has an evening with a woman ended with me refusing to fuck her. I'm the dominant one, I call the shots. The hell is happening to me?

What do you want to watch?" I ask her, scanning through channels.

"Any horror movies on?"

"Mmm, let's see. You like scary movies?"

She nods. "The campier, the better. Halloween is my favorite holiday. What's Halloween like in Scotland?" The mindless chitchat is a nice distraction from plotting all the things I'm going to do to her in China.

"Well, there was no trick-or-treating when I was a kid, I was so jealous of you Americans for that. But some of the towns would have a giant bonfire and we'd still dress up. Mum would find the biggest turnips she could for us to carve."

"You carve turnips?"

"Aye. Put a little candle in them and set them about to keep the spirits away."

"That sounds fun."

I find some old horror movie on tv, the only one I can find in English, and Mallory goes back to ripping envelopes open and telling me who to make autographs out to.

"There's a tradition, too. Two lovers would put nuts into the bonfire. If the nuts burned quietly, they'd be happy forever. If the nuts crackled or broke open, the couple would be doomed."

"Maybe we should put some nuts in a fire and see what happens," she jokes.

"Love, no offense, but I don't want my nuts anywhere near you and a fire."

Mallory clutches her chest and feigns shock, "You don't trust me?"

"No," I laugh, "do you trust me?"

"Absolutely not!" She shakes her head and giggles.

"Well, there you go, then. I had a Nessie costume one year."

"You did not!"

"Aye, I did."

"I need pictures of this."

"I'll see what I can do."

"Can we do a piece on your life back home sometime?" Mallory asks, handing me a tee-shirt to sign.

"No."

"Oh, come on, the fans would love it!"

"No."

"Ugh, you're such a grump." She takes the shirt back from me and hands me a hat to sign next. "Wait," she says. "Put this shirt and the hat on!"

Mallory and I go through every piece of fan mail and she takes photos of me wearing the hats, holding the trinkets, reading the letters people have sent in. She scarfs her burger when it arrives and I steal her french fries. When the movie ends, she's curled up fast asleep on the loveseat.

If everyone crying "Paddock Playboy" saw me now.

Thirteen

"I'd love to be the one to disappoint you when I don't fall down." - Limp Bizkit - Re-Arranged

Mallory

I'm angry.

I thought I would be nervous meeting David, breaking things off with him, but I'm livid as I finish my makeup and prepare to head out the door of Aria's apartment - my old apartment.

I've been back in New York for over a week and he hasn't returned a single call or text until today. I even went to his condo and beat on the door like a crazy person, but no answer. It wasn't until I texted him threatening to show up at Dad's office that he agreed to meet me at the Bean n' Brew. A public place was my idea so there is no chance of drama, but now I'm doubly glad, so I don't murder him.

"He *is* a pussy!" I complain to Aria, who's sitting on the edge of the bathtub as I coat my lashes in gravity-defying mascara. I'm going to look my best while I dump his sorry ass. "Two years together and I can't even get a response to meet him while I'm in town!"

"He probably knows what's coming so he's hiding." Aria nods.

Chasing David down aside, Aria and I have had the ultimate girl's week. We camped out with PJ's and sheet masks in the living room while binging on the new 90210 remake. I treated her to a Thai massage and she insisted we book a waxing session after I filled her in on the change of dynamics between Lennox and me.

She was not surprised.

Lennox is right that the lust between us is inevitable, the stupid sexy asshole. There is no way I can continue kidding myself for the next seven months. I just need to be smart about it. He isn't relationship material and I know that going into it. My heart is safe, I just need to keep my job safe so we'll need to negotiate the logistics.

'Negotiate better,' he said.

The thought of sneaking around in hotel rooms late at night is also kind of hot if I'm being honest.

I think he's on board with this plan, too. He woke me up in Bahrain after I fell asleep on the loveseat and walked me across the hall to my room to go to bed so no one would see me leaving his room in the morning. He doesn't want anyone to know about me, and I can't have Celeritas learn that I'm sleeping with the client I'm supposed to be fixing the media's perception of. I was happy to avoid the walk of shame that otherwise would have occurred the next morning.

"Ok, how do I look?" I ask Aria, who's scrolling through all of my photos on my phone. They're 99% Lennox and 1% scenery of the foreign countries that I pass through but don't get time to explore.

"You look like a woman who should be fucking this sex god," she holds up my phone showing a photo of Lennox peeling off a sweaty race suit, "not David the douche."

"I'm not fucking him." I correct her.

"Yet."

"Yet," I smile and agree.

"Oooo, who is this?" Aria asks and rotates the phone. It's a great photo of Lennox and Matty laughing in the garage in Australia.

"That's Mattias, Matty. The physio."

"Good lord, are they all this hot?"

"Yes, do you see now how powerless I am to resist this? They're a walking, talking trifecta of Big Dick Energy. All swaggering and smelling good all the time. Ridiculous."

"And this one?" Aria asks, showing me another photo.

"That's Jack. He's funny and sweet and gay, so don't get any ideas. How some lucky man hasn't snatched him up yet I don't understand." I suspect Jack has been seeing someone in the paddock, actually, but he's going to have to keep my secrets, too, so I haven't pressed for info. He, Matty, and Lennox tell each other everything but there's no way they would betray Lennox and tell anyone about us. I still think the world would love how loyal Lennox is to his friends, but oh well.

"Ugh, shame for womankind. Tell me more about the blond." Aria taps my phone.

"He's Finnish and super blunt and stoic. It comes off as rude a lot. I'm not actually convinced he *isn't* just rude yet. I don't think you would like him."

"I don't need him to talk," Aria jokes.

"He said personal training is not a real thing and all you do is give aerial yoga lessons to bored housewives."

"What!" She huffs then goes back to examining the photo, "I'd still do him."

"Ok, I'm out of here. Wish me luck."

"That weasel never deserved you, stay strong. Celebratory drinks tonight, right?"

"You know it," I nod back. It's Friday in NYC and we have catching up to do.

The Bean n' Brew is bustling as the lunch rush begins, busy New Yorkers line up for their noon caffeine break or grab takeout before hopping into the nearby subway station. It's not far from the Mitchell Media offices so David used to meet me here for lunch like back in the days when we paid attention to one another and made an effort.

Those days are long past, on both our ends.

Moving past the crowd at the counter, I spot David at a table tucked into the back corner. Good move, David, you do know what's coming, don't you? His laptop is in front of him and he's typing so furiously he doesn't notice me until I'm standing next to him.

"David," I stay standing and expect him to rise and greet me. He doesn't.

"Hey, Mallory, what's up?" He can barely look away from his laptop as I sit down opposite him.

"*What's up?*" I mock his blasé tone, "I haven't seen you in a month, you don't return my calls, and that's what you have to say?"

David purses his lips and huffs at me, "What would you like me to say, Mallory?"

He's right, I don't know why I expected anything else. It's not worth arguing about. Arguing with David is not fun, like arguing with Lennox is, but I shut those thoughts down. That is not why I'm here. "You're right, there's not much left to say. I did want to come home and say this to you in person, though."

"Say what?" His eyes are darting between me and his laptop screen. He could not be less interested.

"David, I flew all the way here. Can you please look at me?"

He lets out an audible huff and looks at me like I'm a petulant child, a waste of his time. "Go on then," he waves at me and stares sarcastically.

"Wow," I mumble and rub my temples. He's making it so easy to break up with him, to see so clearly right now. What the hell was I thinking the past two years? "Things haven't been good between us for a long time, David. Out of decency, I wanted to come home and tell you in person that you and I are done, officially."

His eyebrows shoot up and he laughs, "Yeah, ok, Mallory. Stop being so juvenile. I don't have time for this."

"Juvenile? I'm trying to be an adult here. I don't want any hard feelings or a fight, I just needed to…"

"Could you be more selfish right now?" He snaps. "I am in the middle of a board crisis, our stocks are down, and those plebeians at Cooper Media are making our lives hell!"

I don't know anything about a board crisis or our stocks, but that's because I have never involved myself in Dad's precious dinosaur business of print media and I've barely spoken to Mom and Dad since leaving New York. All I've gotten are snarky texts with vaguely racist comments about the countries I'm visiting or demanding I stop embarrassing and them and come home.

One of Dad's associates had seen me on TV standing behind Lennox during a post-race interview, and he let me know how 'ashamed' he was that a colleague saw me 'associating with such a hooligan.' I told him said hooligan was a world champion and, just because this is what Robert Mitchell really cares about, that his net worth is several times over his. That said hooligan should be embarrassed to be seen with a Mitchell if anything. That was the last text he sent me. Mom knows I'm home and I've met Cody for lunch, but Dad and I may be irreparably broken.

As are David and me.

"Right," I draw out the word in response to David's tantrum. "Ok then, well good luck with that. Good luck to you, David. I wish you nothing but the best." I kind of wish him a raging case of crabs and a receding hairline, but I bite my tongue. It isn't worth it.

"Wait, what are you doing?" David tugs my arm as I stand to leave, pulling me back into my chair.

"Umm, I'm leaving now."

"You aren't serious?" His face is shocked as if he's not heard a word

I've said.

"I'm dead serious, we're over, David. I need to go now."

"Wait, this is all just a big misunderstanding." His voice is low and he reaches for my hand over the table, which I pull away from him and put in my lap.

"No, there's no misunderstanding. Definitely breaking up with you." This is getting weird and I'm glad we're in a public space, after all.

"Mallory, the only reason I've been distant is because your father told me to cut you off, to push you away!"

"What?" I seethe, my face twisted in disgust and shock.

"He said it would get you to stop this nonsense and come home!"

"Oh, did he?"

"Yeah, you and me, Mallory, we're fine!"

I shake my head at him, a mixture of anger toward my father and pity for this shell of a man before me turning my stomach. "And you just went along with it, Daddy's little puppet."

"What choice did I have, be reasonable."

"You could have, I don't know, acted like a man and stood up for me," I wave my hands at him, my voice rising and drawing the attention of people at the end of the counter waiting for their order. "You could have supported my dreams and been proud of me."

"Keep your voice down," he scolds.

"Why? Afraid the people around us might learn what spineless weasel you really are?" A woman behind me adds a loud mmm hmmm and when I turn to look at her she nods at me and gives David a wicked stink eye.

"You're making a huge mistake. Your parents will never allow this."

"My mistake was wasting two years with you. Fortunately, those days are over and Robert and Lydia Mitchell may have castrated you, but I'm a grown woman and I don't answer to them." A second woman behind me utters yeah in support.

I stand up, put my shoulders back, tell David to have a nice life and to never contact me again. The two eavesdroppers behind me give me fist bumps on the way out and I stroll out of the Bean n' Brew feeling like a weight has been lifted. I deserve far better. No more settling, ever again. I know what I want and I'm going to take it.

Weaving in between the commuters on the crowded sidewalks on my walk home, I text Aria and tell her the deed is done. She sends back a gif of Rachel from friends screaming, "Finally!"

Hell with it, I'm on a mission and I'm going to tell Lenox, too. I don't know what time it is in London, but he won't care.

Mallory: I got rid of him. You were right, total pussy.
Lennox: I'm glad you admit I'm always right.
Mallory: Definitely not what I said…
Lennox: Whatever. The only pussy I want to hear about now is yours.
Mallory: lololololol
Lennox: See you soon, payback is a bitch.
Mallory: China's days away yet. You'll have to keep suffering, big boy.
Lennox: China? Have you not checked your email?
Mallory: Not much, I'm scheduled to be off. ??
Lennox: I don't 'lol' but I am laughing now.

I pause in the middle of the sidewalk trying to decipher the cryptic message from Lennox but get elbowed and bumped for impeding the flow of human traffic. I pop my phone into my pocket but it rings before I can put it away. "Mom" flashes on the screen. Wow, that took all of ten minutes.

"Yes, mother?" I answer the phone and step to the side of a building to avoid being trampled.

"What have you done?" She yells in my ear loud enough to hear her clearly over the taxi horns and cars idling past.

"I'm assuming David ran straight to you to tattle?"

"Your father is beside himself, Mallory!"

"Too bad for Dad it's none of his business who I'm sleeping with."

"Mallory! Don't be so crass!" She whispers as if anyone else can hear me. Wouldn't want to tarnish Mom's image anymore, embarrassment to the family that I am.

"Gotta go, Mom."

"Wait, Mallory, we can fix this!" She begs.

"Bye, Mom."

I disconnect and throw my phone into my pocket. Merging back into the crowd, I power walk my way back to my old apartment. I need to check my work email and see what game Lennox is up to now, and then Aria and I are going out on the town. I'm a new woman and I'm done taking orders unless they're the sexy variety from my bossy boss. The thought makes me smile and carries me the rest of the way home.

Ms. Mitchell,

I apologize for the urgency during your time off but a sponsor opportunity has arisen and the timing is exceptional given your location at present. Friday evening there is a charity gala in New York City sponsored by UG Petroleum. Mr. Gibbes' presence has been requested and you will need to accompany him. Mr. Gibbes was uncharacteristically cooperative and is leaving London imminently. Whatever you are doing, Celeritas acknowledges your success to date and your confirmation of attendance will not go unrecognized by the Board.

Dress is black tie. Please see the attached details and coordinate your arrival with Mr. Gibbes.

Best,
   Sandra Alix
   Director of Marketing and Communications
   Celeritas Racing

"No, no, no!" I scream at the laptop on the tiny kitchen counter in our NY apartment.

Aria comes racing into the room as I gape in horror at the email, "What? Did you get fired?"

"No, but I'm going to be if I don't get to a gala in," I check the time, "three hours! Oh my god, Aria! It's black tie, I don't have gown or shoes or... anything!"

"Oh shit. There's no time to find a gown and have it altered. Wait, is Lennox coming?" Her eyes perk up and gleam at the possibility.

I rip the phone out of my pocket and call him but it goes straight to voicemail. Oh god, he's on a plane. I text him instead.

> **Mallory:** WHERE ARE YOU?
> **Lennox:** So eager, I like it.
> **Mallory:** TELL ME WHERE YOU ARE RIGHT NOW!
> **Lennox:** Somewhere over the Atlantic, I suppose. Would you like me to ask the pilot for exact coordinates?

"He's on his way here!" I run my hands through my hair and start pacing in a frantic mess.

"Yes! I get to meet him!" Aria squeals and claps her hands.

"This is not funny! What am I going to do?"

"There is only one thing to do. We need to raid Lydia's closet," Aria nods.

"No!" I whine.

"Yes, it's the only way. Come on, I'll get everything to be your personal glam squad. I'll do your makeup and hair, you deal with Lydia." Aria runs off and I can hear her tearing apart the bathroom gathering up supplies.

Damn it to hell, Aria is right. Lydia Mitchell and I could not be more different inside, but on the outside, she and I are a perfect match and she has an entire walk-in devoted to ball gowns and Louboutins. This is going to kill me, but I pick up my phone again.

"Oh, thank goodness, you've come to your senses," Mom answers, not even saying hello.

"Mother, Aria and I are coming over. I need an emergency ball gown." My stomach is rolling from having to ask her for anything after today's fiasco.

"For the UG Gala? Your father and I are attending, obviously. But why would you need a gown?"

"I need to attend for work and just found out. There's no time to get a dress. I need one of yours." If I bite my tongue any harder I am going to draw blood.

"Mallory, unless you are planning to attend with David and as our daughter who has regained her sense of dignity, I most certainly will not be lending you a gown." The righteousness in her tone, being able to hold something over my head, I can almost see her phony Upper East Side smirk from here in Morningside Heights.

"Mother, so help me god, you will lend me the gown and shoes of my choice or I swear to god, I will drive to Screaming Mimi's and pick out the most fabulous drag queen gown I can find, six-inch studded heels, and I will show up at that gala announcing myself to every patron as Mallory Mitchell, daughter of Robert and Lydia!"

My mother gasps, "You wouldn't!"

"Oh, I would! Just imagine what all the ladies from the club will say, mother!" I roar as Aria comes back into the room with a laundry basket stuffed with makeup, hairdryers, flat irons, and every bottle of product that lives in the bathroom.

"Very well, Mallory," my mother finally concedes and I push disconnect. Nothing is more important than appearances, after all.

"We need to move, honey, time is ticking," Aria balances the laundry basket on her hip and grabs her keys from a hook by the front door.

Fourteen

"When guys see her comin', they start spendin' their money. She's a knockout. But don't you know I'm the only one to call her honey." - Social Distortion - Knockout

Lennox

The sun is low in the sky as we land in New York City. I haven't been here in years and wasn't Sandra the Dragon Lady surprised when I was only too happy to jump on a jet and fly here for whatever pointless event she'd found so important. My cooperation will keep her guessing for weeks or maybe she thinks Mallory has me by the balls.

Which maybe she does, given that I just flew six hours to see her.

I've changed into my tux on the plane, the lame bow tie is tucked into my pocket waiting to be put on at the last possible second, and Sandra has a black limo waiting as I step off the jet at the airport.

"What's the address, love? I'm on my way," I call Mallory and she answers on the fifth ring, sounding panicked.

"Already? Oh my god, Lennox, this is a nightmare."

"I think you'll find I clean up pretty well," I tease her, climbing into the back of the limo and giving the driver the universal sign for 'one minute' so I can get the address out of Mallory.

"I'm at my parent's house but you don't understand. They're awful," she whispers the last statement.

"It'll be fine, I'm quite good with Mums. They find me charming. Give me the address." It's true, never met a Mum who didn't like me.

Mallory gives me the address and we take off into the Manhattan traffic. Twenty-five minutes later we've picked up two flower bouquets at the first florist shop we passed, and have rolled up to a pretentious little neighborhood, the kind where people think buildings that are 100 years old are historic. When a building is 1,000 years old, like half of them in Europe, then it might be historic.

I knock on the door and can hear a little dog yipping at me from inside. It opens and a tall blond with a huge nest of hair piled on top of her head drops her jaw and stares at me like I've just parted the Red Sea. "Jesus Christ," she mumbles and looks me up and down.

"Am I in the right place," I lean back to find a house number on the building exterior, "Mitchell residence?"

"Forget her," the blond grabs my arm and pulls me in the door, "I want to have your babies. All of them."

"Thank you?" I smirk at the quirky blond and look around the foyer we're inside. It looks like a Girl Scout Thin Mint threw up all over. There's antique gold mirrors everywhere and a huge, hideous orange steel circle sculpture against a wall. I know less than nothing about interior design but this place makes my head hurt just looking at it.

"Aria, is that him?" I hear Mallory yell from somewhere in the annals of this funhouse.

"Nope, just the UPS man!" Aria yells back and takes the bouquets from my arm.

"Ah, you're Aria," I smile at her. The one who's been asking Mallory for nudes of me. Well, this should be fun. "I'm here to pick up a special package," I wink at her.

"Speaking of packages," her eyes drop to my pants.

I laugh and put my hands in my front pockets. I can see why Mallory likes this girl, she's bold and hilarious.

"Aria, do not attack him!" Mallory calls from another room and then she rushes into the foyer.

Holy god, she's the most stunning creature I've ever seen. Underneath a slinky champaign-pink velvet gown is every tight curve on display, her porcelain shoulders bare, some sort of ruffle wrapping around her chest and arms, and a slit in the floor-length dress up to her mid thigh. My mind is already imagining sliding my hands up that slit and licking her long neck, totally exposed with her hair up in a fancy bun at the base of her head.

"Tha thu brèagha," I breathe and take a step closer to her.

"Wait, what did you say? What was that?" Aria snaps her head back and forth between Mallory and me, but I can't look away from the vision in front of me, her eyes sparkling with matching eyeshadow and her lips glossy with tint.

"It means you're beautiful," I explain but keep my eyes locked on Mallory and I can see blush creeping up her smooth chest.

"In, like, Scottish?" Aria fans her chest.

"Aye, Gaelic."

"Oh my god, he says 'aye'? Aria gushes.

"Stop it!" Mallory swats her.

"Mallory, aren't you going to introduce us?" An older woman appears in the entryway. As soon as she enters the room, Mallory stiffens and she seems uncomfortable all of a sudden. There's a physical resemblance to Mallory, sort of, but the woman I assume is her Mum is different altogether. Her face is cold and stiff, her pursed lips are overfilled and caked in dark red lipstick. She looks like she's been nipped and tucked within an inch of her life.

"Mom, this is Lennox Gibbes. Lennox, this is my mother, Lydia Mitchell."

"Mrs. Mitchell, a pleasure to meet you. You look radiant this evening," I lie and take her fingers she has outreached to me like I should kiss her ring. She's wearing a much more conservative blood-red gown. "Are you attending the gala this evening, as well?"

"Yes, of course. Robert and I have attended every year since this event's conception." She says like it's some sort of competition.

"I hope Mr. Mitchell won't mind if I steal you for a dance this evening, what lucky men we are to escort two stunning ladies." I lay it on thick. I'd rather dance with Digby than this woman.

"Well," Lydia pips and tries to fuss at Mallory's hair but Mallory smacks her hand away. "Mallory is wearing a gown I just wore last season so that's unfortunate."

What the hell? "You must have good taste, Mallory is a vision." I bite my tongue and force a smile.

"I told her to wear her hair down," she tries fussing with it again and Mallory steps away. "It would look much more... feminine down, Mallory."

"You are gorgeous, love," I reach for Mallory's hand, my patience running thin within seconds of being here.

"Mr. Gibbes," Lydia interrupts, "you will be wearing a proper bow tie this evening, will you not?" She scowls and waves at my neck, the top button of my shirt still undone because I don't want to be choked to death a moment sooner than I need to be.

"Mother!" Mallory scolds.

"What? I'm only being kind so Mr. Gibbes does not feel out of place this evening. Lord knows we don't need anymore gossip about you."

What sort of mum talks to her daughter like this? Mallory is absolutely horrified, her face reddening and her jaw clenching. Aria's eyes are about to roll into the back of her head.

This is the worst mum experience I've ever had.

"Mal, the limo is waiting. Shall we?" I gesture to the door. Please be ready to go, I can't keep my mouth shut much longer.

"Oh, wouldn't you like a tour of the home before you leave, Mr. Gibbes?" The old bat questions. "It's original 19th century," she adds, like I should be impressed with this gaudy nightmare factory.

"How… quaint," I smile, knowing exactly how to play this game. Aria tries to silence a snort behind me. "Please, enjoy the flowers and again, lovely to meet you, Mrs. Mitchell."

I put my hand on the small of Mallory's back to escort her out the door and World's Worst Mom, Lydia, turns and shuffles out of the foyer in a tissy. Aria chases behind us onto the front step outside.

"Holy shit, that was amazing! 'Quaint'!" Aria is nearly jumping up and down in excitement.

"Thank you so much for everything," Mallory hugs her.

"Aria," I take her hand and kiss the back of her fingers, "pleasure." I deliberately smolder at her, in good fun.

I help Mallory into the limo as the driver closes our door and rounds the car.

"I am so sorry!" She puts her hand on my knee apologizing for her snooty mum's abhorrent behavior. And people call *me* an asshole.

"Were you adopted or something, love?"

"No," she laughs.

"You could not be more different from that woman."

Mallory leans in and kisses my cheek softly, "That's the best compliment you could have given me."

The privacy window between the driver is down and I need to get through this event before defiling Mallory anyway, so I settle for slipping my hand on her bare thigh for the ride, as she warns me that her father, Robert, will be at this gala tonight and I can expect more of the same from him. I pour two fingers of whatever swill whiskey is in the decanter in the back of the limo and suck it down in preparation.

This gala is everything I hate.

Phony people telling fake stories, putting on aires trying to impress people they don't even know, everyone looking down their nose at everyone else. This is supposed to be about charity, children's cancer research, but no one is here to help kids.

The suits from UG Petroleum are, surprisingly, the most tolerable folks I've met tonight. I wouldn't dream of embarrassing Mallory in front of her patronizing, condescending parents so I am on my best behavior. In fact, the more nasty glares and snide comments they whisper to her as the evening goes on, the more hellbent I am on being a model guest, someone she can be proud to be here with.

Plus, it's fun fucking with Lydia and Robert.

Mallory's been hitting the champagne pretty hard, but I can't blame her. Her father, a rotund and angry little man, spots us and Mallory slams the rest of her champs as he barrels toward us. "Oh no," she mumbles beneath the rim of her glass. I take her hand in mine in solidarity against miserable pricks everywhere.

"Mr. Gibbes, we have not been formally introduced yet," he shakes my hand and squeezes hard.

I squeeze his harder.

"Dad, Lennox. Lennox, Dad," Mallory waves back and forth between us with her empty champagne flute, her patience clearly long gone. For once, I may be the more civilized person, between the two of us.

"Mr. Mitchell, pleasure. Mallory tells me you are in print media. Newspaper man?"

"Yes, yes," he puffs his chest out. "Traditional media, old fashioned, respectable newspapers, magazines, radio. You get it." He leers at Mallory, his passive-aggressive dig at her career.

I get it, all right. "Of course, how wonderful that you're preserving those antediluvian arts."

"Anti-what?" His face crinkles and Mallory squeezes my hand.

"Indulge a young man, Mr. Mitchell, years ago my advisor switched my print holdings to digital. They've been doing quite well but, tell me, where do you see stocks going as subscription rates continue to plummet?"

"Plummet?" He bellows. "You don't know what you're talking about!"

"Forgive me, sir. I must be mistaken. I just drive a car around in circles."

Mallory grabs another champagne off the tray of a passing server while I keep a deliberately innocent, stupid look on my face, staring at the pompous blowhard in front of me.

"Listen here boy, I don't know what kind of stunt you're pulling with my daughter..."

I do my best to ignore the fact that this asshat just called me 'boy' and interrupt him, "Yes, your daughter. You must be so proud of her. What a job you and Mrs. Mitchell have done as parents to raise such a strong, smart woman with the courage to follow her dreams. Cheers to you, sir." I tip my glass at him.

Mallory wraps one arm around my waist under my tuxedo jacket and Father Time's eyes go wide before he shakes his head at her in disgust and turns to storm off.

"You were raised by wolves," I whisper to Mallory and take another sip of the top shelf scotch that's available, thank god.

"Wolves would have been an improvement. Have I told you how handsome you look tonight?"

"Aye, but you can tell me again."

"Did you really have print holdings?" She asks.

"I dunno, probably."

Mallory laughs and the sight of her smiling despite everything Lydia and Robert have thrown at her tonight is everything. She's impressive. And goddamn gorgeous.

"Dance with me?" She whispers in my ear.

Even in the States where F1 is not as popular, there have been people photographing us together all night, all the couples, but Celeritas instructed Mallory to accompany me so, fuck it. I deposit our drink glasses on an empty table and lead Mallory to an open spot on the dance floor. The instrumental band is playing a slow, bluesy tune, Etta James, maybe.

Mallory wraps her arms around my neck and I pull her against me, just this side of keeping it decent in public. She's stumbling a little but I have a firm hand on her hips, arguing with my fingers not to dip lower and grab her ass no matter how much they want to.

"Say something else to me in Gaelic," she looks up at me, a mischievous grin emerging.

"I am not a piece of meat, Mallory," I twirl her and pull her back against my chest.

"It gets me so hot."

We're gonna need to wrap this event up if she's going to start this.

My tuxedo is not equipped to hide an erection very well and I wouldn't want to scare any of these old bitties looking down their nose at me all night.

"How about French, all women like French?"

"No one's ever spoken to me in French," she purrs.

"Je vais te baiser si fort que tu ne pourras pas marcher pendant une semaine." She waits for me to translate for her, her fingers stroking my neck. "I'm a little rusty, but essentially, I'm going to fuck you so hard you won't be able to walk for a week."

"So romantic," she laughs. "More."

"Uhh, how about German? Du wirst heute nacht auf meine zunge kommen." I bend my head down and whisper in her ear, "You're going to come on my tongue tonight."

"You speak French and German *and* look like this? How is that fair to other men?"

"A little Finnish, too, but that sounds like shit no matter what words you say."

"Mallory Mitchell?" A man in a tux interrupts us just as I'm about to whisper more filth into her ear. "Max Cooper, from Cooper Media."

"Oh, Mr. Cooper! How nice to see you!" Mallory separates from me and the loss of her body contact makes me want to send this Mr. Cooper through the wall.

"Lennox, this is Maxwell Copper, CEO and Founder of Cooper Media. He offered me a job when I was a junior in college but it didn't work out."

"Nice to meet you," I shake his hand. "Guess I should be happy it didn't work out or I wouldn't have her in my corner now." I nod at Mallory, happy to keep heaping praise her way to minimize the emotional fallout from tonight I know she must be internalizing.

"Yes, actually that's why I had to stop and see you. Lennox, we're huge fans and Mallory, my buddies at UG have been raving about you all night. I have to say, we'd love to be involved."

"What do you mean?" Mallory asks.

"We'd like to do an exclusive. Infinity Magazine would be perfect, global digital coverage and print in the US, plus sixteen countries in Europe, and eleven in the Asian markets." Cooper's eyes are big, darting between Mallory and I. He's practically salivating.

"An exclusive?" I ask.

"Yes, your life, your career, the wins, the losses, who you really are. Your story, as you want it told, no bullshit. Mallory, you'd have total control."

"Oh, wow. That means so much that you would offer that, Mr. Cooper. Really, I am honored. But Mr. Gibbes doesn't do personal stories." Mallory smiles but I see the twinkle in her eyes dim a little.

"Damn, that's too bad. I think you have a story to tell, Lennox."

"Everyone has a story, Mr. Cooper," I reply.

"Yeah, you're right about that. Here's my card, if you ever change your mind, please." He hands a card to Mallory and one to me.

Mallory thanks him and I follow her as she picks up another champagne from the open bar and I order another scotch. "What was that about?" I ask her as she downs half her glass in one go.

"That," she comes up for air, "is daddy's worst nightmare, his nemesis, arch-rival. He's Robert Mitchell's Digby DuPont," she giggles. "My dad threatened to stop paying my college tuition if I went to work at Cooper."

"That's messed up," I shake my head and watch Mallory reach for another glass of champagne. "You know, we've done our work here tonight, I think it's probably safe to leave anytime you want now." I've lost count of how many glasses she's had but she's power drinking now and can't be having a good time.

"Ooo, auction time!" She hiccups as the lights flicker alerting the room to focus their attention as another identical man in a tuxedo takes the stage. "Let's go watch horrible people complete to leave as little money as possible to cancer research while still getting credit and one-upping each other!"

Mallory drags me near the stage right next to Lydia and Robert who immediately purse their lips and tsk when Mallory wraps an arm around me and cuddles into my side.

"Mallory, you're drunk!" Her father sticks his fat head into our space and seethes at her. "You look like a tramp!"

"Hey," I shake my head at him and warn him as clear as possible, without causing a scene, that I'm not above causing a scene. Mallory flips him the bird and Lydia gasps.

What kind of father calls his daughter a tramp? This is insanity. I have no idea how Mallory escaped her childhood and became a reasonably functioning adult.

Bidding starts, donation for some specialized medical equipment in a new treatment wing of the local children's hospital. A few people call out their cheap-ass bids, $1,000 here, $2,000 there.

"$10,000!" Robert yells and smirks at me, the crowd claps.

"I hate him," Mallory mumbles into my side, slurring her words.

Something primitive boils over inside of me watching Robert's dumb fucking face glare at his daughter like she's a piece of trash and I'm the scum leading her into ruin.

"One hundred thousand," I yell. The crowd roars. Mallory's eyes go wide and Robert and Lydia gasp and huff, as if it's offensive that a charity make more money.

"One ten!" Robert bellows, putting his hand on hips wide hips, completely convinced that he's just shown me who's boss.

"Two fifty," I shout.

"How dare you!" Robert seethes before Lydia can smack him in the gut because the whole room just heard him chastise someone for donating money to kids with cancer.

"I can do this all night, old man. How deep are those print media pockets these days?" I bait the two most awful people in this room. I probably shouldn't have sunk to his level, using money to make a point, but it's for two good causes: kids and the girl clinging to me who he's humiliated for the last goddamn time.

Mallory snorts as Robert and Lydia's mouths drop open and the room snickers and whispers behind us. Lydia looks around, horrified, then scurries out of the crowd like the shameful excuse for a human she is.

"Sold!" The auctioneer announces over the microphone. "Two hundred and fifty thousand dollars of state of the art medical equipment to treat children afflicted with cancer here in New York City! Your name, good sir?"

"Mallory Mitchell and Lennox Gibbes," I reply.

The other attendees clap, a few random strangers pat me on the back, which I actually do not appreciate, but then the auction moves onto the next item. "Take me home, Mr. Gibbes," Mallory wraps her hands around my neck and presses her tits into my chest.

"I thought you'd never ask, hot nanny."

I lead us out of the crowd of people at the stage and toward the exit when Robert rears his ugly head again. This guy's like a bad case of herpes, there's no getting rid of him. "You've gone too far this time, Mallory! Too far! You are dead to me! Dead!"

"Dad?" Mallory turns to him and slurs slowly. "Gooooo. Fuck yourself."

I can't help but crack up laughing, Mallory swaying like a drunk person and telling her old man off in the middle of this black tie affair filled with New York's elite. A hundred people must have heard her.

Robert storms off and Mallory calls to me, way too loudly for present company, "Lennox, take me home and do those filthy things to me you said in German!"

"Now who needs a nanny?" I laugh and wrap my arm around her to support her as I walk, and she stumbles, out the door as our limo is pulled around.

"Four Seasons, Central Park," I tell the driver and then push the button to close the divider window.

Before the window is even fully closed, Mallory's straddled my lap in the back of the limo and my hands are finally inside the slit in her dress running up her warm thighs and over her smooth ass. "Where are your panties, Mallory?" I growl as she attacks my neck.

"Must have forgotten them," she says in between breaths before she grabs my face and smashes her lips against mine. She tastes like sweet champagne and I need to know what the rest of her tastes like.

With a hand underneath her, I flip her over and lay her down on the back seat. She whimpers and pushes her hips up to mine as I start my descent down from her neck, over the soft swells of her breasts, over her hard nipples. I'm almost to her belly button, kissing and licking through her dress when her hand in my hair goes limp.

I look up and her eyes are closed, her head turned to the side. Out cold.

This can't be happening, this is a new low in my life. I don't think I've ever been rejected. Certainly, no woman has ever fallen the hell asleep on me before. This nanny is going to be the bloody death of me.

Fifteen

"Oh, it's quite clear you're no romantic. Take my hand and we can run, into every setting sun. I'm getting closer, closer, closer to me." - Sea Girls - Closer

Mallory

I'm floating on light, fluffy clouds. Warmth radiates around me. I stretch my toes and crisp, luxurious cotton slides against my calves. A thick down pillow cradles my head as I keep my eyes closed and wiggle blissfully back into the… hard morning wood pressed into my ass?

My eyes shoot open and that's when the throbbing at the front of my brain starts. Curtains are cracked on the panoramic floor to ceiling windows in front of me, hints of the New York skyline beyond coming into view as my eyes struggle to focus. Wrapped around my chest, a strong forearm I've come to recognize. The heat emanating into my back and soothing my muscles, the scent drifting to my senses, my sort-of boss. The man I was paid to supervise last night.

Except, oh god. I was the one needing supervision. The memories of my father slut-shaming me, my mother's face fighting the Botox to grimace in my direction all evening, her club friends sneering, it all comes back as the pounding in my head picks up.

On the nightstand is a bottle of Powerade and a travel packet of Advil. I would smile at the thoughtfulness of the gesture if moving my facial muscles didn't incite the marching band in my temples. I reach for the bottle and rip open the packet of pain meds, scooting out from under Lennox's heavy arm just a bit so I can drink. The sheet pulls down and my naked breasts are exposed, a warm beam of sunlight hitting them and dusting the room.

I sneak a hand behind me and run my fingers over a sleeping Lennox, up his muscular thigh, and I shutter my eyes in relief when I feel the cotton of his boxer briefs. "Keep going, a little higher," his deep, gravelly morning voice murmurs into the back of my head and he moans as he pulls me by my waist back into his impressive length. Everything about this man is rock hard, every sculpted inch.

Except, what he did last night. There was a softness inside of him.

"Did we..." I start, afraid of the answer. If I don't remember the first time I had sex with this glorious specimen of a man, I am going to regret it more than any of the scenes I caused last night.

"You'd remember if I fucked you, love." So smooth and confident, a touch arrogant, but given the girth of what I feel in my backside right now, maybe it's well earned.

He releases his hold around my body and rolls onto his back, stretching and taking up half of the king-sized bed. I pull the sheet up around my chest and sit up against the multitude of down pillows lining the headboard. The suite is exquisite. Rich fawn walls, cream and leather sofas, and purple orchids on mahogany end tables bring pops of color to the luxurious space.

I suck down the Powerade, the artificial cherry flavor replenishing much needed electrolytes and quenching my cottonmouth. I need to do damage control, figure out how bad the fallout is from my behavior last night. I remember leaving with Lennox, but I have no recollection of how I got into this hotel, naked, and in bed. Over the back of a chair in the attached seating area, I see my mother's gown, $5,000 worth of Givenchy, and I peer my head at it because it looks ripped down the entire length.

"What happened to my dress?"

"You were stuck and demanded I get it off you '*right fucking now.*' I obliged." Lennox says, smirking and running a hand over his bare chest. I have a million and one things I should be doing right now, but I can't take my eyes off his abs and the trail of dark hair below his belly button.

"And then I just, fell asleep?" I'm so embarrassed.

"No, then you tried attacking me like a rabid bear. Then I put you to sleep."

"Thank you," I sigh.

"Again, asshole, not monster, Mallory."

"You weren't an asshole last night," I poke his leg under the covers with my toe. "You didn't have to do that, you know, the auction."

"Aye, I know."

I want to cuddle up against him and lay my head on his broad chest, wrap my hand around his narrow waist, but I don't know if snuggling is on the table. We have yet to discuss this arrangement and cuddling might be squarely in the girlfriend zone. We're in the murky inappropriate workplace shagging zone, I think.

"The Maxwell Cooper thing," he says, scratching his head and twisting his face up oddly.

Oh god, I'd forgotten. Max put us both on the spot and personal stories are already a touchy subject for Lennox. "Sorry about that. You've made your stance on the matter clear. No worries."

I change the subject and wonder what else I've forgotten or blacked out. "I need to check my phone. Was it as bad as I remember?" I look all around but don't see my phone anywhere. I have no clothes nearby to throw on so I try pulling the sheet off the bed to wrap around and take with me.

"I turned your phone off and don't bother with the sheet," he yanks it back from me, "already seen it all. Quite lovely, if I may add."

"Lennox," I yank the sheet back, "I have no clothes here! Give me your shirt or something, you brute!"

He groans and gets out of bed, giving me a perfect view of his tight ass in his boxer briefs and, on his return trip with his dress shirt from last night, an eyeful of bulge. He runs his tongue over his bottom lip when he sees me staring at him, and watches me slip his dress shirt on in bed. "Stop looking at me like that, I need to shower," I tell him, rolling up the sleeves.

"I'm just going to dirty you up again," he argues, and my chest tightens. I'm kind of glad he said it so I know where we stand after last night.

"Awfully arrogant, Mr. Gibbes," I inch toward the bathroom and then take off in a mad dash as he tries to grab me across the bed.

"Payback, Mallory. Payback!"

My reflection in the bathroom mirror is enough to frighten the dead. I have raccoon eyes, my hair looks like a woodland creature made a nest in it. "Where is my phone?" I call through the bathroom door as I start scraping last night's makeup off my face with a washcloth. I'm picturing all the nasty messages from my family that await me, but I'm more worried about any harm I may have created for Lennox.

"You won't be needing it today," he calls back.

I mumble to myself thoughts of strangling him while I loot the Four Seasons vanity kit and brush my teeth. If photos of me drunk and hanging all over Lennox come out, Sandra is going to can my ass. I most certainly *do* need my phone today.

I pop out of the bathroom to demand he grow up and return my phone but he's no longer in bed. He's standing a few feet away, arms crossed over his chest, sporting a raging hard-on, and he's looking at me like a lion about to take down a gazelle.

"Lennox," I cock my head at him, "give me my phone."

He raises one finger and motions for me to come hither.

"Lennox," I warn and take a step backward, calculating how far I need to make it back into the bathroom, if I can beat him. I take half a step and then make a break for it. I don't even get two steps before his arms loop around me, I'm flipped around, and tossed over his shoulder.

"Oh my god, you absolute caveman," I scream and wiggle.

"Scream all ya' want, love, just gets me harder." He slaps my ass so hard I let out another shriek.

I'm carried through the suite's living room and he throws me on the bed, sending me flying with a bounce on the firm mattress. I've never seen his eyes so vivid green, so intense. I am the prey and he is the predator, except I want to be eaten, I want him to tear at my flesh and open my soul open. He stands, gaze never leaving mine as I prop myself up on my elbows and he makes his way to a small overnight bag nearby, fishes out a new box of condoms and tosses them on the bed.

"A whole box, oh my," I watch him and start seductively unbuttoning his shirt that I'm wearing. Lennox is at the foot of the bed watching, chest heaving, nostrils flaring. He approaches and takes my foot, pulling me to the end of the bed in a swift tug. His lips press to the arch of my foot, my ankle, up my calf, and he licks a sweet trail behind my knee before dropping my leg back to the bed. He does the same to my second leg and my breathing is already picking up, my pulse racing.

My second leg falls to the sheets and he kneels onto the bed between me, fists my half-open shirt, and rips it the rest of the way, buttons ruined and popping off. He's so toned and muscular I can see every tiny movement he makes reflected in each sinew and tendon flexing. His sculpted abs are tight and the outline of his hardness is pushing up to the low waistband of his briefs.

He inches forward and shoves the tattered shirt off my shoulders leaving me completely bare before him. I've always been the one in control, the aggressor between the sheets, but right now I find myself completely at his mercy. I want to give myself over to him, for him to take what he wants from me. And it's making me so wet for him.

Holy fuck this is hot. How is he so sexy?

Lennox growls at the sight of me so exposed and vulnerable and spreads my legs in his strong arms, holding my knees open and silently taking in the sight before him. He bends and begins licking his way up from my knee, along my inner thigh and traces his lips along the outside of my freshly waxed folds. He barely makes contact with a feather-soft kiss on my mound and I gasp and push myself toward him. But he retreats and works his way down again, trailing his tongue up my other thigh before landing back at my center when he licks me with a touch so light it's barely a breath.

"Lennox" I hiss and push at him again, so desperate for pressure or friction.

My fingers running through his thick hair, I clutch a handful and try to pull him to me. I need his mouth on me, I need his tongue dancing with mine. I need the taste that is so uniquely Lennox. I fall back onto the pillows when he allows himself to be pulled up and he covers me with his body weight, hands and mouth on my breasts. He's sucking to leave marks and god, I want him to. I want his claim branded on me. He circles my nipple with his tongue, then caresses the peak and bites before he takes it between his lips again and smothers it in the heat of his mouth.

Kneading my other breast, he brings his legs up to kneel over me, grips my jaw and finally his tongue meets mine. A faint whisper of last night's scotch melds into my palate. I gasp for air between the assault of our mouths and feel so powerless beneath him, merciless to this dominance and it's the most liberating feeling I've ever known. I want to let go, forget, give in to him completely. His thick cock is pushing into me and I reach for his waist to push his briefs down but he captures my hands and pins them beside my neck.

"Hands above your head," he commands and for the first time, I don't argue. I obey, watching him in a trance and gripping the pillow beneath my head.

Take me, I won't fight.

Sliding down my body, his tongue leaves a trail of heat across my collarbone, the valley of my breasts, the sensitive skin of my midsection. My lungs are on fire and I'm trembling with need, the games we've been playing for weeks are long gone. I'm ready to beg if need be. He can win, he can have me.

"Fucking beautiful" Lennox groans, taking in the full naked length of me before him. "Spread your legs." His voice is so low and gruff, his accent even thicker than normal.

I separate my legs, but he clasps my knees and spreads them further himself before easing himself down with his shoulders between my thighs. He runs his tongue along the outside of my pussy and then makes a long swipe of his tongue from my clit to my opening and I cry out for him. I push up to make more contact but he spreads a hand across my belly and holds me down. His mouth covers my pussy and he's lapping and winding his tongue across every millimeter, through every ridge and valley.

"Oh my god, Lennox..."

"Wider," he tells me, sucking my clit, and I try to open my legs more but they're shaking and trembling and I am not in control of myself. "Fucking wider" he grunts and pins my knees to my side and darts his tongue all the way inside me like a dagger.

Writhing and bucking, I clutch his head, running my fingers into his hair and taking hold for dear life.

"Hands above your head or I'll stop" he lifts an inch and I can feel his warm breath on my core, sending shivers across my abdomen.

I put my hands back up because I will die if he stops. The world will stop spinning and the trapped energy inside me will implode. "Lennox, please."

"Please what?"

"Please don't stop!"

"Payback, Mallory." There's no humor or teasing in his inflection and I'm praying he isn't really going to deny me. When I manage to lift my hips high enough to reach his lips he takes mercy and he pulls my clit into his mouth.

A rough finger slides into me and the sensation of his warm skin gliding in and out, curving upward and massaging me, ignites a fever across my skin starting in the soles of my feet and racing upward. He adds a second finger and I'm so close. My thighs are tense and shaking, I can feel them trembling against his shoulders.

"Yes, yes, oh fuck, yes," I pant.

His fingers stall, dragging so slow I can feel every bit of friction. His tongue flattens against me, deliberately languid and torturous when I was so close. "Goddamnit, Lennox," I whine and try to buck against him but it's no use against his shoulders. I can feel his lips smile against my center.

"More?" He asks sarcastically, licking up the moisture seeping out of me with leisure.

"More," I watch him between my legs and reach a hand for his face. As soon as it leaves the pillow, though, he raises an eyebrow at me and stops his tongue. Oh, this absolute bastard is tormenting me. I don't know how else to surrender to him but there is nothing I will not do, no amount of stubborn fight in me I'm unwilling to submit to him right here and right now.

"Mmm," he licks the length of me, "maybe slow and soft for an hour or two would be the appropriate payback."

I don't dare challenge him because he'll do it. He lives for that shit. "Please, you win. You win everything. Fuck me fast and hard, Lennox."

He growls against me, the vibration of his voice could get me off at this point I'm so desperate. The tip of his tongue circles my clit a few times, never letting me come all the way down. "And what do I win?"

I'm gripping the pillows so hard my knuckles are white and my legs are writhing and wiggling of their own accord. "Anything. Me."

Whatever you want, please just name it and take me.

"How about this perfect smooth pussy?"

God, he's so filthy and it makes me want him even more. "Yes, it's yours."

I've spoken the magic words, Lennox increases the pressure and speed of his tongue and fingers. His tongue is feasting on me, I can't guess how many fingers are stretching me and working my insides to perfection. I'm past the point of no return, cresting on the impending wave. "Come on my tongue, Mallory."

I'm clutching the pillows, my eyes clenched shut and watering as the surge peaks, crashes, and sends me deep below the surface, riptides of pleasure overtaking my body and I scream like I have never screamed before. Lennox keeps licking me, lapping up every bead of my wetness until my screams stop.

I am trembling and panting and insatiable. I need him inside me like I need the air I breathe. Lennox rises to his knees between my legs and I reach for his briefs, this time he lets me. I bend forward at the waist and reach inside to pull his cock free. It's massive and hard and yet so silky and smooth in my hands. The heat coming off is electric.

He stands and pushes down his boxer briefs and I rip open the box of condoms he threw onto the bed earlier. I tear one open with my teeth so eager to feel him deep inside me. Standing at the foot of the bed, Lennox takes his cock in his right hand and starts working it up and down, watching me watch him. Beads of precum glisten on the tip begging for me to taste him, swirl my tongue around the head and take him deep into my throat.

I push myself up on the bed to crawl to him but he shakes his head at me. More wetness seeps from me as he starts tugging on that gorgeous shaft, his bicep and forearm contracting with every pull. Lying back, never looking away from him, I travel my hand down my abdomen and slip two fingers between my lips. Sucking in a deep breath, his eyes dart between mine and my fingers swirling around my clit. Spreading my lips and lifting my hips, I offer him every inch of me.

In an instant he's on top of me hovering his weight on his elbows, prisoning me between his two huge biceps next to my head. I wiggle to reach between us and slide the condom over him and he pushes his rigid length over my core again, running it back and forth over my slick clit. I'm so sensitive my body jerks up to meet him and I grip his back.

He takes my mouth, his tongue strong and probing, the taste of my desire coating him. He's grinding his thick erection against me and I could come again from this exquisite friction but I need him, I need all of him. He lines up the head of his cock at my entrance and I can feel the pressure, the hint of what's to come as he holds steady there, taunting me, hips still. My hands wrap around his biceps beside my head and he stares down at me with complete control.

"What do you want?" He grumbles low.

"You, I want you."

"More."

"Lennox, I want you inside me. Please, I want to feel your hard cock inside me." I beg and clutch him, nails digging into his rock hard biceps.

"More." He commands, his timbre stern and rough.

"I need you. I need all of you. I want to belong to you. I want you to own me, every part of me." I don't know where these words are unleashed from, what part of my subconscious this man has unlocked. I have fought my whole life against being constrained, but this is so different.

He thrusts into me in one swift drive. "FUCK," he roars so loud I can feel the treble of his voice in my bones, "so fucking... tight."

He raises his face to look me in the eyes, still until I can adjust to the size of him stretching my walls. I'm so full but I need him to move, I need more. Lifting my ass up, I try to get every last inch of him deep inside me. He groans and pulls out to spread my moisture over his full length, then drives back into me, hard.

Arching my back and gripping his firm ass, I pull him into me at each thrust, encouraging him to give me everything he has. Curling my free hand around his shoulder, I raise my head to bite his neck, nip his shoulder. I turn my head and bite the rippling bicep next to my head. The taste of his sweating skin is salty against my tongue, and his smell surrounds me, rugged and masculine.

He moans every time my teeth mark him, his pleasure pushing me closer and closer to coming again. He's relentlessly driving into me and my legs start to shake again, my torso tensing in anticipation. He grabs one of my legs behind my knee and pins it to my shoulder, holding it there as he presses deeper into me. The ridge of his cock's head is dragging in and out of me and I can feel every slick movement. I'm so close.

"Look at me," he orders.

I strain my neck to stop thrashing my head back and forth and hold his stare, emerald green seas, depth and passion, fire and embers so hot they glow unnatural colors. It's too much, seeing the blaze inside him and feeling him so deep inside me pressing into my womb.

"Come for me, Mal."

"Lennox" I pant and clench down on him, tightening up.

"Give it," he drives into me, "up."

My pussy starts to spasm and pull him in deeper, "Lennox, oh god."

"Give it the fuck up to me," he demands and with one more ruthless thrust, I'm coming all over him, digging my nails into his back and screaming, crying, shrieking words of pleasure, words of nonsense, words of ecstasy.

He loses control and drives into me like a man possessed until I feel his whole body go rigid above me, every muscle locking up, and his warmth pulses inside of me before he finally collapses on top of me.

I have never been so thoroughly fucked.

Once our breathing settles, he rolls off and drags me into his side, my head on his chest and one leg wrapped over his thigh. I guess cuddling is ok, at least post-orgasm cuddling, the best kind.

"Fuckin' hell," he sighs.

"Aye, fuckin' hell," I tease back, in my best Scottish accent.

Sixteen

Headline: Formula 1 Star Wins Hearts at Charity Gala, Donates Quarter Million to NYC Children's Hospital
Blog: Paddock Playboy Captures New Co-Pilot
Insta: Gibbes and the Girl in Givenchy
PastriesWithPasties: him in a tuxedo, omg, be still my beating heart
46BlackFlags: who's the chick?
BuddyTheElf: I'd do her
CrateNBurro: His new PR person? She's at press with him at races.
DigbyDevotee: She's no Kate Allendale.
GrooveIsInTheHeart: Oh please, at least this one isn't a twig!
RumbleStrip1985: I've stared at this photo for an hour, jaw still not closed.

Lennox

"It's actually not as bad as I was expecting," Mallory says in disbelief, 30,000 feet over the Atlantic. She's been face first in her laptop since the moment the crew turned on the wifi. She wasn't scheduled to fly home with me, she was going to stay in New York for one more night, but she said she'd rather join me on the jet than fly economy.

Fine by me. Mine.

She found her phone I'd hidden yesterday and recoiled in horror when it lit up like a Christmas tree, pings and bings screaming from it. I assume most of it was from her parents given the colorful four-letter words she mumbled back as she scrolled and swiped.

It wasn't hard to distract her, though.

We stayed in the room all day until checking out this evening. I ordered room service, she let me steal one of her pancakes, and I fucked her six ways from Sunday all over the Presidential Suite. She was convinced the glass would shatter when I took her up against the window overlooking Central Park. Given the octave of her screaming my name, I think it was a real possibility.

I shouldn't feel a sense of pride watching her squirm on the white leather couch on the plane as she finds a comfortable way to sit, but I'm full of male ego this evening. The rest of my season is looking up. If I have to put up with the Celeritas bullshit, at least my nights will be satisfying.

"Your parents give it up?" I ask from my recliner seat across from her.

"Oh no, definitely not. But the news, the blogs, everything on social is surprisingly... good?" She keeps twirling her fingers and clicking on the trackpad on a hunt for the disaster she's expecting.

I guess that's a relief, for her. I'm used to handling the hateful comments and trolls. Most days, it rolls off my back. I don't want her dragged under with me, though. Trying to keep Mum, Pop, and Bram out of it is enough work.

"I guess you've done your job, then."

"I think you're right. Despite your best attempts, Mr. Gibbes, the tide is turning on your bad boy image. People really liked all the photos of you signing their fan mail. UG Petroleum is happy with you and we have a new potential sponsor to wine and dine in China."

"I'd rather dine on you." We've got five hours or so left before we land in London, refuel, pick up Matty and Jack, then head to China. Five hours that could be put to much better use than lining the Celeritas coffers with more money.

"Bluewater Tech, a new computer processor company, I believe," she ignores me.

The sliding wood door to the flight crew cabin opens and the attendant asks if we'll be needing anything.

"Just privacy, please," I smile at her.

"Of course, I'll dim the cabin lights for the evening, sir," and she sets out to show Mallory where the minibar and snacks are before pulling out pillows and blankets for the evening and disappears into the forward cabin. Moments later the lights drop and there's only a glow from safety lights and Mallory's laptop.

She takes a deep breath, puts her closed laptop on the worktable in front of my recliner, and squints at me, "Ok, let's get it over with."

Get it over with? That's not exactly a ringing endorsement for my sexual prowess. "There were no complaints earlier," I scoff at her. "I recall a whole lot of begging, in fact."

Her eyes press shut but she has nothing to be embarrassed about. It was hot as hell. Having this strong, stubborn fighter come apart for me, give herself over to me, I feel like I'm on the top step of the podium again. And it's been a long time since I've been there.

"No, I meant we need to discuss logistics. Let's get that over with."

"Ugh," I groan and lean my head back into my recliner. Hot or not, she still harbors a bit of an inner harpy dying to be let out and talk about feelings.

"I want this Lennox, but it can't interfere with my job."

"Ok." I appreciate that she came right out with what she wants instead of making me chase her and guess what's in her head. I want this to continue, too. Problem solved.

"I mean it, this job is important to me. No one can know."

"Why?" I scowl. Who the hell cares? I haven't talked to Jack or Matty but I'm sure they both already know. They aren't idiots and I'm not lying to them.

"It'll be career suicide if anyone finds out I'm sleeping with my clients, Lennox! I want to open my own firm and I need this job. I need the contacts, the experience on my resume. I already have one strike against me." She's talking a mile a minute and I can hear it in her voice how important this is to her. After meeting her abominable parents, I get it.

"What strike? The two ghouls who raised you?"

"No, the last athlete I worked with," she grimaces and my jaw ticks. I don't want to hear about her sleeping with some other dude, some Brazilian soccer player or Australian rugby pro. I need to stop thinking about it.

"The guy you got rid of?"

"No. I told you I've never done this before," she waves between us. I'm more relieved than I have a right to be.

She pauses a minute, fidgeting with the hem of my tee-shirt she's wearing. She does that a lot when she's nervous. The hotel concierge was able to deliver jeans and other necessities for her earlier, but she kept my shirt on. Said it was 'comfy,' as if I've never had chicks steal my shirts before and don't know what that's about. She still has my team jacket from Bahrain, too, now that I think about it.

"So, there was this NBA player," she starts, staring down at the cream carpet of the jet.

"Jesus, do I want to hear this?" I groan.

She tells me the story about this guy, some clown who racked up a DUI and was fighting on the court. Super talented but throwing it all away. She got called in when he was picked up on drug charges. Worked with him for about six months but it kept getting worse.

"We were on our way to an event but he said we had to make a stop first," she continues. "Turns out, the stop was a white supremacy rally."

"What."

"Oh, but it gets worse. Unbeknownst to me, he bought a bunch of coke while we were there. We were filmed leaving this awful, racist rally and then we got pulled over by the cops. He was driving like a crazy person and blew a stop sign."

Now I'm not just shocked, but pissed. This piece of shit was high on cocaine and driving with Mallory in the car?

"The police found the drugs in the car and, in the press, he claimed they were mine, that I had dragged him to the white supremacy group, that it was all my idea."

"Were you arrested?"

"Charges were never pressed against me, it was obvious to the police I had nothing to do with the drugs," she shakes her head.

"What happened with this prick?"

"Oh, he got released from his contract immediately. Last I heard he blew through all his money and was living with friends," she shrugs. "And I was fired."

"But you had nothing to do with it."

"Image is everything, Lennox. I didn't do my job. No one wanted to work with me after that."

"That's bullshit," I seethe. "That's why you came to London," it dawns on me and she nods her head.

I sink into my recliner and run my hands over my eyes. This complicates things, something that was not supposed to be complicated. I don't want to screw her life up more by being my normal dickish self around the track if it can ruin her life like this. But I also need to do what I need to do.

"Sooooo," she continues and I spin my chair back in her direction. "That's why you can't scare me off. You're a marshmallow, comparatively."

"A *marshmallow*..."

"Mmm-hmm, burnt and crusty on the outside but soft and squishy inside," she pinches her fingers together at me like she's kneading dough.

"I'll show you soft and squishy," I threaten her and move to the couch with her. Pulling her onto me to straddle my lap, I run my hands up the back of her shirt, my shirt, against her bare skin.

"You look good in my shirt," I bite her bottom lip and pull it into my mouth.

"You look good out of your shirt, seems we make a good team," she giggles.

Miles pass, huge distances pass beneath us over the ocean while we make out like teenagers. Gripping her ass and dragging her against my dick, which knows no moderation, she winces. "Sore?" I ask against her neck.

She nods, her arms wrapped around me. "That's not exactly a small python in your pants."

Can never hear that enough. "Go on," I tease her and unbutton her jeans.

She grabs my hands and swivels her torso toward the cabin door, "The flight attendant could come back!"

"Trust me, love, she's not coming back here. This is what happens on private jets."

Her plump lips jut out in a pout and she squints her eyes at me. "I don't want to think about you with other women."

"I don't want to think about you with other men," I retort. "If you haven't noticed, playing well with others is not one of my strong suits."

"So, what are you saying?" She runs her fingers over my day-old stubble, wistful thoughts passing over her.

"I don't share, Mallory."

"Well, I don't share, either," she sasses me. Except now I enjoy her sassy mouth and where the quibbling leads.

"Great, problem solved. You done arguing now or you need more foreplay?" I wrap my palms around her ass cheeks and squeeze her softness.

"Seven months left, Lennox, like you said. That's going to be hard for you."

"More foreplay it is," I murmur, rolling my eyes at this familiar myth.

"Can you do it? Be my personal Dick-on-Demand for seven whole months?"

"You're the one who can't keep up," I glance down at her gorgeous pussy, still hidden under the blue denim of her jeans. It's an absolute travesty, one I need to rectify as soon as possible.

She's avoiding the question as much as I am, through the familiar dance of sarcasm. Seven months of banging Mallory across five continents is easy. I don't have an answer for what happens at the end of seven months, though, and there's little point of trying to plan it out. She has plans, I have plans, and they don't line up at the end of this season, as far as I can tell.

"You're an elite athlete, you have an unfair advantage," she gives in a little and bites my earlobe.

"Again, no complaints were had earlier." I bring my hands around to her front and run my thumbs around her nipples. The hotel brought up a lacy red bra in the shopping bag for her, shame it's not likely to survive the next few thousand miles.

"No complaints. Five star review. Would do business again."

"Get these bloody pants off," I pull at the stupid stiff fabric.

Mallory stands in the aisle way and checks the cabin door with a pause as she unbuttons and starts to unzip. "Off," I repeat. No worries, by the time seven months is up she'll be well versed in airplane sex etiquette.

She unzips the jeans and pushes them over her hips, matching little red panties popping into view just before she steps out of the pants. I hope I tipped the concierge enough for going the extra mile with his lingerie selections. Grabbing the hem of my shirt she's wearing, she pulls it up and over her head, tossing it on the recliner's table behind her.

God damn, she's beautiful. Perfect feminine curves, hips to grab on to, those soft, warm tits and an ass I want in my hands at all times.

She cups her mound with one hand, "Be nice to my poor vagina."

I have every intention of being nice, very nice, to that impeccable treasure she's offering me. I stand up and tower over her for a moment, taking it all in and letting her simmer. Taking a seat back in the oversized recliner, I pat the table in front of me. Her eyes go back and forth between me and the table for a split second deducing how she's going to be indoctrinated into the mile high club.

She lifts her hips onto the table and I situate her in front of me like a five-course meal at the finest Michelin Star restaurant. But this is far better. Far more real.

"Lean back," I tell her as I scoot her to the end of the table. She leans backward, pointing her hard nipples toward the sky and putting one hand on the fuselage of the plane for balance.

I wrap my hands under her legs and around her thighs and watch her eyes as I descend upon her, kissing and licking her through the red lace she's already soaked through. I slide the scrap of fabric to the side and let one finger slide up and down her slick channel, watching her ribs rise and lower as her breathing picks up.

And then my mouth is where it belongs, feasting on her pussy, lapping her gently and letting her set the pressure by pushing against me. "Ok?" I ask, not wanting to hurt her.

"Don't stop," she whispers.

Game on.

I curl my tongue deep inside her, dragging out every bit of sweet honey she's giving me before I swirl around her clit. Big circles, little circles, I flick her nub over and over until she's panting and moaning and squirming on the table before me.

"Lennox," she cries.

As hard as it gets me when she screams my name, the flight crew is going to think I'm murdering her if she keeps it up. I stretch one hand up to cover her mouth when her purrs and whimpers become out of control. She sucks my finger into her mouth, swirling around it, holding my wrist so her lips can twirl around and around from my knuckle to the tip.

Her foot goes to my thigh for leverage and she jerks her hips off the table. She runs her teeth down my finger and I pull my hand back before she bites the fucking thing off. She's wild, writhing and bucking her pelvis against me. As fiery as she is when she's fighting with me, she's red-hot combustible when I'm making her come. It's the sexiest thing I've ever seen in my life.

"Oh god, yes, right... right there, don't you dare fucking stop," she pants as her thighs start to quake and her chest arches, her long neck stretched back, chestnut hair cascading down below her. Sensing her impending explosion I throw a hand back over her mouth and she clamps down on my knuckles then spasms and jerks into my face as hard as she can. I slow and run my tongue all around her folds as her hips settle back onto the table and she leans forward running her fingers through my hair.

I give her bare perfection a few more kisses before I lean back into the recliner and revel in the post-orgasm flush that covers her chest, the blissful look of contentment on her face. "Was I nice enough to your poor vagina?"

"Mmmm," she rolls her head to stretch her neck then climbs into my lap on the recliner. "My vagina has never been so happy."

I wrap a hand around her knees, her calves hanging over the side of the chair, "Is that so?" Doesn't matter how much confidence or swagger I act like I have, I want her validation.

She puts her fingers on my chin, "You fuck me like I have always wanted to be fucked."

My eyebrows arch, was not expecting that. I'll take it. "Remember to leave a review, Dick-on-Demand is a new business venture."

"I'll make it a Facebook page," she laughs, burrowing into my chest.

"Jesus, that's all I need." I gather her into my arms and deposit her on the couch, heading into the bathroom to get cleaned up. On my way out I hand her a wet towel and gather up the blankets and pillows. This isn't the long-range jet with sleeping quarters so the couch will have to do.

I lie down against the back and tug her up tight against me, covering us up as best I can and keeping an arm around her to she doesn't fall off if we hit turbulence. My head's resting on a pillow and Mallory's is resting on my curled bicep.

Her breathing slows within minutes. The last time I spent two nights with anyone, I thought I'd be winning my next world championship and I'd eventually be marrying Kate. Glad I escaped the latter, the first I have no idea how to fix. I kiss Mallory's head, tug her in close, and push the thoughts away as I drift off.

Seventeen

Headline: Gibbes Captures Cherished China Pole Position
Headline: Gibbes Outclasses DuPont on Stunning Qualification Lap
Headline: Celeritas Front Row Lockout at Shanghai International Circuit

Mallory

China is kicking my ass.

Between the jet lag, sneaking out of Lennox's hotel room before dawn, and my parents terrorizing me, I am beyond exhausted.

Lydia and Robert aren't speaking to me, which is fine. The manipulative texts from my mother have ended, thank god. Emma could never be bothered with me in any capacity, so she's radio silent. But before the race began today, I had to hear from Cody that my own father met with the company legal department to consider a libel suit against me, saying that my behavior at the gala damaged his reputation.

Cody thinks it's another ruse or Dad's throwing me under the bus because Mitchell Media stock is tanking and Dad needs a scapegoat. He doesn't think Dad has a case but he has in-house legal so he can antagonize me indefinitely at no cost. Even if he doesn't win, my reputation will be dragged through the mud again regardless. I don't know what to do, I don't know how to do it when I'm 7,000 miles away, and I don't know how to keep up with the expanding media and sponsor events Sandra is throwing at me.

At least Lennox is doing well. He was on pole position yesterday during qualifying and took another second place today. Digby ended up in first so Lennox was a bit of a dick for the immediate post-race interviews. But Lennox won the fan's Driver of the Day award and drove an amazing race, so tonight I plan to show him how proud of him I am.

As soon as he gets out of the debriefing they've been stuck in for the last hour, that is.

In the meantime, I'm in the dining hall waiting for him, sucking down as much espresso as I can to keep me awake without causing heart palpitations. I'm Googling 'frivolous libel lawsuit' on my laptop when Jack joins me with a triple espresso plus a giant mug of black Americano.

"I know why I'm tired but what's keeping you up at night?" I point to his caffeine collection.

"The whole paddock knows why you're tired," he says before slugging down the triple shot.

"WHAT," I croak at him. Lennox tiring me out is not what I meant, though he's also technically making me lose sleep. Not just exhausting me with secret orgasms and make-out sessions in nooks and crannies of the track and motorhome when no one is looking, but we've also been talking and actually getting to know one another. Last night I caught myself looking at the old direct messages Kate sent him because I was jealous. I was disgusted with myself and stopped, but I know myself. I know when I'm starting to get a case of the feelings.

Reign it in, girl.

"I'm just teasing you," Jack replies. Thank god. "You might want to keep it down, though. No one on the floor got any sleep last night with your caterwauling." When my jaw drops open he once again tells me he's kidding.

"I'm going to murder all three of you by the end of this season."

"Probably."

I shake my head at him and go back to my laptop. Do I get a lawyer? How exactly does one handle it when a parent sues his child? My phone rings and I expect it to be Cody with more news but it's Sandra. I tell Jack I'll be right back and step outside to take the call. If there's any justice in the world, she's calling with kudos about the Driver of the Day award and new sponsor we met with.

"Ms. Mitchell," she starts. She doesn't sound pleased, but she's the kind of person who is perpetually miserable. "Listen, I'm very pleased with how you are, oh let's say, taming the beast."

I'm getting a little sick of how she talks about Lennox but that's probably my dumb feelings sneaking in again. Also, I sense a *but* coming.

"But... well, our largest backer is getting uncomfortable with so much attention being received by Mr. Gibbes."

"I'm sorry, Ms. Alix. I don't understand." What the hell is she talking about?

"Please treat this as confidential, Ms. Mitchell. The DuPont family is upset regarding a few incidents."

"Digby?" The DuPonts are the largest backers? I assume Sandra means they're mad Lennox ran into him on track, but what am I supposed to do about that? Contrary to my long-running nickname, I am not his nanny.

"Yes, and his family. Chiefly, the problem list includes today's Driver of the Day award, all the fan interaction appearing online and garnering interest, the large donation made at the charity gala..." She may as well run down a list of all the positive work we've done.

"They're upset that Lennox made a donation? To children's cancer research?" I emphasize.

Sandra sighs. "Apparently Mr. and Mrs. DuPont are longtime supporters as well and had to increase the size of their annual donation so as not to be... outshined."

"Umm, ok," I understand enough about people like my parents where it's possible to offend them through competitive social climbing via charitable donation. That was not what Lennox was doing, at all, but I'm certainly not getting into that with Sandra. "And Driver of the Day, that comes from the fans, I can't control that."

"Mallory, personally I think you're doing fine work. It's just that, well, Mr. DuPont is the priority at Celeritas. He is used to receiving the lion's share of attention. The family's toes have been stepped on, that's all."

"Ms. Alix, so I can do my job to the best of my ability, I just want to clarify. Due to financial implications, you want me to decrease the spotlight on Lennox, so as not to offend Digby DuPont." This can't be right, surely I am misunderstanding something.

"Yes, exactly right. Mr. DuPont is a pay driver, that's just how these matters work. Let the men sort that out. You just continue to keep Mr. Gibbes in line, but in the background. Clean but bland, you understand?"

"I understand," I utter, a sick feeling coming over me. I feel gross as she thanks me for my professionalism and hangs up. Clean and bland, Lennox Gibbes is anything but clean and bland. He is shades of gray, real, exciting, tangible, honest. Sometimes he's a jackass, but he is real and that's what his fans have been latching onto, the genuine person he is. Now Celeritas wants me to kill that progress?

I stumble back into the motorhome where Jack is vibrating from caffeine intake. "Jack," I pull up a new browser tab and start pulling up everything I can find on Digby, "tell me everything there is to know about pay drivers."

"Shit," he mumbles.

"Jack," I warn him. "Is he in that meeting getting scolded about being on pole yesterday, ahead of Digby? Is that why he was second again today?"

"I'm not going to speak for him. I will tell you about pay drivers and Douchebag DuPont, though. For your own good."

I nod to accept the compromise as Jack fills me in on the bizarre world of drivers or companies who pay teams exorbitant amounts of money to be allowed to drive. There's a couple on the track each year but Digby is the most notorious, funneling a reported one hundred million per year into Celeritas, three times more than the average pay driver. Most of Celeritas' money comes from sponsor backing but Digby's comes from his family.

"Listen, it's not a secret, pay drivers have been around forever and it's always been controversial. But Dickbag is out of control. He's a totally different level of evil killing the sport." Jack is careful what he tells me, I know he doesn't want to break Lennox's trust, but this is enough to work with.

"I feel sleazy," I admit to him.

"Aye, imagine how Lennox feels." Jack nods his head to something behind me and I swivel to see both drivers and a handful of executives leave the meeting room, Lennox's head is down as he walks down the hallway toward his suite.

Oh, my heart.

I can't tell him what Sandra called about today knowing what I do now. I won't kick him while he's down.

"Thanks, Jack." I close my laptop and start down the hallway after Lennox.

When I make it to his suite inside the motorhome, he's tossing out the little trinkets that have accumulated on his table from the fans he's met this weekend, a lucky cat figure, a jade panda, an opera mask, all into the trash. That isn't like him.

"Hey, I need to discuss the new Bluewater Tech event with you," I lie loudly for anyone nearby to hear, then duck into his room and shut the door. Then I launch myself into his arms and squeeze the ever-loving shit out of him.

"What's this, pity hug?" he mumbles.

"No, you big dummy, I'm proud of you." With my head pressed against his chest, I feel him let out a deep sigh and I know he is arguing with me, in his own head, but he stays silent. Whatever they said to him in the debrief, the fight has been cut out of him right now. He drove a flawless race and those bastards made him feel like shit.

"I'm probably not the best company right now, love."

"Ok," I release my death grip and step back. "You want some space?"

"Is that ok?"

"Of course. I'll ask Jack to drive me back to the hotel."

He nods and I know he's really upset. He's pretty particular on who drives me where now. I've never argued because I like him driving me, being chauffeured around by one of the best drivers in the world is hot even if he's doing it for some machismo, testosterone-fueled reason.

I want to give him a kiss goodbye but I don't want him to think I'm pitying him. I'm pissed off. For him, for me.

"Afraid, but he will not run. Alone, thy will be done. Confessed, but you still feel the shame. Bring me into your arms, again." - Sinead O'Connor - Heroine

It's 10:00 pm and I haven't heard from Lennox. He's in his hotel room, I heard him get back a couple of hours ago, watched him through my peephole like old times. He needs space and I'm not going to take it personally.

Instead, I've spent the last few hours digging up everything I can online about Dickby Dupont. I also refuse to call him by his real name anymore, joining my trio of teammates who call him any other foul version of his name they can dream up. Digby, what a stupid name.

The guy is so squeaky clean online it makes me suspicious. Obscenely wealthy old-money family from Monaco, no photos of him beyond staged social events. No women, or men, in any unseemly photos. All of his sponsors are ultra-conservative brands. He doesn't

140

have any personal social media accounts that I can find, but even his fan-based accounts are as dull as a doorknob.

I heard something from an NHL announcer many years ago. If something's too good to be true, it's probably a fraud.

Dirtbag DuPont is a fraud. I don't know what I can possibly do about it, but I'm a fighter. If Lennox is out of fight, I'll lend him some of mine.

My phone buzzes.

Lennox: Get your ass over here.

There's my bossy, alpha asshole!

I don't bother putting real clothes on and rush into the hall in my pajama pants and a tank top, grabbing just my phone and keycard. Movement way down the hallway catches my eye as Lennox's door opens. Jack and Alessi, one of the drivers from Anora Racing, are about to head into his room. Aha!

"Mallory," he nods.

"Jack," I keep a straight face and nod back, both of us busted sneaking into our respective hotel rooms with our inappropriate workplace romances. Lennox pulls me into his room and shuts the door and I finally let out a grin. Good for Jack, Alessi seems like a decent person from what I've seen.

"Sorry about earlier," Lennox takes me in his arms.

"You can apologize for lots of other things, but you don't owe me an apology for today."

"What else would I be sorry for?" He asks, dead serious.

"How about trying to get me to quit for the longest time?"

"Mmm, that," he kisses my neck. "Well, I'm glad you didn't quit. You're doing a good job and I want you to stay now."

Oh god, he's breaking my heart. My stupid heart that has no business being in this hotel room with him. And now I'm supposed to betray him and not do my job very well.

"Movie?" He asks. He's still not his normal self or he'd have me pinned up against the wall by now, or bent over the nearest piece of furniture. I'm almost glad, though. Not because I don't want him, I do. But because he asked me over for company, not just sex.

"Perfect," I say, grabbing the television remote. I hop on the bed and start scanning through channels.

"Wait, go back," he says, joining me in bed leaning against the headboard. "That looked like Godzilla."

Watching campy old monster movies has become a 'thing' we do. Godzilla is in Japanese, obviously, but I figure out how to turn subtitles on, he kills the lights and I snuggle between his legs and lean back against his chest. He runs his fingers through my hair absentmindedly and I almost forget the nightmare situation I have compounding itself: Celeritas is messing with my job *and* my father is trying to sue me.

"What's wrong?" He asks.

I didn't realize I must have tensed up. "Nothing," I lie. I don't want to pile onto his bad day with my dysfunctional family again.

"Tell me." He starts kneading my shoulders with those amazing strong hands and I roll my head around moaning.

"Just family stuff."

"What now?"

"Ugh," I press my hands into my eyes but Lennox never stops massing my neck. "My dad apparently saw a lawyer today. To sue me for libel."

"Excuse me?"

"He's saying by telling him off in public I was reckless and maliciously caused damage to his reputation. Cody doesn't think he has a case, but…"

"But it's still bullshit. What kind of parent sues their child?"

"They're special, aren't they? I guess this is my punishment for being such a disappointment." Lennox pauses his magic fingers for a second then resumes, running his thumbs along my spine up and down the base of my neck. "Even if a lawsuit is unsuccessful, it'll derail my plans for a firm. He'll keep coming for me until my reputation is shot."

"What do you need from me? Lawyer or,"

"The only thing I need from you," I interrupt him, "is to keep doing that with your hands." We're both quiet for a spell, Godzilla terrorizing Japan on the television. "Are your parents normal people?"

"My parents sacrificed everything for me," he answers immediately.

I wish I could meet them one day but I don't say that aloud because he's been touchy about his family and, well, I'm not his girlfriend. "Tell me about them, off the record? What's it like having parents who love you?" I try to joke at the end but there's a touch of truth to it I try not to think about.

He thinks for moment before he speaks. "Mum worked at a distillery, the oldest on our island. Pop was a marine mechanic. I used to head to his shop after school and help him fix the boat motors. The whole town worked on cod boats, pretty much, so we did a lot of fishing when I was young."

"Did you ever see Nessie?"

"Aye, all the time I'd spot Nessie while wearing my kilt and playing bagpipes, smartass."

He can't see my face but it's covered in a huge grin. "So your dad worked on boats and your mom worked at a distillery."

"Aye."

"And your dad built you a kart when you were three. When did you start racing competitively?"

"Five."

"FIVE?" I try to turn my head and look at him but he turns it back straight, always having to be in control of everything. "And your brother?"

"Sixteen. Thinks he wants to go into F1," he sighs.

"You don't want him to," I say, knowing the answer and understanding a little more of why now.

"No. Be right back." He scoots off the bed and disappears into the bathroom. Water is running and I wonder if he's in the shower, his way of stopping the conversation he might still be uncomfortable with.

A few minutes later the bathroom door opens and Lennox strolls back to me on the bed, stark naked. "Well, hello," I wag my eyebrows at him. Silently, he lifts me up, one arm under my knees and one under my head, and carries me into the bathroom.

He's drawn a bath in the deep two-person soaking tub. He sets me on my feet and looking into my eyes, he pulls my tank off, slides my pajama pants to the floor and helps me into the tub before stepping in to join me on the opposite side. The warm water surrounds me and the bubbles waft up the scent of the hotel's spicy's body wash. Neither of us speaks as he gently runs a bar of soap over my whole body.

Something is different in his face, his eyes, but I can't place it. I study him in silent appreciation.

When he's washed everything on me, I twirl my fingers asking him to turn around. He spins and I take the soap from him and start on his back, massing as I go, though my hands are nowhere near as strong. The soap drops into the water and my hands run over his back tattoo. I've studied it every chance I've had. A massive fish is swirling and trying to eat a smaller fish thrashing to get away. Both fish are thick outlines filled with bold Gaelic designs inside, ropes and knots twisting. *A' bhiast as mutha ag ithe na beiste as lugha* is written, the writing following the curve of the writhing bigger fish. "What does it mean?" I whisper, not wanting to break our silence but needing to know.

"I guess the closest translation would be 'Big fish eat little fish'."

I ponder at all the meanings that could have to a man like Lennox and trace the outlines with my fingers.

"The great devour the small. The powerful swallow up the insignificant." He sighs, his hand trailing up and down my leg next to him.

Boom, mic drop. Take my heart, take it all.

My chest tightens, my heart breaks open and fills with feelings for him I can't control anymore. Nothing about this man is insignificant. I've been made to be the little, insignificant fish my whole life, too. Fuck all of those people who make us feel like this.

Us.

I scoot around to his front and climb into his lap, kneeling over him. I take his face in my palms and stare into his eyes, the green of moss and pine and sage, amazed at the man he really is, the one he lets me see. I kiss him senseless, he reaches for a condom from a toiletry kit on the sink and sheathes himself. I sink down on him in the water. I pull his head into my breasts and he wraps his arms around my waist, helping me raise and lower on his hardness until we both come apart again in each other's arms.

Eighteen

"Yes, I know that love is like ghosts. Oh, and the moonlight baby shows you what is real. There ain't language for the things I feel. And if I can't have you then no one ever will." - Lord Huron - Love Like Ghosts

Lennox

Usually, on my recovery day, which is nothing but a fancy way of saying lay around like a bum all day, I take full advantage and sleep for ninety percent of it. I tossed and turned all night and am kicking around my flat at headquarters now somewhere between restless and ruinous.

I didn't even sleep on the plane. I dragged Mallory next to me on the couch and laid next to her the whole flight while she watched an old vampire movie and slept, daring Matty or Jack to say one word about it. They took one look at my face and knew better.

It should be Celeritas upsetting me, and it is, to an extent. The two hour debrief in which I got reamed out for daring to out-qualify DuPunk pissed me off, sure. The fact that they turned my engine mode down during the race when I toyed with passing him infuriated me. The post-race photos where I had to put my arm around Dingleberry and smile for the cameras, I almost snapped his neck.

But it's her next door.

All morning I've made out bits and pieces of her on the phone with her brother and Aria about her father's latest threats against her. I can't wrap my head around it. And for reasons I can't come to terms with, I need to fix it.

Something has changed. I'm always a bit overbearing but I'm stuck on irrational thoughts of running away from all of this and locking her in my dungeon forever. Primitive, even for me I know, but I just want away from all of this. The absurdity of the situation doesn't escape me either, the woman sent here by the corporate devil himself, sent to make me toe the line, says words identical to those that slam around inside my skull every day.

It killed me when she called herself a disappointment. Watching her in the same endless pursuit of validation you work your ass off to get just so people can throw up roadblocks to kick you back down. The injustice of it all sickens me.

Pacing around the kitchen, I throw some protein powder and bananas into the blender and mash the buttons. Watching everything get pulverized to bits is hypnotizing and oddly satisfying. Reaching for a glass and turning the blender off, I hear a shaky voice from the hallway, "Don't touch me. I said stop!"

My brow furrows and my heart rate picks up. But when I throw my door open, my vision narrows and the only thing I see beyond white-hot anger is DuPont with his hands on Mallory, running his filthy fingers up and down her arm.

Before he can even turn around, my body has acted of its own accord and thrown him up against a wall, his head cracking into a brass sconce lighting the hallway. He screams something, I don't hear the words, as he clutches the back of his head, plaster crumbling to the ground.

I grab the neck of his shirt in my left hand and pull back my right arm with visions of destroying his smarmy face flashing before my eyes when Mallory's screams register to my brain and she wraps half her body around my right arm.

"Stop it! Stop it!"

It allows half a second for my brain to catch up to my body and allows DuPont time to get a few steps down the hallway backing away and holding his head. He looks up and laughs, his sickening weasel voice, "Perfect, that's just perfect, Gibbes! You're done, this time!"

"Stay the fuck away from her," I bellow and take a step toward him but Mallory is standing in front of me trying to block my path. "Did he hurt you?" I ask her, not looking at her but staring down the oxygen thief slowly backing his way down the hallway toward the exit.

"No!" She yells back at me.

"Au contraire," DuPont cackles, "I've only come to offer her an alternative, a real man. You remember how that went last time, don't you Gibbes?"

"You motherfucker," I start but Mallory screams at the top of her lungs for him to get out, standing in between us like a bloody referee.

DuPont continues his backward walk until he reaches the stairwell, a seedy smug grin on his face, then tears down the stairs and the exterior door slams.

"What is wrong with you!" Mallory roars at me.

"Me?" I cry. "I heard you tell him to leave and he had his hands on you!"

"So what! I can take care of myself! You can't go around throwing people into walls!"

"You don't understand," I start.

"No! You don't understand! He's going to get us fired! You're going to cost me this job acting like a wild animal!"

"He cannot get me fired," I try and calm her down, even as my chest is still heaving and my fists clench, but she isn't having it. Her eyes are huge and filled with rage and glass- eyed as tears start filling up inside them.

"That's great for you, Lennox! What about me? He can have *me* fired! Then what? Do you ever think about that? What's going to happen to *me* when I get fired from this job?"

"That's all I...," I pause and suck in a breath, "he won't."

She darts back to her flat and opens the door.

"Mal,"

"No, leave me alone," she says before slamming the door in my face.

Hours pass. Hours of berating myself and listening to Mallory slamming things around in her flat across the hall. All I've thought about for days is how not to screw her life up more, how to get both of us out of this vicious circle.

And I've made it worse.

Even though Dicksnot had it coming and there will never be a point in my life where murdering him is off the table completely, I made it worse for her. I let him provoke me. None of this is working anymore, my coping mechanism of indifference, the playboy persona I don't bother to argue with. I'm letting her down, my family down, my fans down.

Digging around a stack of papers and half-unpacked bags on the dining room table, I finally find it, one thing I can do to protect Mallory from the insidious corruption of Celeritas *and* her father. I make the call and then prepare to grovel.

> **Lennox:** I'm sorry.
> **Mallory:** I'm furious with you.
> **Lennox:** I know. Can we please get out of here?
> **Mallory:** And go where?!
> **Lennox:** Anywhere but here. Please.

Finally, my door opens my door and Mallory walks inside my flat in silence. Her shoulders are slumped and her arms are wrapped around herself. She's small and vulnerable and I wrap my arms around her, dragging her against me. "I'm sorry," I whisper into her hair as I kiss her head.

She nods into my chest and wraps her arms around my waist, "I know. I understand."

She doesn't understand the half to it, but she's here and she's got her arms around me. I can fix anything else.

"Where are we going?" She asks.

"I just want to get out of here, just get in the car and drive."

"That sounds perfect."

A few minutes later I throw our jackets into the car and help Mallory get in since the gullwing doors pointing straight up into the air and harness seat belts aren't the most self-explanatory.

"What the hell is this?" She sinks in and looks at the car suspiciously.

"LaFerrari. Supposed to be a chick magnet, let me know if it's working." She smiles as I get in and fire the engine to life. "You want to drive?"

"I will kill us both. I like when you drive, anyway."

Along the way, Mallory and I return to our normal, whatever that is. I don't have a definition for it yet. She had me stop to feed her, demanding cheeseburgers and milkshakes, but the extra workout I'll need to make up for that is probably a better outlet for my frustrations, anyway.

Dusk will be falling soon as I pull up to our destination. I hope she likes this and doesn't think I'm some kind of creep in addition to knowing what an asshole I am.

"What is this?"

"Highgate Cemetery." I kill the engine and watch Mallory peer around taking in the huge Gothic limestone archways outside covered in moss and ferns and a couple of hundred years of plant overgrowth. "As the legend goes, vampires roam at night. *Taste the Blood of Dracula* was filmed here."

"The movie I watched on the plane?"

I nod at her. Her eyes are wide and I think she's excited, not afraid that I'm an ax murderer or grave robber. "Let me out of this spaceship," she says as she starts trying to get out of her seat harness and open the car door.

Excited turns out to be an understatement. Mallory's holding my hand and strolling the ancient resting grounds calling out famous gravesites for Karl Marx and Douglas Adams. The Victorian grandeur, angels resting atop catacombs, concrete lion heads from the 1800s, every section of the cemetery is more exciting than the next for her. When we get to the Tom Sayres gravesite with a life-sized resting dog statue, it's the first time she takes out her phone to take a photo and she's contemplative spending more time here than others.

"The dog?" I ask her wondering what it is about this one.

She shakes her head. "Tom Sayres was a bare-knuckle fighter, you don't know him?"

I shake my head. I wonder how she does know more about this than I do, but I'm more taken with how beautiful she is, how much I just want to spend time with her, just the two of us. Cemetery, flat, hotel, airplane, I don't even care where we go.

"He was born in a slum, only five foot eight inches tall, only one hundred fifty pounds. He fought men twice his size. In his whole career, he only lost once."

She runs fingers over the stone mastiff on the grave and her eyes grow glassy. "He was a little insignificant fish, too, Lennox."

Her eyes sweep to mine and my heart sinks to my gut, my chest feels like it's on fire. I can't feel my limbs.

I'm either having a massive coronary or I'm falling in love with this woman.

Mallory steps back to me and I take her head in my hands as she looks up at me. I wipe the start of her tears away with my thumbs, "Don't cry," I whisper. The pressure inside my rib cage can't take her tears right now, too.

"They're going to swallow us up, aren't they?" She whimpers, her voice cracking.

I pull her tight against me and cradle her head to my chest, tucking her under my chin. "I won't let them."

I hold her as tight as I can without bruising her until minutes pass and then I feel her start giggling. "What?"

"I'm having wildly inappropriate thoughts about you in a cemetery," she laughs.

"Let's go then, before I get arrested and have to hire a new nanny to clean that up."

The LaFerrari is an impressive car by any standards. However, it has a fatal flaw: it is far too small for the kinds of things Mallory and I want to do to one another. I can't even kiss her without my head jabbing into the roof. Her ass changed every setting on the steering wheel controls, smashed up like a pretzel on my lap. And because I am being punished for something terrible I must have done in a previous life, I don't have a condom.

I stop at the first drugstore I can find to remedy that and Mallory runs inside to make the very important purchase. I argued but she insisted she didn't want to deal with photos of me buying condoms on Twitter tomorrow. The car is conspicuous enough as it is and I'll get mobbed this close to London so I begrudgingly let her go in alone.

It's another fifteen minutes until we'll be back in Aylesbury and I adjust myself for the umpteenth time, my dick smashed up inside my jeans and my whole body pressed into the fitted racing seats. I should have driven a station wagon, panel van, a bloody school bus.

"You know," Mallory theorizes, looking over the low chassis cover between us. "Yep, I can make that work," she mumbles as she starts freeing herself from the seat belts. She's finally free and turns sideways and leans toward me, her foot propping her up on a carbon fiber interior component. She kisses my neck and runs a hand down to grip my dick. I raise my right arm to make room for her and she tucks in to unbutton my jeans.

Fuck yes.

She gets my zipper down and frees my cock, which has been throbbing for an hour now.

"Jesus, you *are* going to get us killed," I watch as her head sinks and brush her hair away. I'm already nearly doubling the speed limit on the bloody A41.

"Good thing my man knows how to drive a car," she purrs.

Her hot breath against my skin sends a rush of blood to my already hard shaft but it's her calling me her man that makes me growl. Her wet tongue circles the head of my cock and I push back in my seat, eyes darting between her beautiful mouth on my dick and the road speeding past us.

Her lips wrap around me as she starts working me up and down, my hand at the back of her head. It's all I can do not to guide her head and I grip her hair in my fist to fight the urge. "Fucking hell," I hiss as she takes more of me into her mouth, her tongue running up and down the underside of my flesh while her lips squeeze tight around me and her cheeks hollow out from sucking me.

My hips jerk up reflexively when the tip of my cock hits the back of her throat and she moans around me, taking me deeper. Her eyelids squint shut as she fights to take me deeper, her head circling and bobbing up and down on me. "Look at me," I growl. Her hazel eyes meet mine, moisture on her eyelashes, and every muscle in my body flexes at the sight. My eyes flash between her and the road, years of reaction time training has never been so handy.

She snakes one hand between my legs and rubs my balls and then sinks all the way to my base, her tight throat constricting against me. "Ugh, yes, love," my head slams back into the seat and the knuckles on my left hand are white from squeezing the steering wheel so hard. My grip in her hair tightens as her pace picks up. "Fuck, I'm gonna come." Mallory moans more, her ass wiggling around and squirming. "Take every last drop," I groan.

Heat surges through me, pressure expands and with a surge, I explode into her throat with a primal roar. Hot ropes of energy and fire and adrenaline and passion shoot out and Mallory swallows and licks and does her damndest to keep up. When I am finally drained and spent she releases her lips and her tongue licks and laps around my crown until she's satisfied and slinks back into her seat.

"So good, love. Incredible."

Mallory is smirking, quite pleased with herself as I catch my breath and tuck myself back into my pants just in time for the last few kilometers. "See, no one died," she teases.

I know she's joking but I need her to know. "You know I won't hurt you, right?" Her eyes fall and dart to the floorboard. "You don't know that?" I question, a twinge in my chest starts up again.

"I want to trust you," she sighs.

"But you don't."

"It's hard for me to be totally out of control."

"You can be out of control and still trust me."

"Prove it then," she goads and smirks at me. She's sassing me, being playful and argumentative because that's what we do. But there's some truth there, like there is behind all of our sarcasm.

Pulling into Celeritas, it's dark and well past the time when everyone has gone home for the night. The LaFerrari rumbles along the brick-lined inner roads, idling past the administration buildings and winding along the dimly lit walkways. I drive us past the factory buildings to the farthest part of the complex and pull up to a heavy iron gate. I push the button for the window to go down.

"What are you doing?" Mallory asks as I pull my wallet out and wave my keycard past the security reader and the gate creaks to life.

"Proving it." Pulling in, the test track comes into view under the headlights. I hop out and throw the switch for the track lights and the expanse of the winding asphalt lights up. Now I'm glad I brought this car and not the school bus, after all, since Mallory wants to challenge me.

Hopping back into the car, her eyes are wide and she's clutching the door panel. "You like when I drive you, yes?" I ask and start tightening down her seat belt harness, snugging her into the seat as much as I can.

"What? Yes, but, what are you doing?"

"In the corners, try as hard as you can to keep your head pushed back into the seat," I push her head back and show her. This car won't pull the g-forces that an F1 car will, but it's still going to be way more than she's used to with that delicate little neck.

"Lennox," she grips one of my wrists cinching her belts and locks eyes with me.

"You know when I'm the most out of control? When I'm in the car on track. And when I'm with you." I tuck back into my seat and attach my harness. "You let me know when you trust me."

I change a few settings on the car's control panels and pull out onto the track. I start slowly and look over at Mallory, still clutching the door panel but she squints at me and then bites her lip. "You want to get out?" I ask just to make sure. Again, asshole, not monster.

She shakes her head no.

Game on.

I nail the throttle to the floor and Mallory screams, the acceleration shoving her back into the seat with force she cannot control, her hands desperate to find anything to hold onto, as if that will help her. In under three seconds, we're past 60 miles per hour and before the first corner a few seconds later, 125.

Mallory screams as we fly into the first corner at speeds that look impossible to most people. My fingers working the paddle shifter, I downshift and slide the rear end out as the car drifts along the width of the asphalt. Mallory's hair is flying out in front of her body and she's board stiff screaming her head off.

I straighten the car out and then upshift through a series of left-right chicanes, the speedometer climbing past 150 as we cut each apex and the screams and four-letter words next to me escalate.

Sailing through the next sweeping corner, the car totally sideways yet going exactly where I intend it to despite the unnatural position of the steering wheel, I taunt Mallory some more. "Say the words, love."

"Fuck youuuuuuuu," she cries, her body board straight and a death grip on the handles she's found to clutch for dear life. The engine is roaring, 950 horses shrieking in the night alongside Mallory. All the instrument panels lite up flashing the status of all the hybrid systems and gears I'm flying us through.

Diving onto the straight, the car opens up and when we pass 200 miles per hour and Mallory sees the number she screams again. Into the next turn, I hold the throttle wide open until the last possible millisecond and throw the car sideways again. Mallory tries, unsuccessfully, to get her gravity-defying hair out from in front of her face.

"Remember KERS, baby? Let's hit it."

"Noooooooooooooo," she screams.

"Oh yes," I laugh and climb past 230mph on the long straight then slam the brakes into the hairpin, Mallory's body now kept in the seat only through the strength of her harness. I throw my right arm over her chest anyway, instinctual move, and swing up through the hairpin with my left hand.

She latches onto my arm and is digging her nails in screaming. "You want me to keep this up with one hand? Fine by me, but your choice." She releases my arm then grips it back then releases, more screaming.

The car rocks and shakes as I keep it in position squirreling around another corner and start the next lap. "Trust me yet?"

Her hands grip her harness and she tries to nod, I think. "Keep your head back. Say the words," into Turn 1 again we go, the tires lighting up, blue smoke pouring off our wheels.

"I trust you!" She finally screams. "I trust you! I trust you!" I back off the throttle and she starts laughing maniacally, bouncing in her seat. "Holy shit, my heart!" The smile on her face is huge, her eyes saucers. I put a hand on her knee and she grips it, her palms covered in sweat. "Go again!"

I bust up laughing, "I've created a monster."

I take us through another few laps until I'm pretty sure all four tires need replacing. Mallory still screams through all of them but she's having the time of her life.

And I'm on top of the world.

At the far end of the track, I do a few donuts for her then bring the car to a stop and kill the engine amidst the plumes of blue smoke surrounding us. "I think I peed a little," she giggles and catches her breath, palming her crazy hair back down.

"You pissed up my LaFerrari? Wow," I tease her.

When her laughs and giggles finally quit, I watch her silently. I want to hear her say it. Again. "You, me. This is more than just screwing around, Mal. At least, it is for me."

"It is for me, too," she breathes.

"You know I won't hurt you? You trust me?" I ask her again, looking into her eyes searching for the honesty, the raw feelings deep inside her.

"Yes," she takes my hand and pulls it into hers.

"Good. I need you to do something for me." Her eyes crinkle at the corners, searching mine. "Maxwell Cooper is expecting your call."

Nineteen

"Baby, I'll take you to an honest place. Darling, I just can't find my honest face." - Inhaler - My Honest Face

Mallory

I haven't been called into the principal's office in well over a decade and that was for putting gum in Rebecca Johnson's ponytail. She was a spoiled mean girl brat and had it coming. I got detention and grounded for a month for shaming my family.

Now I might get fired.

In the two months since I first sat in this office, everything has changed but the room, and Sandra Alix, remain just as cold. The last time I sat in this chair, I was filled with promise. Now I'm filled with suspicion. I don't trust anything they say.

No big surprise, Ding-a-ling DuPont ran right to mommy and daddy and Celeritas to tattle. Lennox and I spent yesterday in meetings with HR and the Celeritas attorneys. They separated us, of course. I felt like a criminal being questioned in a seedy police station, attorneys playing good-cop-bad-cop games like I'm an idiot.

Thank god Lydia and Robert cannot see me now, proving them right about what a failure I am.

"Let's review," Sandra huffs, shuffling mounds of manilla folders and paperwork over her glass desk. Her glasses sit low on her pointy nose and she has more grey roots poking out of her scalp today or I didn't even notice them the last time. "You say Mr. DuPont came, unsolicited, to your flat and propositioned you."

"Yes. He's... propositioned me on other occasions as well, asking me on his yacht," and a few other times I didn't even tell Lennox about knowing he acts like a caveman.

"And he made unwanted physical contact?" Sandra is flipping through pages of typed text but I can't read it upside down.

"Several times, yes. Touching my face, tucking hair behind my ear, yesterday he was running his hand up and down my arms." It's harder than I think it will be to put into proper words what creepy feels like. I'm not going to lie, but I have to do better than 'Digby is handsy and gives me the creeps' if there's any hope for me to stay gainfully employed and for Lennox to keep his contract.

He's not even remotely worried about his contract and it's making me crazy. I know he has enough money for several lifetimes, but F1 is his dream.

"And you asked him to stop?"

"Yes. I asked him to leave and he refused and continued touching my arm." And then Lennox lost his ever-loving mind and slammed his head into the wall.

"You felt uncomfortable during this time?"

I've covered these questions a hundred times already by this point and it's getting difficult to keep my patience. I think I understand how Lennox feels now answering stupid questions from the media. Obviously, I felt uncomfortable, Sandra. I've said so a dozen times. "I did," I say one more time.

"And you are willing to sign an affidavit to these statements?" Sandra peers at me over the top of her glasses.

"Yes, everything I have said is true," I nod.

"Very well," Sandra removes her eyeglasses, sits back in her chair and rubs her eyes. I think the moment of truth is upon me. I'm either about to be fired or, or I don't know what, actually. I don't know how much power the DuPont's have over Celeritas. A hundred million dollars a year probably buys a lot of unethical behavior.

"Given these statements, the DuPont's have elected not to pursue any charges against Mr. Gibbes."

I nod. Lennox told me they wouldn't, said the prestigious DuPont family would never have their name risked in the news, it would be too unseemly. I wonder if my father has thoughts about how he's going to look in the news if he sues his own daughter. Or maybe the Mitchells are just more trashy or more desperate than the DuPont's.

"As for you, Mallory, the UK has very strong employee protection laws and all parties involved wish to avoid such murky waters," Sandra's eyebrows are cocked at me.

"Ooookay," I say slowly, not quite understanding, but I think I am still employed. For the moment.

"As they would say on track, Ms. Mitchell, we will consider this a racing incident."

A racing incident. An accident or collision on track that the stewards decide was due to the nature and chaos of the race, no one particularly at fault. No penalties or fines assessed. I think that's the best I could have hoped for. It's disgusting.

"I understand." Sandra slides over some paperwork for me to sign agreeing that each party agrees to let it go and behave professionally. They'll go in our HR files but that's it.

"Mallory, I would be remiss if I didn't mention this," she pauses for a moment and her shoulders drop. It looks as if she's softened a bit but that would defy everything I know about Sandra Alix, having a heart. Or a personality. "You and Mr. Gibbes seem, oh, more friendly these days." There's the hint of a tiny, tiny smile on her lips but it's stuck like her face is incapable of making such gestures.

"I think we're working fairly well together now, Ms. Alix. After a steep learning curve, as you said," I smile at her with every ounce of fakery in my soul.

Sandra starts cleaning up the shuffled papers all over her desk. "There's nothing in Celeritas policy that prohibits intraoffice dating assuming it is not a supervisor-subordinate position or becomes problematic. With as much travel as the team endures, it's not unusual. I'm sure you can imagine."

I try to school my eyes, my heart rate, the sweaty palms. A closed mouth gathers no foot, so this is a high time for me to sit here and shut up. I've seen those YouTube videos on what to do when the cops stop you, no one talks and everyone walks. I don't know if that applies here, but that's my plan.

"That said, as an old lady who has been in this game for a long time, I would advise you to consider the optics for your career." She taps a pen on a thick folder on her desk in an ultra-rare display of what appears to be genuine human emotion. "And as a woman, use caution."

"Thank you, Sandra." I wipe my palms on my pants and start to rise.

"Ah-ahem," Sandra clears her throat very loudly, glaring at me, her pen tapping furiously.

My brow furrows, Sandra is leering at me, pursing her lips. I follow her eyes to the folder she's tapping against. It's two inches thick and labeled "Human Resources: Confidential. Digby DuPont."

Oh, I see. That's quite a thick HR dossier for the squeaky clean golden boy of the paddock. I knew it. And Sandra Alix, the hard-nosed, stick up her ass, 'dragon lady' as the boys call her, has warned me.

I raise my chin at her in understanding and give her a sharp nod.

Leaving the administration office, I hear cars running on the test track and decide to walk over. It's a brisk spring day but the sun is shining, I'm in London, and I have Lennox's oversized Celeritas jacket on that no one would know is his but us. The scent of his cologne, mossy woods and old leather, mixes with the smell of race fuel in the air.

And, by no small miracle, I am still employed. I don't need to go running back home a total failure. For the moment, anyway.

Security waves as I walk into the track area and take a seat on a section of metal bleachers in the sun. Everyone else is inside the track building, I feel like I'm at my own private race watching two Formula 1 cars circle the track with aero rakes all over both cars measuring airflow over each part of the car.

These cars look older and aren't labeled with driver numbers but I can tell which driver is which by their helmets. Lennox zings past under his blue and white Scottish flag helmet and then Dildo DuPont in his neon green helmet. It's the color of ectoplasm, slime. How appropriate.

Wrapping Lennox's jacket around me and watching him sail around this track he drove me around and around on last night, I don't know how I'm going to handle the latest bomb he dropped on me. He called Cooper Media and agreed to the inside exclusive.

He wouldn't discuss it much last night but I know why he did it. He thinks it would give me security against my father's attempts to sabotage me. And it would, Cooper Media is one of the largest media houses in the world. They're modern too, unlike the crumbling company my father clings to that still thinks newspaper is a viable media and that social platforms are for hippies and miscreants.

Working with Cooper on this would be the nail in the coffin for my family. It may very well kill my father. I'm frustrated that I'm letting myself feel guilty about it, too. Why should I when he is trying to sue his own daughter? Because no matter how many times they hurt me, I still want my parent's approval and love. It makes me feel weak, but it's true.

Every time Mom calls or texts, some naive part of me hopes it will be to tell me she loves me just as I am, that she supports me no matter what. It's never happened in twenty-six years but there's a little girl deep inside of me still holding out hope. One of these days, Dad might come to his senses and see my career as worthy and be proud of what I've accomplished.

Logically, I know it won't happen. Emotionally, I want it. No matter how much I beat myself up right now.

As soon as it was a reasonable hour in New York, I called Max Cooper back. I don't know what I'm going to do, but Lennox said he was expecting my call. They want this exclusive, badly. It would be huge in the European and Asian markets and Lennox has denied every similar request from every publisher his entire career.

If I handed Cooper a story like this that no one else has been able to, worst case, I'd have a job no matter what my dad does. It wouldn't be exactly what I want to do, but it would be a paycheck somewhere in their social media departments. Best case, it would be an incredible stepping stone for launching my dream firm in Sports PR.

I'm not a journalist, technically, and can't write the piece, but Lennox told Max Cooper there'd be no journalists or photographers allowed. Max said that was even better, he wants an intimate expose not a fancy spread. I'd record interviews and take my own photos and work with a writer to develop the perfect story. Lennox mandated I have ultimate control.

I told Max I'd think about it but Lennox has already scheduled our trip to Scotland after the next race.

He doesn't know that I've been warned to back him out of the spotlight. Working with Cooper wouldn't technically involve Celeritas and I don't think they could fire me for it since Lennox set it up, but Doofus DuPont and his privileged family can certainly make his life worse here and on track. If he gets into any more trouble with his teammate, they'll penalize him on track even more, if not outright terminate his contract. I've seen it happen in other sports.

Digby is going to be extra threatened now. It's more important than ever that I keep him and Lennox apart. I can't let Lennox know anything else about my mandate to keep him out of the spotlight.

For both our sakes, I need to figure this out by myself.

Twenty

Headline: Gibbes Points Leader at Celeritas After DuPont Crash in Baku
Headline: Good Job Baku! Good job Gibbes!
Photo: Lennox Gibbes on Podium in Baku, Azerbaijan

F1Scooby: he can spray me down anytime…

HeadSizzlin: sticky!

GingerHippo: Have always been a DuPont fan but I gotta say, I've switched to Team Gibbes this season. He seems like an ok dude.

ScotlandMom: He signed a shirt for me! He's a good boy!

RacingHot: Mom, that 'boy' is all man. :-o

Mallory

I still have no idea what I'm going to do about the Cooper Media situation even as we've just landed at a tiny single strip airfield on the Isle of Skye, Lennox's home island in the Outer Hebrides. Despite that, and the extremely bumpy landing that had me burying my head into his chest, I am giddy to be here.

The flight in, before it became a roller coaster, was stunning. Passing over rocky cliffs, pastels colored homes lining the shores of the coast, and so much greenery, I am almost expecting a hobbit to jump out at me. I want to see everything, but I mostly want to see Lennox's home, where he grew up, his life outside of F1. And I want to know for me, not Cooper Media, or for Celeritas, or even his fans.

We have an hour's drive to his home but it's flying past as I take in the dramatic coastline our route winds us through. Snow peaked mountains rise before deep blue waters, the earth covered in a lush carpet of moss. "Ooo what is that?" I ask Lennox, a question I've asked many times since we got into the "beater" car he leaves at the airport, a gray Audi.

"Loch Sligachan." Part of me keeps asking him where we are because I want to hear him speak all the names of these locations, his accent thicker since the second we landed. It does things to me...

"Can we stop?"

"We have ten days before we're due in Barcelona, plenty of time."

I sigh a contented, happy breath. Ten days alone with Lennox in this incredible, isolated corner of the world. I want to turn my phone off, throw my laptop out the window, forget everything and everyone except the tattooed adonis in the car with me.

Despite driving a phenomenal race in Azerbaijan, it was hard on him because Dumbass DuPont wrecked his car again and behaved like a salty little bitch, making everyone on the team miserable. I stuck with Jack and Matty all weekend like a grade-a clinger, never letting myself be alone so Dumbass couldn't cause any trouble. In any case, I plan to make Lennox feel much better for the next ten days.

Before I know it, we pull off the tiny main road and the car winds down an unmarked gravel drive for several minutes, passing hilly meadows and an old stone fence before Lennox punches in a code and a black steel gate opens for us. Whatever I was picturing in my head as Lennox's home, this is not it.

First coming into view as we keep down the drive is a massive two-story garage built out of round gray and black stones, hundreds of year of weather perfecting their charm. There are at least six black garage door bays blended into the dark stone and the second story is tinted floor to ceiling windows along the front before a peaked thatched roof takes over, covered in green moss that drips down the sides of the building. It is somehow timeworn yet sleek and modern.

We drive past the garage and a few smaller stone outbuildings before pulling up to the main building. "This is your house?" I gasp.

"Aye." Lennox pops out of the car and is rounding it to open my door for me, but I've already gotten it open and have jumped out, my jaw open and trying to take in the spectacular beauty. The house is ancient, more like a castle than a home, all black and gray stone construction, moss growing between some rocks, and a shale tile roof with multiple brick chimneys rising above. Like the garage, there are modern windows peppered everywhere that blend seamlessly into the aesthetic. As far as I can see, it's surrounded by brilliant greenery in all directions.

"How old is it?" I gawk.

"Not that old, it was a diatomite factory built in the mid-1800s." Not that old? I have so many questions I don't know where to start but I'm distracted by an orange tabby cat bounding and leaping over long grass heading straight for us.

"I think one of your fans is charging you," I point.

Lennox turns to see what I'm pointing at as the cat reaches us and starts weaving between his long legs. He bends down to scratch the kitty's ears, one of them missing the top-left point, and coos something to him in Gaelic. I don't need to understand it for my hormones to shift into hyperdrive. "Come on, let's get it over with," he rolls his eyes at me, thinking I'm going to make more cat jokes.

Me, Lennox and the orange cat, who he calls 'Bodach,' traipse all around the property as he stops and refills food dishes in small stone outbuildings along the way. Hearing the kibble hit their bowls, a few more cats appear along the horizon and make their way in for chow as soon as we're out of the immediate area.

I can't help but smile at how adorable this is, the big, strong, tattooed bad boy that he's supposed to be, refilling cat food bowls. "You need a refresher on how secure I am in my masculinity?" He asks me, grabbing my ass and pulling my hips into him along a worn path amongst the fields.

"I would like a refresher course on this," I smirk and cup his package, "but I'm not teasing you about the cats. I'm more woke than that and honestly, my ovaries are on fire."

"There are probably antibiotics for that," he laughs, his eyes bright and alive. He's different here. The way he walks is easy, his shoulders are relaxed. He's comfortable. This is his sanctuary.

He says the cats kind of came with the property and they're all spayed or neutered, a few like Bodach he can touch but the others are wild. His dad even comes by every day to feed them while Lennox is gone. "At the marina where Pop worked, there were always cats hanging around the fishing boats. There's a local group I support, they get all the cats fixed, get 'em their shots," he shrugs.

This man. I can't take any more.

I pull him to me by the waistband of his jeans, "If you don't take me inside and fuck my brains out, I am going to explode. Literally explode, Lennox."

He takes my head in his warm hands and lowers his lips to mine, his tongue sweeping over my bottom lip and then exploring my mouth. I moan and push into him, needing to feel his hardness, his body close to mine, and slide my hands around him. We make out in the middle of the lush grasses, the complete freedom from anyone who might see us makes me want to tear his pants off and go at it right here. I slip my hands under the hem of his shirt and run my hands up his back, needing to feel skin.

"Jesus your hands are cold," he jerks back chuckling. It's pretty chilly here, my panties are not the only thing damp, and there's a decent ocean breeze swirling past us. I've been too preoccupied to even notice I'm a little cold. "Come on, I'll show you one more thing then we'll go inside and I'll warm you up."

Following a worn path in the long green grass, the sounds of the ocean become stronger, waves crashing on the shore. Deep blue water comes into view as we get closer, whitecaps moving their way toward shore, and then we near the steep drop off. "Oh my god," I gasp. Rocky cliffs fall before us and meet the earth with black basalt stones and sand as far as the eye can see. Far below us, the beach juts out creating natural pools where waves crash then slink back out to sea. Gulls swoop the cliffs, the only witnesses to Lennox and I standing at this point. The rugged beauty and isolation are awe-inspiring and humbling.

"Why do you ever leave this magical place?" I whisper to Lennox, standing beside me with his hands in his pockets, brown locks of hair blowing in the wind, gazing out to the sea. I'm wearing a hoodie and have goosebumps whereas he stands in a thin white tee shirt facing the headwinds completely comfortable. He belongs here, of this place.

"I've never brought anyone here before," he says, still watching the horizon.

"No one?" How can that be? Surely he's brought women, girlfriends, Kate the Waif, home before.

He shakes his head. "It's my escape from everyone, everything."

My stomach falls and I wrap my arms around myself. I feel like a monster, I can't do this Cooper Media piece, this is his. No one else's.

"If I didn't want you here, you wouldn't be here," he misinterprets me shrinking in on myself. But his words help another worry, anyway.

"Come on, let's get you inside."

"It's beautiful," I tell him as he puts an arm around me and we start back to the house.

"Yeah well, you haven't seen the inside yet."

Lennox turns off the security system inside the front door while my eyes dart from one side of the massive space to the next. The old factory building has been gutted and turned into an open floor plan home with dramatic two-story ceilings over much of it, original dark wood beams running parallel to the roof, exposed stone over several walls. It is a stunning space that pairs an industrial loft with a warm, cozy cottage. Or, it will be when it's finished?

"Needs a lot of work yet," he says leading me into the kitchen. It's the size of my New York apartment and the windows overlook the coast letting in rays of natural light, elegant white farmhouse cabinets sit below custom concrete counters and copper fixtures pop against the dark stone. The top cabinets are not installed but are still in their boxes piled up against the far wall. Wires for the lighting dangle down and switches in the wall are exposed waiting for the drywall to be finished.

The living room next to the kitchen is an enormous open space with a stone fireplace larger than most cars, its chimney rising all the way to the roof far above us. More windows line the walls and overlook a meadow and a big brick patio space. In the middle of the room is a single grey couch, wood coffee table, and the biggest television I've ever seen, sitting on the floor.

"How long have you lived here?" I ask. Calling this a bachelor's house would be a gross understatement. Even unfinished, it is magazine worthy in design, but it's... empty. It echoes when we walk on the stained concrete floors. There isn't a single photo, throw pillow, or personal item anywhere.

"A couple of years, I guess," Lennox shrugs.

I stay silent as we mill about. I want to ask him why he hasn't had it finished yet, but I don't want to be rude or have him think I don't like it. It's not like he doesn't have the money, a good construction crew could finish everything in a week. It's gorgeous and I'm grateful to be here with him, I wouldn't care if he lived in a tent. I'm also dying of curiosity but keep it tamped down so I don't overstep any boundaries.

He reads my mind or body language and continues, "I haven't really had the time to finish it. Pop and I plug away at it here and there."

"*You* are doing the work?"

"The major stuff I had done, gutting it, framing it out, the windows and roof and whatnot. But I wanted to do the rest myself. I just never get around to it. It was still an old factory inside when I bought it, but it had good bones and character. And I wanted a change."

"I had no idea you were so handy."

"My tool work is second to none," he winks at me, then strides to me and wraps his arms around me from behind.

I lean back into him. "Thank you for bringing me here." His lips drop to my neck and I roll my head to give him access. He takes my earlobe between his teeth and plants soft nibbles down my neck and collarbone, pulling the collar of my hoodie as much as it will give until he growls and tears it off over my head.

I reach my arms behind me trying to touch him but I'm trapped inside his strong arms holding me tight against him as he bites and licks and sucks on the sensitive skin of my neck. I wiggle my ass back into the hardness I feel growing at my lower back. One of his hands moves under my bra and cups a breast.

I moan and arch my back as his thumb works my nipple into a hardened peak and he flattens his other palm across my abdomen then slowly drags it lower and into the front of my jeans. Dipping his long fingers into the front of my panties and into my slick folds, he growls into my ear, "Mmm, who are you so wet for, love?"

"You," I hiss and pull one arm free to bring up behind me and loop around his neck. My nails dig into his neck as he strokes his fingers up and down over my crease and then dip inside of me. "Oh god, I need you." His fingers slide in and out of me, his thumb working my clit.

My body is jerking and wiggling from pleasure but I'm nearly immobile from his tall, hard body behind me, his arms holding me firm against his torso. I'm surrounded and contained by his limbs and completely at his mercy, he's taking away all my control again and it's turning me on so much. I'm going to come from this if he doesn't stop. "Lennox, take me," I beg.

His hand comes out of my panties and he wraps his arms around my waist, carrying me against him until we're back in the kitchen. He drops me next to a counter, windows before me with the ocean beyond. "Bend over," he pushes my back down and goes to work stripping my jeans down and over my feet, then his hard cock presses into me from behind again. He grinds himself against me several times, his hands running up and down my back.

He stops for a moment and I expect the sound of his zipper but I feel the stubble of his chin on my inner thighs instead. "Oh god," his hands spread my legs and his tongue runs over the cloth of my panties before he slips them to the side. His tongue pushes inside my channel and I push my ass back to him and grip the cold concrete counter I'm flattened against.

"So wet, you taste so good," his deep voice rumbles behind me as his tongue laps the length of my pussy. Over and over he strokes me and drives me into a frenzy with the tip of his tongue before he covers me with his whole mouth and sucks my clit. I spread my legs wider for him and he wraps his arms around my thighs practically lifting my feet from the floor and holding me against his shoulders.

Heat begins building in my core, my legs quivering, my grip on the counter intensifying. I want to feel him inside me though, I'm desperate and aching to be filled by him. "I want to come on your cock," I grunt out.

A hand slaps my ass, the sharp sting quickly covered by his warm palm and adding to the intensity of the pleasure overtaking my body. "You'll come all over my face," he lifts for a split second to snarl before his tongue is back, flicking up and down my clit relentlessly. Nothing is hotter than him taking charge of me.

I can't hold it anymore, my sex clenches as a freight train of an orgasm rips through me and I convulse and buck against him. "Ohhhhhh!" I wail and scream and try tearing the counter off the cabinets.

"Good girl," he slaps my ass again. I try to turn to face him but he cups my pussy and holds me against the counter. I hear him rummaging through a kitchen drawer and then his zipper lowering and the telltale sound of a foil wrapper.

"I need your cock, Lennox" I turn my head to the side against the counter but I can't see his face. My skin burns for half a second when he rips the waistband of my panties and they fall away. I hear his ragged breathing before I feel it, the crown of his hard dick at my entrance, then an inch expanding and stretching me. "Please," I beg him and try pushing, wiggling to get more of him.

He leans all the way over me, his cut chest covering my back and he bites my ear, "You're going to take every fucking inch." He stands upright, grabs my hips, and slams hard, all the way into me. Oh god, the burn, he's so big it knocks the air out of my lungs.

He circles his hips, he's so deep at this angle I can feel him pulsing inside of me. He pulls out then pistons into me, driving me into the counter over and over. I lift one leg and try to wrap it around him, he grabs it by my knee and thrusts. My tits are going to have road rash from rubbing against the counter so hard and my insides ripple with pleasure.

"That's it, squeeze that tight pussy." Fuck, I love it when he talks to me like this, it makes me crazy. No one has ever been so filthy with me and it takes me apart at the seams.

I clench down on his dick with everything I have in me and revel in his grunts, the pleasure I know I'm giving him. My body begins to shake all over and I'm seeing white spots from crushing my eyes closed so tight but I want him to come with me. "Harder, give it to me harder."

Oh, shit.

Holy hell, I didn't think it could get any harder but he's giving it to me. Kitchen drawers are rocking, something crashed behind me, and the sound of our flesh slapping together is echoing in this massive house. "Come for me," he orders.

As if accepting his command is my sole job, electricity surges through me and I spasm around him, screaming his name so loud every sheep and neighbor within fifty miles may have heard me. My knees go weak and I nearly collapse to the floor, but Lennox catches me around the waist and flips me around.

He throws me up on the counter like a rag doll and pulls my hips to the edge. His eyes are full of domination and there is no question of who is in charge here. Staring into my eyes that are still watering from the last orgasm, he spreads my legs and drives into me again. I wrap my legs around his hips and lurch forward, wrapping my arms around his neck and hanging on for dear life.

One of his sculpted arms falls to the counter behind me as he tries to get more leverage and drive harder into me. "Need you deeper," he groans before bending down to take my nipple into his mouth. I arch my back and hold my breast up so he can nip and suck it.

I don't know how much more of this I can take, his stamina is insane. I'm ready to beg and plead when his arms slide under my ass and he picks me up, twirls me around, takes a few steps and drives me up against a wall. I dig my heels into his ass and gyrate my hips using his broad shoulders for support. My muscles are exhausted but he feels so good so deep inside of me and I want him to lose control and come inside of me.

Lennox leans his chest back but I'm completely stable between his arms under me and the sheer force of his hips driving me into the drywall. "Touch yourself," he pants.

I bring my arm in from his shoulder and start rubbing my clit but it's too much, I'm so sensitive. "I can't," I whimper and shake my head, my sweaty hair clinging to my face.

"Rub that beautiful pussy or I'm going to fuck you for the next twelve hours."

Oh my god, it's so intense, colors are swirling in my brain and my throat is raw from screaming and grunting. I believe every syllable that he really would, and could, fuck me for the next twelve hours. "Oh gaaa," my body jerks and my hips rise, tears are streaming down my cheeks as I thrash.

"That's it, love, give it to me."

"Oh god, it's too much, oh my god," I cry.

"Give. It. To. Me." He drives into me harder at each word, filling me deep into my womb.

"Lennox!" I wail, a bolt of lightning and heat racing through me, my core finding the last bit of energy it has to orgasm around him one more time. He smashes his chest back against me and drives upward into me one, two, three more times before his whole body tenses and he bites down on my shoulder and howls.

My whole body goes limp, lifeless against him. I can't even pick my head up and I certainly can't think straight. Strong arms wrap around me and I can't even hang on, but he has me. This wonderful strong man has me safe in his arms and I don't have to worry.

As he carries me up a set of stairs, his cock finally wiggles free and drops out of me. I can't keep my eyes open to see where we're going but before comprehension returns to my mind, he's pulled back covers on his bed and gently lays me down. My body sinks into a plush, warm mattress, my head is absorbed into a cloud, every muscle in my body tingling or cramping.

Sleep is about to overtake me when I feel a wet towel cleaning me and then his warm, hard body next to mine. He pulls me into him, covers us up, and my body gives up the fight.

Twenty One

"I know you are the only one, my little tease of heaven. And you know I am the only one, your bitter taste of hell." - Drowning Pool - 37 Stitches

Lennox

Orange and red flames dance across the charred twigs and limbs, glowing embers popping and hissing as moisture inside the wood bursts and explodes. The dance of the fire has me so transfixed I don't notice Mallory's awake until the sliding door opens and she steps outside to join me at the fire pit. A steaming mug of coffee in her hand, she's wearing a pair of my sweatpants rolled up several times at her waist, and my Talisker Distillery hoodie.

"What was in the suitcase I hauled in if not your own clothes?" Honestly, I should throw her suitcase into the bay so she has to wear nothing *but* my clothes, but I still need to tease her.

She smirks at me over the rim of her mug, otherwise ignoring me and taking a seat in one of the wooden Adirondack chairs close to the fire. Her hair is twisted up on the top of her head and she looks like she got fucked half to death then slept for twelve hours, because that's exactly what happened.

"Why are you looking at me like that?" She eyes me suspiciously.

Because the sight of you in my clothes, in my house, in my bed, is doing things to me that I don't know how to deal with. And we're here for a different reason, as much as I'd like to pretend otherwise. "How'd you sleep?"

"Mmm," she moans and rolls her head stretching her neck,

"amazing until I woke up with a sandpaper-y tongue licking my face."

"If I had a sandpaper tongue…"

"Stop!" She closes her eyes and simpers, "Too early for that."

"The black one is Prost, the grey one is Senna. They're siblings and they fight like hell." My super lame F1 pun is lost on her.

"So is this what you do when you come home, do yard work and burn things?"

"Men have to start a certain number of fires each year or our balls fall off." I realize I'm being especially sarcastic, trying to avoid the inevitable.

"You must be a pyromaniac then, your balls are in excellent condition," she gives me a thumbs up, lifts her knees onto her chair and stretches my hoodie over them.

I'd much rather continue making sexual innuendos or just sit here quietly with her by the fire, but I need to rip the bandage off. "So how does this work, you just ask me questions? You record this or take notes or something?"

Her face falls, her expression blank.

"I'll answer whatever you ask but my family still stays out of it, they won't be joining us."

"I won't meet your parents?" She creaks, her voice still groggy from sleep or hoarse from screaming last night.

I feel like a prick but I need to remember that she's here with an agenda, one that I imposed it on her. This is her safety net from her father, Celeritas, and hell, even me when she gets sick of my shit and quits or leaves me at the end of the season. If not sooner. With more edge to my voice than I intend, it comes out, "It's just a hard line for me. They didn't sign up for this life, I won't do it to them."

"I didn't mean…"

"I'm sorry, Mal, that's the only thing off the table. Pick something else. Where do you want to start?" Maybe I should get a knife and slice my chest open for the whole world to see, it'd be quicker and probably less painful.

"Why are you being like this? I didn't ask for this. I said no, you're the one who called Cooper." Her hands are shaking around her coffee mug.

Jesus, I don't know what's wrong with me. I take a deep breath and run my hands through my hair. "You're right. I'm an asshole, I'm sorry."

"I'm not doing it, Lennox. I won't."

"You have to. You said you'd do this for me."

Her lip is quivering and her eyes are glassy. "But you're doing it for me and I don't want it."

She may not want it now but she will eventually. If I can't be there forever I need to do what I can to make sure she has a soft place to land. I walk over to her, kiss her coffee tinted lips, and pull her phone out of the front pocket of her hoodie. Over her protests, I go back to my chair, swipe up and find the audio recorder app. Turning it on, I set it on the arm of my chair.

"Can we just do this?" I ask with as much patience as I can muster.

"Anything I want to know I wanted to know for *me*, not for any other reason." She wipes her eyes with her sleeves. My jaw ticks and I swallow hard to keep myself in my seat, keep myself from storming over there and wrapping my arms around her.

"Let's just start there then, what do you want to know?" She refuses to answer me and is staring off into the grass that's whistling in the breeze. "Childhood, car collection, what do I do in my spare time, girlfriends…" Her eyes dart to mine when I say *girlfriends* and then dart back to the grass. "Ah, there it is. Girlfriends, it is, let's start there."

I wait her out until she finally asks. "Why did you say you've never brought another woman here?" She won't look at me but she's gazing into the fire in front of her now, so at least her head isn't turned in the opposite direction anymore.

"Because I haven't. I bought this place when Kate and I broke up." Her eyes lift to mine. She's been all over my online accounts, she knows all about people I've been with, Kate was just the most public. And the most awful. "Everything went to shit right around then and I needed somewhere to get away from it all. I sure as hell didn't want to stay living in the same house with memories of her in it. Found this place. It was a decrepit pit when I bought it, seemed fitting."

"Why did you break up?" She's speaking so quietly I can barely hear her over the crackling of the fire and the sound of the waves breaking in the distance.

I should have brought scotch out instead of coffee. "Technically? Cheating."

"So you *did* cheat on her." I see her whole body tense up and her teeth gnash.

"Wow," I lean back in my chair. "That's what you think of me." I think this interview, or whatever the hell it is, is telling me far more about Mallory than she's learning about me. I thought I could fall in love with her, but this is how little she knows me.

"Photos don't lie, Lennox," she snarls at me. "And I read the messages she sent to you. Online."

"And? I haven't looked at any of that shit in years. Couldn't even imagine what they say and I care even less."

"Are you saying you didn't cheat on her?"

"If I have to answer that, Mallory, I'll just call the plane and have them take you wherever…"

"You said you'd answer anything," she snaps and interrupts me, her eyes hard and accusing.

I am contractually bound from discussing this, most definitely for any kind of media. But there is lava coursing through my veins and the old familiar roll in my stomach and I'm sick to death of it. "You want to know if I cheated on her, Mallory?" I stand from my chair and yell, pacing along the fire. Her head is tracking me, a tear rolls down her cheek. "I walked in on her fucking someone else in my room in the motorhome, Budapest, two years ago!"

Her hands shoot to her mouth and she gasps. "I'm…"

"No, you want to hear the gory details? You want to know?" I yell. It's too late to stop my adrenaline surge now, it's all coming out. "She was fucking our pal Digby goddamn DuPont. I had one shit season and she jumped ship for the golden boy of F1! Then," I roar as tears stream down her face, "then the little pissant joins our team and I have to play second fiddle to the motherfucker! Not because he can drive, he's a useless twat! Because of money and politics! They turn my engine down during races, Mallory! They've made a fucking joke out of me! Everything I worked for! Everything my parents gave up for me, gone!"

I can't even see straight I'm so furious. Every muscle is clenched and I'm storming back and forth looking for something to drive my fist through.

"Lennox," Mallory sobs and starts toward me.

"Don't!" I put up a hand and she stops. "Just don't." I pace back and forth until my vision returns. "You know what, do me a bloody favor and publish that," I point to her phone. "That'll definitely violate my contract and then I can get on with my life."

Enough time passes that my breathing returns stable and I lean up against the waist-high stone wall surrounding the fire pit. Mallory is still standing there watching me, full-on sobbing with tears soaking her face. She's probably freezing and I don't know why that's the thought going through my stupid head right now.

She takes another couple of steps toward me and I have no idea how I plan to react, but she doesn't come to me. Moving like a catatonic zombie, she grabs her phone from my chair, turns around, and tosses it into the fire without a word.

"What the hell?" I step forward but it's deep in the red embers and already melting, black plastic oozing, green and blue fire wrapping around it and sucking it under.

Mallory moves in front of me, her face is wracked in pain, streams pour from her eyes and run down her neck. "I am so sorry. Please forgive me," she sobs, her shoulders heaving. "I was stupid and insecure..."

Jesus, I can't.

I can't take her crying like this, fighting for breath she's so upset. I drag her to me and crush her in my arms, hold her head tight against my chest. She wraps her arms around my waist and is squeezing the air from my lungs but she won't stop crying.

Needing her closer to me I bend down and lift her up, her legs wrap around me and she clings to my neck. I walk us past the house and to the cliffs overlooking the bay and sit us in the tall grass, her still clinging to me. I don't know what else to do but sitting here watching the waves break gives me peace and we both need that.

I keep my arms around her to keep her warm, running my hands up and down her back, and eventually, she calms. "I don't want any of it, I only want you," she squeezes and mumbles into my flannel shirt. "I want to hide here with you forever and never see any of them again."

Aye, wouldn't that be a dream. If only life were that simple. I kiss her hair. I have to fix this, all of it. I can tie her father up indefinitely with lawyers far better than his but that won't mend what's broken. She'll be stripped of her dream *and* her family. I can break my contract with Celeritas and walk away but then I'll never drive again, Mum and Pop would never understand, it'll all have been for naught.

The sun finally comes out, a rarity for spring in Scotland, and the warmth heats us up. Far out in the water a couple of dolphins or whales surface. I think they're dolphins because the minke whales shouldn't be here until next month, but I've told worse lies for worse reasons. I flip Mallory around, stretch my legs out, which are both asleep and tingling, and point to the 'whales' out in the bay.

She clings to my arms around her shoulders until Bodach, the old-man-cat of the clan, finds us and crawls into her lap like the attention whore he is. "This one's taken, mate, find your own girl," I joke.

"Am I still? Mallory says softly, her head down and her hands busy petting Bodach.

"My girl?"

She nods and I feel her quiver. If she starts crying again we'll freeze to death out here, the cats will eat our corpses.

"Promise me you'll stay away from him. I can handle anything else. Just please trust me and stay away from him." I will find a way to fix everything as long as she trusts me on this.

"I promise you," she swivels her hip to take my chin in her palm and looks into my eyes.

I drop my forehead to hers. "There's something else you need to know."

She pivots on her ass and turns to face me, her eyes swollen and bloodshot. I don't want to see her cry ever again. I'll figure something out, I have to. But at this moment, I can make her laugh, see her smile again. "The nearest Apple store is like, five hours away, love."

"Oh my god, you asshole!" She smacks my chest with both hands and falls into laughter as my arms capture her and we fall back to the ground. I pull her body onto mine and drag her head down until her lips meet mine. She's kissing me with intent, remorse, determination. Damn if I don't take everything she has to give, her tear-drenched hair cascading over us in sheets.

She comes up for air and Bodach sticks his cold nose and fish breath right between our faces. "Bloody cockblocker," I roll over, help Mallory up, and consider how to spend the rest of the day while the sun is out.

"Would you agree we have more trust issues to work out?" I wag my eyebrows at her.

Her eyes close and she takes a deep breath, "Oh god, now what?"

"Let's get you changed."

Twenty minutes later, Mallory comes out of the house in jeans, boots, and the leather jacket I instructed her to put on. I've pulled out my Harley V-rod, the only bike in the garage suitable for a passenger, and I'm leaning up against it in the driveway with one of my spare helmets for her.

She shakes her head at me knowingly but walks up for the challenge nonetheless. "You ever ridden?" I ask and slip the helmet on her head. Like the jacket, it's too big but I strap the helmet down tight. The image of her as my hot biker chick is making me twitchy and hard.

She shakes her head, the helmet bobbing side to side on her neck, "No, but I trust you." Damn it, now the helmet is on and I can't even kiss her for that.

"All you have to do is hang on and enjoy the ride."

"There's a sex joke to be made here but I'm too nervous to think of it right now."

"Hop on behind me," I tell her as I mount the heavy iron monster. She throws one leg over and then I grab her behind both of her knees and pull her frame up close, pressed hard against me and I wrap her arms around my waist.

I fire the bike up and Mallory flinches at the loud roar and thundering idle. "I got you, love," I reassure her and guide us out of the driveway slowly so she can get used to the sensation.

Pulling onto the asphalt road and heading east to pick up the main road that will wind us all along the north coast and past Duntulm Castle, I open the bike up a little bit. She's squeezing me for dear life but the feel of her legs around my frame and her tits pressed into my back is bliss. With my left hand, I cover her hands on my waist and reassure her. I tilt my head back and yell so she can hear me, "Ok?" I feel her helmet nod, knocking into mine, and her death grip loosens.

By the time we're cruising past Loch Harport, Mallory's relaxed enough that her hands have traveled to my hips and I can feel her untucked from my back, her head held up and looking from side to side. It's a smooth, scenic ride along the rugged coastline and she shouldn't be too cold today in her jacket and with me blocking the wind. I still check the temperature of her hands around me every few minutes and keep an eye out for suicidal sheep. "Doing ok?" I yell back to her so she can hear me over the bike.

"Yes," she nods, "go faster!"

I fill with pride and open the bike up, gliding over the old A863 stone bridge that crosses the Amar River and up the sweeping hills past Loch Caroy with the roaring thunder only a Harley can provide. There are a million little feeder roads that lead down to overlooks on the coast and she taps my shoulder or points to at least half of them for me to stop.

We stop to eat, make out, and maul each other near Knott where we head south along Loch Snizort Beag before we zip north again. She can't resist the signs for Fairy Glen, a little town that's capitalized on the unusual landscape, suggesting fairies created all the grassy topped hills and ponds in between. She leaves an obligatory coin on the stone spirals which, one of the tourists tells her, is an offering to the fairies for good luck.

At the ruins of Duntulm Castle at the northernmost point, she's amazed at the 14th-century structures and now understands why my house is practically new construction. I take the long route home down the east coast through the capital town of Portree and by that time, a drive that should have taken three hours has taken eight. Even though she wants to keep going, it's dark and her hands are colder than I'd like.

Back at home, I drop her off at the front door then park the bike in the garage. By the time I get two steps inside the house her sweet lips are all over mine. "Make love to me," she whispers.

And I do.

Not like last night which was hard and rough and we extracted everything from one another over and over in a fury of pent up need. Tonight I kiss her eyelids and caress her face. Tonight she asks me to skip the condom because she's on the pill and wants to feel my skin, all of me inside her. I ease myself into her slowly and I hold her close and let her feel my body over hers, my arms protecting her from anything and everything. When she comes, a tear rolls from the corner of her eye and I kiss it away.

I don't sleep much tonight, but I hold her tightly against me and try to figure out what I'm going to do.

For her, for me.

For us.

Twenty Two

"You can run your whole life but not go anywhere." - Social Distortion - Ball and Chain

Mallory

"As long as you aren't hurt, I won't care."

"Don't you have one that's self-driving? Those are meant for people like me." On our last day in Scotland, Lennox is forcing me to drive a black and orange McLaren up and down the tiny road in front of his home. There are no neighbors near us but if another vehicle comes onto the road, I'm convinced I will panic and launch his million dollar car straight into it.

"People don't need cars in New York City," I argue, going so slow down the road that the car is just idling along.

"Still something you should be able to do, just in case."

I feel a little paranoid when he says things like this, it's happened a few times in recent days. Like he's preparing me for an eventuality no one can stop, or a zombie apocalypse. We have been watching a lot of horror movies…

In an about-face, Lennox brought me to his parent's house, his childhood home, the day after we fought. His 'Mum and Pop,' as he calls them, are the parents I've dreamed of since I was a little girl. They're humble, warm, and the pride in their eyes for their sons is so bright it could fuel the entire east coast power grid. Lennox adores them, and I understand why.

While Pop—I was immediately instructed that I am to call them

Mum and Pop 'like everyone else'—has an accent so thick I missed half of his words, they welcomed me. Part of me felt like one of the strays everyone says Lennox is forever bringing home, but in a good way. He gets that from his parents, who took in both Matty and Jack, and others when they needed help. The modest three-bedroom house they refuse to move from is a wayward home for anyone needing unconditional love, support, and a home-cooked meal.

Bram didn't stay long, he had pressing girlfriend matters to attend to. He's a spitting image of a younger Lennox so it's easy to imagine the trouble he's getting into with girls now that he's sixteen. He idolizes his big brother and now, more than ever, I understand why Lennox is so conflicted about his advancements in karting and path to the junior Formula series.

We traverse the island several times over when it's not raining. By my request, Lennox took me around on the motorcycle several more times. Not only is it a great way to see the beauty of this land, but I felt free on the back of his bike. Worries disappeared for those moments in time. And, in all honesty, it was an excuse to have my arms around him all day.

He drove past the marina where Pop worked from the time he was a kid until he was forced into retirement when Lennox started pro racing. Apparently, tourists, media, and well-intentioned but overstepping fans started turning up more than paying customers and disrupted the business more than the owner could tolerate. Pop maintains Lennox's home and estate while he's away, saying it gives him something to do, allows him to 'earn his keep.' Like his oldest son, who has my heart, sarcasm laced with a bit of truth runs deep in the older generation.

The distillery where Mum worked is the oldest on the island and we had a private tour. Lennox schooled me on the differences between whiskey, bourbon, and scotch. Mum took a job here when he was just a kid because karting is hella expensive. They each took several jobs to afford Lennox his dream that started when he was just three years old and Pop made him that first homemade, tiny kart that still hangs on the garage wall.

Mum showed me pictures of him as a kid at the kart tracks all over Europe and when she pointed to other kids in the photos, snarling words at a few of them in Gaelic, Lennox set back and let her tell the story. They were a poor, working-class family, there's no two ways about it. Good, honest people that Lydia and Robert Mitchell would look down upon. Karting and the path to F1 is rife with money, it's the playground for the ultra-wealthy. Until Lennox got picked up by sponsors, Pop couldn't afford professional gear or mechanics so Lennox turned up in homemade, old beat up karts, used race suits and hand-me-down helmets. The privileged junior Digby DuPont's of the world terrorized him. They'd break parts of his kart so he couldn't race, they called his dad a pauper.

But he showed up week after week and outraced them.

Unlike mine which live inside my heart and stay hidden by my image-obsessed family, Lennox's scars and perceived failures have all been public. From the loathsome way Kate humiliated him to Celeritas debilitating him on track every Sunday. Having to work alongside Digby every single day after what he did, what he continues to do. The way people in my own industry have exploited him, even I tagged a scarlet A on his chest without knowing the whole story. I hope my guilt over that will fade, in time, and that he truly does forgive me.

The weight that must be on his shoulders devastates me. I want to take it all away. The man he is here, on this island, is miles away from all of that stress and pain. I never want to leave here. I want to stay hidden in this fortress with him where we are free of my parents, Celeritas, Digby, Kate, and even the media that has rubbed salt in every wound of his life. I never want him to know that pain again.

I can't point to the day or time on this island that I fell in love with him. His walls have all come down, he's let me in and allowed me to see the real man. The one no one else is lucky enough to see. Maybe I loved him even before we landed here, but I can't deny it anymore. There have been moments where I'm looking into his eyes and it almost leaves my mouth, and I think he's pondering the same words, but there's something stuck in my throat that won't let it come out.

Fear.

This is all so new, so fast. What happens when the season ends and I go back to New York? Do I want to go back to New York? I'd rather stay here but that's a bit premature and I scold myself for the naive fantasy.

What happens if Dickby, Celeritas, or even my father ruin it all before then? That's far more probable.

Lennox has his dream and I have mine, if both don't get crushed before the season ends and send us each our own separate ways. We're too new to survive that and we've made no promises for what happens after the last race in Abu Dhabi.

But for now, I've pushed it all out of my mind as much as possible and have spent this time relishing in his company. I haven't even replaced my phone yet. When we're curled up on the couch in his barren living room watching black and white monster movies, or sitting beside the bonfire he makes every night, I almost forget who he is.

Until his eyes light with fire, his words get filthy, and he issues me sexy commands. Then I very much remember the competitive, bossy, powerful asshole he is.

And I absolutely love it.

For all the jackass things he does during the day, sabotaging his own interviews and letting his false playboy persona run wild, when he takes my clothes off, he makes me feel comfortable, special.

Twenty Three

Headline: Your Barcelona Driver of the Day - Lennox Gibbes

Blog: While the Uber Wealthy Party in Monaco, Lennox Gibbes... Shops at a Bookstore? Wherefore Art Thou, Paddock Playboy?

Headline: Gibbes Presented with Prestigious Fans Choice Autosports Award in Montreal

Mallory

If I ever have the time and money, I need to come back to the south of France and spend time here not working. It is the ultimate irony to be in such a beautiful place and be unable to enjoy it.

Despite the warnings from Sandra and the fact that I have been a good bad-employee, deliberately pulling back from posting so much material on Lennox, he continues to outshine Digby at each race even if he doesn't win. He's been less of an asshole to the journalists. He gives them such long, thoughtful answers that they now joke he's been replaced by a body double. I have no choice but to fake a smile each time because he thinks he's helping me. He spends even more time with his fans at every race. They now mob the hotels the team stays in and he stands outside until every single one has a signed item or a selfie.

Digby's been even worse for weeks because of it. When hundreds of photos and blogs were posted of Lennox shopping in Monaco, Digby's home race, it particularly enraged him. Digby had won that race yet all the internet and the paddock could talk about was Lennox at a freaking bookstore. Insta videos poured in of him flipping through language books because now he wants to learn Italian. Then he signed random books for people and even read to kids in the children's section. He read. To children. In several languages.

I can't control that the world finds that insanely attractive. They're videos posted by the public, I can't make them disappear. And what am I going to do, tell Lennox to kindly go back to biting everyone's heads off and insulting reporters? Please stop being so sweet and wonderful so you don't get us both fired?

I'm certainly not going to heap more stress into his life and tell him what Sandra has me doing. Despite Digby's tantrums, Lennox has been happier since Scotland. He lets more things run off his shoulders, and I'm going to keep it that way.

But now that he's showing the world a tiny fraction of the man he really is, in a misguided attempt to help me keep my job, I assume, the world has latched onto him.

It's out of control.

So out of control that Sandra has scheduled a Skype call with me saying the topic was not an "email appropriate conversation." Corporate speak for someone not wanting to leave a trail of evidence.

While the cars are on track qualifying at the Circuit Automobile Paul Ricard, I want to be in the garage with Matty and Jack keeping my eyes on Lennox. Instead, I am ferreted away in Lennox's suite in the motorhome waiting for the call to come. I am a bundle of shaking nerves, and it's not the sugar rush from all the delicious French pastries Tatiana and Francesca have been stuffing us with.

My mouth goes dry when my laptop screen finally lights up with the call notification. Coming into focus, Sandra is not pleased. Less pleased than usual, even.

I'm so frazzled I don't even let her start, I know what this is about. "Sandra, I'm doing what you said. I can't do anything about the fan awards or the pictures regular people post online, the blogs, the..."

"I realize," she cuts me off waving her hands in front of my screen to stop my rambling. "They're very unhappy, Ms. Mitchell. Very unhappy." Of course, she means the scroogey DuPont's and their sniveling man-child son who throws tantrums whenever he doesn't get exactly what he wants.

"What can I do?" Lennox is going to inadvertently destroy his career at this pace, by being himself, something I encouraged him to do. I can't bear even more humiliation heaped onto him and I've been running myself ragged trying to stay far away from Digby so there are no other head-smashing incidents.

If I thought Lennox was an overbearing, territorial brute before, he has really ratcheted up his overprotectiveness ever since Scotland. I am glue to Matty and Jack at each race, velcro to their sides. It's so bad Matty asked me if I was coming with to 'take a piss' because I followed him absentmindedly even as he started walking into the restroom.

"Mr. DuPont has requested... demanded your services," Sandra says, rubbing her eyes as if this is as painful for her as it is for me.

"Excuse me?" My services? Like, buy me, Pretty Woman style? Is that what he did with Kate, that vile man-whore? Apparently, he can't even get his own women, he needs to steal those from Lennox, too.

"Your social media, marketing services," she clarifies and I let out a sigh of relief. No wait, that's not much better! "As he explained, you must be doing such a good job that the Number One driver should have the best representation."

"No. No, no no, Sandra." I shake my head. "I can't do that!"

"We have no choice, Ms. Mitchell. He..." her head swivels from side to side making sure no one can hear her and then she whispers, "he has the Board in his pocket, Mallory. With the recent err, 'racing incident' in the hallway, we have no choice."

"Lennox will kill him! Literally, kill him!" I'm not even exaggerating. I can picture Lennox burying Digby in the Highpoint Cemetery and god help me, I'd help him dig the grave.

"Be smart," Sandra sneers. "You think that's not exactly what he's banking on?" She taps her pen on her desk, takes her glasses off and rubs her eyes before continuing. "You'll do social engagement and sponsor events with both drivers. We can increase your salary..."

"I don't want more money, Sandra! I c-can't do this to Lennox!" My stupid, stupid eyes are filling up with moisture and I'm so frustrated. I promised him I would stay away from Digby. I learned long ago that life is not fair but this is unreal.

"I warned you not to get involved," she shakes her head but it's not disappointment, I don't think. It's sympathy. "Mr. DuPont has been given your phone number, email, and he'll be expecting your assistance effective immediately."

Sandra wishes me good luck before she disconnects and I laugh. Luck, ha. Maybe I should have put more coins on the stones at Fairy Glen.

I pace back and forth in the tiny suite of the motorhome and stress eat all the little chocolates on Lennox's desk from some fan. Sorry kind stranger, but he can't eat them anyway and I need them.

He can't find out about this, he just can't. If he retaliates, Celeritas will terminate his contract, which is exactly what Digby wants, and then he's done driving, forever. Just like my NBA client who went too far and never recovered, Celeritas will kick him to the curb and he'll never recover. There are only ten teams on the grid and severing a contract will blackball him.

I'm sick with the thought, I can't stand keeping secrets from him. He's been so honest with me, showed me his scars. But that's why I have no choice. I won't open those wounds up, dig my fingers inside, and aggravate the injury. I have to hide this from him, too, for his own good.

Twenty Four

Headline: Disastrous Finish for Gibbes, Engine Failure at France GP
Headline: "No Explanation" from Celeritas for Mechanical Issues Causing Gibbes France DNF

"There's just so much goddamned weight on my shoulders, all I'm trying to do is live my motherfucking life. Supposed to be happy, but I'm only getting colder. Wear a smile on my face, but there's a demon inside." - Five Finger Death Punch - Jekyll and Hyde

Lennox

"Mal, why's your phone locked?" I call to Mallory who's just stepping out of the shower at my place. Only Matty and Jack are in the residential building with us at headquarters, so she's been able to spend the night and not sneak off before morning comes.

I don't like the sneaking at all and wish she'd just come out with it, let us be a public thing, but she's insistent it'll get her fired or ruin her reputation. It doesn't make me feel great that being with me could be career damaging but I know I'm taking that personally when I shouldn't, so I quit bringing it up.

And then I took advantage of the sneaking. Late at night, I took her on the hotel balcony overlooking La Sagrada Familia in Spain. Ate her on the deck of a boat on the Mediterranean Sea in Monaco. Licked maple syrup off her body in Montreal in my hotel room. That one wasn't my most creative, but I was short on time and she had no complaints after the cleanup shower led to Round Two.

I planned to make up for it in the French Rivera but then I was in no mood after my engine blew up and caught fire due to a "mysterious" oil leak and I didn't even finish the race, lost out on all the points. I know what that was all about, more corruption inside the snake pit. But I've bitten my tongue, figuratively and literally, and tried to shield Mallory from it as much as possible.

Plus, Mallory's been exhausted, up late working on her laptop and phone. She's been awake before me the past few days, which isn't like her. She says it isn't her parents causing trouble but I know she's worried about her job here despite me doing my damndest to not cause her any additional stress.

"I didn't hear you, what'd you want?" She steps out of the bathroom with a white bath towel wrapped around her body, another one drying her long, wet hair. She's so beautiful I lose track of my thoughts when she's around. I'm out of my skull for this girl. She's the most real thing in my life standing before me right now. Exposed, wet, raw, honest.

"Come back to bed. Dick-on-Demand is having a big sale. A real blow out. Huge savings." Like the crass asshole I am, I point to the size of the bargains currently tenting the bedsheet.

"As much as I love a good dick sale, I have a meeting with Sandra. Then we have the sponsor event with Hintz-Hegmann in London."

I groan. There's been a lot of phone calls and meetings with the Dragon Lady lately. Maybe sponsorships are picking up since I've been behaving myself, which was half the goal for Mallory's nanny position. I guess that's good, for her. I'll deal with more glad-handing if it helps her. "Hintz-who?"

"Hintz-Hegmann. They're new. Synergized Eco-Centric Middleware." She makes air quotes around the words and I look at her like she's speaking pig latin, which she may as well be. "They reinvent real-time functionalities," she continues.

I may drive cars around in circles for a living, as Robert Mitchell so ignorantly stated, but I am not a stupid man. Another stereotype, of not just me, but all the drivers. We're some of the most honed athletes on the planet and we've been trained and educated for decades to get here, the pinnacle of motorsports. Well, those of us who didn't buy our way in.

That said, what the fuck is eco-centric middleware? "What does that mean?"

"I have no idea, just look pretty and smile for the cameras," she shrugs.

"Mmmmkay," I shake my head. I should probably be a good little boy for Celeritas and Google that before the event. "Anyway, I was going to Airdrop the photos from home to you but the password protection is on," I hold her phone up to show her. Her old phone, the one she burnt to death and sent to an ashy grave in my fire pit, was never locked.

"Oh," she swipes it from my hands, "it's the new phone, must not have updated the settings. Go ahead and send the pics now." She walks back into the restroom with her phone and I send the photos to her from mine.

Scrolling through the selfies she took of us, I find myself lying in bed smiling like a schoolboy. They remind me of better days when it was just us at home. Her in my sweatpants, kissing by the fire, spending the whole day in my bed, watching her investigate tide pools along the shore.

I haven't been home since. It'd be easy to blame my schedule but I haven't made an effort to go home, either. It will feel empty without her now. Even more empty than it already is. When I go back home, I want her with me and she's been too busy. I watch her get dressed and blow-dry her hair through the bathroom door and picture her in Scotland permanently. I imagine her at Mum and Pop's on Christmas morning with Bram and Jack and Matty and I. I'm a lovestruck boy when she kisses me goodbye.

A couple of hours later I've worked out and am dressed in team gear ready to act like a dancing bear at the circus for whoever Hintz-Hegmann are. Mallory has her little black Celeritas skirt on and her ass looks fantastic. I can get through the event if I focus on that visual. We head out of our building and I open the doors to the LaFerrari to help her in for the drive into London.

She seemed off after her meeting with the Dragon Lady but was rushing to get ready. I need to make some serious decisions, Abu Dhabi will be here before I know it and I now accept I don't want her to go back to New York. Like a selfish prick, I find myself wondering if she'd consider opening her firm somewhere in Europe. Even if she wanted to, she'd need to be in London or Berlin or Paris, not on an isolated island in the Hebrides.

I don't know how but we could figure something out. Once I'm out of my contract maybe the next team will be headquartered in a city that would work for her. We'd be apart so much, though, with me on the road more than half the year. I sigh, knowing I'm jumping the gun, but I could make something work.

"Oh Ms. Mitchell, will you be joining me for the drive to London?" The hair on my neck stands up as I spin to see Dickhead DuPont prancing through the parking lot in his boat shoes, the lights of his Hummer flashing as he unlocks it with the key fob.

"And why would she be riding with you in that monstrosity you drive to compensate for…" I wave at the ugliest vehicle ever to drive onto the Celeritas lot, but Mallory cuts me off.

"No, I have work to discuss and will be riding with Lennox," she calls back and scurries into the car. "Please just get in, Lennox," she looks at me with pleading eyes while trying to pull the gullwing door down.

Dickhead winks, actually winks at me, but I close Mallory in the car and get in my side, not letting him provoke me again. "The hell is that about?" I ask her as I start the car up.

"I don't know, he's an idiot. Please ignore him, Lennox." Her foot is tapping against the floorboard and I sigh, hating that he's making her uncomfortable, that this situation between us is making her life more difficult.

Pulling out of the parking lot and swerving around Dickhead's Small-Dick-Mobile because sometimes testosterone wins the battle and because today I'm not in an F1 car my team has crippled, I drive us the hour into London. Mallory's so tired she sleeps most of the time, her time awake spent doing god knows what social media duties on her phone and sighing.

"Ok, so you need to schmooze the founders, Chase Hintz and Bernie Hegmann," Mallory rattles off as we head inside a snooty bar and restaurant that's marked as closed for a private event. "All the company exec's will be there, but those two are your targets."

I mm-hmm and roll my eyes and let her out of the car. Another day, another bullshit glad-handing.

"Sandra wants me to take extra photos and stuff today. So, just so you know," she fidgets with her purse strap and looks at the ground as we walk, "I'll be floating around the whole event, you may not see me much."

"Ok," I mumble. "Are you ok? You're acting weird."

"Yeah, just tired." She squeezes my hand then lets it go before anyone sees us. "They're a really important potential sponsor."

Sure enough, I don't see much of Mallory during the event. I spotted her by the bar a bit ago, standing with one of the H founders and Dickhead and my blood pressure rose but she tapped her iPad and mouthed the word "photos" to me before disappearing. I forced myself calm and wished I was drinking something stronger than club soda but I'm driving her home and probably don't need alcohol clouding my judgment in this close proximity to Dickhead.

Another hour later, I still don't know what reinventing real-time functionalities means but I have been perfectly polite nodding my head and charming the employees and two founders. Whatever real-time functionalities are, they're a definite fit for the F1 target audience, I agreed.

Even the Dragon Lady would be pleased and hopefully, she'll lay off Mallory. The club sodas are running through me and I excuse myself from the thrilling conversation about eco-centric middleware. Two employees stop me on the way to the bathroom for selfies. I smile. I deserve some kind of phony-fuck trophy for this. Eh, on second thought, no, I don't want that tarnishing the real trophies in my garage.

And then the smile is gone as I open the bathroom door. Dickhead is tucking himself back into his pants in front of a urinal and Mallory is standing inside the men's room clutching her iPad, her back turned and looking up at the ceiling. Seeing me, her jaw drops and her eyes go huge.

"Lennox," she gasps.

"The fuck?" I look between her and Dickhead who is wearing a smug grin as he strolls to the sink.

Mallory stands in front of me and puts her hand on my arm, "Lennox, please..."

"Get in the car," I growl at her, staring at Dickhead, my whole body getting twitchy.

"Aw, don't be a poor sport, chap," Digby gloats, shaking his hands off over the sink.

"Lennox please, let's just go, come on, please," she begs and pushes against my chest urging me out of the room.

Every cell in my body wants to give Dickhead something to gloat about and it takes every ounce of self-control to let Mallory pull me out of the room by my arm. I do, but I'm livid even as she gets into the car and I slam the door down, fire the car up, and tear out of the parking lot.

She's looking at her knees and clutching the iPad to her chest. "It's not what it looks like," she finally mutters.

"Yeah? Why don't you tell me what it was, then?" This goddamn Ferrari cannot go fast enough no matter how much I mash the pedal down and snap the paddle shifter.

"Please slow down," she grabs the door handle as I swerve between two cars and the car rocks back and forth.

Her shoulder seat belt strap is loose so I reach over with my right hand and jerk it down with one quick pull, squealing us around a corner with my left hand on the wheel. "Thought you liked when I drive, love, or was that a lie, too?"

"Not like this! And I didn't lie!"

"What the bloody hell were you doing? I asked you to stay away from him!"

"I told you, I had to get some extra collateral. For Sandra."

"Really, Sandra wanted dick pics, or what?" What possible excuse could there be for being in a men's room with the devil incarnate with his dick out? I asked her to do one fucking thing, stay away from him. The car lowers to the asphalt and the wing opens as soon as we hit the M1 in seventh gear.

"You're scaring me," she whimpers and clenches her eyes shut.

I take a deep breath and back off the throttle, somehow made to feel like *I* am the asshole in this situation. "How could you?"

"I swear to you, nothing happened. I just, I needed a quote and he made me follow him in there to get it." She's still staring at her knees. If everything were Kosher she'd be looking at me, yelling at me, arguing back.

"After everything I told you? I told you who he is. I fucking told you everything, Mallory! He's the dangerous one and you're scared of *me*? I asked you to stay away from him, just stay the hell away! Why can't you do that?"

"Nothing happened! Please just let it go! You can't act like a madman or Celeritas is going to fire you!"

"Fuck Celeritas!" I smack the steering wheel. "I don't give two shits about Celeritas, Mallory, I don't want you around him!"

"Then I'm asking you to let this go and don't let him provoke you for *me*. So that *I* don't get fired."

There's a tear rolling down her cheek again but I can't look at her. I am too furious. I don't think she really fucked Dickhead in the bathroom. I mean, minimally, Mallory's not exactly a bathroom quickie kind of girl. But something is going on. She's lying to me.

Goddamn this noise inside my head. I can't go through this again, it'll kill me this time. She'll kill me.

I don't speak the rest of the way home, my mind going faster than the car as I think about the locked phone, the increase in the number of alleged meetings, all the text messages from Aria and Cody all of a sudden. Hell, in France after I blew the car up and wanted to leave the track, she told me she wanted to stay and watch the rest of the race with the guys, that she'd meet up with me later. Why didn't that tip me off?

Because I've been an idiot.

A thousand times last night I almost got up and stormed into her apartment. All night I fought the urge to argue and demand answers. All night I went back and forth asking myself if I am seeing things, being paranoid because of past transgressions.

But she lied. At the bare minimum, she made me a promise and is choosing her job duties over everything I told her. I've never brought anyone home or told her the things I told her. Years together with Kate and I never let her meet my parents.

In a particularly low and gross moment in my life I can never get back, I poured over all of DuPrick's media and the Celeritas pages looking for any incriminating evidence, photos of them together. I went through all of Mallory's accounts. I don't even know what I'm looking for but I didn't find it and then I felt even worse.

I didn't even do that when I saw, with my own eyes, Digby banging Kate on my bed. I saw it with my own eyes so I didn't have to go looking for proof, but I realize I also never felt like this about Kate. I was pissed, not hurt. Now it's pain pressing down on my chest like a million tiny daggers.

She had to know it would hurt me to find her in the bathroom with DuPrick, his dick in his hands. But she wouldn't cheat, leave me for him, would she? What else is going on if she's lying to me, if she can't keep the simple promise to stay away from him?

My phone buzzes again and I assume it's another message from Mallory that I read over and over but can't respond to yet. But it's Matty and I'm late, I was supposed to be in the gym fifteen minutes ago. I run my fingers through my hair. Work, Matty, and Celeritas will have to wait, this is more important.

Lennox: Help me understand. Can we talk?

Mallory: I'm in a meeting. Later? Please?

Another meeting. How convenient. It's just as well, I need to do something with this frustration and making myself crazy isn't helping.

Two hours of cardio, boxing, and the speed-bag has helped to take the edge off even if my mind is still in warp speed. I'd prefer to stay longer, keep at it, picture Digby's face on the heavy bag. But Matty's pissing and moaning about strained muscles and I don't enjoy ice baths. And I need to resolve this with Mallory, now.

Matty's been eying me suspiciously the whole time but the nice thing about Finnish culture, they don't talk a lot. Small talk is considered rude and worse, inefficient. I appreciate that when he does speak, it's the truth, there's no hidden agenda. What a rarity.

I consider asking his opinion as I sit on the weight bench and wipe the sweat off, but he's just going to reiterate that I'm an asshole. He won't expand or go into details, because being an asshole pretty much sums it up perfectly.

My entire life has been dominated by my career since I was old enough to walk. She's entitled to the same. I can deal with that, I'll support her. I can't deal with her around Digby and not trusting me to stay away from him. Lying to me, hiding things from me. Just act fucking Finnish and tell me the truth so I can fix it.

"Phone's been going off all day." He tosses it to me and goes about re-racking weights.

I set it down next to me on the bench, not wanting to look, and run the towel through my sweaty hair. Buzz buzz buzz. Buzz buzz buzz. Over and over. I just want a minute to think but it's relentless. I give up and glance sideways at it on the bench. A picture of Mallory flashes on the screen then disappears.

What is that about? I pick up the phone and swipe it open. Sixteen messages from some foreign phone number not in my contacts. I look through the first few photos.

Mallory on a couch. Mallory bent over plugging a cord into an outlet. A side profile of Mallory tying her hair up. What the hell is this?

"Matty, you recognize this number?" I hold the phone up so he can see it.

"377, that's Monaco's country code," he answers immediately, throws another weight onto the rack, then makes the connection at the same moment I do. He's over my shoulder in an instant, watching as I swipe through the rest of the pictures.

Mallory with a glass of wine next to her laptop. Mallory smiling at something. Someone's hand on her knee. Then I get to Mallory in a bedroom, her back facing the camera. Then one of her pulling a Celeritas shirt over her head, her back naked except for red bra straps. I don't make it any further.

I recognize those brick walls now, the old leaded windows in the photos.

I storm out of the gym with Matty beside me. We don't speak but we both know where we're going.

Past the administration building, through the garden, past a parking lot, all of it in silence storming over the brick walkways until we round the final corner and pass through a cluster of evergreen trees.

Mallory's back is to us. She's looking up at a shirtless Digby in the entryway of his residence building as he lets her out.

They say something and she starts down the sidewalk toward our building in the opposite direction. Digby catches a glance of Matty and me, adjusts his dick in his pants, and lets the door close in front of him, smiling at me like a fool.

"Don't," Matty puts an arm over my chest.

Black stars creep in from the corners of my eyes, my blood runs cold. If any of my internal organs or systems were working I would throw up. I should want to kill him, drag him out of that brick house and beat him within an inch of his life like I did the last time.

But I'm overwhelmingly hollow, a shell of a man standing here looking down on myself like an out of body experience.

"I'm sorry, man," Matty mutters.

Twenty Five

"Take me back to the night we met, and then I can tell myself what the hell I'm supposed to do. And then I can tell myself not to ride along with you. I had all and then most of you, some, and now none of you" - Lord Huron, The Night We Met

Mallory

I cannot wash the filth off my body no matter how hard I scrub or how hot the shower water gets. I've been lather, rinse, repeating for an hour. That vile pig kept touching my leg, touching my arm, then he dumped a whole glass of red wine down my chest. I'm pretty sure he did it on purpose after I repeatedly told him I did not want his wine. The weasel probably roofied it. I refused to put his disgusting shirt that he offered on and wore Lennox's Celeritas jacket home zipped all the way up to my neck like a nun.

I hate this so much I am sick to my stomach. I hate that I left Lennox in bed this morning, lying to him as he was being so sweet to me begging me to come back to bed. Making up meetings, secreting around, this is not who I am. But I have to do this, for both of us. I will get us through this if I have to take a million showers every day to get Digby's stench off me.

Digby DuPraved suddenly decided he needs to launch new social media accounts and demanded I come to his flat. I tried meeting him in the admin building, the cafeteria, I tried flat out refusing.

And that's when he showed me his true self, sending me copies of Lennox's contract illustrating all the ways he could ruin him. If I played nicely for the next three months, the rest of the season, he said, Lennox would be out of his contract and free to drive for any other team without damage to his reputation. And without incurring the fifty-million pound fine that was laid out in black and white if he walked out of his contract.

Of course, Digby made sure to specify that he would not ruin my career either, as long as I did what was asked. He made it clear he could do that, too. I don't even care about that anymore, but I won't let him do this to Lennox again. I won't let him take away everything Lennox has worked for since he was a little kid in those karting photos. I just need to get through these next three months and somehow not destroy my relationship with Lennox in the meantime. Keep Lennox away from Digby and not let him be provoked, that's exactly what Digby wants, just like Sandra said. If I can do that, three months, ninety days, I'm out. My dreams will be intact and Lennox will be out, away from these sick bastards, and he can go to one of the other nine teams, wherever a seat is open. They'd be lucky to have him. He's a world champion, for god sake.

He can race for a real team again, make his fans and his parents proud again. Even if I know his parents are proud of him no matter what, well, I understand how he feels all too well.

Ninety days, Mallory. You can do ninety days. You have to.

Getting dressed, I pull on a pair of tight jeans I know Lennox likes and his Talisker Distillery hoodie. I know it's silly but he has a weakness for me wearing his clothes and I need all the help I can get. I spend more time on my hair and makeup, too. My eyes are puffy and bloodshot but, through the wonders of black mascara, I try to hide that.

As good as it's going to get under such duress, I knock on his flat door. He doesn't answer but maybe he's still not speaking to me despite his text? I use my key and open his door, calling for him. Damnit, he's not here.

Marching back into my apartment I find my phone and enter the dumb passcode I had to put on to keep Lennox from seeing all the godforsaken texts from Digby which he always kept just professional enough to not be incriminating, but slimy enough to make me queasy.

Douchebag: Ms. Mitchell, I don't like to be kept waiting…

Douchebag: Great post, Mallory. I'd like to see you tonight about a different kind of post requiring your attention.

Douchebag: Thank you for a productive afternoon, Ms. Mitchell. Oh, you forgot your blouse in my flat. Whoops! ;)

The last one is from today, that pig. I'm so mad. I've screen-capped everything but it's not going to do any good. Even Sandra said he has the whole board of Celeritas in his pocket.

Backing into my iPhone messages, there's a blue dot next to "Lennox." Thank god, he finally replied.

Lennox: Guess you were right, photos don't lie.

There's a picture attached and I blow it up and squint at it. It's... me? With my shirt off. In Digby's flat changing from my wine-soaked shirt into my jacket.

Oh my god, Digby took photos of me? The picture is taken from the door, but I closed it! That fucking pervert! And Lennox thinks... oh god, how could he not?

Mallory: Where are you? Please let me explain!

Three grey dots appear, then they're gone. Then they appear again, hover endlessly, and then his reply comes through:

Lennox: Lose the number and move on. I am.

My fingers are frantic flying over the screen, he has to understand, I did not do this. I would not do this to him. I lied but I would never sleep with Digby! I'm going to throw up. I hit send but the message won't go through, it's hung up trying to send. Send you bastard phone, send!

I can't wait, I call him. It doesn't even ring, I get an automated message that my call cannot be completed as dialed. Did he, did he block my number?

I check my signal, four bars. I call again. Same automated message.

Just to make sure my phone is working, I call the only person who will always answer my call.

He answers on the first ring.

"Cody?"

"What's up, sis'?"

"Nothing, never mind," I disconnect and start dry heaving.

In a panic, I call Lennox again and again, but it's the same thing. He's blocked me. What does he mean he's moving on? Please don't mean what I think it means.

I race back across the hall to his apartment, my hands so shaky it takes me three tries to open the door. His suitcase is gone, most of his clothes are gone. No, no, no! I have to talk to him!

Not even closing the door I race down the hallway and fly down the stairs.

"Jack!" I beat on his door on the floor below us. Tears are flowing from my eyes so hard I can't see straight. "Jack, I know you're in there! Open the fucking door!" I pound on the door more so hard my fists are red. "Please, Jack!" I wail and sob.

Finally, the door opens and Matty stands in the entryway, Jack behind him on the sofa with a beer. Matty has ice in his veins, he looks like he wants to kill me. I have never seen him look so cold. And Matty always looks cold.

"Where is he?" I try to move into the apartment but Matty puts his hands on the door and frame to block me. I push him and wiggle through his arms, he huffs in disgust.

"He's not here," Matty says as I go from room to room like a crazy person calling for him. I'm out of my mind.

"Where is he?" I scream at them again. They both just stare at me like a raving lunatic. Because I *am* a raving lunatic. "Jack, please!" I go him and beg, prey on the fact that he's always been kinder, more emotional, than Matty.

"You should go," he utters and picks at the label on his beer bottle.

"Please, I did not do this!"

"At least the last one fucked him over after one bad season. You, he has one bad *race* and that was all it took," Matty crosses his arms and sneers at me, his eye twitching.

"What? No! I did not do this! Please, just tell me where he is!"

"We saw you. With our own eyes," he's disgusted and shakes his head at me. "He's in London. Likely a club. There are fifty thousand of them, good luck. Now leave." Matty holds the door open and points the way out.

I collapse at Jack's feet at the couch, literally begging. "Please tell me," I whimper and don't even bother wiping away the snot I know is running out of my nose.

"You have to know where our loyalty will always be. You should go, Mallory." Jack runs his fingers through his hair then goes to the door, his arms crossed too, but staring at the floor.

I feel like a garden snake slithering past them out the door into the hallway where Matty slams the door in my face. I know they're right, he's gone. But I check the parking lot anyway. His car is gone.

Making my way back to my flat, I have no idea what to do. He doesn't check any direct messages, doesn't do email, his inbox had over 16,000 messages the last time I logged into it. I handle all of his digital communications. I'm the only one who will see it if I contact him in any way.

I could call an Uber and head into London. But, as usual, Matty is right. London is enormous. There are tens of thousands of places he could go, if he even went to London. Why would Matty or Jack give me a hint, no matter how trivial? They think I'm worse than Kate.

I pace from room to room in my flat until I collapse on the bed. There's no way he will ever forgive me for lying, even if I explain it to him. "Photos don't lie," he threw that back in my face, the same thing I accused him of. Stupid, stupid, stupid. How could I be so stupid?

All I can do is lie here and cry until it hurts, until my eyes are raw, and hope he comes home. Alone. Not with anyone he's 'moving on' with tonight. But he's hurt and angry. The thought wretches my stomach so violently I barely make it to the toilet in time to throw up.

Halfway through the night I get up and move to Lennox's flat. I know he hasn't come home because I would have heard it. It's not like I can really sleep even though every couple of hours my body shuts down for a few minutes. In his flat, I'm at least surrounded by him, wrapped in his sheets that smell like him, sweet torture.

Because I am stupid and desperate, I keep calling and texting him through the night. I send him a thousand messages that don't go through. I admit it in writing and tell him I love him. That I would never hurt him like that. I beg him not to throw us away and hurt me tonight.

None of them go through.

Despite exhaustion, my body launches upright when I hear the doorknob jiggling the next morning, or whatever time it is. It's daylight, that's all I can tell. My pillow is soaked and black from pools of my mascara.

"Lennox?" I run into the living room as the door opens, still in yesterday's clothes.

"Oh, sorry, Ms. Mitchell." One of the Celeritas security guards has let himself in. "Um, boy, this is awkward."

"What?" Has he been hurt, did he drive like a madman and wreck that stupid time machine car?

"Umm," the man in Celeritas security gear scratches his head. "I'm real sorry ma'am but I've been sent to remove all the personal effects and change the locks on this flat."

I don't have any words forming in my mind, just colors and swirls and stars. I race to the bathroom and throw up the only thing left inside me, putrid bile. I stagger back out and look at the man. "Do you…" I mumble.

He puts his hands up, "I don't know anything, ma'am. Just changing the locks. Do you need assistance moving any items to your flat?"

"N-no, let me just get my phone." Walking back into his bedroom I find my phone in the sheets and like a pathetic little girl, I take his pillow with me and walk past the security guard, full of shame.

In my kitchen, the tears start again. He's really serious. He's done with me.

I tap my phone screen awake to try him again. There are a series of Google Alerts waiting for me. I have them set up to ping me whenever certain keywords hit the web's search index, "Lennox Gibbes," "Gibbes Celeritas," "#LennoxGibbes2019." There's a smattering of those alerts covering my screen now.

My fingers are shaking so bad I can hardly click the links.

Headline: Celeritas' Lennox Gibbes' Wild Night in London!
Blog: The Paddock Playboy is Back, Baby!
Insta: Look who I met last night! #LennoxGibbes
PoeticPoppy: There's videos everywhere, he was sooooooo drunk lol
5FingerDiscount: Come on, dude, that's like 8 hot chicks hanging on you. Leave some for the rest of us!
PhoenixRysing: when u look like him maybe u'll have a harem 2
ManchesterUfan: is that Kate Allendale with him again? Score!

There are photos and videos on Facebook, Twitter, Instagram, Snapchat - they're everywhere. Several bars and pubs and clubs were geotagged. There are fan selfies with him on the streets of London at all hours of the night. He's stumbling drunk in one of them. In another, he catches a bra someone offscreen throws at his head. Countless women wrapping their hands around him, smashing up to the side of him for photos.

I don't even recognize the look in his green eyes, vacant.

I have nothing left in my stomach to throw up but my body somehow keeps producing tears. Those never leave me. The finality of it hits me, there is no recovering from this now. Up until this very moment I was holding onto the smallest shred of hope, but this is the end.

They've swallowed us up. And now it's too late.

It's dark when I wake up on the couch and, like a moth to a flame, I make myself check the usual platforms. There's nothing new. No messages or missed calls, either. I've been ghosted and replaced. I have no idea where he might be, not that it matters. I have no one in my corner on this entire continent and have never been so alone. Do I even have a job anymore?

With delirious thoughts speeding through my mind and the worst pain I have ever had in my head, or my heart, I check my work email.

Ms. Mitchell,

As I understand it, this email will not come as a surprise to you. Effective immediately, there has been a staff restructure. You will now solely represent Mr. DuPont. Mr. Gibbes issued this request and Mr. DuPont has accepted. In the best interest of Celeritas, I have made all the necessary arrangements. You will depart for Austria in two days with the other DuPont personnel.

Best,

Sandra Alix
Director of Marketing and Communications
Celeritas Racing

I don't have the strength to throw my phone so it slips from my hand to the floor.

Twenty Six

"See, honey, I saw love. You see it came to me, it put its face up to my face so I could see. Yeah, then I saw love disfigure me into something I am not recognizing." - Phosphorescent - Song for Zula

Lennox

Release the car. Release the car. Release. The. Bloody. Car.

I grip the steering wheel tight. I have to get out of this garage. I can see her in my periphery vision no matter how much I lock my face straight ahead, out of the garage and onto the pit lane in Austria. Standing on *his* side of the garage in *his* #16 Celeritas apparel, her head is hung low.

I had to quit drinking days ago to drive this weekend. Conveniently, I was presented with a cup to piss in this morning. I've never had a drink within days of driving but that's never stopped the 'random' tests after DuPont knows I've been out. I'm the only driver on the grid who's been tested in years. Fucking douche.

Unfortunately, without the burn of liters of scotch in my gut, things aren't numb anymore.

I focus on hating him, all the ways I want to hurt him, as I chase his car around and around the track today. I can picture it in my head, I can hear the sounds it would make, visualize the carbon fiber shattering if I just run right the hell into him at full speed.

The people watching, the factory workers in Aylesbury who would only have to rebuild everything and who depend on his farce of a team to pay their mortgages and send their kids to college are the only reasons I back off. It certainly isn't the engineers in my ear telling me to back off.

"Fuck off, don't talk to me," I bark at them through the radio in my helmet. That'll be a fine.

Good.

It's easier to fixate on one thousand and one ways to murder Digby than think about *her*, anyway. Digby has always been a prick, always will be. But *she* was supposed to be different. I let myself believe she was. Even though she showed up as another media cretin, another nanny sent to stuff me into the perfect Celeritas mold, I tamped down my suspicions and fell for it, believing she was real.

She's no more real than the rest of them. Even Matty and Jack I pay to be here, for christ's sake. That's all I have to offer anyone, money and fame. I thought that lesson has been ingrained in my brain real good the last time, but nope. Had to touch the hot stove one more time and now I'm surprised when my hands are burnt.

Wonder how long it'll be before my face is plastered all over Infinity Magazine, photos of the inside of my home across the Cooper Media websites, stories Mum and Pop told her printed in thirty-five languages for global distribution. I stayed holed up alone in a London hotel until I flew to Austria, I don't even want to go home and see the sanctuary she's ruined.

I'll stay in hotels, for now. Maybe I should get disposable apartments, at this point. I'm certainly not staying at Celeritas anymore so I can see her strolling out of Digby's flat every morning.

Jack's been running interference, assuring me she's staying on the opposite end of the current hotel - *his* floor, of course. In a fog, Jack and Matty direct me through the motorhome and paddock in a strategic dance to avoid either one of them. We're men, we don't discuss it. It just happens.

In the post-quali press pen, there's no avoiding her proximity, though. All the drivers, including Dickless, are there along with their PR people. Journalists surround us on the opposite side of the metal crowd fencing. At least I can go back to being my normal asshole self now though, there's no incentive to give these senseless questions any dignity.

"Lennox, has the team determined the cause of the engine failure in France?"

"Beats me," I shrug and down a bottle of water with as little regard as I can muster.

"I'm sorry, you don't know happened?"

"Don't know, don't care. Next question." I look behind me to toss my water bottle into a bin. Mallory's next to Digby holding her voice recorder in front of him as he speaks to another journalist but I catch her eyes for the smallest measurement of time. They're glassy and shaking.

Yeah, that doesn't work anymore, love. Sell the lies somewhere else.

"Lennox, it looks like you had other things in your mind last week. Several photos surfaced of you clubbing in London. Do you have a comment?"

"Aye, there were other things on my mind but they've been worked out of my system, all better now," I wink at the journalist and speak loudly enough for *her* to hear me. She thought I was an asshole before? Ha.

"Some online comments suggested supermodel Kate Allendale was spotted with you. Can you confirm if you've reunited?"

"Pff," I exhale and scratch my head, "there were a lot of women, mate, I couldn't tell you." The British journalist's jaw drops and he tries to stifle a laugh but out of the corner of my eye, I see Mallory turn and dart out of the media pen, her chestnut hair floating out behind her.

I could tell him I stumbled to a hotel room alone, as usual. That I haven't seen Kate in over a year and I wouldn't fuck her with Digby's dick, much less let her near mine ever again. But that wouldn't hurt *her*. That wouldn't make *her* feel even an ounce of how she's made me feel. Plus, she's full of shit.

She'll give up the act eventually. Unfortunately for her, hitching her wagon to Digby isn't going to be the saving grace she thinks it is. He'll ditch her as soon as he gets bored with her, just like he did with Kate. And all the others.

Not my problem.

From here out, my head's down. I'll do my contract for the rest of the season. There should be four open driver seats next season and Jack has scheduled meetings with two of those teams already to discuss the move. I don't care if they offer ten pence and a free beer every Sunday as a compensation package, I'm out.

I'll race again, legitimately, for any other team and that'll be the end of this bloody nightmare. I won't have to lie to Mum and Pop again, be embarrassed in front of my fans. I'll redeem myself on track like I always have.

As for *her*, she can fulfill her agenda, get her experience and references, spite her parents and build her brand with Cooper, then fuck off back to America.

"Sorry, your name is Candy?"

"Yes, but with an i."

"Candy with an I..."

"Right. C-A-N-D-I."

It's Sunday post-race and I'm leaning on the sidepod of my car in the garage bay. I blew the race and couldn't care less. Jack is rubbing the bridge of his nose with his eyes closed and shaking his head. Matty is watching us like he's witnessing a car crash.

Across the garage bay, on the devil's side, Mallory is pretending to swipe through yet another new phone after Digby berated his assistant, but I notice her glancing our way when she thinks I can't see her.

"This is the new nanny. Candi. With an I," Jack sighs.

"Nanny?" The tiny barbie thing in front of me tee-he's, "I'm a PR professional! I just graduated!"

"From high school?" I chuckle.

"From college, silly," she slaps my arm and twists her shoulders. "I'm perfectly... legal," she winks.

My shoulders heave with laughter and I slap Jack on the back. "Bloody perfect!"

Candi with an I is about 125 centimeters tall with a chest circumference to match. Her hair is down to her ass and bleached bone white, she has gigantic hot pink lips and fake eyelashes. Her voice could shatter crystal. She won't stop touching me.

I absolutely loathe her.

"Can I get a selfie?" She smashes herself into me without waiting for my answer, holding her pink bedazzled iPhone up in front of us. Looking straight ahead for the camera, I can see steam coming out of Mallory's ears. She glares at me and takes a step toward Digby and... runs her hand up his arm to his shoulder.

Oh, that's how it's going to be.

I school the tick in my jaw and the lump in my throat. I silence the spike of adrenaline that just surged into my bloodstream.

"Did your mum name you candy because you're so sweet?" I ask and watch her making duck lips in the phone screen. The words coming out of my mouth make me sick but I force them. Or, the nausea could be from the copious perfume wafting off Candi with an I. She does not smell like jasmine.

Stop it. She chose him over you. She's choosing him right now, over there, smiling up at him.

Duck Lips giggles, "You're so funny! My mom is your biggest fan, I can't wait to show her this!" She wiggles into me.

"Your mum..." I mutter as she springs up and turns to her next victim. What the hell parallel universe am I in?

"Jackey, you're next!" She tries to back into Jack to get a selfie with him, too.

"My name is Jack. And I'm gay. Extremely gay," he puts a hand up to stop her and makes a heaving motion with his shoulders feigning being sick.

Duck Lips pouts then bats her eyes at Matty.

"Stay away from me," he deadpans.

I haven't been sleeping for shit and maybe I'm delirious but I can't stop myself from laughing as I rub my exhausted eyes. I mean really, what the fuck has happened to my life?

"Ahem," Jack clears his throat, "Candi with an I is apparently the best candidate the Dragon Lady could find on short notice." His eyes swing to Mallory, then back.

"I'm very eager to please," Duck Lips pips at me, swiveling her upper body back and forth on her hips. I don't know if she thinks that's attractive or if she has to piss.

"Are ya' now," I raise an eyebrow at her. "Go fetch me a bottle of water, will you, Candi with an I?" I almost called her 'love' at the end but even though Scots call everyone 'love', I couldn't do it. I called the bloody trash collector 'love' last year when I was half asleep, but now I can't speak the word.

The woman I thought I loved is presently twenty feet away from me running her hand up Digby's back, oblivious to me. He puts an arm around her and runs one finger through her long brown hair.

"Go on, get," I swat the most vapid nanny on earth on the ass and she squeals and skirts out of the garage giggling. As I thought, Mallory couldn't ignore that, a flash of her eyes gave her away.

This feels like shit. I feel like shit acting like this but there's nothing else to be done about it. As much as she hurt me, I called Sandra the Dragon Lady and had Mallory transferred to Digby so she wouldn't even lose her precious job. So her dream would be intact when she leaves after the final race in Abu Dhabi.

Now I can either mope around like a pussy or I can keep the mask up for the next three months.

"Come on," Jack slaps my arm and I suck in a breath and jerk awake. I hadn't realized I was leaning up against the car in a vacant trance for who knows how long, staring at her. Staring at her staring at me.

I can't read her eyes. They're swollen but I can't place the emotion. Fuck, I'm exhausted and out of my skull. Pity, it's probably pity in her eyes.

"She looks like shit," Jack mumbles when we're out of earshot and walking back to the motorhome to pack up and leave for the night.

"Aye, and how do I look?"

"It's not a competition," he snaps.

"Everything in my life is a competition." I don't want to talk about this. I want it to go away. Unless I keep up the sarcasm and facade every waking minute, the pain in my chest returns.

"You can't do this the rest of the season."

"Do what," I grumble as a statement instead of a question because I know damn well what he means.

"She's hurting, mate. *You're* hurting her."

"Me?" I snarl. "What the fuck, who's side are you on?"

"I'm just saying, this isn't going to work for the next three months. Just let Sandra fire her if this is how you're going to act."

"No," I fire back immediately. I'm filled with rage and hurt but I won't steal her dreams like mine have been taken from me.

"Christ mate, figure your shit out." Jack throws open the door to the motorhome and leaves me standing in the entryway alone.

Figure my shit out. What is there to figure out? I have my plan.

Twenty Seven

"I hope you're happy now, I could never make you so. You were a hard man, no harder in this world. You made me cold and you made me hard. And you made me the thief of your heart." - Sinead O'Connor - You Made Me the Thief of Your Heart

Mallory

I can't make it ninety days.

Not being this close to him, watching him take alternate routes around the paddock to avoid me. Not when I have to stand in the garage with him so close I could take ten steps and shake him, slap him, scream at him, wrap my arms around him, kiss him.

Despite the awful things he said to the media today, despite how much I hate him right now, I have memory flashes of being held in his arms. Fantasies that he'll come to me. He'll wake me up. He'll tell me this has all been a nightmare, a sick joke. I'm in an endless loop going back and forth between angry and agony.

He won't come to me. He won't forgive me and even if he did, I couldn't forgive him now. I may not be able to find it at this exact moment, but I know I have a small scrap of dignity deep inside that wouldn't let me take back a cheater. I can't take back someone who could hurt me so badly and so deliberately.

The Paddock Playboy, what was I thinking? He was never going to change.

It's over. There will be no happy ever after, no leaping into his arms and being carried off into the sunset. But that doesn't keep the thoughts away when I have to see him. I wish there was a switch to turn it off loving someone, but there isn't.

Between fractured thoughts of Lennox, I have Digby to deal with. I'm so tired and disoriented I can't even keep coming up with nasty names for him. He is a horrible human on every conceivable level. He is vicious to his own personnel, terrible to any Celeritas staff he finds beneath him, and yet when he goes before the media he acts like a prince. Prince of darkness is more like it.

Fucking fraud.

He has me launching brand new social media pages for him in some twisted pissing contest to outdo Lennox. The idiot never had any personal pages but now it's suddenly priority number one. Well, it may fall secondary only to his priority to get into my pants. Oddly, I feel better knowing that he only wants me to destroy Lennox. His preoccupation isn't really about me.

On the wrong side of the garage today, I'm working on Digby's new Facebook page and grinding my teeth trying to dream up anything positive to say about this piece of trash pervert. He can't stop to answer my questions for thirty seconds without yelling at William, his poor beaten down assistant. Everything and anything William does is seemingly unacceptable.

"Do you have personal photos from Monaco you want me to use?" I squeeze my eyes closed and force my mouth to speak the words to Digby. I need to get through this godforsaken Facebook page and leave the garage before Lennox shows up and makes me cry again.

"Of course I do, Mallory. I live there. William! How many times do I have to tell you? Take this back and bring me an Evian!" Digby sends the battered William away again. He must jog a hundred miles a day on these demeaning errands.

"Now then, where were we? Monaco, yes?" He turns back to me and blathers.

Yes, Monaco. Where Lennox borrowed a boat one night and just the two of us went out alone onto the sea, far enough to be away from telephoto lenses, and he made love to me and whispered sweet things in my ear.

Like he's done with half the free world, you naive girl.

I clear my throat and try to concentrate. "Yes, I need photos if you want me to backfill your feed from all the earlier races this season."

"If you'd have listened to me and left that uncultured lout in Melbourne, you would have had all that you need by now, wouldn't you?" His lips flatten into a line. I have never punched a human in my life, but he's going to be the first one. This is all his fault.

"Why do you hate him so much?" How much hatred and jealousy can live inside one person?

"Oh Ms. Mitchell, I don't think I hate him as much as I imagine you do these days after he humiliated you in such spectacular fashion!"

"Why?" I ask again, my voice getting growly.

"It's simply sport at this point, darling," he puts a finger under my chin and I close my eyes, try to keep my fists from connecting with his face. "I'll take everything from him, even his women!" He laughs like the maniacal bastard he is.

I grit my teeth and shake my head.

"You'll come around, Mallory, they all do. The sooner you forget that unrefined dolt, the better off you'll be. I can take you places, you know. Sky's the limit."

Before I can respond to Digby's asinine comments, Lennox, Matty, and Jack stroll into their side of the garage and the air leaves my lungs. Lennox is leaning up against his car acting so calm and cool, so unaffected, like I was nothing to him. I guess I was. And those two friends of his that do his bidding, they can eat a bag of dicks, too.

"Just give me the photos, Digby." I try not to look at Lennox.

William has returned with a warm bottle of Evian. I don't know if William is so abused his brain no longer functions, if he's not the brightest bulb in the box, or if he's just being spiteful. They're all valid possibilities.

Digby takes the warm bottle of water from William and shoves it in his face. "You absolute imbecile. Why do I pay you? I'll get my own water, like a peasant! Do something useful and send her the Monaco photos!" Digby points his head at me then slithers his way out of the garage. God forbid he get his own fucking drink.

William reaches into his pocket and hands me an iPhone, "I guess they'd be on here?"

I swipe and open up the phone as William steps back and enjoys his moment of silence from his tyrannical boss. Is this Digby's phone? Are the photos he took of me on here? I look around nervously and find the photo folder, my fingers going as fast as they can. I can't find the photos of me, damn it. Pictures of yachts, pictures of women in bikinis on yachts, oh my god he's such a douche.

Maybe they're in the Recently Deleted album if he's as stupid as I think he is. Scroll, scroll, scroll. I don't see them. More yachts, parties, and several videos. My thumb hits one of them and it blows up on the screen and starts playing.

A party? No wait, there's a half-naked girl on a table. Is this sick fuck recording other unsuspecting women? The phone is propped on a surface and I have to crane my head to keep the perspective. A shirtless Digby comes into view on camera he bends over the girl, taps a vial of something onto her abdomen, then - oh my god. He's doing coke off her!

"What are you doing?" Oh fuck, Digby's back.

I drop my hand with the phone and hit the home button over and over to hide what I was looking at. I don't think he saw. "What are you doing with my phone?" He jerks it out of my hand.

"Getting the Monaco photos, like you said," I smile at him with as much phoniness as I can muster.

Holy shit holy shit holy shit.

My gut is rolling, between this and the turmoil I have been in for days now over Lennox, I feel like I'm going to faint. Lennox, I have to tell Lennox. This would solve all his problems at Celeritas.

"William, are you stupid? Nevermind, don't answer that. You are, indeed, stupid," Digby goes back to flogging William. I lose track of what he's even going on about, something about the private plane, maybe? Who cares, there are videos of Digby doing cocaine on his phone! It was definitely him! I'd recognize that pasty white chest and smarmy face anywhere.

Between my racist NBA player and other naughty clients of the past, I know what a video like this can do to an athlete's career. Steroid use alone has brought down legends, Digby doing blow off some women's stomach has to be enough to tank him.

I knew he was a fraud, I knew it! Mr. Squeaky Clean apparently can't keep his nose clean!

Fuck, they're in the Recently Deleted folder and are going to auto-delete themselves. I didn't even notice how many days they had left.

I don't know how but I have to get those photos and videos. I'm going to take this trash to the curb. Douchelicker Dupont, you're going down! You've fucked with the wrong New York nanny.

I need access to that phone, which means I need access to Digby. *More* access to Digby. I swallow hard.

In that moment I hear a shrill giggle from Lennox's garage bay, or it could be a seabird being strangled. A blond-haired Oompa Loompa has her triple D's plastered up against Lennox, who is laughing like a hyena and taking selfies with her.

I want to claw her eyes out. I want to slap the hell out of Lennox. I can't deal with this right now. My brain goes into survival mode. It's fight or flight time. I hear Cody's voice telling me I've always been a fighter. I'll cry more later but right now, I fight.

I touch Digby's arm, I run my hand up to his shoulder. I smile at his surprised reaction.

"What is this, Ms. Mitchell?" He licks his lips.

Stay down, bile. Stay down.

"He humiliated me in front of the entire world," I act like a wounded butterfly. It's not a had act to play right now, quite honestly, and the Oompa Loompa is illustrating my point all too well.

"Ah, a woman scorned?"

I nod to the blond bimbo nanny behind us with her pink fingernails all over the love of my life. "Two can play at this game," I shrug suggestively as Digby glances behind him.

I need to play this cool. He's stupid but I can't risk being too obvious.

"Interesting. You're a wicked one, Ms. Mitchell."

"Mr. DuPont, you have no idea." I run my palm up and down his back and he puts an arm around me while he continues his assault on William.

Across the garage, I catch a glance at Lennox slapping the Oompa Loompa's ass. I've tried to avoid looking him in the eye for days now, but mine are drawn to his. I want to tell him so much.

Why are you doing this to me? How could you?

Despite it all, I am still going to help you, you stupid asshole. I will do this for you.

It's past three in the morning and I haven't slept. At this point, I may as well stay awake for my early morning flight back to Aylesbury. But there's nothing I can do but plot so I continue to lie here and stare at the smoke detector light on the hotel room wall that blinks every three-point-six seconds.

Tomorrow, or today I suppose, I go back to the Celeritas headquarters until the next race two weeks away. Lennox will not be in Aylesbury with me. He won't be across the hall from my flat. He isn't across the hall from my hotel room now, but at least he is in this building, somewhere. I think. Is he alone like I am each night?

Doubtful. You've seen how women throw themselves at him.

Stop thinking about him. Focus on the plan.

My stomach growls. I don't remember eating today.

Knock knock. Knock. What the hell. I check the clock again. Then I sneak out of bed to see what's going on. If it's Digby at my door, I'm not ready for this. What if he doesn't have his phone? No, I'll have to stay in here and hide.

I patter in the darkness to the door and look through the peephole. My heart drops and the damn tears start to flood my eyes. Lennox is in the hallway with his long arms stretched above my door frame, his head hanging down. He has no shirt on, what the hell is he doing?

I can't leave him out there, Digby is on this floor and if he sees Lennox outside my room, it might ruin my plans. He has to believe I am anti-Lennox. I *am* anti-Lennox, damnit.

You lied but he put the nail in the coffin.

I take a deep breath and open the door to my dark hotel room. He stands upright and his face meets mine. He looks like I feel, bags under his hooded eyes, sagged shoulders. The green of his eyes is shattered.

I move aside so he can enter and he staggers two steps inside and bumps into the small office desk just inside the entry. My door closes and I turn the desk lamp on. "Are you drunk?" I whisper.

He looks around my room like the dumb asshole is expecting Digby to be there, then he shrugs. His reddened eyes are transfixed onto my shirt. His shirt, the damn Talisker Distillery hoodie. Don't ask me why I'm wearing it. I know the right thing to do is burn it.

I cross my arms and draw myself in when I catch a hint of his cologne. His hair is unruly and looks like he's been running his hands through it over and over again. Or maybe someone else has been running their fingers through it tonight. "What do you want?" I ask him when he doesn't speak.

His gaze drops from the logo of my sweatshirt to my bare legs. The hoodie comes up to my mid-thigh. His eyes come back to mine and he whispers, "You."

A tear rolls down my cheek, I can't stop it despite how angry I am. He lifts a hand to wipe it away but I smack his hand back, "Don't."

"Don't cry," his voice cracks.

My anger rises, heating my flesh and building pressure in my brain. He's been making me cry, deliberately, and now he shows up acting like he gives a shit. "What do you care? Why are you here?"

"Creature from the Black Lagoon is on TV." He mumbles.

"Are you fucking serious," I bark. "That's what you came here at three in the morning to say to me?"

"What do you want me to say?"

I could think of a million things I want him to say. But what's the point? "Nothing. I don't want anything from you. Get out."

"Please," he whispers. His nostrils flare for a breath and his chest shudders.

"Please, what? What do you want?" Despite being angry, the tears keep coming. He looks so broken I can't stand to look at him. I want to hit him and I want to hold him, not in any particular order.

"Argue with me, call me an asshole, anything."

"It's too late, Lennox. I don't want to fight with you anymore," I shake my head. These stupid tears, they sting my eyes from all the broken blood vessels.

"Don't say that," his hand comes to my face and I try to slap it away but he brings it back and his warm palm cradles my cheek. I close my eyes and try to control my breathing. "I miss you so fucking much," he whispers.

My shoulders heave, there's so much pressure in my chest. His thumb runs under my eye and he wipes away each tear that falls.

"I don't know what's real anymore, Mal." I blink through the haze and look up at him. "I don't know who's here because they care and who's here to fuck me over."

"Why don't you ask them?" I sob.

"Because the truth hurts, maybe I don't want to know." He brings his second hand up to tuck my hair behind my ear, but it's too much. As much as I want his touch, it reminds me.

"Go ask your Big Tits, your new nanny," I smack his hands away again.

"She quit."

I huff. "That's great, even she has more sense than I did."

"I told you I was an asshole," he speaks softly.

"It's not funny, Lennox. You said you were 'an asshole not a monster' but you *are* a monster!" I make air quotes about the little joke he'd always make while doing something obnoxious than sweet two seconds later. "I was real. You hurt me. You destroyed us."

"No," he grabs my hand but I pull it away. "Jesus, please stop, please let me hold you."

"You lost that privilege when you fucked half of London!" I back away from him.

He follows my steps, "I didn't. I wouldn't. You know that."

"I don't know that! Have you seen the fucking photos? How could you!" I am yelling now. If hotel security comes, that's fine with me, they can haul him away.

"All I ever wanted was for you to trust me and you still can't." He takes a step back and grabs fistfuls of hair on his head.

"I did, and you broke it!" I poke my finger at him. I am quaking from emotion.

"I know I was an asshole but I did not touch anyone else. I don't want anyone else. Mal..."

"Tell it to Kate," I snarl at him.

"Oh fucking hell," he turns his back to me with his hands on his hips. He paces a few steps before turning back. "There was no Kate! There *is* no Kate!" He's yelling too now.

"It doesn't matter, you are deliberately being cruel and I will never believe you!" I scream and look him in the eye and watch his face change. He looks like I slapped him. Like he's just been hit with the finality I've already come to realize, if not accept.

There's a long pause where all I can hear is my heartbeat before he finally says, "Well, I guess that's that, then."

"Looks that way." I stare at the wooden desk. He moves toward the exit but pauses. My insides are turning inside out, panicking because once he walks out of this room it's really over. I have to fight my body to not beg him to stay.

"You know, no matter how pathetic it makes me, I still wanted you. Even after you made my worst nightmare come true. I still wanted you. I would have forgiven you." He reaches for the door.

"I did not betray you!" I scream and stomp my foot.

His head hangs down to the floor and he nods at his feet, then looks back to me. "But you did. You've been lying to me just like the rest of them. I begged you to let me handle this. I would have given it all up for you."

"Given it up?" I rave at him. "Are you mad? This is your dream! Everything you've worked..."

"No," he interrupts me. "I just needed you to trust me. You were my dream." He opens the door and starts to leave but turns back. "I love you, Mal. Goodbye."

Twenty Eight

"These are just flames, burning in your fireplace. I hear your voice and it seems as if it was all a dream, I wish it was all a dream." - The Head and the Heart - Another Story

Lennox

I don't know why I bought this house. I envisioned a home, but it isn't. It's a house. A giant, empty house with black stones as dark as my heart. It's been almost two weeks now since I've locked myself up here like the monster in the castle. How fitting.

I quit checking my phone, no good has ever come from it. I feed the bloody cats then slip back into bed and sleep all day. The cleaning service had long since changed all the sheets by the time I pulled up the drive so any traces of her were long gone. Just as well, there are enough memories lingering to haunt my every step no matter where I go here.

I don't go to the cliff because I remember holding her there. I can't walk into the kitchen without picturing her making breakfast and wrapping my hands around her from behind, nuzzling her neck. The living room where we made love on the floor, Mallory trying to pin my hands down and teasing me into losing my mind, which was inevitable. I need to sell that stupid Harley, too. Give it to charity or something. I don't want to see it.

Eventually, it'll fade away.

I can either lay around streaming Netflix off the satellite internet and do my best to avoid old horror movies or I can pick up another house project that I've started but never finished. Or I can continue to sit outside at the fire pit drinking scotch all day and watch the flames dance and flicker and listen to the wood crackle.

It's as warm as it gets in Scotland now, when the grass is long and lush and the seabirds are busy with their hatchlings along the cliffs. Warm salty breezes pass over me and make the brush whistle. When I built this fire pit I thought I'd sit around it in weather like this, but with friends and family, a woman I hadn't yet met who would fill this place with love and make it a home. But it's still just me kicking around the ninety-six acres by myself.

Isolating myself because no connection is better than an inauthentic one. Hollow is better than hurt. No words whispered in my ear is better than lies.

I hear rocks crunching between tires and swivel to stare down the long, winding gravel drive. Pop's old blue Mitsubishi pick up truck is ambling down the path. I don't know why he insists on driving that damn thing, it's beat to shit and I bought him a new one ages ago.

I haven't been to see him or Mum or Bram. They know I'm here, they know why—more or less—they know I flew straight home after Austria. There's nothing else for me to do except finish up the season and then I'll be back here for winter break. Several more months by myself.

"Hey, Pop," I say as he strolls past the garage and takes a seat in a wooden Adirondack chair that surrounds the oversized stone fire pit. He looks older than I remember, I wonder how many of his grey hairs I've contributed to his silver head in my life. Between the races, the crashes, and all the rest of my bullshit.

He and Mum sacrificed so much for me. Even though their house is paid off and neither has to work anymore, Pop looks particularly disappointed with me today. It's one of my greatest fears and adds to the malaise that's overtaken me since I told Mallory I loved her and then walked out of her life.

"Your Mum sent me," he starts.

I nod. That sounds about right. I don't even know where my phone might be today and Mum's probably worried. Because that's what I do to my parents, make them worry and embarrass them. Let Celeritas bring shame upon them, too, when all the Scottish papers talk shit about me.

"She wants details," Pop says.

"I don't know what to tell you," I swirl the amber liquid around in my glass tumbler.

"You know I can't go home empty-handed."

I sigh and get up, taking a few steps to the small bar area built into the stone wall surrounding the fire pit. A few feet from where Mallory threw her phone into the fire and said she knew me. "Drink?"

"Aye."

I pour Pop two fingers and slouch back into my chair to stare mindlessly at the fire some more. If it has any words of wisdom for me, the fire hasn't said shit yet. But I'm still going to stare at it.

"It's different this time," he announces after taking a slug of the peaty scotch.

"What is?"

"It's different from when it ended with Kate. You were mad then. You aren't mad now."

He's right, I'm hollow, but not mad. "No, I'm not mad, Pop."

"Why not?" Christ, this is going to turn into the Spanish Inquisition, just what I need.

"Ah hell, I don't know." I huff and throw a splinter of wood from my chair into the flames. "I guess because last time it hurt my pride more than anything."

"And now?"

"Now? Now there's no one to be mad at." Besides Digby, of course. Fuck him. But they don't know about that. They just think I'm a shitty driver and a shitty son, both are probably true enough.

"But yourself."

"Aye."

Pop leans forward, elbows on his chair arms. Even his eyebrows are grey now. "That's much harder than being mad at someone else."

"No one to beat the shit out of, that much for sure." Just that one assclown waiting for me to lose my mind and beat him senseless so he can take the very last thing from me and ensure I won't drive for anyone next year, or ever again.

"Oh, you're beating yourself up plenty, son."

I shrug and continue my lifeless gaze into the flames. "I wish I could." That part is true enough and I ponder the physics of physically beating the hell out of myself.

"Is it over, for sure?"

"It's over, Pop."

He sighs and sits back into the chair. "Mum won't be happy. She liked her."

"You only met her once." I know that's a crap excuse as soon as it leaves my mouth. I've only known Mallory for five months and I've loved her for at least half of them if I'm being honest.

"Aye, but she's the only one we ever met. Mum was so happy she cried," he waves his arm.

That's bloody perfect, now I am making Mum cry, too. Way to go, asshole. There's apparently no depths you will not sink to. Mallory's right, you are a monster.

"She made you happy," Pop continues.

"Yeah well, apparently the feeling wasn't mutual." I take a long gulp of my scotch and let it burn my throat.

"You sure?"

"Real sure, Pop. No room for interpretation."

"But you love her?"

I kill off the last swallow of drink, lean forward and set my tumbler on the ground. I put my hands on my knees, my head down, and rub my eyes and forehead. "Listen Pop, I'm sorry to disappoint you and Mum and everybody else but it's over. She doesn't trust me. Has never trusted me and said she will never trust me. So that's the end of it."

He pauses a long moment, maybe he understands now and this conversation can stop. "Well, what are you going to do about it?" He asks.

I raise back up and turn my head to Pop, "I just told you, she doesn't want me. It was over the minute she started lying to me, anyway."

"Ah," he nods, "she done you wrong?"

I shrug. I don't know how to explain this to him but for some reason, it's important to me that he doesn't think Mallory is like Kate. I know she isn't. "No," I mumble.

"What was that?" He questions and puts a hand to his ear dramatically. Smartass.

"There's nothing to be done about it." I lean back in my chair and slink down.

"You're just going to sit here drinking by yourself all day and night, eh?" Pop has his arms crossed over his chest and I feel like I'm a kid who's just failed an algebra test and is getting a lecture about living up to one's potential.

"Aye. Then I'll leave for the next race and that'll be that." I can't bear to upset Mallory anymore so I'll have to avoid her until she goes home. To New York. I'll stay in different hotels. I'll tell Jack not to give me her hotel room number next time, no matter how much I beg him.

"Just gonna leave for the race..." he mocks me.

"Exactly. It's the only thing I'm good for."

"That's rubbish," he purses his lips and shakes his head at me.

"Is it, Pop? Is it really? Take a look around. What else do I have going for me? Got this stone monstrosity here, it's been sitting in disrepair for ages." I shrug and wave across the expansive property stretched out before us, "but I'm hardly here. Barely see you and Mum and Bram. Bram wants my help with karting and I push him away because I don't want this for him. I can't even," I stumble and pick my words carefully. "I can't even race like I want to. And now, I've fucked everything up with the only woman I..."

"Well, you've got quite the self-pity speech prepared," he interrupts and does a slow clap a few times for dramatic effect. I wonder if I am this annoying when I act like a sarcastic jackass.

"It's not pity, it's just the truth."

"You have things other men would kill for," his voice gets sharp and he points at me. Ha-ha-sarcasm time is over.

He's right and now I'm offending Pop on top of it all. "I'm sorry, I don't mean to be ungrateful to you and Mum."

"Ahhh," he waves his hand to brush me off, "this isn't about us. All we've ever wanted is for you to be happy."

"I know, thank you."

"Guess we didn't do our jobs very well then," he says, matter of fact.

"What? No. You and Mum gave me everything, you were wonderful parents. You *are* wonderful parents."

"But you're not happy."

"Pop, come on," I sigh.

"Well are ya'?"

"I thought I was."

"And now it's gone and..."

"And now I know what I don't have and what I really want." Too bad I've fucked it all away.

"So let me ask you again, what are you gonna do about it?"

"Pop, I can't, you don't understand. There's more going on and I've messed it all up too badly."

Pop sits back in his chair and stays silent while he kills off his drink. I know better than to get another refill for myself. I don't want to hear that lecture, too. "Aye, I'm just an old man, I wouldn't understand," he rolls his eyes at me.

"Fucking hell," I huff, this isn't over.

"I may not know everything but I'm the one who was beside you at every race since you were a lad. I know the type of horse shit that goes on, that has *always* gone on. And I know how my own bloody son drives!" He fumes at me, his face getting red.

My head jerks up, I search his eyes.

"I'm old but I'm not stupid," he answers my question.

Fuck. He knows about Celeritas. He knows enough, anyway. I drop my head in shame. "I'm sorry," I murmur.

"You're a bloody eejit, is what ya' are," he waves his hand at me again and looks off into the distance.

"What?" I'm not necessarily debating that I'm in idiot, but hearing it from him is surprising, still.

"You want to make us proud, eh?"

I look away and swallow hard. I'm a grown-ass man and will not tear up in front of my pop. I nod.

"Then be happy. Your mum and I don't care two hoots about how ya' do it. Never did. If you wanted to be a ballerina, I would have made ya' a dress. But you wanted a kart so that's what I built."

I rub my eyes and can't stop a chuckle with the thought of Pop sewing pink tutus. Mum would have loved it, though, stuck in that house with the three of us boys.

We sit quietly for a long time watching the fire. Millions of thoughts race through my mind.

Eventually Pop stands. "Well, then come on. I need help fixing the tractor and I want to get the yard mowed before it rains again."

I don't know why he won't just let me pay someone to mow the fucking yard. Or let it go feral for all I care. He says it gets him out of the house and I don't argue because I suppose he is bored being forced into early retirement because of me. He does seem to enjoy the behemoth riding tractor, which, as a man, I can support.

We make our way to the garage and Pop enters the alarm code and raises an overhead door, flips the lights on. My championship car is in here, wrapped in her cover. A couple of supercars sit inside too, covered in an inch of dust, the only clean one is the McLaren Mallory drove up and down the road. The damn Harley is here, resting on the custom hydraulic motorcycle storage rack.

I'd give anything to pull it down and ride all over the Hebrides with her again. Not do anything but drive along the coastline and feel her against me again, feel her trusting me to take care of her and keep her safe. But I can't even offer her that now because her trust is gone.

She's countries away working for Digby DuPont and she's doing it because her dream is still alive and she's fighting for it. I feel like the biggest piece of shit on the planet.

"Grab a pry-bar and come help me get the deck off this thing, eh?" Pop has made his way to a far corner of the garage where he's got the big diesel tractor and mowing deck pulled inside.

I open a toolbox and grab the pry-bar and the socket set I know we need and shuffle over to him. "What's my old kart doing down?" I pause in step and ask him.

"Oh, I was just tinkering the other day and thought I'd see if it still fired up."

"Does it?"

"Dunno, didn't get around to it before your Mum called me home." He goes back to leaning over the tractor deck and starts loosening bolts.

My old kart is down on a work stand, rusty exhaust pipe and the plastic side pods sticky from garage grease and grime. It's been hanging on the wall ever since I bought this place and finished the garage. It was the first vehicle I made a spot for in here. Now the hand-painted #15 on the front and sides is faded and the plastic cracked.

The fiberglass seat is so small, from five year old me. The span of my outstretched fingers now covers the circumference of the steering wheel. The engine components still look decent only because they always leaked, they were all used parts Pop and I scavenged from other projects. But that leaking oil has kept the key engine parts from rusting.

If I replace the spark plug, flush all the fuel and lines, maybe it would start. I'd never fit in it to drive it again and the tires are long since dry rotted, but I can almost hear its high pitched whine and I kind of just want to hear that sound again and remember the simpler time.

Pop looks up from over the tractor deck and wipes his greasy hands in a shop rag and watches me running my hands over the kart. "Always regretted I could never afford a real pro kart for you. We didn't have one until you got sponsored."

"It was perfect, Pop."

"You always fought hard for what you wanted on the track, Lennox. Even when you were a kid, they messed with your kart because they couldn't beat ya' fair."

"I know," I nod.

"You quit fighting," he tosses the rag onto a shop bench.

"I'm so fucking tired, Pop." I lift my head from the kart and glance at him.

"Then you're fighting for the wrong thing."

Twenty Nine

"When the bombs drop, darling, can you say that you've lived your life? Oh, this is a high time for hypersonic missiles." - Sam Fender - Hypersonic Missiles

Mallory

"It has to be soon, I can't keep this up in front of Lennox, even if he deserves it," I tell Aria as we plot and scheme from my tiny flat.

"You don't want to be even more of a hypocrite, you mean?" She mumbles at me and sashays her head.

"You're supposed to be here to be supportive, not reasonable and mature," I put my hands on my hips. "You were never this big of a fan of David, you know."

"David is not the hottest man alive. Lennox Gibbes is," she retorts.

"I wish that were enough," I sigh and my mood immediately sours. I'm like a fish out of water flopping back and forth between emotions these past two weeks. Angry, sad, angry, sad.

"I know, honey, I'm sorry," she rushes to my side and hugs me. "I'm only saying, you have no proof that he really did cheat."

"He has no proof that I slept with Digby, either, but here we are." I sniffle into her shoulder.

"Two wrongs don't make a right. Do you want to be right or do you want to be happy?" She takes me by the shoulders and forces me to look at her, "Happy and in bed with that delicious man candy?"

"Don't say candy," I chuckle and think of Big Tits the nanny who lasted for twelve whole hours. "Besides, it doesn't matter. If we can't pull this off with Digby, Lennox will never be out from under this corruption. He'll never be happy and it will all have been for nothing."

Except for the memories. Despite everything, how much I hurt, I wouldn't trade them. I would do it again, god help me.

"Well, then let's get back to scheming."

Aria flew over when I hit rock bottom after arriving home to Aylesbury. Lennox had told me he loved me, then he left me. The next forty-eight hours were bad. There was ugly crying and I am embarrassed to admit that in a moment of weakness, I got out of bed and tried to break into his flat desperate for anything of his to hold in my hands. I blamed sleep deprivation, but as soon as I told Aria about my B&E, she was on the next flight.

She brought me tea in bed and forced me to eat. She let me wallow until she'd deemed that the appropriate amount of time had passed, and then she dragged me up and made me take off Lennox's clothes. We even burned the stupid Talker Distillery hoodie in the meadow out back in a wine-fueled feminine war cry. And then it became time to get to work on the mission at hand.

Operation Destroy Digby.

I have flirted, fawned, inappropriately pawed, giggled, batted my eyelashes, and led that pig on for nearly two weeks now. When he got suspicious, I posted photos of him and me on my social media knowing Lennox might see it. I said horrible things about Lennox to Digby that I did not mean. I hope when this all goes down, Lennox will hate me a little less and know what I was really doing.

The door buzzer interrupts Aria and me and we shoot one another a knowing glance.

"Hello?" I speak into the security unit on the wall.

"It's Digby, let me up." I press the buzzer and wave my arms frantically at Aria to hide any evidence of our plotting. The coffee table has notebooks full of Digby's daily schedule, anything useful we've dug up on his family, friends, or personal life. With all of our recognizance work, we would have made fine detectives.

Slamming the last of the evidence into a kitchen drawer, I open the door for the biggest douchebag the world has ever seen. "Hi handsome," I place my hands on his chest and croon up at him.

"Mallory," he wraps a hand around my ass and pulls me into him. "I stopped by to ask if you're coming to my place to work tonight?"

"Hi, Digby!" Aria waves like a rabid fangirl from the kitchen, drawing his attention away. Not only is she the best friend a brokenhearted girl needs, but she's been my scapegoat. I can't possibly stay at Digby's place because Aria is in town. Never a moment of intimacy because that darned Aria is always underfoot.

"Aria," he sighs when he sees her. "Still in town, are we?"

"She's your biggest fan, be nice, baby," I gush at him and pull his chin back to look at me and nibble my bottom lip. I know exactly how to work this idiot. Just dangle a shiny object in front of him and stroke his ego and he can't help himself.

Moron.

"Mmm," he moans at me, "she could join us, you know." He wags his eyebrows in Aria's direction.

"I want you all to myself," I purr and run my fingers along his belt loop. I want you all to myself alright, in a prison cell, you creep. I don't imagine the spoiled rich boy will actually do any time, his kind of money can buy all the fancy lawyers he'll need to avoid jail. He just needs to get permanently ejected from Formula 1. But it still brings me unbridled joy to imagine this spoiled rich boy in prison with proper inmates.

"Naughty girl," he runs a finger down my throat and past my cleavage.

"Soon," I whimper like an Emmy Award winning actress on a daytime soap opera.

He tells me we'll be traveling together to the race in Silverstone in two days. I feign excitement. Then he slaps me on the ass and slithers out of the flat to whatever rock he lives under.

As soon as we hear the exterior door shut, Aria and I jump around as if we're covered in spiders and trying to brush them off.

"Did he seriously just suggest a threesome?" Aria shakes her arms and shivers in disgust.

"I'm going to throw up, oh my god he's such a creep!"

After we've both washed our hands and arms with antibacterial soap and Aria comments that we're going to have to sage the flat to get his evil out of the building, it's time to get back to plotting.

This has to happen quickly. I don't know how long his phone will keep those videos in the Recently Deleted folder and I don't know if they can be recovered after that. Plus, the Silverstone race is the home race for Celeritas. I want to take them all down on their home turf where it will hurt the most.

They're all going to pay, like in one of the greatest horror movies of all time, Stephen King's 1976 classic, *Carrie*. When they dumped a bucket of blood on her at prom and girlfriend had had enough, these fuckers are going to pay.

Ok, so maybe there won't be buckets of blood, I don't think, but they're gonna pay.

After an exhaustive Googling, like the professional sleuths we are, I've decided that I need to just take the whole phone. There might not be time to send the videos, the wifi could be down, there are too many variables. I need to take the whole phone and pray the videos are still on there or else we'll have to get high tech. Aria is still investigating what our options look like if we have to pay someone to get deleted files off or figure out if the videos are in Digby's cloud.

I'm going to have to take the phone and make a run for it. It has to work, it just has to.

"Ok, so Stage One is finalized. We need to cement the steps for Stage Two, you have to be sure." Aria says.

"You're frightening when you're so cold and calculating," I snicker.

"Me? You're the one over there cackling about buckets of blood!"

But, she's right. I've been dawdling over Stage Two. It's time to put up or shut up. I pick up my phone.

"Hey, Cody, can you talk?"

I am trembling with nerves, shaking so bad my voice is wavering. It's time. Stages One and Two have been finalized. Stage Three depends on how tonight goes but my crew and I are ready to pull the trigger.

I have a crew, because that's how I roll, now.

"Buck up, buttercup," Aria tells me from our hiding location outside the Celeritas administration building where we've stalked Digby to. We've monitored his schedule and he's right on time where he should be. There's no more time to spare. Everything is in place. It's now or never.

Aria takes my hand. "One last time, are you sure? There's no coming back from this..."

"I'm doing it," I tell her.

"Then I've got your back, girlfriend," she nods stiffly. "I'll be ready."

"Thank you," I whisper and wipe the sweat from my palms.

I take a deep breath, fill my lungs, clench my fists to get them to stop shaking, and then I leave Aria behind in the bushes and take my first step toward the admin building and whatever awaits me after this.

I waive my keycard and enter the building, taking the path I know well now. Opening up the gym door, right on schedule, Digby is on a treadmill and should be finishing up any minute. I'm wearing a short, tight-fitting red dress with a plunging neckline and heels, which I'll have to ditch quickly if things go according to plan.

Digby pulls his earbuds out and raises an eyebrow at me. Excellent, those earbuds are attached to his phone just as planned. I swing my hips and stroll toward him. I look like a two-bit hooker, which I think is exactly his type. He rakes his eyes up and down my body.

"My, my, what is this?" He asks pushing buttons on the treadmill to slow it down.

"Like what you see, sir?" I run my hands down the sides of my torso.

He steps off the treadmill and stands before me. A drop of his sweat hits my arm. Antibacterial soap isn't going to cut it this time. I'll need bleach. Industrial strength bleach.

"I like it very much, what's the occasion, Ms. Mitchell?" His sweaty finger traces the neckline of my dress.

"We're finally alone," I run my palms up his disgusting wet tee shirt.

"Is that so?"

I nod and bite my lip. "Take me to your place, I can't wait anymore."

He moans at me and analyzes my face for a moment while fiddling with my hair.

Come on, you stupid little weasel.

In a second he grabs a towel from his treadmill, wipes his face off then throws the sweaty towel back on the treadmill and puts his phone and earbuds in his short pockets. Taking my hand in his, we're off.

You don't even wipe down your equipment, pig.

Outside, we begin the walk to his residence building. His hands are all over me. I giggle loudly knowing Aria is following the sound of my voice from the bushes. She's sneaking like a prowler in case things go south and I need an emergency extraction. I'll need her skills for our exit plan. God, how did I get so lucky rooming with her in college when everyone else got stuck with some psycho?

Digby lets us inside his building and I'm doing my best to keep an eye on that phone in his pocket without being obvious. His hands are all over my ass as we climb the stairs. My gut sinks as he opens his flat door and we step inside. This is happening.

Don't delay, get to it then get out.

"I want you, Digby," I lie through my teeth and wrap my arms around his neck.

"And what of my teammate, the disgraceful Mr. Gibbes?" He asks, squeezing my ass.

Shit, is he buying this? Ramp it up, Mallory. Fight.

"He's humiliated me for the last time," I look in his eyes and prey on his sick need to destroy Lennox. He likes that. I continue. "I know where my bread is buttered." He smiles. He likes this game.

Please, Lennox, forgive me.

"He's not half the man you are," I reach down and cup his groin. Newsflash, Digby isn't a quarter of the man Lennox is, by any measurement.

Digby hisses and his lips drop to my neck.

"Mmm," I moan, "go take a shower so I can run my lips all over you."

"I thought you liked it dirty," he mumbles around my neck.

Damn it you filth pig, just get in the shower so I can destroy your life already.

"I'm the dirty girl, you're the sexy powerful man, Digby. Come back smelling like a gentleman and do very ungentlemanly things to me."

He lifts his head and I'm not sure if I've been made or if he's going to humor me. "I expect you naked on my bed in two minutes," he says as he holds my chin and then he heads to the bathroom.

"Hurry," I fake giggle and kick off a high heel past him. I won't need them anyway and it sells my story.

The shower turns on and he hasn't even closed the door. Great, one less thing, I was prepared to kick that fucker down. All the flats have the same hollow remodeled interior doors and well, Celeritas will need to replace mine after I practiced.

Creeping toward the restroom and pretending to unzip my dress in case he sees me, I pass the breakfast counter and snag his keys. I tuck them into my cleavage and keep creeping toward the bathroom where water is running. I wait until I hear the glass shower door close and pause a few seconds to be sure.

I peek my head in. His back is turned and he's soaping himself up.

Boom, the gym shorts are on the floor with the wires of the earbuds dangling out! I crouch down and take two steps in, reach for him gym shorts, and I've got them, the phone is in there!

"Hey!" Oh no, Digby has turned in the shower and sees me.

I grab the shorts and run for my life. Through the living room, I fling the front door open and tear down the hallway.

"You bitch!" I hear him scream in the distance; he's not in the hallway yet.

I skip several stairs at a time and haul ass out of the building clutching his filthy gym shorts with the phone inside. I dig his key out of my cleavage and sprint barefoot across the campus. I just need to round this corner and the parking lot will be in sight.

I turn back and Digby is running out of the residence building door with a towel around his waist. Fuck, hurry hurry hurry, I won't be able to outrun him!

I round the corner and see her right where she should be. Of course she is.

"Throw me the key!" Aria screams.

I fling it to her and through an act of god, the throw connects and she catches them and unbeeps the doors. She has two small bags we packed on the hood and throws them inside moving at the speed of a woman possessed. She opens the passenger door then as she gets in the driver's side, "Hurry!" She screams.

I don't look back, I just hear Lennox's voice saying, "He's dangerous, Mallory." I put everything I have into my legs and run like I have never run before in my life. I dive into the open car door and Mallory already has it in reverse and hits the gas before my door is even shut.

She throws the Hummer into drive and as I sit up and get the door closed, Digby lunges just feet away, but it's too late. The doors are locked and we're speeding away while he stands in the parking lot wrapped in a towel.

I'm lit up with adrenaline, on fire. I roll the window down and hang my head out and scream as loud as I can, "Ha! Fuck you, you fucking wanker!"

"Holy shit, holy shit, holy shit," Aria chants as she keeps the Hummer floored and we make it onto the main road off of Celeritas grounds. "We just stole a car, Mallory!"

"Go two miles then take a right. We ditch it at the end of that road," I tell her as I fish the cell phone out Digby's gym shorts and find the photo folder.

"I remember," Aria pants, clutching the steering wheel and racing this behemoth, idiot vehicle down the road. I would never have been able to be our escape driver. I'd have wrapped us around the very first telephone pole we came across. Lennox would be proud of how Aria's driving. He would have been prouder if it were me driving, but he can't have everything. I know when I'm bested.

"They're here, the videos are here!" I scream.

"Do it!" Aria yells, never taking her eyes off the road.

I select the videos and start following the upload instructions I memorized. I watch the bar move as they upload and Aria fishes my cell phone out of her back pocket and hands it to me.

My fingers are shaking but I dial the number I programmed. He picks up on the first ring.

"Mallory?"

"Max, do you have it?" I yell into the phone.

"It's coming through, you did it."

Thirty

"I've been around the world, I've seen a million girls. Ain't one of them got what my lady she's got. She's stealing the spotlight, knocks me off of my feet. She's enough to start a landslide just walking down the street." - AC/DC - Girl's Got Rhythm

Lennox

It's Thursday before race weekend, press day. All of my life I've hated this day the most, the day a roomful of journalists in a stuffy conference room grill us for an hour about the upcoming race. Today I'm looking forward to it. Today I start the fight that matters, to get her back and redeem myself in the ways that matter.

"Are you sure?" Matty asks inside the motorhome at Silverstone. The support staff is buzzing with the extra preparations for the home race celebrations. The executives and team bosses are out of sight though, behind closed doors dealing with the situation I handed them this morning on typed letterhead from my attorney.

"Aye, I'm sure. It's done."

Matty puts his head in his elbows on the table and rubs his eyes. His forehead wrinkles. "There has to be another way."

"There isn't. I can't stay here anymore. I don't like the person it's turned me into. I need to focus on what's important and I can't do that while I'm not even worthy of her. I definitely can't do it watching her work for DuPont the rest of the season."

"Why can't we just get Celeritas to fire her, again?" This would be one of those times Matty says things that offend people and he doesn't mean to.

"He's in love," Jack slaps Matty on the arm and grins like a fool.

"Aye," I pause. "I won't help destroy her dreams. If I leave, hers are still unbroken. She'll be able to do anything she wants, go anywhere she wants. If I leave, DuPont won't be able to use her as leverage and will lose interest."

"If you stay?" Matty asks.

"They'll destroy us both."

"You're falling on the proverbial sword," Jack clutches his heart and I roll my eyes at him. "Hey wait, what about my dreams?"

"Your only dream is to get paid," Matty grimaces at Jack. "Though this does bring up a valid point," he raises an eyebrow at me.

"You can always move back in with Mum and Pop," I laugh. I'll do whatever I can to help Matty and Jack land on their feet, wherever they want to go or whatever they want to do. Both will surely be able to stay in F1 if they choose. Good physio's and PA's are hard to find.

Jack is more optimistic. "There's always next season, right?"

"Not likely with me resigning and breaking my contract like this. There are more important things in life."

"Like what?" Matty asks, horrified at my response. Such a bloody pessimist.

"Like her, for starters. Like having pride in myself again. I used to stand for something but along the way, I've forgotten what that might be. I can't be complicit in this shit anymore or I'm no better than DuPont."

Matty and Jack both cringe at my last statement, but it's true. I want to be a man my parents are proud of. I want to be a man Mallory can be proud of. I want to be happy and I need her for that. I guess that makes me a selfish asshole, but I can live without racing. I can't live without her.

"The fine?" Matty asks.

"50 million. The lawyers can work it out," I shrug. I may have to cool it on the supercars, but I'll be fine. I'd live in a bloody fort and drive a Yugo as long as Mallory was in the passenger seat.

"This is an awfully big risk, mate," Jack rubs his head. "What if she won't even forgive you?"

I nod. I've thought a lot about that, but this is still something I need to do. "Guess I'll spend the rest of my days trying. Maybe go back to karting. Maybe I'll be a ballerina," I smile.

Jack checks his watch, "Now that I have that image fried into my brain, we have five minutes until press time, shall we go?"

"Aye, let's enjoy the last one."

Mallory

Max had the driver waiting for us right where he said it would be. By the time we made it to our prearranged hotel room under someone else's name in London, all the files were uploaded and Max was headed to the airport. Sixteen videos in all and Max says there may be a lot more his team can access when they finish analyzing the hardware. His reporters are already knee-deep digging into every nook and cranny of Digby DuPont's life.

But of the sixteen videos we have now, it's more than I could ever have imagined. Prostitutes, drugs, and enough seedy shit is in his search history to make a trucker blush and to tank a career politician.

Maxwell Cooper thought I was calling him about the piece on Lennox, but what I gave him instead is far bigger. He's been only too happy to help. Very soon, it'll all be public.

Cody has called several times to check on me and remind me that no matter what happens, he'll be there to pick up the pieces. The fallout will be intense, but I've never been so sure of anything in my life. We talked all night about what this means for me and my parents. It will be the severing of our relationship, permanently, as was always threatened. Cody says Mitchell Media is on its last legs, the board is threatening to fire my father, and his daughter giving a blockbuster exclusive to his largest competitor may be his push off the cliff.

He didn't need to tell me that Dad has seen several lawyers now trying to find anyone who would take his libel case after his in-house attorneys refused. My mind was made up before hearing that, but it does ease the guilt I'll probably always carry. I'll handle that on my own two feet with my head held high, though.

I'm doing what's right despite the personal consequences. And while Lennox will never forgive me, in a million years, for what I had to do to get these videos, he'll be able to race again. He'll be a world champion again. I believe in him and will watch him on TV every other Sunday from wherever I am in the world. I'll be his biggest fan quietly supporting him in secret, for the rest of my life.

I just need to get through this press conference.

Max and Aria are here by my side because we have no idea what Digby is going to pull. Celeritas has called a special press session ahead of the normally scheduled driver interviews, so he knows something is up and we're expecting a real shit show. We've been on the lamb, only just turning up for the press conference, so it'll be a surprise for everyone. I'll never see my little flat back in the London countryside again, but it will all be worth it.

"It's time. Ready to do this, kid?" Max asks me.

"Damn skippy." I link arms with Aria who I couldn't imagine not coming with for the piece de resistance, and the three of us walk through the 'Press Entry' door.

The room is filling up with journalists from around the world, far more than usual because of the special session Celeritas called. Several Celeritas bosses are lining one wall but I can't see Lennox, he's nowhere in the room. I guess he never was one to attend any press meetings he was not forced to be at, but I had hoped he would be here. This is for him as much as it's for me.

"Incoming," Max taps my arm and looks toward our favorite coke fiend storming toward us, his red face scrunched up and so mad he could spit.

"What are you doing here?" He seethes at me. "You were fired! You can't be here!"

"Oh, I'm sorry, Dickby, you must not have seen my new paddock badge." I hold up my neck lanyard for him to see. "I know reading is not your strong suit so let me spell it out for you. See, it says Cooper Media, VIP All Access." I run my finger along the words like a real smart ass. It's glorious.

"What? This is outrageous! You can't do that!" Digby huffs. This may be the first time in his life he isn't getting what he wants. Welcome to the real world, pervert.

"I can do that, and I did to that. I win, Dickface, you lose." I probably should be more professional standing next to Maxwell Cooper, CEO of one of the most influential media corporations in the world, but my need for justice outweighs workplace etiquette.

"Lose? We'll just see about that. Your caveman lover boy will be the biggest loser this sport has ever seen by the time I'm done with you two!" Digby has his hands on his hips and sashays his head at all three of us.

I snap when he insults Lennox. I've had to be quiet for too long.

"That caveman is more of a man than you will ever be!" I poke Digby in the chest as hard as I can. Aria tugs on my arm but I am on a roll and Digby is going to hear me.

"You have to buy your way in here and fuck with his car in order to win. You're a pussy!" I poke him again. "Also, your dick is fucking tiny! Tiny! That's right, you have a tiny little dick! Your arch-nemesis, though, that caveman you speak of, huge dick, I mean huuuuu..."

Aria is tugging at me again despite me swatting her away while I unleash my fury on Digby. "Mallory!"

"What!" I finally snap at her. Her eyes are huge and she points behind us with one finger.

Oh shit, Jack and Matty are behind us and have heard my out of control rant that devolved into dick sizes. Their jaws are both hanging open in stupor. Even stoic Matty is slack-jawed.

"What is happening right now?" Matty asks no one in particular as my face flushes from embarrassment.

I come to my senses and focus on the mission at hand. "Is Lennox here?" I ask them but they're both looking at me like an insane person. Of course, I look like an insane person, they don't know anything yet other than whatever Celeritas told them about this press conference, and I just announced to the room that I know Digby has a tiny, tiny dick.

Shit. If I ever got the chance to talk to Lennox again, I wanted him to hear the explanation from me, but now he'll be blindsided and hurt again when his friends inevitably tell him what his psycho ex has done now.

"Please take your seats," the FIA Press Officer says over the microphone at the podium.

Max takes my arm and starts leading me away. "Come on, let's move upfront. We'll let Celeritas do their schtick first so we can respond after. The AV guy has the file and is ready to put it up on screen at your command."

Aria, Max, and I move to the front of the room while Jack and Matty continue to squint their eyes at me like I have two heads. I'm so nervous, I've never seen the press room this full. It's standing room only with media personnel from every sports network around the world.

Fake it 'til you make it, girl.

"Ladies and gentlemen, let's get started," the Press Officer states and the room gets quiet. "As you know, this is a special media session requested by Celeritas Racing. We will start with driver number fifteen, Lennox Gibbes."

"What?" I say aloud, to no one. The Press Officer steps from the podium and Lennox enters the room from the side door the drivers use to enter at the last minute. He's in jeans and a grey button-down I bought him to make up for stealing half his clothes. He should be in Celeritas gear. There are so many people packed in this room he doesn't even see me.

He clears his throat then starts speaking. "Thanks for coming, everybody. Over the years you and I have had our disagreements." The room of reporters chuckles. "So, some of you will probably enjoy what I have to say today and some of you may not. But honestly, as long as the right person hears me today, that's all that matters."

"What is he doing?" Aria whispers.

"I have no idea," I whisper back and keep my eyes transfixed on Lennox. He looks bright and strong and healthy, better than he looked the last time I saw him at my hotel room door. He's so blindingly handsome, his brown hair perfectly messy in that way that looks deliberate.

His voice is deep and strong, there's no hesitation. He has no script and looks the reporters in their eyes. "I started racing when I was five years old, competition is all I've ever known. But someone recently taught me that there are more important things in life. I'm here today to tell you that this weekend will be my last Formula 1 race. This morning I resigned from Celer…"

"No!" I scream, my vocal cords possessed, my body acting without thought. Every journalist in the room turns their head toward me at the front of the room.

Lennox scans the crowd until he finds me. "Mallory?"

"No!" I scream at him again, my body flushes with a surge of adrenaline. Every emotion I have encountered over these past weeks rises in me and they boil over as I scream, "You will not! You will not do this!"

Lennox leans back from the microphone and stares at me, totally confused by this inexplicable outburst. Every eye in the room is on me as I march to the podium ready to plow my way through any idiot who dares to try and stop me. A few long strides and I am astride the podium.

"I will not let you do this!" I yell at Lennox as if it's just the two of us in this room.

"It's ok," he speaks at a normal volume, of which I am not capable of right now, and tries to take my hand but I don't let him. He must think I've gone completely insane, a jilted ex-girlfriend gone mad. "Please, just trust me, it will all be ok," he whispers.

"I do trust you, you stupid asshole!" A symphony of laughter breaks out in the audience. "*You* should have trusted *me!*" I point my finger at him.

He tries reaching for my hand again. "Ok, ok. Let's just go somewhere and…"

"No! I'm not going anywhere! You're going to listen!" I turn to the crowd, "All of you are going to listen!" There are dozens of cameras facing me, journalists pointing oversized microphones to the front of the room and leaning forward in their chairs.

Oh god, I am screaming in front of a room of media. I look unhinged.

No buckets of blood, Mallory.

This is not the speech I had prepared to give. I'm going to have to wing it. I glance at Lennox beside me in a power stance ready to take control, throw me over his shoulder, ready to handle whatever arises. I imitate his strength and square off my shoulders, raise my chin.

"This man," I speak into the microphone and point to Lennox, "is not retiring from Formula 1. He misspoke and he's very sorry." The room collectively laughs again. From the corner of my eye, I see the tiniest of smirks start at the corner of Lennox's mouth and he crosses his arms watching me, waiting to see what else I'm going to say.

"This man," I continue, "is a World Drivers' Champion. He holds nine FIA records. His talent is beyond reproach. But he is also a good man, an honest man who loves this sport. He has dedicated his life to racing. Because of his integrity and his passion for F1, out of concern for the safety of other drivers and track personnel, you will understand why Mr. Gibbes called this press session when he learned of the illegal and immoral activities happening on-track, and off, by his teammate, Digby DuPont."

"What the hell are you doing?" Lennox whispers to me, his eyes growing round.

"Will the audio-visual team please play the Cooper Media video file now?"

Lennox rocks his head back in shock and looks around as the room lights dim and the video Max prepared starts playing on a drop-down screen. Max's staff cleaned up the images so it's crystal clear what's happening and then he spliced several of Digby's videos together to make one file that will sum up Digby's offenses quite nicely.

As Digby comes onto screen, it's him snorting coke off that woman's stomach. She turns out to be a prostitute in video clip number eight, but we'll get to that. In the back of the room, I catch the sight of Digby running out of the exit doors. I smile because he can run, but it's too late for him.

Then we see Digby cutting up cocaine in the motorhome with the Celeritas logo on the wall right behind him. Reporters gasp and cameras flash. Moving on, we see Digby in his race suit and helmet doing a finger full of cocaine right before he gets into the car in Melbourne.

Alessi from Anora stands from his seat and shouts, "What the fuck? He's doing coke in the car? That fucker hit me at that race! He could have killed me!"

The video continues as Digby appears to buy a brick of a 'powdery white substance' on his yacht in Monaco and rubs it all over his teeth and gums. Another driver in the audience stands to yell. Then we see Digby bragging about the prostitute he just bought who's going down on him in his Hummer. The video goes on for several minutes with several clips as the audience gasps and journalists grow frantic.

As the videos play, I feel Lennox take my hand. I grip it hard as he stands beside me at the podium.

When the video ends the lights come back on and the room is in a frenzy. All the Celeritas staff is long gone, they scurried out like rats on their own sinking ship. Reporters start yelling questions out over one another and clamoring to get to the front of the room. There's going to be a stampede.

Max comes to the podium and is smiling from ear to ear. "Want me to take over from here?"

In a daze, I nod and then everything is a flurry as Lennox pushes past the mob of people in the room, pulling me behind him as we escape through the side door.

Thirty One

Lennox

My elbows are out as I push past media crew and support staff and the crowd of people who stuffed the conference room for Mallory's bombshell. As soon as the video started rolling, a herd started amassing in the room. Everyone from team bosses to cleaning crews are packed in like sardines. I'm clearing a path and dragging her behind me. It's a fucking frenzy.

I push the conference room doors open with my shoulder and break into the hallway. I feel Mallory's hand jerked out of mine and look back. A journalist I don't recognize has her arm and there's a giant camera in her face. "Back off!" I roar and shove him away from her.

"Go, go!" She scurries to my side and we take off again. We jog through the building being chased by a flock of cameras and take the first exit door we come across. Outside there are more cameramen waiting and I search up and down the paved path behind the track buildings but there's nowhere to go to get away from them. The motorhome is absolutely out of the question now.

"Hey!" I hear Jack yell behind us. He, Matty, and Aria have pushed through the crowd and are jogging toward us outside. What the hell is Aria doing here?

"Do you have my keys?" I yell to Jack as the trio hustles to catch up.

Jack digs into his pants pocket, "Does Raggedy Anne have a cotton crotch?"

He hands me the keys and I pull Mallory to continue our escape but she tugs back, "No, I can't leave Aria."

"Girl, go!" Aria is between Jack and Matty and slips her arms around both of their waists smiling like the Cheshire Cat.

"Take care of her," I tell them both, nodding to Aria, and grab Mallory's hand.

We need to get the hell out of here. There are reporters and cameras everywhere, circling us like buzzards. They're trying to tug on both of us to ask questions. I make long strides through the track and into the parking garage when I feel her arm pulling on mine to match pace with my long legs. "Keep up or I'll pick you up," I tell Mallory as plow through the crowds. If someone else grabs her or she gets hurt in this mob we're going to have another scene.

By the time I hand her into my car there are only six or eight cameramen filming us but Mallory is out of breath and shaking. "Are you ok?" I speed out of the parking lot.

She takes several deep breaths with her eyes closed, "Yes. Holy shit, holy shit," she pants.

I have no idea where I'm going or what just happened but I need to get us away from the track first, away from the crowds, the news teams. My hotel won't be safe from them now. Silverstone is in the middle of bumfuck nowhere England and soon there's nothing but cows and crops on both sides of the road. Mallory is silent beside me but I know she's freaked out.

"Where are you going?" She finally asks me.

"I don't know, just, away from this," I wave with my arms to convey the gravity of everything we need to escape right now.

"Just pull over somewhere, I'll call Max to come get me." She pulls out her phone and her hands are shaking.

"What? No. Mallory, we need to talk." I put my hand over hers on the phone but she pulls it away. Now that she's had a spell to calm down, she's pissed. I spot a dirt road up ahead and pull off and far enough down the road to be out of sight from the main road. There's nothing around us but orchards of some kind of fruit trees.

I pull to the side with branches hanging over the car and kill the engine. Mallory is looking at her knees and gripping her phone. I run my hands through my hair and try to focus. I don't even know where to start. This is absolute insanity and thoughts sprint across my mind faster than I can keep up with, but no. That's not what's important.

Unclipping my seatbelt so I can sit sideways to see her, all I want to do is drag her into my arms and make sure she's ok. "There's so much I need to say to you but I'm not sure where to start," I admit.

"Same," she nods and stares out the windshield.

"Do you mind if I go first?"

"Since when do you ask?" She's defensive and won't look at me.

I wish I could deliver an impassioned speech on her like she gave to that conference room of reporters, but I've always been better about showing her how I feel rather than tell her.

And that shit stops now.

"I meant what I said in Austria. I love you. I know I fucked up. I swear to you there's only been you since the day I met you and I think you know that. I know you don't trust me, though, and I'll do whatever..."

She shakes her head and interrupts me, "That's not it anymore."

"What is it, then? Tell me and I'll fix whatever it is."

"You can't fix this," a tear runs down her eye.

I put my hand on her face and she lets me keep it there, "There's nothing off the table anymore, Mal. Please. I'm fucking miserable without you. Will you look at me?"

"I can't," she closes her eyes and it guts me that she can't even bring herself to look at me.

"I'm so fucking sorry, please believe me. I'll earn back your trust, I don't care how long it takes. I might have a lot of free time now." I'm not trying to be a smart ass, I just want her to stop crying. I don't ever want to make her cry again.

"Why did you do that?" She wipes her tears away and brushes my hand off in the process.

I watch her in her seat and I have no doubt that it was the right thing to do. None. "I can live without driving. I can't live without you. If you want to live in New York and open a firm, or work for Cooper, whatever you want to do now, I'll support your dreams. I just, I know how it feels to have your dreams crushed and I couldn't let you go through that, too. And I want to be someone you're proud to be with, not some asshole fraud." Like Digby, I think, but I don't want to speak his name.

"I've always been proud of you."

My chest tightens. "I didn't deserve it, but I'll spend the rest of my life trying to be the man you deserve, if you let me."

All of a sudden she bursts into tears and her shoulders are heaving, her hands cradling her head. I try to console her but I can't reach her to hold her and she's trying to get out of the car door. She finally pushes the right button and the door rises and she shoots out. I jog around the car where she's pacing back and forth along the car, red-faced and trying to get control of her emotions.

"Love," I reach for her and try her to pull her in.

"No, don't call me that," she snaps and turns away from me wrapping her arms around herself.

"Why?"

"You won't love me anymore," she sobs.

"Mallory," I take her by the shoulders and make her face me, "there's nothing that will make me stop loving you. I know, Christ, I know a lot has happened and I don't understand it all right now, but I don't care about any of it."

"You will when I tell you what I've done."

All of my breath escapes me and my heart sinks to my stomach. I don't know if I can hear this. "Whatever it is, if it's over now then it doesn't matter."

"You don't mean that." She throws her arms up. "Jack and Matty are going to tell you anyway, let me just get it over with then you can leave me again. Leave me in this, this fucking apple orchard this time!"

"I will not leave you. I will never leave you again," I stand before her and take her tear-stained face in my hands.

"Just, let me get it over with," she breaks away and starts pacing again. As much as I don't want the details of whatever the hell has happened that culminated with videos playing of Digby with drugs and prostitutes, she wants to talk and I need to listen. I lean up against the side of the car and brace myself.

"You have to know I was doing it for you," she starts. I close my eyes and swallow. I can't live with myself if she did something to make her this upset and she did it for me. "I, I found videos on Digby's phone and I had to get them away from him, I had to get him alone."

I'm channeling all of my self-control to stay still and silent and stand still against the car, let her get it all out and then we'll deal with it.

"I had to lead him on, let him touch me," she sobs. "I did terrible things, Lennox."

The thought of him touching Mallory is unbearable, every nerve in my body is on fire. She's staring at me now waiting for a reaction. "I'm listening. I'm not leaving."

She's watching me closely, "He, he grabbed my ass, he touched my chest, he kissed my neck. I let him. I didn't want him to, but I let him."

"Still here," my eyes track her. This is killing me but I won't leave. Being without her is the only thing that has ever felt worse than this.

"I touched him, Lennox. I groped his disgusting little Digby dick." Her body recoils and the disgust she feels recalling this is all over her face. "It was the only way, I hated it. I hate *him*."

"Aye, I know," I dip my head and agree quietly.

"That's it. You can go now." She turns her back to me and takes a few steps away toward the trees.

"That's it?"

She turns back around. "What do you mean that's it?"

I shrug my shoulders, "Ok. I'm still here, Mal."

"You're not mad?"

"Oh, I'm plenty mad," I stand up from the car and take two steps so I'm inches from her, "but I'm mad at myself that I let this happen to you. I don't know how I'll ever forgive myself, but I'll figure it out."

"You didn't make me do it," she looks up at me.

"But you did it for me."

She nods.

I run my fingers through her long hair and hold the back of her head. "I wish you would have just let me handle this so I could keep you safe. I would have done anything for you. I *will* do anything for you. But I understand why you did it." I pull her body into mine and hold her head against my chest. This is the first time in weeks I've held her and there's no power in the universe that I'll let take her from me again.

"I'm sorry, I had to do something. It wasn't fair, I had to fight." Her arms are to her side and she goes back and forth with them wanting to wrap around my waist, then back to her sides.

I chuckle into her hair, "I think I fell in love with you the first time you fought with me. So fucking sassy."

"It's the competitive streak in you, you like the challenge," her arms finally go around my waist and my eyes close in relief.

"You're probably right." I kiss her hair and whisper to her, "I love you, Mallory. You don't have to love me back right now. One day I hope you will."

She pulls back and looks up at me, "You didn't see my texts."

"What texts?"

"You blocked me, on your phone."

"I was out of my mind, Mallory. After everything that happened in the past with him, I thought you were the last person who would lie to me and it just, it fucking wrecked me. I couldn't bear the thought."

She nods and looks to her side at the apple trees again. "Can you take me back to the track now? Or I can call Max, I guess."

"Max? Why?" The track is the last place on earth I want to be right now, and we have so much more to talk about.

"I have to figure my life out now, Lennox," she says with no small amount of frustration. "I have no job, no home, my dad is probably having a heart attack as we speak, I stole a car and the cops could be looking for me for all I know!"

"What?" Stole a car, what the fuck? None of it matters. "I'll come with you, then, wherever you want to go. New Y..."

"No," she cuts me off.

"Then Scotland, move in with me. Please. I don't even know if I'm supposed to race on Sunday now or not but, fuck it."

"No, Lennox." Her face is stern and she's holding her elbows across her stomach. "It's not that simple. You hurt me."

Her hazel eyes are glossy and bloodshot. Knowing I put that look in her eyes guts me and is a shame inside me worse than any of the bullshit I've ever done in my life. "I know, love, and I'm so fucking sorry."

"You did it deliberately. You want me to trust you, but you didn't have trust in me either. You were hurt and you lashed out to hurt me on purpose. I have never felt so terrible, Lennox. I don't know if I could go through that again."

"I swear to you it will never happen again. I want to spend the rest of my life with you, Mallory. I don't care where we go or what we do, but I need you. I know I'm selfish but I won't give you up. I can't."

"I don't know if I can," she shakes her head. "I don't trust myself right now, much less you. Running away with you to your castle won't solve anything. I ran away once when I came here to escape my problems. I'd feel like I'm always waiting for the other shoe to drop. The next time you'll throw some supermodel in my face."

"Don't do that. Look at me," I take her face. "You are the only woman I have ever felt this way about, I have never loved anyone like this. I mean it, I want to spend the rest of my life with you. You're fucking everything to me."

"I need time. Time away from you. Everything is completely out of control and I don't know which end is up."

Time apart is the last thing I want. I'd cut off my right arm if I could just take her back home right now and marry the shit out of her. But I came prepared to do whatever it takes and I will. I need her to trust me and be all in with me. "There's nothing I won't give you, tell me what you want and I'll do it. Just promise you'll come back to me."

Her gorgeous, hazel eyes with flecks of gold and brown pierce me, "I can't promise you that."

"I will make you love me, Mallory. I will never give up. Trust that." I will chase this woman across the earth if I need to. All the resolve and fight I used to have is back and every ounce it will be directed to this mission. This is the only race that matters anymore.

Thirty Two

Mallory

The first week I was back in New York I didn't get to enjoy it much because everything was blowing up back in London. My phone never knew a moment of peace.

After we left the orchard outside Silverstone, I filled Lennox in on the whole story, from Sandra's original request to stop outshining Digby, all the way through the stolen Hummer and how Max helped us. He laughed when I talked about Aria speeding us away like a total badass, calling us Thelma and Louise.

He held my hand the entire time and kissed the inside of my wrist every so often. I felt weak for letting him, but I couldn't deny his comfort and strength putting me at ease. I felt his body tense up during certain parts of the saga, but he was silently supportive the entire time. The only thing he'd feed me was that it was over now and we would be ok, no matter what happens.

Aria and Jack called to update us as we drove and everyone agreed it would be best to avoid the track so we went straight to London. Digby had gone AWOL, the FIA launched a formal investigation into Celeritas and barred them from participation in any events until the matter was resolved. Lennox was subjected to a battery of drug tests as part of the immediate investigation but was cleared. He was hung up in London dealing with attorneys and fallout but went home to Scotland as soon as he could.

Saying goodbye to him in London was the hardest thing I've ever done in my life. Every cell in my body wanted to take him up on his offer and run away to the isolated coastline of the Isle of Skye. Move into that half-finished home and hide away with him forever. But my head was in no condition to make rational decisions and I wouldn't be able to think clearly if I was around him. I wasn't strong enough to resist him begging and telling me he loved me. And I know I will not survive him breaking my heart again.

He asked if he could call me and I asked him not to. I said that I would call if and when I want to talk to him. I need to figure out what I want.

Today, the start of my second week home, it's the first day I'm moving on from everything. I've decided it's time. As I walk into Angelo's Pizza to meet Cody, I feel my appetite return at the smell of New York thin crust.

Cody jumps from his seat when he sees me and gives me a big bear hug. "My sister the felon," he jokes. We didn't get charged with stealing Digby's car after all. I guess he had enough sense to not involve the police at the time. It'll be a fun story to tell one day, I suppose.

"I've missed you so much," I beam at my brother as I take my seat. Cody already has my favorite slice and a Diet Coke waiting at the table for me, though I'm considering switching to Diet Pepsi these days.

As I fold my slice up and relish the gooey greasy pizza, Cody fills me in on the Mitchell Dysfunctional Family Saga. The board at Mitchell Media is in the process of replacing dad, which Dad's blaming me for. Cody says it's been a long time coming and I'm just the handy scapegoat. My parents have not contacted me and I've made no attempt to contact them. I won't say it's been easy and I have guilt that may never go away, no matter how misguided it is. But I need to focus on me, not let my decisions be influenced by trying to live up to their expectations, nor trying to spite them. I've been guilty of both.

"So, you going to take the job at Cooper?" Cody asks as he wipes cheese off his chin.

"I haven't decided yet. I have some cushion in the bank again and I want to be sure of what I do next. Max said the door is open and to take as long as I want."

"No more firm?"

I sigh and think about my answer when I finish chewing. "I don't know Cody. I don't think I want to work with athletes in trouble anymore. My track record has not been so hot. And who would hire me after I ratted out an athlete with a drug problem? No one."

"You loved it, though."

"I loved sports and liked telling the athletes' stories, but if I'm honest, when I got my journalism degree and went into social media, there was a big part of me that did it to defy mom and dad. Now, the thought of logging into my own social media accounts turns my stomach, much less someone else's."

Cody squints his eye at me and motions his hands that I should continue since his mouth is currently otherwise engaged with pepperoni.

"It's all... bullshit. All of it. None of it is real. It's like Mom with her snooty friends from the club. The only reason they go is to show off how wonderful their lives are. I don't want to lie about people's shitty lives so they feel less shitty and make other people feel more shitty in the process."

"That's a lot of shit," he laughs.

I almost say the word 'aye' but catch myself.

"And Speed Racer?" Cody asks, lifting an eyebrow in question, using his nickname for Lennox. We should have been twins the creepy way he always knows what I'm thinking.

"I haven't talked to him since I've been home."

"He hasn't called you?"

"I asked him not to," I defend Lennox and realize I'm defending Lennox and now I'm confusing myself. "I just asked for some time."

"How much time?"

"Now you sound like him, Cody. I don't know how much time. Why?" I'm inexplicably frustrated with his question. I don't want to be pressured into anything, one way or the other.

He shrugs, "Argumentative as always, I see. Just saying."

I squint at Cody and spend the rest of our time catching up with that seed planted in my brain now. Am I being argumentative for the sake of it?

When I get home, Aria's out with a client. I throw my keys on the kitchen counter and notice a box on top of the pile of mail. I recognize Lennox's handwriting immediately but the return address verifies it. It was post-marked the day I left.

Is he sending me my shit back?

I take the box to the couch and pause for a moment before tearing it open. If it contains something I left at his house, I guess I'll have my answer if there's any hope for us.

There's a folded note and a big metal tin of Twinings tea. What the hell is this? I open the note.

> *My Dear NILM (that's Nanny I'd like to Marry),*
> *I know you said no calling, but you did not say no writing.*
> *Negotiate better.*
> *The first time I met you was in Britain so I'm sending you a*
> *reminder of that time. The queen buys her tea at this shop, so while*
> *that's still not good enough for you, I hope you'll enjoy it.*
> *You are my queen.*
> *I love you.*
> *L xoxoxo*

My hand covers my mouth which is hiding a huge grin. Negotiate
better, oh that smart ass. This is sweet, I don't remember the last time
anyone sent me an actual gift in the mail. I only get bills and jury duty
summons. But I'm not ready to talk to him and a box of tea doesn't
change what he did. I haven't processed what Cody said and I've just
dedicated this week to figuring out what I'm going to do with my life.

But, I also want to talk to him. I'll text him. That's not as dangerous.
I won't be able to hear that accent that makes me wobbly in the knees.

> **Mallory:** The first time I met you, you started dirty
> talking to me about being put on a leash...
> **Lennox:** Please come home and put me on a leash. I'll
> go buy one right now.
> **Lennox:** Also since you initiated, I am assuming it is
> ok to text you.
> **Mallory:** Yes, as you've pointed out, I need to
> negotiate better.
> **Lennox:** I love you.

Aria comes home and walks in on me smiling like a doofus with my
package. She brought the mail in earlier so she must have known
about it and has probably been waiting all day to find out what was
inside.

I hand her the note and she clutches her heart. "So, I'm not
supposed to tell you, but chicks before dicks, right?"

"Tell me what, Aria?" My voice drops as I imagine the possibilities
of what she's been scheming now. After seeing her detective work and
get-away driving, I'm a little frightened now of what she's capable of.

"He's kind of been texting me, a little bit," she bites her lip and moves out of striking distance.

"What? About what?"

"Well, at first he just wanted to thank me for helping you and keeping you safe during Operation Destroy Digby. He said he heard I was a hell of a driver," she giggles.

"And then what?" I yell, "I can't believe you didn't tell me this, Aria."

"Umm, well, he's sent gift cards to spas and restaurants and I'm supposed to take you out and help you relax, I think he used the word 'pamper' which is freaking adorable."

"Oh my god, just give me your phone!"

"Ok, but I am sworn to secrecy," Aria pulls her phone out of her purse and hands it to me after making me promise I won't rat on her.

There aren't many messages but they started the day I left London, again. He thanks her. He says he's emailed her gift cards to all the places I ever talked about loving in New York. He says not to tell me because it's about me taking care of myself and not about him getting credit for it. And one message saying he wants to get to know her better because getting to know my friends is important to him.

"I didn't feed him any info about you," Aria tells me. "I'm trying to remain impartial here but do you see this shit?" She waves to her phone and fans her chest.

"Wait, how did he get your number?" I ask her and ignore the fact that Aria, of all people, saw what condition I was in after Lennox broke my heart. Being charming and swoon-worthy was never Lennox's problem.

"Oh, umm, the boys and I exchanged numbers after you ditched me at Silverstone. He must have gotten it from them," she takes her phone back and puts it in her pocket suspiciously.

"Are you talking to them, too?" I gasp.

"No! No, we have not forgiven them yet, those naughty, naughty boys. I am definitely *not* talking to the hot Nordic Viking guy."

"Oh my god," I throw a couch pillow at her and we both laugh.

I missed her while I was gone.

The next day, I get two packages. It must be the mail catching up from weekend delivery. I may, or may not, have been waiting for the mailman to appear after we used a gift certificate to a spa that Lennox sent. He can afford it and since he's the cause of my shoulder tension, I didn't argue when Aria insisted we go.

I take both packages to my bedroom and climb into bed to see what he's done today.

There's a small stuffed koala bear and, oh my god, one of the calendars from the charity photoshoot I made him do at the cat rescue. He's on the cover shirtless with a cowboy hat and a kitten in each arm. I never got to see the finished calendar and I don't know if I want to read his note first or look at more shirtless pictures of him. Why does he have to be so freaking hot? It does not help my resolve.

Love,

Do you know how hard it is to find a koala bear in Scotland?

In Australia, I knew you were different. For a moment in time, you made me forget everything that was wrong. It was the first time you rode in the car with me and you were checking me out the whole time. (You think I didn't notice, I did.) I always noticed you. You're impossible to miss. You're the most gorgeous woman I've ever seen.

I love you.

L xoxoxoxo

Inside the next cardboard shipping box, a bigger one, is one of his grey tank top shirts, a black Carhartt jacket he wore when we were in Scotland, and a beautiful handmade fabric scroll with Arabic writing on it.

Hot Nanny, Love of My Life,

I know how you like to steal my clothes, so here is the shirt I was wearing when you creeped on me in the gym and sent me home with the worst blue balls I've ever had. The jacket is for the one I put on you in the garage in Bahrain (which you also stole) and is where you taught me about your family and I taught you about cars. In Bahrain, I also kissed you for the first time but you stole something from me. Please come home and reclaim it. It's yours forever.

PS - I mean my heart. Also applies to other things, see aforementioned blue balls.

PSS - You'll have to google the scroll.

PSSS - I now have fans waiting for autographs at the post office daily, but I persist.

I love you.

L xoxoxoxo

I text him again and realize I was looking forward to more mail deliveries because it gives me an excuse to text him. Sneaky...

> **Mallory:** The clothes will come in handy since I burned your others.
> **Lennox:** You burned my clothes?!
> **Mallory:** The Talisker Distillery hoodie went up like kindling. There may have been wine involved.
> **Lennox:** note to self: send only non-flammable gifts in the future
> **Lennox:** [photo] which color do you like better?
> **Mallory:** the one on the left, why?
> **Lennox:** Kitchen paint. I'm working on finishing the house so you have a proper home. If you don't want to live here though, we'll sell it.
> **Mallory:** Send more pics so I can see
> **Lennox:** [photo]
> **Mallory:** Not of your abs! The kitchen! lol

I called Lennox that night and we talked for hours until I fell asleep on the line to his deep voice and the accent I've missed so much. I didn't realize until this morning that it was the middle of the night in Scotland when I called, he never mentioned it. He told me about all the house projects he and Pop are finishing, texted me a ton of photos. I told him about my parents and trying to figure out what I want to do for a living.

We agreed we didn't want to talk about Celeritas, but he did say he's not driving the rest of the season. Celeritas has been taken over by solicitors pending dismissal of most of the board and executives. He said he isn't upset about it, but I have a hard time believing it. Projects around the house will only keep him entertained for so long.

He didn't pressure me about anything, we just talked. It was nice.

I want him to be happy.

This morning I finally Googled enough to find out what the scroll he sent me says: "Darling. Light of my life. I'm not gonna hurt you." It's a quote from *The Shining*, one of countless movies we watched curled up together. I laughed for a good half an hour and can't imagine how much time he is spending on these silly, sweet mementos every day.

Most men would have sent flowers. He could afford to send expensive jewelry. But Lennox sent me horror movie quotes, memories from small moments we shared. He'd been paying attention.

Today's package was small, a padded mailer with a thong that had "Mrs. Gibbes" ironed on and another sweet note, this one saying he wants me to be the real Mrs. Gibbes. I am both endlessly entertained and horrified wondering where he is getting these things at the little shops on the Isle of Skye. If I would log onto Instagram or Snapchat or Facebook I could probably find out. I would probably find photos of him asking some little old lady about getting a custom thong made.

But I'm blissfully disconnected from it all. I'd rather know the real him and spend my time in the real world. With real people. He was right about this, it's too hard to see what's real when you surround yourself with fake.

Late at night, an express mail package came, a brand new Talisker Distillery hoodie that he said he wore all day until the cut off time for overnight delivery and, of course, a joke about not lighting this one on fire. It smells like him.

Every day there are packages and notes. A little boat from Monaco, maple syrup from Canada, a Godzilla action figure from China, everywhere we've been he's sent something with sweet and funny notes about loving me in those locations.

Every day we text and call at least twice per day. He still doesn't pressure me. He ends every call telling me how much he misses me, loves me, and will never stop. But he doesn't ask for an answer or make demands. It must be killing him not to be the one in charge.

Every day my heart heals.

Three weeks and some days since I've been home, I'm in bed in his tank top and we're Skyping and watching the remake of *IT* together. Lennox is making jokes about catching glimpses of my side boob. Apparently side boob is the hottest thing ever, who knew.

"Be quiet and watch the movie," I smile at his handsome face.

"Just sit here and look pretty, eh?" He jokes and throws a piece of popcorn at his laptop camera.

"Lennox Gibbes, are you eating popcorn?" I gasp with extra dramatic flair.

"Aye, extra butter," he shoves a handful in his mouth.

"Matty is going to kill you," I giggle.

"Ah but that's another perk, I can eat now and Matty can't do shit about it. By the time you come home, I'm going to be big and fat."

Every so often, Lennox says things like this. Comments about *when* I come home. He finished *our* room today. *We* have a new cat who showed up outside and needed to get neutered. *We* need to buy a Tesla because they're self-driving and I can't kill myself or anyone else while driving it.

"I know what you're doing," I purse my lips and smirk at him.

"Getting fat?"

"Sneaking in subliminal comments about when I'm coming home. You're not that clever."

"Ms. Mitchell, are you suggesting there's a method to my madness?" He smiles and throws more popcorn at the screen and I flinch in reflex, which just makes him smile more.

"I'm surprised you didn't call me Mrs. Gibbes," I tease him.

"I will one day," he says.

"So arrogant," I shake my head at him. He's irresistible when he's in these moods, which are more like his daily personality now. They're not just flashes of the man I'd only get to see sneak peeks of from time to time.

"Nope, confident. It's inevitable, Mallory. Told you that in Bahrain." He grins from ear to ear chewing his popcorn. He's quite pleased with himself tonight.

Stupid sexy asshole.

"Watch the movie," I roll my eyes at him and bite my cheek to keep from smiling.

Going back to *IT*—and trying to focus on the movie, not Lennox who's making a show of licking his fingers—all the kids from The Losers Club are in the street. Ben says he thought they wanted to get out of this town, too. And Beverly, arguably the best character, the girl bullied over rumors of promiscuity, argues, "I want to run toward something, not away."

I need to write Mr. Stephen King a thank you note.

Thirty Three

Lennox

Most of the house is done now. Just some small finishing touches left to finish. I had hoped Mallory would be home by the time it was ready to furnish so she could decorate it however she wants. I'd just have helmets and trophies scattered about if left to my own devices. I'll start feeling her out to get hints on furniture. I'd rather be over-prepared.

She didn't answer my call this morning. Maybe she was asleep or out with her friends or her brother. Or working with Maxwell Cooper. Whatever she's doing, I trust her. Hopefully, she'll call tonight, or better yet, FaceTime me so I can see her beautiful smile. She smiles at me again, these days.

I need to get this new interior door I stained finished and hung and then head into town to ship out today's package to Mallory: a stuffed Loch Ness monster, a book about hunting Nessie, and some brochures for tours I promise to take her on when she comes home. I'm pretty sure they'll deport me from Scotland for participating in that tourist bullshit, but she's been teasing me about bloody Nessie for six months. So a-Nessie-hunting we will go. When she comes home.

And she will.

I have the rest of my life to keep this up, to earn her trust back and prove I'm not an asshole or a monster. That I'll never hurt her again. Patience has never been a strong suit and every day I have to stop myself from flying to New York and dragging her home, but it has to be her choice. When she comes back to me, wherever in the world that is, I want all of her with me. Not just pieces because she's afraid to give me everything. I can't live with her holding herself back from me. Every day is a workout to be the man she wants to come home to, one day.

A green light is flashing on the far wall of the garage and I walk over to investigate. Ah, just the wall charger blinking to say she's full up. I hate this bloody Tesla. I have no idea how to work on it, there's nothing to tinker with. It's not natural, though I'll admit that Marvin Gaye Mode is pretty cool. The bloody thing starts playing love songs while a fireplace video crackles on the huge computer screen. Ridiculous. But it's safe, it parks itself, can drive itself, and has all kinds of heads-up alert systems to prevent bad drivers from doing bad things. I've only driven it a little to set it up for her. I want it to still have the new car smell when she gets home.

Turns out, I didn't need to cool it on buying the supercars, but instead I bought Mallory a Tesla. My contract with Celeritas is pretty much null and void now after the world of shit they're in. Administrators are saying the whole company will be sold off, hopefully intact to a new team who can take over. Pretty much all of the executive staff was let go after HR documents came out about all the sleazy things Digby had been up to, harassing staff, inappropriate touching, and unwanted advances.

What a prick.

Authorities finally caught up with him, he failed all the drug tests, like *all* of them. He'll never drive again. Last I heard he was on house arrest in Monaco. I told Jack I don't want to hear the salacious gossip anymore, though. Don't ever put me in the same room as DuPont and expect me to not bury him in a shallow grave for what he put Mallory through, but that shit is otherwise done. Over.

Moving on to better things.

The power drill drives in the last screw of the new door hinge when a god awful noise sneaks into the garage. Sounds like down the road someone is grinding the shit out of the gears of their transmission. The clutch is slipping and sputtering, metal is rubbing together, gears being ground down to shavings. Christ, it makes my blood run cold. I wonder if Mrs. MacDonald, the mail lady, is having trouble with the post truck.

I set the drill down and walk out of the garage, down the gravel drive and toward the street. When my drive gate comes into view, there's a small red car coming up the drive. No idea who this is, paparazzi or fans have never shown up here. It's too bloody remote for the paps to warrant making 50 pounds on a boring photo of grass and trees, and the locals have always respected my privacy and played stupid when anyone asks how to find my house.

But, this car isn't slowing down as it nears the gate. No, it keeps its ambling speed with no signs of stopping. I pick up a jog and when I'm about ten yards away, the car runs right into the damn gate. The engine sputters out and the car lurches forward in one final death throe as the clutch is let out. "What the fuck?" I yell and jog faster.

The car door opens as I reach the gate.

Mallory.

Her head pops out of the car, gorgeous chestnut hair with bits of honey woven throughout catching the sun. "Oh my god! I'm so sorry! It's a stick shift! That's all the rental place…"

Those are all the words she can get out before my lips meet hers and silence her complaints of the rental car. Both of my hands on her head, my fingers in her hair, I bring my head down to hers and she stands on her toes to meet me in the middle.

Soft, full lips and a hint of cinnamon meet my tongue, dancing, probing, communicating so many words of desperation, relief, adoration. She makes a tiny moan and her body softens into mine, her hands around my neck pulling me into her more. Fuck, the noises she makes, the little moans and noises, the way her body goes limp and she gives herself to me—it undoes me.

She pushes her body into mine and every muscle comes alive and she reminds my body of what she felt like pressed up against me. Our mouths still frantic at one another, I start to move her out of the open door of the car and press her against the rear door so I can feel more of her, harder up against me, I need to feel everything.

Shit.

"Are you ok?" I pull back and run my hands up and down her arms, her face her head. I don't see anything hurt and she was going pretty slow, but…

She launches herself back at me gripping at my shoulders, fingers digging into my neck, then clutching my hair as her tongue moves past my lips and into my eager mouth. Coherent thoughts are gone, replaced with fire, the heat of an inferno combusting through my veins. She pushes her hips into me and her left leg starts to lift over my thigh. I grab it behind her knee and press her hard into the side of the rental car.

The tips of my fingers are buzzing with electric current feeling every detail of her skin. The memory of her taste and that sweet jasmine smell makes neurons fire in my brain that had been asleep for weeks. "Lennox," she pants when she lifts her mouth away an inch for oxygen, the whisper of her breathe passing my lips.

Taking her head in my hands and searching her eyes, those hazel orbs alight and dancing back and forth as she searches my own, I whisper her name, "Mallory." She's so fucking beautiful. Is she really here, is she back, is she mine? "Are you..." I have to know, I have to know now what this means for her, her coming here, these kisses, the way she's looking at me.

"I'm home," she whimpers, her eyes locked with mine.

Everything in my body that's been under lock and key explodes, overwhelming relief, ecstasy, joy, love, it all floods my being as I smash my mouth into hers again. I bend down and wrap an arm under that perfect round ass and pull her up, her legs wrap around my waist and I slam us hard into the car. She rocks her hips into me and I feel her heat radiate into me.

"I love you so fucking much," I groan into her neck as I run my tongue from the base of her neck to her ear, reveling in her taste.

"Show me," she whines.

I turn us and start carrying her back up the drive. I'll show her, show her how much I love her, now and for the rest of my bloody life. Her mouth is on my neck sending shivers up my spine.

"You're squeezing the life of out me," she giggles into my neck, and I realize how tight my arms are wrapped around her.

"Aye, you realize there's no escape now, I'll never let you leave." Never. Never will I let her go.

She's writhing against me, licking and sucking my neck as I carry her past the garage toward the house. "Mm, Lennox, now," she points to the garage, the nearest structure.

Jesus fuck, the idea of making love to her in the bloody garage is my teenage fantasy come true. May as well do this right, I carry her to the hood of her new car and set her down, lean her back and kiss the ever-loving hell out of her. She leans her hands back onto the hood and arches her back.

"What is this?" She realizes the new addition to the stable amongst the other cars. "Did you? You seriously bought a Tesla?" she laughs. Her face is so alive, her smile lights me up and that laugh will warm me on the coldest of nights.

"Have you seen our gate?" I tease her and point in the direction.

"Yes, you need this dumb vehicle."

"I need you," she clutches my shirt and pulls me back down to her. Her words make me swell with pride. They push out all the fears and darkness.

She tears the shirt off over my head as my fingers work her button and zipper down. She kicks her shoes off and I push everything past her hips, down her smooth, toned legs and rip it all off over her feet.

I savor the taste of her skin up her legs, her inner thighs, the curve of her hips, her stomach that's rising and falling with desperate breaths. She pulls her shirt over her head and those soft, perfect breasts are mine again. Rosy round nipples turn to peaks under my fingers and tongue again. She says she's the one who's come home, but this is my home.

I kiss my way back down her body breathing in her intoxicating scent, my mouth salivating as I'm about to taste her but her fingers in my hair are pulling me back up. "Need you up here," she whines.

"Mmm," I groan into her flesh, "I want to take my time, savor you."

"We have the rest of our lives, I need you inside of me."

Fuck, I love this woman.

I take one long swipe of my tongue through her folds and growl as I move back up and cover her body. I kiss her and she moans as she tastes herself on my lips and pulls my cock out of my pants, her warm fingers gripping me tight. I'm so goddamn hard and throbbing, I need her like the air I breathe.

Her hand grabs my ass and grips my jeans, pulling me into her. Her hips rise toward me with urgency and I line myself up and slide into her slick heat in one smooth thrust. Mallory clutches me, her back arches and those perfect tits reach for me while sweet moans and whimpers fill my ears. "Oh, fuck," I groan into her, so wet I slide fluidly in and out, so tight wrapped around me I can feel every clench of her walls.

Her skin squeaks against the hood of the car every time I rock into her and her pelvis rises up to meet mine. I swivel my hips while deep inside of her and cover her length with my body, hold her tight inside my arms. I can't get deep enough inside of her. I can't hold her tight enough against my heart. I'll spend the rest of my life trying to get closer and deeper into her.

"Love you so mmm..." I try telling her again but her fingers are clawing my hair out and she crashes her mouth into mine rendering me speechless as she whines and pants around my lips.

I can feel her heart pounding in her chest when her wet core tightens around my shaft and starts spasming. Her nails dig into my back and I hiss, grinding deeper and harder into her. She arches and her cries grow louder, her body tensing up around mine, "Oh god, Lennox, yes, fuck, come with me!"

Watching her face twist and distort in pleasure, her gorgeous naked body before me, hearing her scream my name in ecstasy, feeling so full of pride to make her feel good, a volcano rumbles inside me and I thrust. I hold myself inside her tight walls as a flood of lava erupts and fills her. "Fuck!" I roar as she continues to spasm around me, wiggling her hips riding out aftershocks as I collapse against her soft tits.

Our breathing is still sporadic and her fingers are running through my hair when she giggles, "Holy shit I missed you."

"Mmm, Dick-on-Demand was in danger of going out of business there, for a while," I mumble into her warm mounds.

"Never," she laughs, my head rising and falling with her chest.

Blissful moments pass even though the hood of this car is not the most comfortable place. Elon Musk should work on that.

I take Mallory's head in my hand and look in her eyes, kiss her lips softly. "I'm so in love with you, Mal. I'll spend the rest of my life trying to earn your love, please know that."

"You idiot," the corners of her eyes crinkle and she smiles, rubbing her fingers through the stubble along my jaw that's gotten quite long in my laziness. "Where's my phone? I think it's in my pants."

She grunts and points to her pants flung on the floor. I groan at the loss of her skin pressed up around mine but I sit up and reach for the pants before settling down again on my back and handing them to her.

She pulls her phone out of her pant pocket and starts swiping through it. I grumble at her and the bloody phone, but keep my mouth shut as I've been working on. She snuggles into the side of me and hands me the phone, "Here."

She has the messaging app pulled up. There's lots of messages in green instead of blue, red exclamation points next to them, *message not delivered*. "What is this?"

"Read," she taps the screen with a fingernail.

Lennox, I love you. I love you so much. You stupid asshole I'm in love with you.

"You... love me?" I lower the phone and turn my head to look at her. Her full lips are curled up, her eyes soft and happy, her face flush with contentment.

She holds my face in one hand and caresses a feather-light kiss across my lips. "I've always loved you, Lennox Gibbes."

I capture her in my arms and drag her onto me, kissing her with every ounce of passion from deep within as her long hair cascades over my shoulders.

"That's what you get for blocking me," she giggles and bites my lip.

Epilogue

"If you need a light, I'll be the match to your candle. My darlin' I'm ready to burst into flames for you." - Vance Joy, 'I'm with You'

Fourteen Months Later

Mallory

The trees are rich oranges and auburn and the gentle breeze making leaves dance in the grass is crisp on my skin, but the fire keeps me cozy. Surrounding the fire pit that we use more nights than not, when we're home, are now deep wooden benches so we can sit together.

Pumpkins and a few carved turnips line the stone border wall. My second year attempting to carve a turnip didn't end up much better than the first. Mine look like rats gnawed through them versus the little intricate faces hollowed out of Lennox, Jack, and Matty's turnips.

That's ok. I know when I've been bested and they can win the turnip battle.

"Warm enough?" Lennox has an arm around me and snuggles me closer into his warm chest.

I'm plenty toasty but I lean into him anyway, let the smell of his woodsy cologne mix with the scent of the fire and the ocean. "Mmmhmmm," I nuzzle him and run my hand up his muscular thigh.

"Mallory," his fingers thread through my hair and he warns me, "don't rub the lamp if you don't want the genie to come out."

I silently chuckle at the ridiculous things he still finds to say to me every day, all the ways he makes me laugh. "Does the genie grant me three wishes if he does come out?" I look up at his green eyes dancing, reflecting the light of the fire.

His warm hand comes to my face and his thumb traces my jaw, "There's no limit on the wishes I'll grant you."

God, I love this man.

This castle on the island is our sanctuary but home is wherever he is. We find a way to keep home with us no matter where in the world we are. And when we are back on the Isle of Skye, the time spent here is extra special. Our home is full, not just with furnishings now, but with Aria who has become a frequent flyer, Matty and Jack, Mum and Pop, Bram who is graduating soon, old karting friends Lennox has reconnected with, and new local friends I've made. My sister is a lost cause, but Cody's been here a few times for the holidays and we're closer than ever.

"We should get started," Lennox gives me a quick kiss, "I'd like to take the bike out one more time this year."

"I'd like that," I smile into his lips looking forward to another afternoon with him along the coastline. Pods of minke and orca whales are frequent this time of year, coming in closer to feed. More than that, it's just the comfortable quiet time with Lennox, letting everything slip away and letting him guide me wherever we're going, knowing he always has me.

I feel his hand slip into my pocket and he pulls my phone out, turns on the voice recorder, and smirks. I know he's about to make another joke about me throwing my phone into the fire the last time we tried this.

"Yes, haha, Mr. Gibbes," I roll my eyes and pull my legs up underneath me on the bench so I can sit facing him.

"Mm, Mr. Gibbes now, is it?" He smirks at me in that smoldering way that melts my insides.

"Yes. I'm a professional. Ahem," I clear my throat for emphasis. "Now, then. Mr. Gibbes, tell me, how does winning your second world championship compare to your first three years ago?

He leans back on the bench and considers his answer. If he treats this like he does most media now, I expect a fair answer, sometimes brutally honest, often peppered with sarcasm. "There's no comparison at all," he answers, his voice deep and strong.

"How so?" I reply in my best journalist voice.

When Lennox was offered contracts to race the season following the demise of Celeritas, there was no way I was letting him give up his dream. He signed with Anora Sports and drives alongside Alessi now, who has become another dear friend. Alessi and Jack still sneak around, except around us and a few precious others they trust. Maybe the motorsports world will get with the times one of these years.

But Lennox is happy, so I'm happy. I took a long time to think about what I wanted to do. Spent the rest of the season Lennox had off getting to know him more, getting to know my new home, my new family. Time passed falling in love with him even more and with this beautiful new country he's given me. And when his new season began I took the job offer with Cooper Media as one of the only female F1 journalists in the paddock.

Now I get to tell the stories of the athletes that I always wanted to and travel the world alongside the love of my life who clinched this year's championship by a landslide with four races remaining. I couldn't be more proud of him and I tell him daily. I'd be proud if he'd come in last, though. I'm proud of the man he's become. It was always inside of him but he's more liberal with sharing now.

Usually.

There's still a lot that is only shared with me, like his family—our family—who he remains fiercely protective of. I don't blame him, or mind. Some things are just for us.

"The second championship will always mean more," he continues answering my question. "This one was about redemption."

"Redeeming yourself on the track after three difficult seasons. That must have been particularly meaningful after the chaos of last season, the chaos of the Celeritas scandal."

"Nah, fuck them," he brushes the concept away and I bite my cheek to not smile. I said Lennox was happy, not a different person. I wouldn't want it any other way, even if I have to be very careful what I ask him during live coverage because I know he will give me his exact truth.

"I redeemed my records on track, yeah, but it was off-track that meant the most," he explains. His broad shoulders are back, exuding confidence and conviction with his body language.

"Off track?" The journalist in me asks him while the lover in me swoons.

"Aye, I almost lost myself. Thank god I had this nanny walk into my life. Hottest chick you've ever seen. Sassy as hell, razor sharp. Whipped my ass into shape." He winks at me.

"Lennox," I laugh and extend a leg to kick him on the bench. "I cannot print that!"

He grabs my leg and drags me back close to him, his lips moving to my neck to nip and kiss. "I should get perks for answering interview questions when the reporter is my girlfriend."

"Then you should have negotiated better," I squirm as he tickles me and my palm floats over his bumpy stomach muscles.

"Aye, I agree," he gives me a sweet kiss on the lips and stands. He takes a few steps over to the bar area of the fire pit. I assume he's grabbing a drink and I look forward to tasting the scotch on his lips, but he said he wanted to take the motorcycle out, so that's not it.

"What's this?" I look up at him when he returns, holding his palm open before me with a handful of brown, shiny chestnuts.

"They're nuts, Mallory."

"I see that, smart ass. Why do you have nuts in your hand—ugh, don't answer that," I groan.

"The tradition," he reminds me. "We won't be home on Halloween, we have to do it now." He takes my hand and helps me stand.

"Is my big, strong man feeling insecure all of a sudden? He needs to throw nuts into the fire to know if we're going to live happily ever after?" I tease him and run my palms up against his chest.

"Nope," he grins and beams down at me. "Toss 'em in."

"You're ridiculous," I tell him and turn to toss the chestnuts into the fire. They fall through the sticks and charred wood and I lose sight of them. "They're not doing anything."

Lennox doesn't respond and I turn to look at him. "Oh," I gasp and my hand goes over my mouth. My heart pounds and the sounds of the fire and the whistling winds cease to exist.

Lennox is before me on one knee, a black box with a ring in one hand. My eyes dart between it, a shining antique solitaire catching the sun, and Lennox's deep green pools staring back at me.

Oh my god, is he doing this?

"Love, you gave me my dreams back but you'd taken them over long before. You're my entire world, my everything. If you let me, I will spend the rest of my life loving you beyond your wildest imagination. Watch monster movies with me, cross the globe with me a million times over, always come home to my arms. Be my hot nanny the rest of my life. Marry me, Mal."

Warm tears contrast the cool air on my cheeks before he has all the words out and I throw myself at him, both of us falling back onto the brick pavers before the fire. Our mouths lock, arms entwine, fingers grasp and heat is transferred, everything else falling wayside.

"Is that a yes?" His strong arms wrap around me as I cover his face, neck, any skin I can get to, with kisses.

"Yes," I smile and hold his face, "it was always yes." I taste his lips again, "I love you so much, Lennox."

I didn't realize until weeks later that my phone recorded the audio of his proposal. Lennox did that on purpose, of course. I'll cherish it for the rest of my life. I was too busy planning the wedding he gave me two months to arrange. He didn't care where or how, just soon. He didn't want to wait anymore and neither did I.

After a panicky week researching exotic locations in dreamy locations around the world, I realized I wanted something real. And I have the most real thing in my life right here. We got married high on our cliff at home with just those we love the most at our sides and Bodach the cat who made an appearance halfway through.

I was wearing the 'Mrs. Gibbes' thong beneath my simple strapless gown with a sweetheart neckline and wrapped in an elegant wool throw, because Scotland cliffs are cold as fuck in December. Despite all the teasing, Lennox would not wear a kilt. He stood before me tall and handsome in a tailored suit that accentuated his wide shoulders and narrow hips.

And we promised to always make each other's dreams come true.

**

Be sure to sign up for the Kat Ransom Newsletter for exclusive content, sneak peeks, and up to date information on new releases.

Kat Ransom writes steamy romances filled with strong, sassy men and women who bring them to their knees. She lives in Cowboy Country in the Southern US with her husband and two jenky rescue cats. When she isn't writing, she's exploring isolated corners of the world or curled up with a wool blanket and a stiff whisky trying to warm up her perpetually cold toes.

Kat loves to hear from her readers! Contact her at authorkatransom@gmail.com
Follow along at katransom.com or find her on:
Twitter: @katransomauthor
Instagram: @authorkatransom

Join her mailing list for the latest updates, sneak peeks and fun freebies: https:// katransom.subscribemenow.com

Before you go, please consider leaving a review!

Fast & Wet

Coming Soon!

Join Kat Ransom's Newsletter for the
sizzling sequel!

Made in the USA
Monee, IL
23 January 2022

89654561R00163